Nothing But Velvet

Kat Martin

St. Martin's Paperbacks

To my mother, Helen Kelly, for her unfailing love, friendship, and support. Thanks, Mom, you're the greatest.

NOTHING BUT VELVET

Copyright © 1997 by Kat Martin.

ISBN: 0-312-96243-6

Printed in the United States of America

St. Martin's Paperbacks edition / July 1997

10 9 8 7 6 5

CHAPTER ONE

∾

"*I* forbid it! Do you hear?" The duke of Carlyle's face turned a mottled shade of red beneath his mane of snowy hair. "You are a Sinclair," the duke said, his eyes locked on those of his handsome defiant son. "You are an earl, a peer of the realm, and heir to the duke of Carlyle. I will not allow your sordid relationship with that harlot to continue!"

Jason's spine went rigid. Standing in the ornate, walnut-paneled study at Carlyle Hall, the duke's lavish country estate, Jason clamped his jaw against the anger surging through him, the muscles tight across his broad shoulders.

"Forgodsakes, Father, the lady is the countess of Brookhurst—not some light-heeled tavern wench!" He was twenty-one years old, tall and well-built, a man fully grown, yet his father treated him as if he were still a half-witted child.

"She is also eight years your senior, a widow who has slept with half the ton. It is clear that she is also a woman who will settle for nothing less than the Carlyle title and fortune."

Jason's hands balled into fists. "I refuse to let you speak of Celia that way. And whether you forbid it or not, I'll see whomever I choose." Ignoring the sound of his father's meaty hand crashing down on his rosewood desk, Jason turned and stalked out of the study, his angry strides echoing on the black marble floors. Fury pumped through him, and humiliation, and an icy resolve to thwart his father by whatever means he could.

Outside the hall, his sleek bay hunter stood waiting, pawing the earth in restless anticipation. Jason gave the stableboy a curt nod of thanks and swung up into the saddle. In the window behind him, the oil lamp flickered in his father's study as the big man strode out into the hall, then the sound of a slamming door echoed clearly through the massive stone mansion.

A thread of uneasiness snaked along Jason's spine. Surely his father wouldn't follow him back to the inn. Surely not. Even a stubborn, arrogant man like the duke of Carlyle would never go so far.

Jason watched a moment more, but his father did not appear. Breathing a little easier, he reined away from the house, grateful the confrontation was over at least for the present. He set the horse into a canter, then relaxed a little more at the animal's steady, rhythmic pace. Stark rays of moonlight slanted down through the branches of the trees, and a slight breeze ruffled his dark brown hair, cooling the last of the anger that still burned at the back of his neck.

As the miles slid past, his thoughts moved away from his father's bitter words to the woman whose warm, pliant body awaited. Celia Rollins, Lady Brookhurst. Tall, slender, and beautiful, from the top of her elegantly coifed, black-haired head to her shapely breasts and narrow waist, all the way down to the high, feminine arches of her feet.

They had been seeing each other for the past three months, often meeting at the Peregrine's Roost, an intimate, well-appointed inn halfway between Carlyle Hall and the countess's country estate, Brookhurst Park. Tonight they had planned just such a tryst, and Jason grew hard inside his snug black breeches just to think of the pleasure he would find when he joined the countess in bed.

It was less than an hour till the familiar ivy-covered arch marking the inn appeared above the courtyard, setting his blood to pumping again. He rode into the walled interior, the horse's hooves clattering on the cobbles, dismounted, patted the bay's sleek neck, and handed the reins to a stableboy waiting out in front.

With long, eager strides, Jason started walking toward the rear of the building. Accessible from inside the tavern, as well as having a second private entrance outside, the room often served wealthy patrons. Jason hurried even faster, but a stirring at the corner gave him pause.

"A coin, sir? Spare a coin for a blind man and God is sure to bless you." He was a mangy creature, sitting hunched over on the ground, his body swathed in rags from head to foot, an old tin cup in one hand. Even in the darkness, Jason could see the sores on his pasty skin. He tossed a coin into the metal cup, made his way to the back of the inn, and took the stairs to the second floor two at a time. A single brief knock and Celia beckoned him in.

"My lord," she whispered, smiling as she went into his arms. She was slim yet voluptuous, a vision of loveliness in the glow of the small fire blazing in the hearth. "Jason, darling, I'm so glad you've come."

She pressed her lips against his and kissed him with eager abandon, making him instantly hard. Jason kissed her back with the same hot need he sensed in her, dragging the pins from her silky, waist-length hair. It shone blue-black in the lamplight and hung straight down her back, a midnight curtain that contrasted his own chestnut, not quite shoulder-length hair worn in a queue at the nape of his neck.

"Celia . . . my God, it feels like years instead of only a week." He kissed the spot below the rim of her ear, trailed kisses along her bare shoulders, and frantically began to work the buttons on her gown, a heavy sapphire silk, nearly the same shade of blue as his eyes.

For a moment Celia faltered. "I-I was afraid . . . I know how your father feels . . . I thought you might not come."

"My father's opinion doesn't matter. Not in this." He kissed her again as if to prove it, then began to kiss a path along the arch of her throat down to her breasts, but a pounding at the door stopped him cold.

He wouldn't, Jason thought, imagining the angry, mottled face of his father. But as he feared, when he opened the door, the duke stood there in the opening.

"I've come to have a word with you. Both of you." Blue eyes clashed with blue, his father's gaze darkened with a hint of steel. The duke's fierce glare took in the countess's dishevel, her uncoiffed hair and rumpled gown. "I won't leave until I do."

Jason clamped his jaw, fury warring with humiliation, for Celia as well as himself. "Say what you came for, then leave." He stepped back as his father walked in and closed the door. Sliding a protective arm around Celia's waist, he silently cursed his father, and thanked God they were at least still fully clothed.

The duke of Carlyle fixed them with an icy stare and opened his mouth to speak. Then he frowned, his eyes shifting toward a movement at the door on the other side of the room. For a moment he just stood there. The echo of a gunshot ended what he might have said, the deafening blast filling the chamber, the lead ball taking him square in the chest.

The countess stifled a scream, and Jason gasped in horror at the scarlet blossom erupting in the middle of his father's silver waistcoat. The old man grasped the spreading stain as if he could keep his lifeblood from spilling out and pitched forward, both knees buckling beneath him.

"Father!" The word exploded from Jason's throat. He spun toward the duke's assailant, stared with horror into the familiar face of his half brother, Avery, who had climbed the outside stairs and fired through an open window, then Jason felt an agonizing pain burst in his head. The room began to spin and his legs refused to support him. Bright spots darkened his vision and began to close in.

"Father . . ." he whispered, fighting the black swirling circles that rose in front of his eyes. With a groan, he slumped forward, landing unconscious a few feet away from the duke's lifeless body.

The countess stepped over the shards of glass from the broken pitcher that lay scattered on the floor, opened the door, and the fashionably dressed man outside walked in.

"Very good, my dear." Avery Sinclair smoothed a fat silver curl at the side of his elegant, tied-back periwig. "You've always had a quick wit about you." Ignoring the pounding that began on the door leading into the inn, he knelt and pressed the still-smoking pistol into Jason's limp hand.

The countess smiled thinly. "One should always be prepared when opportunity presents itself."

Avery simply nodded. "I hoped you'd be smart enough to realize the old man would never allow you to marry his son."

"I knew it, even if Jason didn't."

"Well, now your problem is solved." He surveyed the bodies on the floor with grim satisfaction. "I had no idea the old man would make it so easy."

"Open this door!" The innkeeper's husky voice rang from the hallway. His heavy fists banged on the thick oaken planks of the door.

"Let me handle this," he said.

Celia arched a sleek black brow. "Oh, I shall."

"And remember, a bit of scandal is a small price to pay for your share of a considerable fortune."

Her pretty mouth curved up. "Never fear, I will remember . . . your grace."

CHAPTER TWO

∞

ENGLAND, 1760

A duchess! She was going to be a duchess! Their desperate scheme had actually succeeded.

Velvet Moran stood at the tall mullioned windows in the entry, watching the duke of Carlyle's ornate gilded carriage depart, waiting until it had finally disappeared down the poplar-lined road. Pondering the hour she had spent in company with the elegant blond man who would soon be her husband, she barely heard her grandfather's footfalls as he crossed the black-and-white marble floor, approaching where she stood beneath the crystal chandelier.

"Well, my girl, you've done it, eh?" The earl of Haversham was having a good day today. No memory lapses, no forgetting where he was or what he had been saying. Days like this were infrequent and growing more so, but Velvet cherished every one. "You've saved Windmere, just as you said you would. Saved us both from ruin."

Velvet smiled in spite of the trepidation that still churned inside her. "Only two more weeks and I'll be married. I feel terribly guilty for deceiving him. I wish there were some other way, but we certainly can't risk telling him the truth."

The old man chuckled softly. He was snowy haired where he wasn't going bald, and lean as a bone, his skin so thin blue veins showed through in his hands and face. "He'll chafe a bit when he discovers the debts he'll incur as your husband, but your dowry is a fine one. That should appease him some. And he'll have you. A man couldn't want for a finer wife.''

''I'll make him happy, Grandfather. He won't regret marrying me—I vow that on my honor.''

The old man cupped her cheeks between his wrinkled hands and stared into her pretty face. With her upturned nose and slightly tilted golden brown eyes, Velvet was the picture of her long-dead mother. She was petite and shapely, with high full breasts and a tiny waist. Her hair was long and wavy, the color of polished mahogany when it was left unpowdered, alive with reddish highlights.

Her grandfather sighed. ''I know it can't be helped, but I was hoping for a love match, not a marriage of convenience. What your grandmother and I once had . . . that was what I wanted for you. I wish it could have been so, but life is never easy. And one must do what one must.''

A wistful moment stole through her. She, too, had hoped to marry a man she loved, though she hadn't really believed she would ever be that lucky. ''The duke and I will get on well together. He has wealth and position. I'll be a duchess, live a life of luxury. What more could any woman ask?''

The earl smiled forlornly. ''Only love, my girl, only love. Mayhap in time, you will find it with the duke.''

She forced herself to smile. ''Yes, Grandfather. I'm sure I will.'' But thinking of Avery Sinclair, of his self-righteous ways and pompous, overstarched manner, she didn't believe it was true. ''It's drafty in here,'' she said, taking the old man's arm. ''Why don't we sit for a while in front of the fire?''

He nodded and she led him toward the rear of the house, passing the formal drawing room with its opulent red flocked walls, barouche painted ceilings, and heavy carved furniture, then another small salon, also lavishly furnished, hung with silk moiré draperies, and centered around a green marble hearth.

As soon as they rounded the corner, the opulence disap-

peared. The hall no longer glittered with golden sconces and
gilt-framed portraits, for the sconces and gilded frames had
long been sold. The beautiful Persian carpets that had once
warmed the floors had garnered a price that had kept them
in coal through the winter. Stained, threadbare versions had
been laid down in their stead to stave off the bitter cold.

To the occasional visitor, with its warm redbrick exterior
and beautiful parklike grounds, Windmere looked as magnificent as it always had, standing three stories tall and overlooking the river. In her father's day, its big square towers,
gabled roofs and chimney stacks, and hundreds of acres of
meadowlands had made the house a showplace.

The last three years had changed all of that. The debts
her father had acquired before his death had come as a shock
to Velvet and the earl. Even in his misty state of mind, her
grandfather realized what a terrible mistake he had made in
turning management of his estates over to his son. But the
old man's health was failing. With no one else to rely on,
he'd had no other choice.

Now George Moran was dead, as his wife had been for
more than ten years. He had been killed in a carriage accident on the Continent while traveling with his mistress, an
actress by the name of Sophie Lane.

It was Velvet who'd discovered, to her horror, their dec-
imated funds—and the mountain of debts her father had left
them. All but her dowry, the only unselfish thing he had
done in the years he had managed the estates. Since the
earl's fortune had been vast, the dowry was quite sizable,
in fact one of the largest in England, certainly enough to
keep them living well for years.

The only catch was, Velvet had to marry before the funds
were released from the iron-clad provisions of her trust fund.
Her husband would acquire a small fortune.

He would also acquire Haversham's vast array of debts.

Her grandfather paused in the hallway. "Where are we
going?"

"To the Oak room. Snead will have started a fire." Snead
was one of a half-dozen trusted retainers who were all the

staff they could afford to keep at Windmere. "It will be warm and cozy in there."

"But the duke . . . I thought he was coming to pay a call?"

Velvet's heart sank. The lucid day was over. "He already came, Grandfather."

"What about the wedding?"

"We'll be traveling to Carlyle Hall at the end of the week. His grace insists we arrive several days early so that everything may be properly in place before the day of the wedding." She had said all this before, but of course he had forgotten. And what did it matter, if it pleased him to hear it again?

"You'll be a beautiful bride," he said with a sentimental smile.

And he'll be one very surprised duke, Velvet thought. But she would cross that bridge when she reached it. In the meantime, she would keep up the facade that would ensure her marriage to a very wealthy husband. She would ignore the cold that pervaded the house, the smell of musty rooms that had been closed up, the stench of cheap tallow candles.

Thank God she would only have to pretend for another two weeks.

Jason Sinclair paced the floor in front of the slow-burning fire in the marble-manteled hearth, the crisp white lace on the cuffs of his full-sleeved shirt brushing his fingers as he moved. He had always been a tall man, broad-shouldered and lean-hipped. In the past eight years, the leanness of youth had been honed by hours of backbreaking labor into a hard-muscled body as solid as steel.

He turned to the man across from him. "God's blood, Lucien, we've brought the bastard nearly to his knees. We can't falter now and let him win."

Lucien Montaine, Marquess of Litchfield, leaned back in his tapestry chair. "I realize this news is not what you wished to hear, my friend, but brooding over the matter will do you no good. It may take some time, but sooner or later, we'll find another way to reach him. A leopard doesn't change his spots, and a jackal like Avery will once more fall prey to his vices."

Jason paced toward his friend, the one man who had stuck by him through the hell he had suffered these past eight years. "I've waited long enough, Lucien. The man may wear a facade of wealth, but we both know it for the lie it is. His money is nearly all gone. The time to strike is now."

"I can't disagree with your thinking. 'Tis the reason he's so determined to marry."

"I want what is rightfully mine, Lucien. Carlyle Hall is the first step in getting it. I want justice for my father. I want my brother to pay for what he's done. I'll do whatever it takes to see that he does."

"You've only two weeks before the wedding. The girl is one of the wealthiest heiresses in England. Once Avery acquires her dowry, he'll be able to pay off his debts—including the mortgage you hold on Carlyle Hall. You won't be able to foreclose. Unless you can find a way to stop the marriage—"

"That, my dear Litchfield, is exactly what I plan to do."

A thick black brow arched up above eyes as black as pitch. He was nearly as tall as Jason, but leaner, his features more harsh, his hair an ebony black. "Just how, may I ask, do you plan to accomplish that end?" They had known each other since boyhood, their country estates not far apart. The marquess was the one man Jason would trust with his life.

Which was exactly what he had done by returning to England when he was supposed to be dead.

"You said the girl would be traveling to Carlyle Hall with her grandfather, that they would be arriving the end of the week."

"That's correct."

"Then I shall simply detain my brother's precious betrothed until after the wedding. The grace period on the note is almost up. When my brother isn't able to make the payment, we'll be able to foreclose and the property will belong to me."

Lucien steepled his long dark fingers. "You actually intend to kidnap the girl?"

"I don't have any other choice." He smoothed back a lock of his wavy dark hair, loose from the narrow black ribbon at the nape of his neck. "I'll need your help, of course. I'll have to find a place to keep her until the property is mine."

"You're serious," Litchfield said.

Jason sat down in the chair across from him, stretching his long legs out in front of him. "I'm always serious. Any humor I once might have felt was beaten out of me over the last eight years."

Litchfield eyed him darkly. "She's only nineteen, an innocent by all accounts. She'll be frightened out of her wits."

"I won't hurt her. I'll do everything in my power to see that she's made comfortable." He toyed with the lace on his cuff then rubbed the scar on the back of his left hand. "I'll tell her I'm holding her for ransom, that I have no reason to harm her as long as her fiancé is willing to pay." He smiled coldly. "By the time she figures out it isn't the money I'm after, the wedding day will be past and the note foreclosed. Carlyle Hall will belong to me—and my brother on his way to ruin."

Litchfield shifted in his chair, his brows drawn together in thought. "Under normal circumstances, I wouldn't condone your actions, but this time you may well be right. The girl will be saved—at least for a time—from marrying a murderer. If she's lucky, she never will. That in itself, justifies what you plan to do."

Jason's smile came easy this time. "I knew I could count on you. You've stood by me through the worst times a man could have. Now you're risking your reputation by helping me again. I won't forget this, Lucien. You're the best friend any man could have."

"And you, my friend, deserve a chance to regain what bitter fortune—and your murderous half brother—so cruelly stripped away." Standing, he walked over to the carved wooden sideboard and lifted the lid off a crystal decanter of brandy. "The girl will be coming from Windmere, traveling the road that passes between Winchester and Midhurst. I've a hunting lodge in the forest near Ewhurst, not far away. It's small but neat and well cared for. We'll stock it with whatever provisions you and the lady might need."

He poured brandy into his snifter, then carried the decanter over and refilled Jason's empty glass. "There's a lad who lives nearby who can help you. He's loyal to a fault. You can trust him to carry messages and help out wherever he's needed. Aside from that, you'll be on your own."

Jason merely nodded. "Once more I am in your debt."

The marquess took a sip of his brandy and his lips curved faintly. "I've met Lady Velvet. She's quite a charming little baggage. I trust you'll keep the lady's virtue as safe as you do her person."

Jason grunted in response. "The last thing I want is another so-called lady. Celia was lesson enough, one most bitterly learned." At the mention of her name, the scar seemed to burn on the back of his hand. Absently he rubbed it. "Give me a romp with a lusty whore. The price of bedding a lady is too steep to pay."

Lucien made no reply. Jason Sinclair had changed in the last eight years. The youthful man he'd once been had been eaten away by his anger and the pain he had suffered in the Colonies. For four of the past eight years, he had worked like a slave on the swampy Georgia plantation where he had been transported, a turn of fortune at its oddest, since he had been sentenced to hang.

The years had changed him, hardened him into a man Lucien barely recognized as his friend. The cold blue eyes Jason saw through held none of the warmth of the younger man. They were predator's eyes, distant and as hard as his powerful body. Every movement spoke of the change, from his long, pantherish strides to the keen-edged awareness that came over him whenever he sensed danger.

Four years working as a convict, then finally escape. For the last three years, he had prospered, working his own plantation on a small island off St. Kitts. Only one year was missing. A year Jason never spoke of.

Lucien wondered if it accounted for the darkness that stole over his friend's features whenever he thought he was alone.

CHAPTER THREE

∞

*V*elvet Moran fidgeted on the plush velvet seat of the glossy black Haversham carriage, the last of half a dozen her family once had owned.

"How much longer, Grandfather? It seems as though we've been traveling for hours."

"We *have* been traveling for hours—it's nearly dark outside. Usually you barely notice the time. You plague me incessantly to travel about. Now that we're actually on the road, you've done nothing but fuss and fidget."

Velvet sighed. "I suppose you're right. Part of me wants to hurry, to get this whole thing over. The other part wishes we never would arrive."

"Chin up, my dear. Once you are married, things will settle into place."

Only the two of them rode inside the carriage. Though the air had turned chill, her lady's maid, Tabitha Beeson, had ridden up top with the coachy. She had been there since their stopover at an inn for an early supper and a place to change out of their wrinkled traveling clothes. Velvet suspected the woman carried a *tendre* for the driver and thought the coachman might feel the same.

She sighed as she rested her head against the deep velvet squabs. What would it have been like to fall in love? There were times she had dreamed about marrying a man who loved her, but just as often she thought she didn't want to marry at all. In the past three years, she had come to value her independence. Marriage meant giving it up.

Most of the time she simply wished she could remain on her own as she had been, without the restrictions of a husband who would govern her every move.

"Velvet?"

"Yes, Grandfather?"

"It seems to have slipped my mind . . . where did you say we are going?"

Velvet reached over and squeezed his thin, veined hand. "Carlyle Hall, Grandfather. To marry the duke, remember?"

He nodded and smiled. "The wedding. Yes, yes, of course. You'll make such a beautiful bride."

Velvet didn't answer. Instead she fiddled with a lock of her powdered mahogany hair, smoothed the front of her apricot silk moiré gown beneath her heavy lap robe, and tried not to think of her wedding night. Or what the duke would say when she told him her dowry was all that was left of the Haversham fortune. Then again, Avery Sinclair appeared a somewhat reasonable man. He was wealthy as Croesus and he truly seemed fond of her. Perhaps he would understand.

Velvet leaned her head back once more and closed her eyes, hoping she could also close off her thoughts. She did for a while, until the sound of hoofbeats began to intrude into the quiet of the cool March evening. They grew louder, thundering even faster than the carriage horses' hooves, then the sharp report of a pistol brought the vehicle to a sliding, jolting halt.

"What the devil . . . ?" The earl frowned as he regained his seat, and Velvet leaned forward, sticking her head out the window.

"Good evening, my lady," said a tall man astride a big black horse. A spent pistol smoked in one hand, a cocked gun pointed toward the driver. Velvet sucked in a breath at the fearsome sight the dark rider made in the thin sliver of moonlight cutting through the cloudy night.

"Saints preserve us!" Tabby cried from atop the carriage. " 'Tis the 'ighwayman, One-Eyed Jack Kincaid!"

Velvet ducked her head back inside the coach, her body beginning to tremble. Good sweet God, it was him! She had heard about him, everyone had. He had robbed hapless travelers from Marlborough to Hounslow Heath. Now here he was in the flesh—black patch and all!

"There's nothing to be afraid of, my lady," the outlaw said in a quiet tone that carried an edge of steel. Leaning down from his horse, he turned the latch on the door and pulled it open. "Just hand over your valuables and you can all be safely away."

He was a big man, muscular, tall, and powerfully built. One eye was covered by a heavy black patch, the other was the fiercest shade of blue she had ever seen. She glanced at her grandfather, who looked totally befuddled, then back to the man on the horse. He was dressed in snug black breeches tucked into knee-high jack boots. A full-sleeved white linen shirt stretched over a wide, brawny chest.

"Believe it or not," she said in the steadiest voice she could muster, "we are traveling with very little money and not even much jewelry. You would be far better served to rob someone else."

He studied her a moment, then his gaze fell on the gilded crest on the carriage door, a dove in flight above two crossed swords. Peace and Strength. The Haversham motto.

"Perhaps. Then again, perhaps not. Hand over the old man's purse and yours as well."

She hastily did as he asked, her hand shaking as she handed him the pouches. She had told him the truth: There wasn't much in them. He frowned as he stuffed them into the waistband of his breeches.

"Now your jewels."

Her grandfather's heavy gold watch and a big ruby ring with the crest that also appeared on the door. It galled her to give them up. She unfastened the brooch on her bodice with an inward smile. The diamond pin was paste. The original, her mother's, had long been sold to pay off debts.

"That's all there is." She grudgingly handed it over. "I told you there wasn't that much."

A corner of his mouth curved up in a smile that really wasn't. His lips were nicely formed, she noticed, the bottom one slightly fuller than the top, but there was a hardness about them. His nose was straight, his brows dark and finely arched. A thin scar ran along the edge of a jaw that looked rigid and unforgiving.

"As you said, there isn't all that much." He stared again at the crest, and she wondered if he knew whose it was. "Since that is the case, I suppose I shall have to make the best of a bad situation." The smile slid away. "Get out of the carriage, Lady Velvet."

Dear God, he knew her name! "W-why? Wh-what is it you want?"

"I want you to do as I say."

"Not . . . not until I know your intention."

He surveyed her a moment, surprised at her bravado perhaps, assessing her it seemed. A hard look came into his features. "What I intend, my lady, is to ransom you to your bridegroom. You must be worth a fortune. Now get down from the carriage before someone gets hurt."

His last final words filled her with dread. *Before someone gets hurt.* Grandfather was old. She didn't want him injured.

"What is happening?" the earl asked as she bent and started unsteadily toward the door. "Where are you going?"

"It's all right, Grandfather." She tried to keep the quiver out of her voice. "This gentleman simply wishes a word with me. You mustn't fret yourself. I'm sure he means me no harm."

She looked up at the outlaw and caught a surprisingly earnest expression.

"I will not harm you, my lady. I give you my word on that."

"Your word? You expect me to accept the word of a brigand? You're telling me a highwayman has honor?"

"This one does."

Why she believed him she could not say, yet some of her

fear receded. He simply wanted money. She understood the lengths to which a person might go in order to get it. She stepped down from the coach, straightening her wide panniers and wishing the bodice of her gown wasn't cut quite so low. The outlaw took in her fashionable attire and she caught the hint of a frown.

He swung his gaze to the driver. " 'Tis time you were on your way. The lady will come to no harm as long as you do as I say." He brandished the pistol, leveling it straight at the coachman. "Stop once between here and Carlyle Hall and I cannot promise the outcome of her fate."

"Oh, my poor dear child!" Tabby whined. "To be ravished by the likes of One-Eyed Jack Kincaid." She was crying, dabbing her eyes with her handkerchief yet the words had a surprisingly wistful ring.

"I told you I mean her no harm," he snapped. "Now be gone!" The pistol roared and he tossed it aside, then another one magically appeared. Tabby shrieked, the coachman slapped down the reins, and her grandfather fell back against the squabs as the carriage thundered away.

Velvet watched it disappear round the bend with a heart that had turned to lead. Slowly she lifted her eyes to the outlaw's face.

"Take off that blasted cage you're wearing."

"Wh-what?"

"Your undergarment . . . that infernal cage beneath your skirt. Take it off."

Velvet felt sick to her stomach. He did mean to ravish her. How could she have been foolish enough to believe he meant her no harm?

"Here?" She stared at the winding road that disappeared into the forest, at the tall yew trees that formed a curtain along the way. An owl hooted from atop a distant branch, the eerie sound echoing in the darkness, sending a chill down her spine.

"Just do it."

Her bottom lip trembled but her chin went up. "Turn around."

"What?"

"I said turn around. I'm not about to disrobe in front of you."

"Good Christ, I'm not asking you to disrobe, just to take off that horrible contraption so you can ride in front of me." But when Velvet didn't move, he turned the horse the other way and sat staring off toward the woods.

Maybe he was telling the truth, maybe he wasn't. Velvet was no longer willing to find out. With a last glance at the outlaw, she lifted her skirts out of the way and started running. She wasn't about to meekly submit, not when she might escape.

Night was full upon them. The strip of moon dipped behind a cloud, leaving it so dark she could barely see the ground in front of her feet. Still, she only got a few paces away before she heard him swearing and the sound of his heavy jack boots hitting the dirt. Good sweet God, she couldn't let him catch her!

Plunging wildly ahead, pebbles cutting into the bottoms of her soft kid slippers, vines tearing into the lace at her elbow, Velvet raced on. She dodged a tree to the left, darted into the darkness off to the right, came into a clearing and ran even faster. Her side was aching, her heart threatening to pound through her ribs.

As fast as she ran, his thundering footfalls closed the distance. In seconds he was on her, knocking her to the ground, both of them rolling in the dirt. Velvet shrieked in anticipated pain, her breath rushing out in a woosh, but somehow he had managed to take the force of the fall and amazingly she remained unhurt.

Flat on her stomach beneath his bruising weight, but unhurt all the same.

"Get off me!"

"Dammit, hold still!" His big hands encircled her middle, slid between the waistband of her skirt and the tightly fitted bodice. He jerked the tabs that held up the skirt, then those that kept her panniers fixed in place. He certainly knew his way around a lady's wardrobe, she thought bleakly, struggling to wrench herself free.

"Let me go!"

Before she knew what was happening, he was off her, gripping the panniers at the bottom of her gown and jerking them neatly out from beneath it.

She was still fully clothed, she realized, still somewhat dazed as he helped her to her feet, only the bulky whalebone petticoat was gone.

He took in her dishevel, the dark reddish hair that tumbled around her shoulders, the rips in her bodice, and the dirt on her face.

"It's time we were away," he said. "For your friends' sake as well as your own—it would be better if we aren't here when they return."

Staring into that single fierce blue eye, Velvet shivered. Jack Kincaid might be a man of his word, but an edge of danger surrounded him like a cloak. His threats might be subtle, but she didn't doubt for a moment his ability to carry them out.

Ignoring the dust that still clung to her clothes and the pins that had fallen from her hair, she walked in front of him back to his horse. Lifting her up on the animal's back, he positioned her in front of him, then swung himself gracefully up behind her. Against her back, thick slabs of muscle flexed across his chest, and steel hard arms surrounded her to gather the reins.

A sliver of fear slid through her. The man was even bigger than he had first appeared and she was out here alone with him. Trying not to think of what he might yet have in store for her, Velvet gathered a handful of the horse's coarse black mane and clung desperately to the saddle.

In minutes they had disappeared into the forest, moving at a faster pace than seemed possible in the inky darkness, the outlaw unerringly finding his way. He was a remarkable horseman, she realized, sitting the animal with an easy grace, moving with all the bearing of a nobleman. For the first time, it occurred to her that his speech was that of a gentleman. Velvet wondered where he might have come from, what might have led him off the path of righteousness to the doomed fate of a rogue.

She wondered what her own fate would be, and if he would remain true to his pledge that he would not harm her.

Whatever occurred, one thing was certain. Her wedding was only a few days away. She had no idea what the duke would say to a ransom, or if he would be willing to pay, yet she had to go through with this marriage.

The first chance she had, she would have to escape.

The tall black gelding stumbled and Jason tightened his hold on the girl he held in front of him. She was small but not frail, with tilted golden brown eyes and an upturned nose. Her lips were full, her cheeks the color of a soft, ripe peach. High lush breasts nearly spilled from the top of her apricot gown, the underside occasionally brushing against his arm where he held on to the reins.

In their struggle in the dirt, her hair had come loose from its pins and long tendrils hung past her shoulders. A dark reddish hue, he thought, though he couldn't quite make out the color for the dusting of powder in what had once been an elegant coiffure. It tumbled free now, soft and silky where it curled against his hand, and he found himself wondering if the auburn color was correct.

The horse eased down a hill, forcing the girl more firmly against his chest, and his body tightened in response. Litchfield had warned him—a charming little baggage, he had said. But his description had hardly done the lady justice. Velvet Moran was as tempting a morsel as he had ever seen, fiery yet feminine, soft and sensual in all the right places—and he had been too long without a woman. Jason shifted in the saddle, trying to ease the hardness that had risen inside his breeches, and inwardly he cursed.

It had never occurred to him he would find his brother's intended attractive. It was the farthest thought from his mind. Now he found himself thinking what it might be like to bed her.

He wouldn't, of course. He had done a lot of things in the years since he had left England, despicable things just to keep himself alive. But he had never harmed a woman, never taken one against her will. He didn't mean to start with this one.

Besides, easing his lust was hardly important. What mattered was regaining his heritage, taking the first step that would see justice done.

Beginning the long painful journey that he hoped would clear his name.

He felt the girl shiver and reined up long enough to untie his cloak from the back of his saddle and wrap it around her shoulders, then he started off again. At first she held herself away from him, determined to avoid his touch. But the hours made her weary and now she slumped against his chest, her head tucked into his shoulder.

A pang of guilt slid through him but it didn't last long. He would do what he had to. The girl was safe, as he had promised. He was the one who would suffer. She stirred a little and wisps of her long silky hair brushed his cheek. He could smell her soft lilac perfume. The week would be hellish, but then it would be done. Over the years he had suffered far worse than an unwelcome measure of lust.

They rode a little farther and Litchfield's hunting lodge finally appeared. Thank God, he silently muttered, eager to get the sleeping woman out of his arms. He reined up in front of a small two-story structure built of pale yellow stone that sat at the edge of a meadow. There was a single bedchamber upstairs and an open-beamed great room with a big rock fireplace, which served as a kitchen.

The stableboy, Bennie Taylor, waited out front. As Litchfield had promised, the lad was capable and loyal to a fault. He would do whatever Jason asked.

"Evenin', milord." The youth was perhaps twelve years old, a sturdy young man with sandy brown hair and a distant, uncertain smile. Litchfield had introduced him to the boy as the earl of Hawkins, the name the marquess had given him. Since Hawkins was the name he had been using since he had left England, it was as good as anything else.

"See to the horse, lad. I'll take care of the lady."

"Aye, milord."

She awakened when he lifted her down, stiffened in his arms as he set her on her feet. "Where . . . where are we?"

"A place in the forest. I've tried to make it comfortable."

Her eyes tilted upward, accusing eyes that peered at him from beneath a thick fringe of lashes. "You planned this. You meant to take me all along."

He would like to take her, he thought, watching the flush creeping over her breasts, but not the way she meant.

"As I said, I hope you'll be comfortable." He tipped his head toward the lodge. "This way, my lady."

With obvious reluctance, she followed him into the house, stopping a moment in the entry, surprised it seemed that the place was so well cared for.

"Not exactly the sort of spot one would associate with an outlaw," she said.

"What did you expect? A garret above some seedy tavern?"

"Exactly."

"Sorry to disappoint you." He started toward the stairs, presuming she would follow.

"How much will you ask?"

He stopped and turned. "Beg pardon?"

"The ransom. How much will you ask?"

He smiled thinly. "How much do you think you're worth?"

Not nearly as much as you believe, Velvet thought with a surge of panic. Her safety depended on the coin she would bring him. She wondered what he would do should he discover how nebulous her worth really was.

"The duke may not value damaged goods," she said, thinking of her ruined reputation and the incorrigible prig Avery Sinclair could be. "He'll have no way of knowing that you haven't . . . that you haven't . . ."

A sleek dark brow arched up. "That I haven't what, my

lady? That I haven't ravished you? That I haven't carried you off and stolen your virtue?''

The heat rose into her cheeks. ''I'm telling you he might not be willing to pay.'' And her grandfather certainly couldn't.

But he simply shrugged his shoulders. Inside the house, they looked as broad as the beam above the door. ''I guess we'll just have to wait and see.''

Oddly, he didn't seem overly disturbed at the prospect. In fact so far nothing he had done seemed to fit one's usual perception of an outlaw. It should have been comforting. Instead she found it oddly disconcerting, as if something were happening just outside her range of vision, something she couldn't quite see.

''There's a room for you upstairs,'' he said, starting up to the second floor. ''Follow me.''

She did as he said, dragging her now too long skirts along the way. With her panniers gone, they trailed in her wake, weighing her down as if fashioned of lead instead of expensive moiré silk.

The outlaw must have noticed for a frown creased his brow. When they reached the top of the landing, he turned to face her. ''Stand still.''

Velvet shrieked at the glittering blade he pulled from his high black boot, and nearly toppled backward down the stairs. A long arm snaked out, barely catching her. The highwayman cursed.

''God's blood, I told you I'm not going to hurt you.''

She was shaking but she lifted her chin. ''That's a little hard to believe when you're standing there holding onto *that*.'' She pointed at the gleaming blade, and he smiled with a hint of malice.

Bending forward, he caught the hem of her dress and used the knife to cut off a good three inches across the front. ''Turn around.'' Eyeing him warily, she did as he commanded and more of the gown fell away. ''At least you'll be able to walk without tripping over the blasted thing.''

''If you hadn't practically undressed me—'' She stopped

midsentence at the look in that penetrating eye. Her cheeks
heated up and she glanced away. "I gather this is where I
am to sleep."

"The linens are fresh. I think you'll find the bed is comfortable."

She turned toward the window and for an instant hope
flared.

"Forget it. They've all been nailed shut, just in case you
get any ideas. And I'll be sleeping downstairs. Behave yourself, Lady Velvet, and soon you'll be on your way. You'll
merely be inconvenienced for the next few days."

Inconvenienced, she thought. If that were the only consequence she would pay. Still, she gave him a nod of resignation. "As you wish . . . my lord."

A dark brow arched up. She hadn't been sleeping, as the
outlaw had believed when the boy had addressed him as a
nobleman. And she wasn't going to simply sit by and wait
for him—whoever he was—to send word to the duke. To
hope that Avery would pay, to chance missing her wedding,
to lose Windmere, to destroy her family and her future. She
had to find some means of escape.

Velvet felt like pacing. Instead she sat curled in the center
of the deep feather mattress that covered what would have
indeed been a comfortable bed—if she had been able to
sleep. Instead she sat waiting, huddled in the darkness, still
dressed in her cumbersome gown, her uncomfortable whalebone stays poking into her ribs, secretly grateful that at least
her bulky panniers were gone.

Outside the window the clouds had grown more dense,
rolling, flat-bottomed thunderheads marked by distant
flashes of lightning.

It wasn't the kind of night she would choose to make her
escape, but every hour she remained only made her situation
worse. Though she had no idea where she was, surely sooner
or later, if she kept on walking, she would come upon a
village or a hamlet, or simply a cottage where someone
would help her.

All she had to do was get away.

How long had she been waiting? Long enough for the outlaw to fall asleep? She had checked the door but found it locked. The nailed shut window was her only escape.

Careful to keep the wooden slats of the bed from creaking, she swung her legs to the floor and slowly stood up, her heart picking up its pace now that the moment was at hand. Gathering the linen sheets she had knotted together to form a length of rope, walking on tiptoe, she made her way across the room, pausing at the bureau to pick up her makeshift hammer—the silver-backed hairbrush that along with a lovely silver comb, had been placed on the table for her use.

She glanced skyward, hoping someone up there would hear her worried prayer. "Dear Lord, I'm not very good at this sort of thing. I hope you'll consider helping me."

He must have agreed, for when she pressed the wad of linens against the pane and cracked it ever so carefully with the back of the hairbrush, the glass split neatly and only one small piece fell noiselessly away.

"Thank you." Her hands were shaking. She steadied them as best she could, then, piece by piece, lifted the splintered shards away from the sill, slowly increasing the size of the opening, then breaking off the wooden strips between the small panes and working to lift out the rest of the ragged glass. It took longer than she planned. A light rain had started by the time she had the last of the broken window stripped away and the length of linen tied to the leg of the heavy wooden table against the wall.

Praying the linen and the table would hold her weight, she wriggled through the window and, hand over hand, lowered herself to the ground. Her foot wound up in a puddle of mud and she gasped as the icy water filled her slipper and soaked through her white silk stocking.

Stifling an unladylike oath, Velvet made a quick survey of the grounds, trying to decide which way to go. Nothing looked familiar. She wished she had been paying more attention. Well, there was no help for it now.

Lifting her rapidly dampening skirts, Velvet started running toward the woods.

Jason blinked and blinked again, unable to believe what he was seeing. But the small figure he had seen dangling in front of the window, the figure now running toward the woods, would not go away. How the devil had she done it? He had nailed those panes shut himself. She had to have broken the glass, but he hadn't heard a sound. Now she was running again, headlong into what looked to be a rapidly building storm.

"God's blood." The woman was definitely a pain in the neck. Working the last button on his breeches, he pulled on his boots and grabbed up his cloak, tossing it around his shoulders as he raced out the door. Lightning flashed and thunder rumbled a warning. The damned wench had surely picked a foul night indeed to make trouble.

By the time he crossed the meadow following the direction she had taken, rain pelted down with a vengeance, and a fierce wind whipped through the trees. Lightning continued to flash and the rapid echo of thunder said it wasn't that far away.

One glance at the sky and Jason hurried even faster, beginning to worry in earnest. Cursing his petite captive with every frosty breath that whitened the chilly air, he raced into the forest. Rain stung his face and the wind tore at his hair, but his determined strides only lengthened. He caught the flash of her apricot skirts ducking behind a tree, heading deeper into the woods, saw the jagged edge of a bolt of lightning, heard it crack and sizzle as it knifed through an overhanging branch.

He started running flat-out, his heart pounding as loud as the thunder, slamming wildly against his ribs. What if something happened? What if she were injured, perhaps even killed?

Jason's stomach knotted. He had brought her here. It was up to him to protect her. He would, he vowed.

And prayed he could keep his word.

* * *

Velvet dragged in great burning gasps of air. The stitch in her side ached unbearably and her legs shook until she thought they might not hold her up. Her hair was a sticky, sodden mass that stuck to her bare shoulders, and her gown was a limp, wet rag that clung to her legs, weighing her down. Dear God, the storm had worsened so quickly! A light rain might have aided her, hidden her tracks from pursuit. The tempest raging around her, the fierce winds battering her arms and legs and tearing at her hair, threatened her very life.

Sweet Jesu, she hadn't planned on this! And yet she couldn't go back. The danger was just as fierce back at the hunting lodge.

She turned at the crack of thunder, fear prickling her spine, then lightning flashed again. Velvet stood frozen at the sizzling yellow spike arching toward her, so near she was certain the white-hot, jagged menace meant her death. The bolt slammed into the top of the tree above her, and a terrified scream tore from her throat. Twisting away from the flames that erupted among the branches just inches away, she whirled to run in the opposite direction.

Colliding instead with a solid wall of flesh, she screamed again.

"Damn you, Duchess." Hard arms closed around her, dragging her away from the flames above her head, dragging her to safety. He sheltered her against him, wrapped her in his cloak and pressed her face against the hard warmth of his chest. Her body was shaking, but she felt him trembling, too.

In some strange way she found it comforting.

They stood that way for several moments, his chest rising and falling beneath her cheek, his clothes smelling of rain and moist dark soil.

"Please," she said at last, "you must let me go." She lifted her eyes to his rain-slick face, her pulse running fast, her breathing ragged. "I-I have to get back."

He only shook his head. The leather thong had slipped

from his hair and dark waves fell to just above his broad shoulders.

"Please—I must get to Carlyle. I have to marry the duke."

He stiffened at the words, pulling a little away, and a harshness settled into his features. "You can marry whomever you wish . . . once you're returned. Until then, you'll stay here with me."

She started to struggle, tried to break free, but his hold only tightened. He shook her—not gently—forcing her to look up at him. "Listen to me, you little fool—don't you know you could have been killed!"

Before she could answer he lifted her up in his hard-muscled arms and started striding back toward the house. She could feel his heart pounding, matching the swift, thudding cadence of her own. Burnished dark hair fell over his brow and his jaw looked stern. Strangely, it occurred to her that even with the ominous black patch, Jack Kincaid was a very handsome man.

It didn't take long to reach the house, not with the long strides he was taking. Once he did, he kicked open the door and stepped in, setting her on her feet in a spot that quickly puddled with rainwater and mud.

She was shaking all over, numb with cold and the residue of fear and her failure. Her teeth were chattering so much she barely heard the foul oath he swore.

"Christ's blood, woman. How did you think to survive out there?"

"If . . . if it hadn't started raining . . . if it hadn't turned so cold . . ."

"Aye, and if pigs could fly you would have gotten away."

She lifted her chin. Perhaps leaving as she had was a stupid thing to do. Perhaps she should have planned things better, but she had been too upset to think clearly. She clamped down on her teeth to stop the noisy chattering and looked longingly toward the fire, where the outlaw knelt to stoke the flames.

More logs were added and in no time at all, a warmth pervaded the high-ceilinged room. Even though it did, soaked as she was, she continued to shiver.

"You've got to get out of those clothes." His deep voice rose above the crackle and hiss of the fire. Turning away, he jerked a blanket off the sofa where he had been sleeping. "Tomorrow the boy will bring you something clean to wear. In the meantime, you can wrap yourself in this." He handed her the blanket then stood there waiting, an implacable look on his face.

Velvet chewed her lip. Her fingers were numb; she couldn't even feel if her thumbs were still attached to her hands. Unfastening the buttons at the back of her bodice would be impossible. "Perhaps the gown will dry," she said, knowing there wasn't the slightest chance.

The outlaw scoffed. "Don't be a fool. Take it off. You can go upstairs if that is your wish, though if I were you, with that window broken in your room, I'd stay down here where it's warm."

She gnawed her lip. "Perhaps you are right, but . . . the truth is, unless you wish to play lady's maid . . . I won't be able to do it. My fingers are too cold to unfasten the buttons." Which she couldn't reach without help even if they weren't.

He muttered a curse then scowled, his single blue eye going dark. "Turn around."

Knees still shaking beneath her skirt, she did as he instructed. Modesty had its place, but this wasn't one of them. Biting back her embarrassment, she ignored the tickle of his big hands brushing her skin, and caught the gown against her bosom as the fabric fell away. When she turned, she found his broad back facing her, his eyes trained the opposite way. A gentleman outlaw. She had heard of such things, though not in connection with One-Eyed Jack Kincaid.

Hurrying, hoping not to test his patience, she stripped to her chemise and wrapped the blanket snugly around her.

"What about you?" Shuffling toward the fire, she released a deep sigh at the satisfying warmth that enveloped her.

"I'm used to a little discomfort." But he turned toward the fire, lifted his arms, and stripped the soggy linen shirt off over his head. For a moment, Velvet stood frozen. She had never seen a man's bare chest and certainly never imagined one that looked like *his*. In the light of the fire, it rippled with thick bands of muscle. A furring of dark brown hair covered the upper part and arrowed down past the waistband of his breeches. Not for the first time, she noticed the network of scars across the back of his left hand.

"I'll go fix the window," he said, sitting down to tug off his boots. Velvet turned away, trying not to notice the rustle of fabric that meant he had stripped off his breeches. "Then maybe we can both get some sleep."

Velvet said nothing to this. Her mind was still churning with the image of his hard male torso, of what it must feel like to touch a body like that, of whether that curly brown chest hair was as soft and silky as it looked.

She heard more rustling as he pulled on dry clothes, heard his footfalls climbing the stairs, then the pounding of wood while he boarded up the window she had broken. So much for her clever escape. She hardly felt guilty for making the effort, yet she couldn't shake the memory of the way he had protected her in the forest, the worry she had seen on his face.

Who was he? she wondered.

Why had the stableboy addressed him as a peer?

More importantly, now that her first attempt had failed, how was she going to get away?

CHAPTER FOUR

∞

*J*ason dumped the last heavy pail of hot water into the wooden tub he had set before the fire. In the tropics, he swam nearly every day. Bathing was a pleasure that over the years had somehow become a necessity. Already that morning, he had cleansed himself in the icy water outside. Now he figured, after her muddy attempt last night, the girl might appreciate a chance for some cleanliness, too.

And secretly he wanted to see what she looked like. She'd been lovely when he had first seen her, though his damnable eye patch had obstructed his view. How would she look with the heavy gray powder washed out of her hair, her pretty face freshly scrubbed, instead of smudged with dirt?

It was dangerous, he knew. He only had so much will and the lady tested it sorely. Last night, even muddy and bedraggled, he had wanted her. In the light of the fire, he had ached to caress her smooth skin, to bare her lush breasts and fill his palms with their pale, heavy weight.

It sickened him to think that his brother might have touched her, kissed her, perhaps even made love to her. His jaw clamped at the image even as he heard the sound of the door being opened at the top of the stairs.

Her head popped out. She surveyed him a moment before speaking. "Good morning, my lord."

"Good morning. I trust you slept well."

"As good as could be expected . . . considering the circumstances."

Jason ignored a twinge of guilt. "I brought you some clean clothes. I thought you might like a bath before you put them on." Young Bennie had provided them, since the lady's trunk had been too large to carry on the back of his horse, an oversight both he and Litchfield had made when planning the abduction. Fortunately, the lad's sister was nearly the lady's small size. Jason had paid the pair handsomely for a simple brown woolen skirt, white peasant blouse, and chemise, as well as a clean white night rail.

"A bath, did you say?" She glanced down at the tub and her face lit up with a smile that transformed her face. "I should quite love a bath."

Jason smiled, too. He had thought she might believe as so many English did that bathing led to illness. Apparently, she was willing to take the risk.

"Are you hungry?" He tried not to stare at the bare skin above the blanket, to notice the bedraggled mass of her hair instead, but the image of smooth pale flesh remained.

"I'm starving. Apparently being abducted hasn't affected my appetite."

"There's some cheese on the table, some bread and a mug of tea. I'll wait outside until you've finished."

Velvet said nothing, just stood on the stairs until he was gone and the door closed firmly behind him. An exhausted sigh escaped her. Her body ached from last night's misadventures and she had slept only a little, tossing and turning before falling into a brief, drugging sleep. She had awakened just after dawn to the slanting of the sun through her boarded up window, the storm having passed as quickly as it had appeared.

For a moment she'd forgotten where she was. Then memory crept in. Her abduction. Her thwarted escape. The storm. The dangerous highwayman. She'd glanced at her surroundings, the bedchamber with its ruffled muslin curtains, the wooden dresser against the wall, the blue willow porcelain bowl and pitcher resting upon it. Oddly, a tiny bouquet of

yellow daffodils bloomed from a cut crystal vase sitting beside it. Last night she hadn't noticed, nor paid attention to
the colorful blue quilt upon the bed.

As a prison the place wasn't really so bad.

Still, she was hardly safe here. Her abductor was just that,
and until she was free, she remained in danger. Her comfortable prison might wind up her tomb. Who was to say?

Descending the stairs, Velvet crossed to the window and
peered outside. Spotting the highwayman splitting logs some
distance away, she closed the curtains, then walked over to
the small copper bathing tub. Nervously, she chewed her
bottom lip. She was taking a chance, but the dirt and grit
had to go, and the outlaw was so strong he could have ravished her already if that was his plan.

She tested the water, found the temperature to her liking,
tossed aside the blanket, and stepped in.

A sigh of sheer pleasure whispered past her lips. Exactly
warm enough. She settled herself as deeply as she could,
enjoying the silky feel of the water against her skin, then
leaned forward to wash her hair. A cake of lilac soap had
been set out for just that purpose, and relaxing with con-
tentment, she lathered the heavy strands to wash the mud
and the last of the sticky powder away.

She scrubbed her face, recalling that the small heart-
shaped patch she had placed near a corner of her mouth had
been lost during her scuffle with the outlaw in the dirt.

She soaked for a while, till the water turned cold, climbed
out and dried off with a small linen towel. A clean chemise,
a brown woolen skirt, and white muslin blouse, the neckline
gathered above the breasts with a drawstring, rested on the
arm of the sofa. She dressed in them quickly, surprised to
find they fit, ate the bread and cheese, then sat on a stool
in front of the fire to drink the tea and dry her hair.

She had just about finished when the highwayman
pounded on the door.

"You had better be in there, Duchess, and you had better
be dressed. I'm coming in." The door slammed wide. Jack
Kincaid stood in the opening.

Velvet tossed her dark auburn hair back over one shoulder, set down her mug of tea, and straightened to face him. "You didn't tell me I needed to hurry."

The outlaw said nothing.

"I-I'm sorry if I took too much time. I'm afraid I wasn't paying attention. I . . . I was simply enjoying myself."

Jack Kincaid just stared.

"My lord?" she said.

He stepped into the room and closed the door. When he spoke, his voice sounded deep and a little bit rusty. "My apologies, Lady Velvet. I had begun to believe you had somehow gotten away. I—" He cleared his throat, one penetrating blue eye fixed on her face. "I can see I was mistaken."

She moistened her lips. "Yes . . . yes you were. Thank you, sir, for the bath. It was much appreciated, I assure you."

"Your hair . . ." he said. "It's like fire . . . the most remarkable color I've ever seen."

Something warm trickled through her. Why, she could not say. "Thank you, my lord."

"There's a brush and comb upstairs if you need them."

"Yes . . . thank you." The words sounded breathless, which was exactly the way she suddenly felt. He was looking at her strangely, making odd little flutters rise in her chest. "I was just on my way up to get them."

He remained where he was. Taking a moment to steady herself, Velvet walked toward him, passing him on her way to the stairs, catching the smell of woodsmoke and leather. Her hands were trembling. Why was her heart pounding so hard?

By the time she returned downstairs, her hair pulled back in a tidy little bun at the nape of her neck, he was kneeling near the flames, cutting up freshly washed vegetables and dropping them into a heavy iron pot, adding bits of mutton to what appeared to be the makings of a stew.

She watched his dark head bent to the task, his wavy hair tied back as it usually was, and remembered how wild and untamed he had looked the night of the storm. He seemed slightly more civilized now, yet the undercurrent was there, the barely leashed power. The danger.

It forced her to remember her peril, the jeopardy she was in every moment she stayed there, the ruin she and her grandfather faced should she fail to marry the duke.

The weather was clear: cloudless blue skies, a cool, gentle breeze. In the long hours just before dawn, she had come up with another plan of escape. All she needed was a means to see it through.

"I don't suppose you've heard from the duke."

He turned to face her. "The duke? You mean your beloved future husband?"

"I mean his grace, the duke of Carlyle."

"No." He went back to seasoning the stew, but beneath his white shirt, the muscles across his back appeared to be drawn more tightly than they were before.

"I suppose there hasn't been enough time—but you *did* send the ransom note."

He looked at her and his bottom lip curved faintly. "Why would I not? That is the reason I brought you here, isn't it?"

"I suppose so. That is what you have said." But he only glanced away. Why was it every time she mentioned the ransom, she got the feeling it had nothing to do with the reason she was there?

Morning passed into afternoon. The outlaw spent much of the day outside while she remained cooped up indoors. At least he had provided her with a stack of books, reading each title as he handed them over. *The Works of Milton.* Bunyon's, *Pilgrim's Progress.* A book of Shakespeare's Sonnets, and Defoe's, *Robinson Crusoe.* Though he played the role of gentleman, might even be a peer, she was still a bit surprised that he could read.

The next several hours she spent leafing through the volumes, but the pages failed to hold her interest—she had more important things to do. When he finally came back inside the house, she was pacing, determined to get on with her plan.

"How much longer before dinner?"

He glared at her over a wide, muscled shoulder. "Take it easy, Duchess. I'm not one of your servants. I'd suggest you ask nicely or you'll be doing the cooking yourself."

Her chin went up. "I've never cooked a meal in my life."

"Why am I not surprised?"

"Are you really a lord?" The change of topic caught him unawares. "I have a feeling you're used to the title."

He shrugged those powerful shoulders. "Perhaps I was . . . once. Now it has an odd sort of ring."

"But you *are* a member of the peerage?"

A dark brow went up. "Why? Does it make a difference? But then of course it would—to a woman who's supposed to marry a duke."

The phrasing struck her oddly. "What do you mean, *supposed* to marry? I *am* going to marry him. Neither you nor anyone else is going to stop me."

He dropped the spoon into the stew pot with a clatter. "That determined are you?" His jaw went tight. "I didn't realize you fancied the man quite that much." He rubbed the scar on the back of his hand. "I suppose there are times he can be charming. And I guess he is handsome enough. Are you telling me this is a love match?"

Velvet moistened her lips. In love with Avery Sinclair? Avery was hardly a man to love. He was too much in love with himself. Velvet sighed and stared into the flames. "No. I'm not in love with Avery. I wish I were. The marriage was arranged by my grandfather." *More or less.* "It suits both of us and it suits our families."

Some of the tension eased from his body. She wondered why he cared.

"The stew is ready." He filled a pewter bowl and handed it over, then filled one for himself. They said nothing during the meal and as soon as they had finished, he gathered up the bowls and carried them outside to wash them.

The time had come. Her heart skipped several beats then

started thrumming. Scrambling up from her seat, Velvet reached toward the fire, grabbed the heavy iron poker he had used to stoke the flames, and raced upstairs. She couldn't afford to wait any longer. She should have acted first thing this morning, but something had held her back.

She glanced toward the boarded up window, noted the bright rays slanting in through the cracks. The sun remained high; there would still be plenty of light before nightfall. This time she was taking his horse, and if all went as planned, he wouldn't be in any shape to follow.

Her hand felt sweaty around the long iron poker she carried. She wiped her palm against her brown wool skirt and pressed an ear to the door, listening for his return downstairs.

It wasn't long before she heard him moving about. She had already removed the bright yellow daffodils from the vase on the dresser and poured the water into the chamber pot below the bed. Now, holding the poker in one hand, she knocked the vase to the floor, unleashing what she hoped would pass for a shriek of pain as the glass crashed into splintery shards.

"Duchess?"

She made a weak little sobbing sound that was supposed to sound like crying, then quickly climbed up on the chair she had dragged behind the door. Her stomach felt tied in knots, her mouth cotton-dry, but her resolve remained strong.

"Duchess, are you all right?" His heavy boots took the stairs two at a time.

Velvet sucked in a breath for courage, raised the poker with shaking hands, held it aloft and waited till he burst through the door. Her stomach felt leaden—dear God she didn't want to hurt him—but she tightened her hold and the poker swung down toward his head.

A blazing blue eye caught the movement, went wide with astonishment. At the last possible moment he twisted. The poker caught the side of his head and glanced off his shoul-

der. Still the blow did its job and he went crashing to the
floor.

"Oh, dear Lord." Scrambling down from the chair, her
legs weak and trembly, Velvet tossed the heavy length of
iron away, knelt down and touched his cheek.

"I'm sorry," she whispered, trying to ignore his pitiful
groan of pain. "I had to do it. I have to get away." His
skin felt warm. She hadn't killed him, thank God. Hopefully
he wasn't hurt too badly.

Trembling all over, she raced down the stairs, stopping
only long enough to snatch up his heavy cloak and the bread
and cheese she had managed to stash away. Then she was
out the door and running toward the stable. The big black
horse was there but thankfully the stableboy was gone. She
had prayed he wouldn't try to stop her.

"Come on, Blackie," she whispered, remembering the
name the highwayman had called the horse, leading the animal from the stall by his halter, fastening the lead rope
around his head to use for reins. The saddle pad was all she
had time for. Pulling the horse through the door of the barn,
she climbed up on the fence and dropped down on its back,
adjusting her skirt around her, ignoring the stockinged legs
she exposed below the hem of her skirt.

"Good boy, just take it easy." He was a spirited horse,
but she was a passable rider. Better than most women, when
she was properly mounted. Surely she could manage the big
black gelding well enough riding astride to make it to some
sort of town.

At least that's what she told herself as she dug her heels
into the animal's ribs and leaned forward, but at the first
leap the tall horse made, big hands seized her waist and
jerked her roughly off its back. Velvet screamed as One-
Eyed Jack Kincaid swung her to the ground in front of him,
his face a dark mask of rage. Her breath caught. She whirled
to flee, but his fingers caught her arms, dug into the tops,
and halted any possible movement. A trickle of blood ran
from his hairline, and as much as she wanted to escape, her
insides clenched to see how badly she had hurt him.

"Going somewhere, my lady?"

Fear pumped through her at the cruel set of his jaw. Sweet God, mayhap now he would kill her. She bit down on her trembling lips. "I-I'm sorry. I had to get away."

His mouth twisted cruelly. "Sorry to disappoint you."

Her fear increased, a chilling tingle that slid down her spine and settled like cold steel in her belly. She stared into his features and for the first time it occurred to her that instead of a single blue eye glaring down at her with menace, this time there were two.

"Sweet Jesu," she whispered, suddenly transfixed. "Who are you?" Certainly not One-Eyed Jack Kincaid.

His features turned even more harsh. "Your nemesis, my lady. A man who has underestimated your will for the very last time." A shrill whistle brought the return of the horse. With a death grip on her arm, he led the animal back to its stall, dragging her along in his wake. He jerked off the pad and unfastened her makeshift reins, then dragged her back toward the house, his big rough fingers digging into her flesh all the way.

She tried not to cry, but his painful hold combined with her failure had her cheeks wet with tears by the time they reached the door.

The highwayman saw them, cursed, and surprisingly his hold on her gentled. "Get inside," he said gruffly.

She did as he commanded, taking several wary steps out of his reach.

He rounded on her with the full force of those penetrating eyes. "Dammit, woman. Can't you understand? I'll let you go when it's time and not before then. Make it easy on us both and resign yourself—you aren't leaving until I say!"

She sniffed and wiped the wetness from her cheeks.

"Bloody hell!" He stalked back outside, slamming the door so hard it rang into the smoke-darkened rafters. Through the window she saw him heading for the watering trough. He ducked his head beneath the surface, then shook the water from his wavy dark hair like a dog emerging from a chilly stream. Streaks of pink ran along his cheek, and guilt sifted through her.

Good Lord, she had never hurt another human being. She hated herself for it, yet couldn't deny she'd had good cause. She retreated several paces as he strode back in, but he made no move to approach her, only sank down on the sofa, closed his eyes, and rested his head against the back.

Velvet eyed him warily. A bruise was beginning to form on the side of his face, and another spasm of guilt lanced through her. She moved a little closer.

"I never wanted to hurt you," she said softly.

Two blue eyes cracked open. She felt them on her face as if he touched her. "You're a woman. I should have known better than to trust you."

Velvet sighed. "If you would tell me the truth, tell me what this is about, perhaps I could help you. I don't believe you are really Jack Kincaid. I'm not even sure you're after the ransom. Please . . . if you would just—"

"Lady, if you would just keep quiet, maybe my head would stop hurting."

Velvet bit down on her lip. The man was in pain and she was the cause. Making her way to the bucket of water by the fire, she dampened a cloth then returned to the sofa, carefully placing it across his injured head.

Those piercing blue eyes slid open. Something dark and turbulent swirled in their depths, something of hurt and betrayal. Something that made her wish she could change what she had done.

"I had to do it," she whispered. "I wish you could understand."

They drifted closed again. "Perhaps I do," he said without looking at her. "Perhaps I even admire you for it. I still can't let you leave."

Velvet said nothing more. She had never met a man like this one. She couldn't begin to understand him, and yet she was drawn to him. Fascinated by the danger that seemed to surround him. Touched by the gentleness she had glimpsed in him more than once.

She would continue to fight him. She had no other choice. But she knew no matter what happened, she would never hurt him again.

CHAPTER FIVE

∞

Carlyle Hall glittered like a jewel in the darkness of the crisp March evening, every window lit by glowing beeswax candles, strains of harpsichord spilling into the quiet of the night.

Built in the early part of the century, the house was Palladian in design and fashioned of Portland stone. With its lovely Venetian balustrades and stylish pedimented windows, it was a showplace in the surrounding West Sussex countryside.

Beneath the painted ceilings of the King James Room, Avery Sinclair paced in front of the gold brocade sofa where Bacilius Willard, a big, burly, ex-Bow Street Runner, stood with his tricorn hat gripped nervously in his hands.

"Where the devil is she?" Firelight played on the silver cadogan wig that covered the duke's golden hair. "By God, we've only three days before the wedding. Guests are beginning to arrive. So far they haven't realized the chit is missing, and even the old man forgets about half the time. But sooner or later they are bound to figure out that something is wrong."

"We should 'ave found her by now," the hulking man said. "We've set a dozen lads to tramping the roads betwixt 'ere and where the lass was taken. We're bound to run across them sooner or later."

"Well, it had bloody well better be sooner!"

Baccy nodded his big shaggy head. He had worked for Avery for more than six years, ever since he'd been caught in for petty thievery and been tossed into Newgate prison. "Coachy said the bloke took the lass for ransom, but nary the sign of a note 'as appeared."

"She's a comely little baggage. Mayhap the man's cods overruled his senses."

Baccy's broad, pockmarked face turned red. " 'E's touches 'er and 'e's a dead man. I'll track the bastard down meself and slit 'is throat from ear to ear. You've me promise on that, yer grace."

Avery waved the big man's words away. "In the scheme of things, whether or not he tups her is hardly important." Though the thought of being thwarted by a common thief sent a shot of fury through him. "What counts is that we find her—and soon. I can't keep the old man stashed away forever. In the meanwhile, there is the wedding. Time is ticking away."

Baccy turned his tricorn hat in his hands. "I won't fail ye, yer grace."

"I'm certain you won't." In truth, Avery believed the man's promise. Baccy Willard was as loyal as a hound. Avery had saved him from the gibbet at Tyburn Hill, plucked him from the jaws of death, and in return there was nothing the huge man wouldn't do for him.

It was exactly the result he had intended.

"Be gone with you now," Avery said, slapping a hand over one meaty shoulder, a pat much like tossing a spaniel a bone. "Bring the chit back and you'll find a nice fat pouch of golden guineas waiting for you."

Baccy made no answer. Unlike Avery, money meant little to him. He worked for a kind word, a moment of praise, or a smile of thanks.

Avery watched him leave and felt a jolt of satisfaction, thinking it the best sort of bondage he could imagine to imprison a man.

*   *   *

Another day had passed. Jason brought the currycomb through his horse's thick black mane, using the slight task to take his mind off the girl inside the cottage. His head still throbbed whenever he moved too quickly. Damn, he couldn't believe he'd been gull enough to fall prey to her scheme.

Once, eight years ago, Celia Rollins had unmanned him in much the same manner. She had nearly been the death of him. God's bones, he should have learned his lesson.

And yet the circumstances were nothing the same. Velvet Moran had not betrayed him, hadn't pretended feelings for him she did not have. She wasn't in league with the devil in the form of his conscienceless brother. She wasn't after control of his fortune.

She was simply trying to escape. She was fighting to save herself from a man who posed an unknown threat, a man whose intentions she could not guess, nor what end for her he might have planned.

In the same set of circumstances, would he not react the same?

In truth, as he had said, he admired her for the courage to take action. Other women would have swooned at the sight of him riding full tilt toward the fancy Haversham carriage. Most of them would have dissolved into tears to see him firing his brace of pistols above their heads.

Velvet had done neither. She had sacrificed herself for the safety of the others, then fought him with every ounce of strength she possessed.

She was too much woman for his murderous half brother and in the past few hours he had determined the bastard would not have her. She deserved to make a decent marriage. Once she was free of the duke, she could find a respectable husband, a man befitting a woman of spirit and fire like Velvet Moran.

He glanced to the door of the house and a reluctant smile touched his lips. He wondered what, even now, she was planning, for he didn't believe for an instant that she had given up trying to thwart him.

She wouldn't succeed. Of that he was certain. He had too much at stake to succumb to a slip of a girl.

The smile on his face grew broader. Considering the lump he carried on the side of his head, he found himself oddly eager to see where next her reckless courage might lead him. He began to think of finishing his self-imposed currying task and heading back to the house.

Velvet peered through the slats of the boarded up window in her bedchamber. The highwayman remained yet in the stable. The highwayman. That was how she still thought of him, though with his two good eyes he was definitely not Jack Kincaid. And he was even more handsome than she could have imagined. So tall and imposing he took her breath away.

Velvet sighed. Whoever he was, he was still her opponent, a man she must somehow outwit. It wouldn't be easy, as she had already discovered, but if it could be done, she was determined to find a way.

Bearing that in mind, she eased the bottom drawer of the dresser closed, disgruntled that she hadn't found anything useful inside.

An old wooden chest sat along one wall. She crossed the room and knelt before it. She wasn't afraid he would catch her. She could hear him if he returned to the house, and even if he came upstairs, he had made no effort thus far to invade the privacy of her bedchamber.

The chest creaked as she lifted the lid. A tray of sewing items: a ball of wool not yet spun to thread, needles fashioned from the antlers of a deer, a skein of colorful embroidery thread, several lengths of simple undyed woolen cloth. Nothing there to aid her. She lifted off the tray and searched a portion of the chest below. Medicinal supplies: strips of bleached muslin for bandages, a hartshorn of ammonia for swoons, several jars of salve. She pried the lid off one of the jars, then wrinkled her nose at the smell of rancid lard mixed with horseradish and dark flecks of nameless herbs.

Several more packets of herbs lay in the bottom. She opened one of them, recognized the smell of dried nettles, opened another packet and frowned. It was a type of fungus found in the woods, a narcotic plant that was often crushed into powder and mixed with mulled wine as a sleeping potion. Cook had shown her how to fashion such a draught for her grandfather, when the occasional need arose.

A shadowy thought teased the back of her mind. She tried to shake it, but it wouldn't let go, mushrooming instead into a full-fledged notion. She had vowed not to hurt him, but how hurtful would it be if he simply fell into a deep and relaxing slumber?

In time he would awaken.

By then she would be gone.

Velvet grinned and clutched the packet to her chest. They took their main meal midafternoon. Earlier, the stable lad had brought cold pigeon pie, mutton pasties, some Stilton cheese, and a flagon of wine. Wrapped in a cloth, the food and wine sat on a table beside the hearth.

She glanced once more out the window. No sign of the outlaw. Placing the packet of herbs on the floor, she crushed them to powder with a slippered foot, then pounded them even finer with a heavy pewter mug that sat beside the water bowl and pitcher on the dresser.

As soon as she had finished, she headed downstairs. The flagon of wine sat exactly where the boy had left it. She pulled the stopper from the flask and started to pour in the powder, but her hand stilled at the top of the jug.

How much to put in?

He was a big man. It would take a goodly portion, but he never consumed more than a goblet or two of wine. As far as she knew, the powder wasn't deadly. She closed her eyes and dumped in the entire contents of the packet, then restoppered the jug and shook it until she figured the mixture had dissolved.

Footsteps sounded just as she finished. She whirled away from the hearth and rushed to the sofa, grabbed up the book she was supposed to have been reading, and buried her nose in the pages, hoping the guilty flush in her cheeks would fade before the highwayman—whoever he was—had time to notice.

The outlaw paused in the doorway, eyeing her a moment longer than he should have, then he stepped into the room and closed the door. She forced herself not to glance up at his approach, though his long, predatory strides never failed to capture her attention.

"Shakespeare's Sonnets." His dark brows pulled together. "I thought you were reading Defoe."

Her heart began racing. Sweet Jesu, how could she have forgotten? She feigned a weary sigh. "In truth, not a one of them holds my attention. All I can think of is how much longer must I stay locked up inside?" The testy remark seemed to satisfy his suspicions.

"Sorry, Duchess." A corner of his mouth curved up. "Think of it as respite from the heavy responsibilities you'll be facing as the wife of a duke."

Velvet tossed back her hair, growing a little too fond of wearing it loosely tied back and completely devoid of powder. "La, I'll have a hundred servants at my beck and call. I imagine I shall be able to suffer along."

The outlaw scowled.

She set the book away and looked into his handsome features. "You have two good eyes, not just one. I don't believe you are really Jack Kincaid. At least will you tell me your name?"

For a moment he said nothing and she didn't think he would answer. Her heartbeat quickened as he moved toward the table where the wine sat, unwrapped the food and began to set it out. He looked at her over his shoulder.

"Jason," he said. "My name is Jason."

Velvet smiled. "Jason," she repeated, letting the name roll off her tongue. It had a softness to it at odds with the man, a veneer of civility that didn't fit his dangerous persona. "Not an outlaw's name, yet in a way it suits you."

Jason said nothing, just stacked two pewter plates with food and poured them each a goblet of wine. Velvet accepted the food and drink, carried them over to the sofa and sat down. She nibbled at the cold pigeon pie, but her stomach rumbled with nerves and she couldn't really eat. Instead, she pretended to sip the wine, careful not to swallow a single drop.

Jason polished off his plate and downed his wine, poured a second gobletful and drank it down. When he refilled his glass a third time, she went tense.

"My, you're certainly thirsty today."

He looked down at the glass then at her, caught the way she unconsciously nibbled her lip.

"You fear I'll get drunk and ravish you? You may trust that I will not." He finished the contents of the goblet. "Rest assured, my lady, a few glasses of wine will not turn me into a ravening beast." But he blinked even as he said the words and the glass came sluggishly back to rest on the table.

Velvet watched him from beneath her lashes, saw his tall frame sag down in the chair beside the low-burning fire. He stared into the embers, the wine forgotten, her presence seemingly forgotten as well. Sweet God, it was actually working!

The minutes slipped past. Little by little, his eyes began to close and Velvet's speeding pulse began to hammer even faster. It was going to work. Dear sweet Lord—her plan was actually going to work! His head slumped forward, sagging slowly toward his chest. Lower and lower, he sank in the chair, his body growing limp, the heavy muscles relaxing, his eyelids now completely closed.

Only a little while longer, Velvet thought, her nerves stretched taut with excitement and the urge to run. Only a few minutes more and she could be away.

His head tipped forward, eased down until his chin came to rest on his chest. Velvet leaned forward as well, poised on the edge of the sofa, her heart pounding, waiting . . . waiting . . .

She was almost on her feet when the outlaw made a heavy lurch sideways then jerked upright. He blinked, blinked again, ran a hand over his face, then groggily turned in her direction.

The minute he did, those fierce blue eyes read the guilt in her expression and he knew in an instant she was somehow responsible for his state.

"What did you do!" he roared, bolting to his feet. "Forgodsakes, did you poison me?" Two long strides and he had her, his big hand clamping around her wrist.

She tried to break free, but his hold was like iron. "Sweet Jesu—no! I would not do such a thing! You are not going to die—'tis simply a sleeping draught. It isn't going to hurt you—you will merely fall asleep!"

He staggered and nearly fell, but he didn't let go of her wrist. "Vixen!" he shouted. "Bloody little vixen!" He dragged her a few steps closer to the fire, then his hand shot out and he grasped the leather thong that had held the cloth tied around the food.

"Wh-what are you doing? What—" She shrieked as he jerked her against him, wrapped the thong around her wrist and his own, and tied it tight, clumsily poured a measure of wine over the knot to soak the leather then jerked it even tighter.

"I may be sleeping, Duchess, but you may rest assured that while I am, you will not be leaving." He staggered toward the sofa, meaning to lie down before he fell, but he didn't make it that far. He caught her against him as his eyes rolled up. His knees buckled, and the two of them crashed to the floor, landing in a tangle of arms and legs, the highwayman's crushing weight atop her.

"Oh, dear God." She could hardly catch her breath. It took considerable effort to move him the necessary inch to allow her lungs to fill with air. It took a moment more to get her bearings. Once she did, her face went hot with embarrassment. Her cheek was pinned against his shoulder, his thigh wedged intimately between her legs, and a big callused hand lay on her breast. Long fingers curved around it, saved only from touching her skin by the barrier of her thin muslin blouse.

The tip of a finger brushed her nipple.

The moment she felt it, the soft peak tightened and a strange, soft heat slid into her belly. Good sweet God! She shifted but she could not move, and only succeeded in pressing her feminine parts more closely against his leg. She was riding the long hard muscles in his thigh, and with the knowledge, a burning heat began in the core of her.

Her heart pumped with maddening force, yet an odd curiosity began to swell inside her. One of her hands was solidly bound, but she could move the other. She lifted it a tentative inch then another. She could feel his linen shirt beneath the tips of her fingers, which skimmed across a wide, powerful, vee-shaped back down to a waist that was narrow and also swathed in muscle. With a will of its own, the hand moved lower, over a rounded buttock, testing the curve and the firmness. Guiltily, she jerked it back to his waist, but the memory of his solid flesh lingered.

Velvet gritted her teeth. A worse torture for herself she could not have devised. Hours of lying beneath him while his warm breath fanned her cheek and his hard body held her immobile. Hours of these strange, tingly sensations coursing through her blood and pooling low in her belly. As the long minutes passed, a soft ache arose, one in her breast, tempting her to press herself more fully into his hand, one in a place lower down.

Sweet Jesu—what was the matter with her? The man was a highwayman, a robber, perhaps even worse. Still the ache persisted, and as the hours crept past, she cursed him. She also cursed herself. How had she let this happen?

By the time darkness descended, his heavy weight had begun to take its toll. She was exhausted from straining away from him, from fighting to get free. From trying to ignore the heat of his big body and the soft tingly aching in her own. Uncertain how much longer she would be trapped beneath him, she welcomed her fatigue and eventually drifted to sleep.

Though the fire had long died, she didn't get cold, and in her sleep she felt oddly protected.

* * *

Jason stirred. His head was pounding as if a dozen andirons were banging inside it and his body felt strangely lethargic. All but one part.

He was hard as a stone, throbbing with the same pulsing rhythm that pounded inside his head.

God's breath, what the devil was the matter? He shook his head, trying to clear his muddled thoughts, opening his eyes with a Herculean effort. Christ's bones, he was lying on the floor! The room was dark and cold and he was starting to shiver. His head snapped up, his thoughts careening toward the woman, frantic to think she might have escaped and if she had, where she might have gone.

Then events came rushing in. Even before he moved, he felt her soft body beneath him, saw that her skirt was hiked up and her legs splayed by his, saw that one of his hands cupped a breast.

Jason groaned, his arousal going stiffer, pressing into the warm vee between her legs. Flame dark hair brushed his cheek and long soft tendrils curled around his neck and shoulders. He moved instinctively and the nipple beneath his palm crested against his hand.

His body throbbed in response and Jason swore a silent oath. Swiftly, he came up on his knees, rousing her with the movement, causing her to blink and stare into his face.

He gave her a reckless smile. "Enjoying your slumber, my lady? I should have thought you would prefer your nice, comfortable bed."

"Bastard!" she shouted, rolling away from him, only to be brought up short by the coil of leather around her wrist.

"Easy, Duchess. This was your little misadventure, not mine."

"Y-you are saying this is my fault? You are blaming me? Nothing that has happened is my fault! You are the one who abducted me!"

"And I am the one who grows weary of your attempts to thwart me." He came unsteadily to his feet and helped her climb to hers. "Hear me well, Duchess—try another reckless stunt like this and I will not be held accountable for my actions." He forced her chin up with his hand. "I can promise you, however, next time I will not be nearly so forgiving." He looked at her hard. "Do I make myself clear?"

For a moment she said nothing and he released his hold on her chin.

"There is a simple way to end this," she finally replied, easing herself away. "You could simply just let me leave."

"When the time is right, I will."

"And, pray, when will that be? *After* it is time for my wedding?"

He glowered down at her. "Exactly so."

"What!"

"Believe it or not, someday you will thank me."

"Thank you! Have you gone insane?"

But he simply ignored her. " 'Tis cold in here." He bent and pulled the knife from his boot, brought the blade up and used it to slice through the thong binding their wrists. She looked as if she would like to sink the blade between his ribs.

Foraging through the logs beside the fire, he stacked them carefully atop the coals, then used the bellows to rekindle the last of the nearly dead embers into flame. "A blaze will be welcome."

"You . . . you are insufferable!" Turning away, she marched toward the stairs. Jason tried not to notice the way her long reddish hair floated down her back, to ignore the trim stockinged ankles beneath her raised skirts. He tried most of all not to think of how her breast had felt cupped in his hand.

As she stepped inside her bedchamber and slammed the door, he was suddenly glad he had slept so long and so soundly. With memories of the woman's soft body plaguing him for the balance of the evening, he wouldn't be getting much sleep.

Jason glanced toward her door at the top of the stairs. Of that he could be certain.

*   *   *

The duke smiled effusively at the Viscount Landreth and his fleshy wife, Serena, who topped the broad granite stairs and sashayed into the entry.

"Good of you to come, Landreth. Devilish journey, what with the roads so blessed muddy."

"Wouldn't have missed it, what?" He winked broadly, causing the quizzing glass to fall from the thick folds of skin around his eye. "Tempting little morsel you've snared. Hoped for a match between her and my son, but I daresay he hadn't much chance against a man of your standing."

Avery smiled politely. "I'm a fortunate man, indeed." He turned to the butler, standing a few feet away. "Show his lordship and his lady up to their suite of rooms, Cummings. Lord Landreth and his wife must be tired. I imagine they will wish to refresh themselves after their journey."

"Quite right," said the viscount. "Gout's paining me a bit and all that."

Avery smiled. "I look forward to seeing you both at supper."

The butler inclined his graying head toward the guests, and the viscount and his entourage of servants were ushered away, affording Avery the chance to escape.

He headed straight for his study, where Baccy Willard stood waiting like an errant schoolboy in front of the duke's carved rosewood desk. Avery closed the door with an edge of force and saw him cringe.

"All right, where is she? You said that you would find her. You promised me that, and yet you have failed."

Baccy hung his head. "We've scoured the bleedin' 'ills, yer grace, but we 'aven't found nary a sign of 'er."

Anger surged but Avery forced it down. "He must have ridden farther than any of you imagined."

"Aye, yer grace. We believed 'e would stay close by to pursue the ransom."

"Well, obviously he didn't."

"No, yer grace."

Avery clamped his jaw. "Day after the morrow is the day

of the wedding. By eventide, the house will be swarming with guests. What do you suggest I tell them?''

Baccy shrugged his massive shoulders. ''The truth?'' he suggested lamely.

''The truth! What truth? That the girl was abducted, or that if this marriage does not take place I shall be ruined?''

His thick head hung slack at the top of his stout neck. ''I didn't mean that truth, yer grace.''

''I'm sure you didn't. Now I suggest you get back out there and find her. Her grandfather is becoming a problem, and a note arrived just this morning from the solicitor in London who represents the holder of the note on Carlyle Hall. If we don't act soon, the mortgage will be foreclosed. I will be facing poverty, and you, my dear man, will be well on your way back to a life on the streets.''

Baccy shivered. ''I'll find 'er, yer grace.''

Avery picked up a heavy glass paperweight on his desk and stared into it with icy eyes that mirrored the cold crystal depths of the glass. ''Then do so.'' When Avery said nothing more, the burly man turned away from the threat he had seen in the duke's hard features and loped toward the door.

Avery watched him go. For reasons even he didn't quite understand, Baccy Willard was the one man he confided in. Though the man's intellect was barely above that of a child, Avery said things to him he said to no one else. Mayhap he knew the man didn't really understand. Or perhaps it was the knowledge Baccy's tongue could be cut out before he would breathe a word of anything Avery said.

Mayhap it was merely that every man needed someone to talk to and there was simply no one else.

Whatever the reason, he didn't concern himself about it. Not the way he was worried about the disappearance of the Haversham heiress. He needed Velvet Moran. He needed her bulging dowry to save his skin.

Where the devil was she?

Avery paced back and forth, cursing the highwayman who had taken her, cursing Baccy Willard for his failure to return her, cursing the twist of fortune that had forced him to mortgage the house and the merciless holder of the note, whoever he might be.

"God's teeth!" He shook his fisted hand, wishing the outlaw to bloody perdition, wishing he didn't have to face his growing stream of guests. By day after the morrow, the wealthiest members of the ton would be ensconced at Carlyle Hall. He had spared no expense to impress them, his creditors more than eager to assist, his debts held at bay by rumors of the fortune that would soon fall into his hands.

And Velvet Moran, what of her? Sullied or not, as long as she was breathing, he would marry her. He would redeem Carlyle Hall, get a brat on her, and leave her to repine in the country. He would spend his time in the city, use her fortune to rebuild his own, and his power would be as strong as it was when his father was the duke of Carlyle.

Until then, he simply had to persist. Avery pasted on a smile and returned to his guests.

CHAPTER SIX

∞

*T*wo days passed. Today was the day of her wedding. Velvet wondered what Avery had told the guests, how he had explained that his betrothed had not arrived, that there would be no marriage as had been planned.

She had failed to escape, failed to return in time to marry the duke. All morning, Velvet felt the weight of defeat like a millstone across her shoulders. She glanced toward the door, but it remained tightly closed. The highwayman lurked outside, careful to stay away from the house and out of the path of her fury. Only the stableboy had appeared, emptying chamber pots, delivering foodstuffs, but saying nothing, his manner making it clear his loyalty lay with the man named Jason.

The lad was upstairs working now, tidying her bedchamber and freshening her pitcher of water. She watched as he descended the stairs, his eyes carefully averted from where she sat reading.

She marked her place in the book with a finger and turned to look at the boy, whose eyes were carefully fixed on the floor in front of him.

"Your name is Bennie, isn't it?" It was all she could think of to say. She wished she could think of a way to convince him to help her.

"Aye."

"Are you a friend of Jason's?"

His sandy-haired head snapped up. "Are ye speakin' of 'is lordship?''

"Yes, I am."

" 'E pays me, that's all. I'm to do as 'e says." Bennie started uneasily toward the door.

"It's very pretty out here in the forest . . . don't you think?"

"It's terrible cold in winter, but I s'ppose it's nice enough."

"I've forgotten the name of that little town along the road not far from here . . . what is it called . . . ?"

He eyed her warily. "Don't be tryin' yer tricks. 'Is lordship warned me, said you was a wily one . . . that I was to pay you no 'eed."

Velvet lifted her chin. "What else did he tell you? Did he tell you he kidnapped me? That I'm being held here against my will?"

The boy stepped toward the door, shaking his head, sandy hair falling over his eyes, hiding most of his thin, angular face. "Ain't no business of mine why 'e brung ye 'ere. 'E 'asn't 'urt ye none that I can see. You're 'is woman. You should mind what 'is lordship says."

"His woman! Is that what that lying cur told you?" But the boy merely started toward the door.

"I could pay you," Velvet called after him. "If you would help me get away, I would give you twice the sum he is paying."

The boy ignored her as if she hadn't spoken, opened the door, went outside, and closed it firmly behind him.

So much for her efforts to sway him. She had guessed from the start Bennie's loyalty could not be bought and in a way she liked him better for it.

Still, it didn't help solve her dilemma. With a sigh of despair, she returned to the sofa, glancing at the clock above the mantel along the way. Two in the afternoon. By now she should have been married. Never mind that if she were, she would be frantic with worry over the wedding night she faced with Avery Sinclair.

Though his cool demeanor was unnerving, and none of his unappealing kisses had stirred her, she would have done her duty. It was simply part of the bargain, a price she would have willingly paid to save her family and the home she loved.

Perching restlessly on the sofa, Velvet picked up the leather-bound volume of *Robinson Crusoe* she had been trying to read, but the letters on the page seemed to blur. Anger and disappointment sat like a rock in her stomach. In a burst of temper, she slammed the book closed, tossed it aside, and watched it land with a thunk on the floor.

Curse him! If she didn't marry the duke how on earth would she and her grandfather live?

They were nearly out of money. They were behind in the servants' wages, and there wasn't that much left in the house to sell, not and keep up the facade she would need to snare herself another rich husband.

She glanced out the window, saw the highwayman in the distance, exercising his tall black horse at the end of a lead rope. Why did he want to stop the wedding? What could her marriage to the duke possibly have to do with *him?*

But no answers came.

Frustrated, she flounced off the couch, stooped to pick up the heavy volume from where it had fallen, and noticed the flagstone beneath it appeared to have been knocked loose. Velvet looked closer. The stone had been purposely set in the floor that way; it had never been firmly mortared into place. She moved the book out of the way and began to dig out the stone, wondering if some sort of hidden cache might lay beneath it.

Grunting with the effort, she lifted the heavy rock free and spotted a small leather pouch that had been stashed in the dug-out impression. It jingled of coins when she hefted it, but it was the weapon lying in the hole beside it that snagged her attention.

Excitement trickled through her. With hands that were suddenly clumsy, she picked up the old blunderbuss, carefully lifting it out of its hiding place and unwrapping its protective cloth.

Her fingers smoothed over the worn, polished wood. "I wonder if you work?" The piece had been well-cared for, she saw, the barrel still blue, the brass fittings still pungent with the scent of oil. It was primed and ready to fire, she realized, studying the weapon more closely. Whoever put it there had meant to be prepared for any threat that might arise.

She hurried to the window, saw the outlaw begin to lead his horse back inside the barn. He could return to the house at any moment.

She lifted the weapon once more, assessing the weight of it in her hands. It appeared opportunity had arisen yet again—she couldn't merely ignore it. Still, she could hardly shoot him. She smoothed the polished wooden handle. What to do . . . ?

Velvet bit her lip as the door swung open and Jason walked in, carrying an armload of wood. There was no way to hide the gun, no way to postpone the action she must take—if she truly had the courage. Swallowing her uncertainty, she forced back the hammer, needing both hands to do it, raised the heavy blunderbuss, and aimed it at Jason's broad chest.

"I-I don't want to hurt you."

He dropped the load of wood he was carrying, the logs rolling out in front of his long legs. "What the hell . . . ?"

"All I want is to leave. 'Tis all I have ever wanted. But if you force me, I will use this. Step away from the door and let me pass."

A muscle jumped in his cheek. "Put the gun down, Duchess, before someone gets hurt." Hard sapphire eyes moved over her face. She found herself memorizing the exact shade of blue, stamping an impression of his features into her mind so that she would be able to remember.

"You are the one who will be hurt," she said, thinking that in a very few moments, the man called Jason would be gone from her life for good. The feeling brought a tightness to her chest. "I repeat—step away from the door and let me pass." Her heart thundered. The blunderbuss shook in her hands. She tightened her hold to steady it.

She wouldn't pull the trigger, but he didn't know that. She hoped she sounded convincing.

He moved a little closer. "I'm tired of your games, Duchess—put that cursed thing away."

She gazed longingly at the door, which still stood open behind him. "I can't do that." She began to circle around him, making a path toward the opening. When she glanced at his face, she saw his jaw clamp with fury. A muscle twitched in his cheek, and a trickle of fear shimmered through her.

"Please . . . Jason . . . get out of my way."

His big hands balled into fists. Blazing blue eyes snapped with a fire he made no effort to hide. "I've told you time and again that I will not harm you, that in a few more days I will release you. You refuse to listen. You have dragged me through the mud, hit me over the head, and nearly poisoned me. Now you threaten to shoot me. I'm warning you, Duchess, put that blasted gun down—this very minute—or you won't like the price you will pay."

She cocked a brow, intrigued in some perverse way by the challenge. "The price, my lord? You seem to have forgotten, I am the one holding the weapon."

His mouth twisted up. "And I am the one who will haul you over my knee and thrash you within an inch of your life if you don't do what I say."

Her bravado wilted. Velvet chewed her lip. The look on his face was pure menace. If he caught her he would beat her. The breeze wafted in through the open door. She looked down at the deadly weapon. Would he actually risk his life to stop her?

"The gun, Duchess."

She looked at the door with longing. It was simply just too tempting. Pointing the blunderbuss in his direction, she bolted past him toward the door. A harsh growl erupted and a hand snaked out of nowhere, knocking the barrel upward so quickly it discharged. Velvet screamed as wood and plaster rained down on their heads, as a muscled forearm wrapped around her waist and he dragged her roughly against him.

"I warned you," he barked, hauling her toward a chair, sinking down on the edge and hauling her across his lap.

"Let me go!" But he paid no heed. His big hand went up and three hard smacks fell across her bottom, burning through the simple woolen skirt, each stinging smack carrying the full force of his temper. Then he gripped her shoulders and jerked her over on his lap to face him, breathing heavily as he met her furious glare.

Velvet opened her mouth to unleash the vile oath she was thinking, but his hard look stilled the words. Their eyes clashed, held, steely blue and furious golden brown. An angry pulse throbbed in a vein at the side of his neck. His chest moved in and out, expanding the sinews across it, reminding her how solid it had felt pressing into her that night on the floor.

Unconsciously her tongue slid out to moisten her lips and she heard the highwayman groan.

"God's blood, woman." He caught her chin between his fingers just before his mouth crushed down on hers.

Stunned disbelief. Outrage. Then awareness of his firm lips over hers, the hard-soft feel of them, the warmth, the fierce way they took possession. A soft gasp allowed his tongue inside and he claimed the right as if it belonged to him.

The room seemed to spin. Her stomach fell away as if she had stepped off a cliff. Jason's hands sank into her hair and he dragged her toward him, dislodging the ribbon holding it in place, encouraging the heavy reddish mass to spill loose around her shoulders.

His mouth continued its plunder and a sweeping warmth slid through her. Her heart was hammering, pounding inside her chest. Beneath her thin blouse, her breasts began to swell, becoming sensitive and heavy.

Jason deepened the kiss, delving with his tongue and

starting little fires that shimmered across her flesh, making her feel trembly and weak. Her hands lifted up to his shoulders, her fingers digging into the muscles there, clinging as if his solid strength were the only thing holding her up.

"Jason . . ." she whispered when his mouth left hers to move along her jaw, down her throat, and across her shoulders.

"God, Duchess . . ." Then he was kissing her again, the hand at her waist moving upward until he cupped a breast. She shifted toward him, breathless and moaning, and her nipple stiffened beneath his hand. An ache rose up. She pressed herself more fully into his palm, and a husky sound rose in his throat.

Velvet didn't realize he had untied the drawstring at the front of her blouse, felt only the merest whisper of fabric as the blouse slid off her shoulder. Then the fires of Satan erupted in her stomach at the feel of his warm palm surrounding her naked breast. Good sweet God! She wasn't prepared for this, felt helplessly out of her depths.

"Jason . . ." she whispered, beginning to squirm, fighting for the remnants of control that seemed to be sliding ever further from her grasp. Her body felt on fire. Her breasts throbbed, and liquid heat burned in the place between her legs.

He kissed her deeply, ravishing her lips, then lowered his head and took her nipple into his mouth. Heat scorched through her. His tongue gently laved the sensitive end, a tiny sob escaped, and she arched upward, reason receding beneath a tide of pleasure like nothing she could have imagined. She knew she should stop him yet she could not summon the strength. Her hand shifted over the muscles across his back and they tightened at her touch. She dragged her fingers through his silky dark hair, dislodging the thin black ribbon that held it back, freeing the wavy strands to shadow his powerful neck.

She was trembling all over, her head thrown back, her hair a wild dark cloud, tendrils of it spiraling around his wrist. She could feel his hardened arousal beneath her as he held her in his lap, yet even the threat implied by his turgid flesh could not penetrate the haze of fierce sensations.

Only God, it seemed, could do that, and she silently begged for His intervention. It came in the guise of Bennie Taylor—or at least that was whom she imagined had set to pounding on the door.

"What the devil . . . ?" It took a moment for Jason to rouse himself, to end his drugging kisses and tear his mouth from her heated flesh. When at last he did, a draft of cold air rushed over the place he had abandoned and with it an icy jolt of reality, ending her passion-numbed state.

"Oh, my God," she whispered, her eyes going wide with the horror of what they had done.

"God's blood," Jason swore, pulling her blouse into place with a shaky hand, his eyes dark blue and stormy, looking nearly as chagrined as she.

"It's all right, Duchess," he said softly at the stricken look on her face. "I won't let him in." He began adjusting his clothes, the thick bulge in his tight-fitting buckskin breeches a blatant reminder of what had nearly occurred.

Velvet turned away, her face flaming, her insides churning with embarrassment, and the warm, tingling sensations that had led her down the fiery path of temptation.

She said nothing to the highwayman as he walked to the door and dragged it open. Nothing as he started speaking to Bennie, who stood a few feet away. When the boy pointed toward the barn, Velvet saw a lean gray horse tied to the fence and a tall man lurking in the shadows. He took a step out of sight before she glimpsed more than a portion of his face.

"I'll be right back," Jason told her. With a last sweeping glance, he stepped through the door and closed it behind him, leaving her in dishevel, her thoughts in turmoil, her body still embarrassingly warm.

Walking into the stables, Jason spotted Lucien Montaine waiting in the coolness of the shadows. Willing his pulse to slow, he shoved his hair back out of his face, wishing he had thought to bring the ribbon that held it in place. Wishing he didn't look like a man who had just been interrupted in the act of tumbling a maid. Cursing himself for doing just that, hating himself for the way he had behaved.

"And here I was . . . worried about you rusticating out here . . . afraid you might be getting bored." The heavy sarcasm in Lucien's voice wasn't lost on Jason.

He simply shook his head. In the scheme of things, the marquess of Litchfield missed little. Obviously, he knew exactly what had been going on inside the cottage.

"Boredom is the least of my problems." Jason raked a hand through his wavy dark hair. "Thank God you arrived when you did. I don't even know how it happened. One minute we were fighting, the next thing I knew I was kissing her. God, she has the softest, sweetest mouth I've ever tasted." He shook his head again, still not quite able to believe it. "At any rate, the fault is entirely mine, not the lady's. I never meant for anything like that to occur. I give you my word, Lucien, it will not happen again."

"I presume that means I arrived before you went so far as to deflower our pretty little innocent."

Jason closed his eyes, wishing he could blot out the memory of his hands on her beautiful breasts. "The girl is still a maid." But she wouldn't have been, if Lucien had not come when he did.

"Then it's good you've only a single day more in confinement with her. I trust you'll be able to control your baser instincts that much longer."

Jason sighed. "I can't believe I behaved as I did. I knew I had changed since I left England. I didn't know quite how much."

A bold black brow arched up. "Surely you were not in the act of taking the girl by force."

Jason's eyes went wide. "Forgodsakes, no. Even I wouldn't stoop that low."

Lucien's mouth curved faintly and he clapped him on the back. "Then relax, my friend. The lady is a comely little

baggage, a temptation for any man. Do not castigate yourself for simply being human.''

Jason smiled at that. "Her virtue will be safe, as I have
said. Still, I'm glad this business is almost done.''

"Which is what I have come to tell you. Avery has received the missive which alerts him to the final hours before
foreclosure. By tomorrow at midnight, Carlyle Hall and its
surrounding fourteen thousand acres will once more belong
to you.''

Jason nodded with satisfaction. "What of the wedding?
What have you heard?''

Lucien chuckled softly. "I daresay, it was priceless.
When I arrived at Carlyle Hall early this morning, Avery
was spreading on the sentiment so thickly it would have
covered the red heels on his shoes. He was grief-stricken to
discover his betrothed had fallen into the hands of high-
waymen on her way to the wedding. He was sparing no
expense to find her, but the marriage would have to be post-
poned.''

Jason frowned. "He still plans to marry her?''

Lucien assessed him for several long moments, then
shrugged a pair of shoulders nearly as wide as Jason's own.
"If she will still have him. Then again, perhaps she will
discover the truth of his circumstance. I doubt the Haversham heiress will be much interested in allying herself with
a poverty-stricken duke.''

Jason's shoulders relaxed as the notion sank in. He hadn't
realized how tense he had grown at the idea of Velvet marrying his brother. "Then I shall see her safely returned to
Carlyle Hall day after the morrow. No need for her grandfather to worry any longer than necessary.''

Lucien nodded. "If there is a problem, I'll send word,
but I don't expect any. As soon as the girl is home, you can
join me at my estate. From there we'll continue our efforts
to clear your name.''

Jason extended a hand and the marquess shook it. "Thank
you, Lucien. I'll never forget what you've done.''

"We've only just started, my friend." He inclined his

head toward the cottage. "In the meantime, I don't envy you the next two days."

Jason rolled his eyes. "You have no idea."

Lucien just laughed. Careful to keep his back turned toward the windows, he swung up on his horse. "Take care of yourself. I'll see you soon."

Jason watched him ride away, then sucked in a long slow breath and started back to the lodge. He expected the girl to be locked away in her room, wreathed in remorse and embarrassment, blaming him—however rightly—for the things that had occurred.

Instead she sat quietly on the sofa, her eyes fixed on the pages of her book. He eased the door closed behind him and crossed the room to the place in front of her, but she didn't glance up from her reading.

"I know you are angry."

The girl said nothing.

"I'm not saying you don't have every right to be upset. I want you to know I never meant for any of that to happen. I never meant to touch you. I apologize, Lady Velvet. And I give you my word that it will not happen again."

She lowered the book and he noticed the flush that pinkened her cheeks. "I did not think to hear an apology. Coming from a highwayman, it is quite unexpected." She moistened her bottom lip. For the first time he realized how hard she was working to remain in control. "Your speech was very gallant, my lord, but in truth, the fault was also mine. I behaved very badly." She shook her head, swirling the burnished dark hair that still floated cloudlike around her shoulders.

"I don't understand it," she said. "It was as if I were not myself. Perhaps the confinement, or . . ." Her cheeks went even pinker. There was another slight shake of her head. "I hope you do not believe that it is the norm for me to act in such a fashion. I assure you, my lord, it is not."

He almost smiled. "I may be jaded, my lady. I may not always hold women in the highest regard, but I realize an innocent when I see one. I should not have taken advantage.''

She glanced away from him, staring off toward the window, still not meeting his eyes. ''That man who came ... The hour of the wedding is past. Did the ransom arrive?''

''No ransom note was sent. It wasn't the reason you were taken.''

''Then the time has come for me to go home.''

He nodded. ''Day after the morrow I will see you safely returned to Carlyle Hall. I believe your grandfather is still in residence. I'm sure he'll be eager to see you.''

''Day after the morrow?''

''You have my word.''

She looked at him then, assessing him closely, not quite certain whether or not to believe him. ''But I have seen your face. Are you not concerned that I will tell them who you are?''

He did smile then. ''Who am I, my lady?''

''Why you are ... you are ...'' She tossed back her fiery dark hair and he tried not to remember the silk of it wrapped around his hand. ''You are a tall, brawny, blue-eyed highwayman. Your point is well-taken, sir.''

''Velvet?''

Her head came up at the intimate address. ''Yes?''

''There is something you should know about your future husband.''

She eyed him warily. ''And what might that be, my lord?''

''The duke is very nearly impoverished. Even Carlyle Hall does not belong to him.''

''What!'' She jumped to her feet, the book tumbling out of her lap. ''But that is absurd.''

''I'm sorry. You may have your solicitors verify what I'm saying, but you will discover that it is the truth.''

''I don't believe you. That is not possible. The duke is a very wealthy man.''

''There was a time he was. I'm afraid that time is past. The man is marrying you for your money. He needed it to prop up his flagging business interests. Over the years he's invested poorly. One failed scheme after another. He put a small fortune into a method for turning saltwater into fresh. Obviously it did not work. He invested heavily in a company which claimed it could extract silver from lead. Another time he tried to change quicksilver into a usable malleable metal. He has traded in human hair, imported jackasses from Spain, and backed an inventor who claimed to have constructed a wheel of perpetual motion.''

Her face slowly turned ashen. ''Dear sweet Lord.''

''None of these endeavors produced the least return. In business, the man is an utter failure. If you marry him, you will be risking your fortune in the hands of a man who most likely will see it destroyed.''

She sank back down on the sofa, her face even paler than before. ''Why are you telling me this now? If you wished to end the betrothal, why did you not say so before?''

''I never said I wished to end your betrothal. Suffice it to say, I could not take the risk of your money falling into his hands . . . at least not until after the morrow.''

Her hands began to tremble. She clenched them in her lap. ''You're telling the truth, aren't you?''

''Aye, Duchess, I am.''

Velvet fell back against the sofa. She started to shake her head and a small bubble of laughter escaped. ''I cannot believe it.'' Thinking of Avery, thinking of the marriage she had thought would have saved her, her mirth grew and grew, filling her head, ringing clear into the rafters. ''This is rich! Truly rich!''

The highwayman was frowning, watching her laughter erupt into tears, watching her scrub them away with a fist. All the while the laughter continued, a harsh sort of pain-filled bark that held a tinge of irony only she could hear.

The duke was marrying her for her money! She laughed harder, doubled over, slapped her thighs, and burst out again.

She was laughing so hard she could no longer see for the tears flooding her eyes.

"Stop it," Jason said softly, but she only laughed harder. "Stop it, I said!" He jerked her upright, off the sofa, and the movement startled her to silence. It halted the laughter but not the tears, which continued to trickle down her cheeks.

"Ah, Duchess . . ." Jason pulled her into his arms and held her protectively against his chest. "He didn't deserve you."

She cried harder then, sliding her arms around his neck, clinging to him and letting his warm strength flow into her.

"It's all right," he said. "You'll find someone else to marry, and he'll be a far better man than Avery Sinclair."

Velvet listened to his words, but it was the gentle tone of his voice that seeped through her despair. He felt so warm, so solid. His big hands were so impossibly gentle. The tears began to fade and the tightness in her throat began to ease. Slowly, awareness returned and she noticed the hard arms surrounding her, the steady heartbeat beneath her hand. With a last tremulous glance into his face, she eased herself away.

"I-I'm sorry, my lord." She sniffed, bringing the last of her tears under control. " 'Twasn't merely the duke and my failed marriage plans. 'Twas a bit of everything, I suppose."

He wiped the dampness from her cheeks with the pad of his thumb. "It's all right. You'll be home soon and able to put all this behind you."

Velvet nodded, but her chest ached with the knowledge of all she had lost, and the smile she gave him felt pasted on her face.

Everything wouldn't be all right. Unless she found another man to marry—one with money enough to clear the Haversham debts—it would never be all right again.

Velvet fought not to cry fresh tears but it wasn't easy. She wished more than ever that she could go home.

CHAPTER SEVEN

∞

The last two days passed quietly. Jason thought perhaps he had made a mistake in not telling Velvet the truth about Avery at the start. Of course in the beginning she wouldn't have believed him. She probably would have thought him demented and tried even harder to escape.

At any rate, she knew the truth now—at least part of it—seemed to believe him, and had accepted his promise that he would take her to Carlyle Hall. She gave him her word as well, said she would remain at the lodge at least until the day they were scheduled to leave.

With their fragile truce in place, he gave her more freedom, let her go out to enjoy the crisp March sunshine. She seemed happier out of doors, wandering beside the tumbling brook next to the lodge, listening to the chirp of an early returning blackbird, or watching a doe in the meadow.

She behaved differently now, resigned to making the best of the few days she had left, determined, it seemed, to enjoy her brief interlude in the country before returning to the structured life she faced back home.

Even Bennie had let down his guard and accepted her overtures of friendship. In the last two days, the pair had formed a tentative bond, the two of them laughing together, Velvet telling him stories, even helping the boy with his morning chores.

Jason relaxed a little himself, letting his guard lapse a bit more, perhaps, than he should have. Once as he had finished chopping wood, he glanced at the sun hanging low on the horizon and realized that Velvet had been gone from his sight for more than an hour. Clamping his jaw, he set off in search of her, worried that she might have run away after all, his mind sifting through possibilities of which route she might have taken.

He found her in the stable and breathed a sigh of relief.

"So there you are." Approaching the stall where he spotted the top of her glossy dark head, he rested a foot on a rung of the fence and leaned his elbows on the top rail to look down at her. "I thought mayhap you had decided to leave after all."

She sat cross-legged in a nest of fresh straw, a hint of silk stocking exposed where her skirt was ruched up, three tiny black and white puppies snuggled contentedly in her lap.

Velvet looked up at him, unruffled by the slight edge to his voice. "I accepted your word that you would see me home on the morrow. I gave you mine in return. I do not mean to break it."

Somehow he knew that she would not. He smiled, relaxing even more, enjoying the way she looked sitting there with the puppies. "I see you have made some new friends."

Her soft mouth curved prettily. "Are they not beautiful? This one is called Marty and this is Nigel. Bennie named them. He left this one's naming to me."

"And?" he asked, quirking a brow.

"I decided to call him Winky, since he is the smallest of the litter." She pressed her nose into the ruff of soft black fur around the animal's neck. "I should love to have a puppy. I had a lovely little blond spaniel once, but she died some years ago. Her name was Sammy—short for Samantha." Her smile slid away. "Even after all these years, I still miss her."

Jason said nothing. She looked so damned fetching sitting there in the straw he found it hard to concentrate. He watched the care with which she held the puppies. There was a dog he had loved as a boy. His father had given him the pup as a gift on his twelfth birthday, a hunting dog, a magnificent setter with sorrowful eyes and silky red hair. They had done everything together.

He hadn't thought of Rusty in years. Not since he'd been hauled in chains aboard the battered old brig that had carried him away from his homeland.

"Do you like dogs, my lord?" Her voice brought him back to the present, its clear, sweet ring carrying a note of warmth.

"Yes," he said, his voice a little gruff.

She set two of the puppies gently in the straw and rose to her feet, cradling the third pup carefully against her as she walked toward him. "Would you like to hold Winky?"

He started to say no but instead found himself reaching for the puppy, a mixed breed of unknown origins who looked suspiciously like the dog who occasionally followed at Bennie's heels when he worked around the lodge. The pup was still tiny, small enough to fit in one of Jason's big hands. It felt soft and warm and smelled of fresh milk and puppy, a smell like nothing else.

He found himself smiling again. "Mayhap you could take him with you. I imagine Bennie would be glad to find the little mongrel a home."

She sadly shook her head. "I don't think I should. I must settle this business with the duke and there is my grandfather to consider. He has become . . . forgetful. Caring for him takes a great deal of time. Even on his good days, I worry about him. He hates what is happening to him. I wish I could help, but there is nothing I can do."

Jason stroked the pup, whose long-lashed eyes had drifted closed, the small body limp and relaxed under his gentle attentions. "What of your mother and father?" he asked.

"Mother died when I was nine. Father passed on three years ago this autumn." A bitterness crept into her tone. "He wasn't a very good father. He was rarely around, but I loved him. In his own way I suppose he loved me."

The puppy whimpered in its sleep, and Jason soothed it

with a soft stroke over its fur. "My father was the most incredible man I've ever known. He was wise and strong, honest and forthright. He was demanding, but he was also giving. I always knew he loved me. He was the best father a man could have."

The memory was so painful his voice came out rough. When he glanced down at Velvet she was staring at him with a look of compassion. He handed her back the puppy, uncomfortable with what he had revealed. "The hour grows late and it begins to grow cold. We'll be leaving early on the morrow. It is time we went back in."

Velvet watched him as if she tried to read the thoughts he had once more locked away. He'd said more than he had intended already. He didn't like to speak of the past. It was no one's business but his own and it was simply too painful.

"I'll only be a moment," she said. Kneeling down, she carefully replaced the puppy along with its brothers in the warm circle of straw. As she left the stall, the stray that was the pups' mother trotted in.

Velvet seemed to approve, smiling though she made no comment. Running to catch up, she hurried her footsteps to match his longer strides. He slowed a little and together they headed back toward the lodge. The breeze had come up, stirring the leaves and ruffling the branches of the elm outside the door, but the sun remained warm. Late-afternoon rays cast a reddish glow to Velvet's auburn hair and made her brown eyes look golden. They tilted up at the corners, he noticed, or at least they did when she smiled.

He thought of her sitting in the stable, laughing as she cuddled the puppies, her soft peach lips smiling with pleasure as she held one out for him to hold. It took all his force of will not to stop on the doorstep, turn her into his arms, and crush that soft mouth under his. The image sent a surge of heat racing through him, made his blood grow thicker, begin to pool in his groin.

He grew hard inside his breeches and an ache throbbed there. Clamping his jaw, he strode into the lodge, leaving Velvet to wonder at his abrupt change of mood—and the foul disposition that stayed with him for the balance of the evening.

Tomorrow she would go home. Or at least be returned to Carlyle Hall. Velvet believed that Jason had told her the truth, that he would see her safely returned as he had promised. She pondered the time she had spent with him this afternoon, and the bit of himself he had unexpectedly revealed. Beneath the hard exterior, there was a gentleness in Jason that appeared at the oddest times, moments like those when he had held the puppy, the love reflected in his eyes when he had spoken of his father.

He had withdrawn from her after that, barking orders all through supper, grumbling and finally stomping out of the house. By the time he had returned, she had already retired upstairs. Perhaps that was what he had wanted.

From the silence that had finally settled belowstairs, she guessed that he was now sleeping. She undressed and pulled on the soft cotton night rail he had provided, no longer worried about his unexpected appearance in her room. Jason was a man of his word. Since their heated encounter and his unexpected apology, he had played the part of gentleman. He would not touch her again, she knew. He would not break his word.

Velvet climbed up in bed and leaned over to blow out the candle, but a noise downstairs gave her pause. She heard someone speaking and swung her legs to the side of the bed. Quietly, she crossed the room, pressing an ear against the door Jason locked each night before retiring.

Not that it mattered. On the rare occasions he dozed, he was such a light sleeper the smallest sound usually roused him to full alert.

The voice continued speaking, Jason's voice, she realized, and wondered with whom he was conversing. Knowing it was futile, she tried to lift the latch and was surprised to discover that he had left it unbarred. Apparently he believed she would wait at least until morning to see if he meant to keep his word. Or perhaps he had simply forgotten.

Whatever the case, she eased open the door, saw Jason stretched out on the sofa, and no one else in the room. He was deeply asleep, she saw, the covers shoved down below his lean waist, his thick chest bare and covered with a sheen of perspiration.

The sight brought a flush to her cheeks. Then worry set in. Sweet Lord was he ill? She crept down the stairs, certain he would awaken as he usually did, but he merely tossed and turned and continued to mumble unintelligible words. He was dreaming, she realized, speaking to someone only he could see, in the midst of some terrible nightmare.

"Jason," she called softly from the stairwell, but he paid her no heed. He was caught in the throes of the dream, held captive by some dark menace that sent shudders through his powerful body.

Velvet slowly descended the stairs, hoping he would awaken, trying not to think how virile he looked lying there half-naked, trying not to remember how those slick hard muscles had felt pressing against her when they had been kissing.

She arrived at his side and he still did not awaken. "Jason . . . ?" She reached toward him, beginning to worry now that something was seriously wrong. She touched him lightly on the shoulder then gently began to shake him. "Wake up, my lord. You're having a night—" She shrieked as he jerked wide-awake, bolting upright, his hand snaking out to grab her, his overwhelming strength hauling her hard against his naked chest.

"It-it's Velvet!" she cried out. "Let me go!" It took a long moment for him to get his bearings, a moment to realize he was gripping her painfully hard.

"Good Christ," he growled, releasing his hold, wiping his sweat-dampened face with the palm of his hand. "What the devil are you doing down here?"

Unconsciously she took a step away. "Y-you were tossing and turning, talking in your sleep. I thought perhaps you had fallen ill."

He released a weary breath and leaned back against the sofa. "I didn't hurt you, did I?" Absently, he rubbed the scar on the back of his hand while she rubbed the bruise on her arm.

"It's all right. You didn't mean to." She saw the way he frowned. "It must have been a terrible nightmare."

"I've had worse. I'm sorry I hurt you. Go back to bed."

"Are you certain you are all right?"

"I'm fine." His eyes shifted away from her face, ran down the length of her body, barely covered by the thin cotton nightgown, and a smoky look came into the startling blue. Jason glanced away, fixing his attention on a spot above her head. "I said go back to bed. You shouldn't have come down here in the first place."

It occurred to her that standing in front of the low-burning embers of the fire, he could perhaps see nearly through her white cotton night rail. She flushed and turned away, starting toward the stairs, wishing she had left him alone.

"We'll be leaving here early," he called after her, grumpy again as he was before. "You had better get down here well before dawn, or I shall come up and rouse you from your cozy bed myself." He cast her a wicked half smile. "Then again, perhaps that is the better idea. I promise you that would be a far more enjoyable way to start the morning."

Bright heat rose in her cheeks and a curling warmth slid into her stomach. Dear sweet God! Turning away from him, she crossed the room and hastily climbed the stairs. When she reached her bedchamber, she closed the door and slumped against it, feeling breathless and suddenly far too warm.

Surely he wouldn't really come up there. Surely he would not dare! But for the balance of the evening, though she sorely needed her rest, she tossed and turned, unable to think of anything but the tall virile highwayman coming into her bedchamber as she lay sleeping, of him awakening her with more of his fiery kisses.

CHAPTER EIGHT

∞

*V*elvet walked purposefully down the glittering marble-floored passageway of Carlyle Hall, heading for the impressive Queen's Salon and her meeting with Avery Sinclair. She had asked him for a place where they could be private. This was not a conversation for the servants to overhear.

Her footfalls quickened as she approached the gilded twelve-foot doors leading into the salon, one of the most ornate in the house and one of Avery's favorites. Her arrival two days earlier had been greeted with damp-eyed effusiveness on the part of the duke, and heartfelt tears of relief shed by her grandfather, who immediately forgot that she had been missing.

She had come to Carlyle Hall across the meadows, riding on the back of the highwayman's tall black horse. He had left her off at the edge of the trees, pointing her toward the back of the mansion, his face unreadable as he bid her farewell.

"Well, Duchess," he'd said, "I guess this is good-bye." Absently he fingered the bruise at his temple. "I cannot say I enjoyed our confinement." Then he looked at her with those searing blue eyes and flashed her an arrogant grin. "But I cannot truly say that I did not."

She found herself blushing, knowing he was thinking of the intimacies they had shared. "You are quite a rogue, my lord."

"And you are quite a woman."

She smiled at that, unable to resist the compliment. "All in all, I suppose I am better for the adventure. If Carlyle is impoverished, as you have said, you have saved me from a disastrous marriage. That in itself is enough to earn my silence and a measure of my gratitude."

His eyes ran over her face, taking in each of her features. "Oddly enough, Duchess, I believe I shall miss you."

An unexpected lump rose in her throat. Insanely, the sting of tears pricked behind her eyes. "And I you—my lord outlaw. God protect you, Jason."

He said nothing for the longest time. Velvet finally turned away, trying to ignore the heaviness that had settled in her chest. She started across the fields toward the manse, her slippers growing damp with the early evening dew, but the thunder of hooves coming from behind brought her up short. She turned to see the highwayman pounding toward her. He bent low in the saddle and scooped her up, set her before him in the saddle, turned her into his arms, and his mouth came down hard over hers.

His kiss was hot and possessive, taking command of her lips, making the heat unfurl in her stomach. Then the hard kiss gentled, became a tasting, a savoring, the creation of a memory. It went on for timeless, aching moments while Velvet clasped her arms around his neck. A last fierce ravishing of her mouth, and Jason set her free, lowering her back to her feet in the meadow.

"Good-bye, Duchess," he said in a voice gone rough. "I vow I won't forget you." Then he whirled the black, dug in his booted heels, and rode like fire in the opposite direction.

Velvet stood there trembling, watching him ride away, her eyes suddenly awash with tears. It was insane to feel this way, so empty all of a sudden, so completely alone. For days, she had been his captive, surrounded by his indomitable presence. She hadn't imagined what it might feel like when his powerful essence was gone.

Her eyes trained on the spot where he had last been, she

stood alone in the meadow, her chest aching, a thick lump clogging her throat. It was crazy, but that didn't make the ache go away.

It was there again now, the dull throb of memory, as she stood in the Queen's Salon waiting for the duke, that sense of something missed, something vital and strong that she would never have the chance to experience.

Who was he? she wondered as she had a dozen times. Why had he stopped the wedding? She had sent one of the Haversham footmen into London with a note to her solicitor. Soon she would know the truth of the duke of Carlyle's circumstances. And yet she really didn't need that final confirmation. She had no doubt the man called Jason had told her the truth.

From the moment he had abducted her, she had sensed an honesty about him. He had no reason to lie about this. And so she stood waiting in front of the marble-manteled hearth, beneath twenty-foot honeycomb ceilings, for the impoverished duke who would have ruined her life.

She was dressed in her finest, an ivory brocaded gown shot with gold and trimmed with black Mechlin lace, part of the expensive trousseau that had taken the last of their money, a necessity if she was to wed with a duke. Her hair was powdered and dressed in high curls atop her head. A small black oval patch marked a spot beside the corner of her mouth, and her bosom thrust upward from the square-cut bodice of her gown.

She was ready for this meeting. It was imperative it end successfully and she knew exactly how to make that come about.

The tall double doors swung open and in walked the duke. A pair of footmen dressed in red satin livery closed the portal behind him and he strode toward her smiling, his mouth a thin slash, reddened with a hint of rouge.

"My dearest lady." He brought her fingers to his lips as she swept into a deep curtsy before him.

"Your grace." He was dressed as finely as she, in the stylish *habit à la française* that was the vogue, the coat and breeches of dark green silk edged with gold, the waistcoat heavily embroidered. His hair was powdered instead of wigged, as he usually wore it, hiding the gold that was visible in his eyebrows and thick blond lashes. The fleeting thought occurred that by Society's standards he was not unattractive, his features fine, his heavy-lidded dark brown eyes adding to his genteel appearance.

"Shall we sit?"

She nodded. "As you wish." She allowed him to seat her in a large brocade chair near the hearth, then waited as he took a place across from her.

"Shall I ring for refreshments?"

"No. This shouldn't take long, and as I said, I prefer that we be private."

He leaned back in his chair, crossed one leg over the other. She had never paid attention to a man's calves before. Now it occurred to her that beneath his stockings, Avery's appeared to be padded. The highwayman's, she recalled, had been well formed and heavily corded with muscle.

"This business you wish to speak of . . . I gather it is rather of a delicate nature. Do I dare to guess that this has something to do with your abduction?" He leaned forward. "Dear lady, if your virtue is the issue of this meeting, never fear. I am not so hard-hearted as to allow such a loss to come between us. It is hardly your fault that you were ruthlessly wrenched away from your betrothed. From this day forward, whatever might have occurred shall remain our secret, never to be spoken of again. The wedding will take place—"

"The wedding, your grace, will not take place at all."

Avery frowned. "Don't be absurd. I told you I care nothing for—"

"My virtue remains intact. That is not the issue at hand."

The frown deepened, pulling his blond brows together till they almost touched in the middle of his forehead. "Then what, may I ask, *is* the issue, my dear?"

"I'm afraid I have learned a very disturbing truth, your grace. Normally my grandfather would be discussing this matter with you but as you know at present he is . . . not quite himself. The fact remains, however, that I have, by whatever means, discovered your true circumstances. I wish finances were not an issue, but in a marriage such as ours, we both know they are. I understand your need of funds, your grace, and I am more than sympathetic. Unfortunately, my dowry will not be used to solve your problems."

His expression did not change but the color slowly ebbed from his cheeks. "I'm sorry, my dear, but I haven't the faintest notion what you are talking about."

"You know exactly what I'm talking about." She allowed a soft note into her voice. "I'm not faulting you, your grace. As members of the nobility, we all face grave responsibilities. Marriages formed to solve financial problems are commonplace. However, in this case, that is not going to occur." She shifted in her seat, smoothing the skirt of her ivory brocade gown. "As I said, I am well aware of your problems. I do not intend, however, to discuss them outside this room."

Avery said nothing.

"In exchange for my silence, there is something I must have from you."

His eyes sharpened, became pinpoints of black. He understood a bargain. He was back on solid ground, she saw, exactly where she had led him.

He leaned forward in his chair, plucked at a piece of lint on his dark green coat. "I am not, dear lady, confirming any of your ridiculous charges, but if you are in need of some sort of assistance, perhaps I may be of help."

Velvet stood and moved to the fire, placing herself a bit above him. "These past few days have been trying for all of us. As I'm certain you well know, this abduction has done nothing to benefit my reputation." She looked him in the face. "Should our betrothal suddenly end, people will speculate as to why. Just as you did, they will question my virtue, and though it remains undamaged, the odds of my making a suitable match will surely be lessened."

"Go on," the duke said.

"In exchange for my silence, I simply ask that our relationship continue for the next several weeks as it has in the past. Let it be known you are still willing to marry me. You may say that you paid some sort of ransom. Tell them money purchased my safe return." It sounded far better than the version she had told, that she had simply been able to escape.

Avery pursed his lips. "I see no problem in that."

"It will take time to reschedule the wedding. People will expect a delay. Before the new date is set, I shall simply cry off. We will remain close friends, of course, and by then, perhaps we will each have found another suitable candidate to fulfill our marriage requirements."

Avery assessed her as if she were a woman he had never seen before. His smile was more a curling of his lips. "I assure you, my lady, the rumors you have heard concerning the duke of Carlyle are patently false. Still, if you would prefer to end our betrothal, I am certainly willing to abide by your wishes. And of course I will allow you to cry off, as any gentleman would."

"Then we are agreed?" She daintily extended a white-gloved hand.

"Exactly so, my lady." He bowed extravagantly over it. She didn't miss the edge of malice in his voice or the fact that beneath his polite veneer, he was angry. She had thwarted his plan to save himself, and Avery Sinclair wasn't a man who liked to be thwarted.

"I'll be returning to Windmere on the morrow. It is my understanding, however, that you had planned a gala to be held here at Carlyle three weeks after our marriage."

A grim smile surfaced. "I had thought to have a costume ball, our first such affair as a married couple. The invitations have already been sent. As you said, it is scheduled for three weeks hence."

"Good. The Season has not yet really begun. Shortly after the ball, I shall cry off, leaving us both free to pursue our interests."

"As you wish," he said tightly.

Velvet dropped into a curtsy. "Thank you, your grace. I trust I haven't broken your heart too badly."

A golden brow arched. "*Ah, contraire,* Lady Velvet. I shall linger in despair for the pain I suffer at your refusal." He flashed her a look of pure malice. "Fare thee well, my lady, until next we meet."

In a glitter of dark green silk, he was gone, his angry strides carrying him from the room. She had made an enemy in Avery Sinclair, yet now that he was out of her life, she felt a joyous sense of relief.

A memory of the vicious look on the duke of Carlyle's face came to mind, and she thought perhaps the highwayman had saved her from more than a disastrous marriage. Velvet shivered to think what menace those icy dark eyes might have held for her, once she had become his wife.

Seated before the fire in the walnut-paneled study of his country home, Castle Running, not far from Carlyle Hall, the marquess of Litchfield watched his friend, Jason Sinclair, restlessly pacing the room.

"You seem distracted, my friend. You have been so since your arrival. It wouldn't, perchance, have anything to do with a certain young lady of our mutual acquaintance?"

A muscle tightened in Jason's jaw. "The girl has been safely returned. She knows the truth of Avery's finances. 'Tis no concern of mine if she hasn't the good sense to end her betrothal."

Lucien's black brow rose a fraction. "I believe she will do so . . . in time. The matter is a delicate one and Velvet Moran is no fool. Eventually, she will end her relationship with your brother and return to the marriage mart." He eyed his friend over the top of his brandy snifter before he took a drink. "Perhaps once she does, you will be interested in her yourself."

Jason made a rude sound in his throat. "I'm a candidate for the gibbet at Tyburn Hill, not for marriage, Lucien."

"Forgive me. For whatever odd reason, I thought perhaps the girl had caught your fancy. As I recall, you weren't opposed to trysting with her. She must have held a certain amount of appeal.''

Jason turned to face him, his expression dark. ''I would have liked to bed her. She was a fiery little vixen and I lusted after her practically from the moment I first saw her. She is ripe for a man, and had she not been an innocent, I would not have hesitated to take her. If I had sated my lust, she would already be far from my mind.''

''Which means you continue to think of her even though she is gone.''

''Which means I would still like to bed her. Since it would hardly be the gentlemanly thing to do, I will do my utmost to forget her.''

Lucien smiled faintly. ''I thought you said there was nothing of the gentleman left in you, that you had abandoned those genteel qualities years ago, in the muddy swamps of Georgia.''

Jason almost smiled. ''For the most part I did. While I remain in England, I am doing my best to resurrect them. I assure you, Litchfield, it is not an easy task.''

''You mean to leave then, even should your name be cleared?''

''I don't belong here anymore. I'm no longer part of this life and it is no longer part of me. I'll remain here only as long as I must.''

Lucien sighed, reading the impatience stamped on his friend's dark features. Jason wanted his name cleared. Over a year ago, he had hired a Bow Street Runner to investigate his father's murder, but nothing of any value had been unearthed. Another man, this one chosen by Lucien himself, had been hired when Jason had first arrived in England.

''I realize,'' Lucien said, ''that in this case, no news is hardly good news, but I assure you the man we have working for us is competent. I've used him on a number of occasions and he has yet to fail at his task.''

''I don't doubt his expertise. But eight years is a very long time. Nothing came of the first investigation. Even if there is someone who saw what actually happened that night, finding him won't be easy.''

"No, it won't. But money is always an inducement. A word here and there . . . a marker called in. Who knows what we shall discover?''

Jason smiled, but Lucien read it for what it was. The odds were against success and Jason Sinclair knew it. He was risking himself in returning to England, but it was a risk he was determined to take.

For the past eight years he had vowed to clear his name, to see his family's holdings returned, to see his father's murderer pay. He had taken the first bold step and Carlyle Hall once more belonged to him, though he had allowed Avery to remain. The owner was traveling on the Continent, they had told him. The duke could stay until the man returned.

In truth it was simply better if Avery remained in residence at Carlyle Hall, or at the duke's town house on Grosvenor Square, so that they could watch his movements.

Lucien leaned back in his overstuffed leather chair and took a sip of his brandy. Jason's glass sat untouched on the mantel. He was pacing again, restless as he was before, his mind filled with thoughts Lucien could not begin to fathom.

"Perhaps we should travel to the city,'' Lucien suggested. "The Season is just now getting underway. Even if it weren't, there are always amusements. From the look of you, some female companionship would not be amiss.''

"The city?'' Jason's gaze swung in Lucien's direction.

"Aye. As long as you stay clear of your brother, once he arrives, there is little danger you'll be recognized. Your own mother would hardly know you for the boy you were back then.''

Only too true, Jason's eyes said.

"I notice you have wisely avoided Celia Rollins. A lady rarely forgets a man she has known as intimately as that one knew you.''

Jason paused and reached for his glass, cradled it in his wide palms, then brought it to his lips. "Lady Brookhurst is safe for the present. In time I intend to seek her out, but not just yet. First I mean to return to the inn. Perhaps a memory will surface, something of value that I have forgotten.''

The Runner had been to the Peregrine's Roost, of course, on more than one occasion, but according to him, few of the original servants remained and none remembered anything useful about the night of the murder.

Lucien warmed his glass between his long-fingered hands. ''In truth, you are probably better served to remain at Castle Running for a few more weeks. Avery is planning a lavish costume ball—though I can't imagine how he thinks to afford it. The outcome might prove interesting.''

Jason's jaw flexed. The look in those fierce blue eyes could have frozen the brandy in his glass. ''My half brother has always loved to entertain. He thinks himself the height of fashion, and of course Carlyle Hall provides exactly the setting for his lavish excesses.''

Lucien casually stood up from his overstuffed chair, setting his empty glass down on the piecrust table beside it. ''Lady Velvet is certain to attend,'' he said with deliberate casualness. ''Being seen with the duke will help dispel the gossip. It is imperative she put the scandal of her abduction to rest.''

Jason's mouth curved wickedly. ''Would that I had given the lady something to be scandalized about.''

Lucien merely smiled. Whether or not his friend was willing to admit it, he cared for the girl in some fashion. Feelings he hadn't allowed himself since his ill-fated affair with Celia Rollins. Lucien intended to encourage him. Jason Sinclair had suffered enough in the past eight years. He deserved some measure of happiness.

He deserved to know the tender side of a woman, instead of simply suffering a woman's betrayal.

Though Lucien was hardly an expert, and cynical in the extreme, some deeply hidden part of him still believed his friend deserved to know a little of love.

* * *

Jason shoved open the door to the Peregrine's Roost and walked in. He couldn't shake the notion that the answer to his problem lay here at the inn. That someone must have seen something besides what Avery wanted them to see—the duke of Carlyle murdered by his eldest son during an argument over his son's latest mistress.

More than the face of his grief-stricken half-brother, whose heroic efforts could not save their father but had at least disabled the villain who had killed him. There had to be something. Yet so far no one including himself had unearthed a single clue.

Jason ducked his head and stepped into the low-ceilinged taproom. Eight years hadn't changed it: the smell of smoke and rancid ale, the rough-planked wooden floors, the heavy oaken beams, even more age-darkened than they were before.

The scarred wooden tables sported a new coat of varnish, but the nicks and grooves were the same, the benches still uneven or perhaps it was the floor. The upstairs room he had shared with Celia appeared much the same, or at least it had seemed so when he looked in through the outside window. The curtains seemed a bit more worn, the bed a little smaller, the mattress in need of feathers, but perhaps without Celia's glittering presence, it would have looked that way back then.

He thought of her as he sat down at an empty table and ordered a tankard of ale. She was living in London, he knew, living high on the fat yearly allowance Avery provided. He wondered how she would take the news that the duke of Carlyle was broke, or if she had already figured it out.

He wondered what she looked like now, thought of her tall, willowy, raven-haired beauty and found himself comparing it to the petite, full-breasted charms he had discovered in the person of Velvet Moran.

They were as different as any two women he could imagine, one using her dark allure for seduction, the other spirited, determined, arousing his lust simply by her fiery nature. Celia was wickedness personified. In Velvet passion warred with innocence, her appeal more powerful by her very naïveté. And there was a sweetness about her, a goodness he sensed that was lacking in most of the women he had known.

There wasn't an ounce of goodness in Lady Brookhurst, not a single dram of compassion, but at the time he had been too much in lust to see her for the woman she really was.

Jason pictured Celia and his hold grew tighter on the handle of his tankard. Celia knew the truth of what had happened to his father. Celia could be his salvation, yet he dared not go to her yet. He could offer her money, which if she weren't in need of now, odds were she soon would be. But even a large sum of money might not ensure her help. A little scandal was one thing. Admitting Avery Sinclair's guilt in the death of his father meant implicating herself in a murder.

Ruination among her peers was not something Lady Brookhurst would willingly do, no matter how well it might pay. The timing had to be perfect, the threat of exposure so real she would have to take heed. He needed a way to force her into admitting the truth—he needed a witness to come forward.

Jason glanced around the tavern, studying the faces of the serving maids, the occupants in the taproom, the stout man behind the bar. He finished his ale and wandered into the kitchen, his pulse speeding up at the sight of the cook's familiar round face.

"What can I do for ye, luv?" The short, beefy woman smiled. Waving a heavy iron spatula in the air, she walked toward him. She'd been friendly to him back then, too. Perhaps that was the reason he recalled her.

"Something smells good. I could use a bite to eat."

She eyed his snug buckskin breeches and navy blue riding coat, the lace that hung from his cuff to the tips of his darkly tanned fingers. His queued-back hair was unpowdered but his clothes said he was, at the very least, a member of the gentry.

" 'Tis spitchcocked eel ye be smellin' and a haunch of venison, roasted. I can have ye a plate served up in the blink of an eye."

Jason smiled. He wasn't really that hungry, but if it kept her talking he would eat. "My thanks, mistress. Mind if I sit in here?"

She frowned. It was an odd request, coming from a man dressed as he was. Then her mouth curved into a grin. "If yer lookin' for my Betsy, she won't be back for a time. Gone to the village, she has. Won't be home afore eventide. I can tell her ye come, though, if ye give me yer name. A fine lookin' gentl'man like yerself, my Betsy will be sorry she missed ye."

"My name is Hawkins," he said, the name coming easily after the last eight years. "Jason Hawkins."

She simply nodded and began to dish up the food. The kitchen was warm and steamy. A big black kettle bubbling with liquid hung from a hook above the fire, and for a moment the stout little cook disappeared behind a thin wall of steam. She reappeared carrying a pewter platter heaped with meat and a chunk of rye bread, which she set down on the heavy wooden table in front of him. She disappeared again and returned a few minutes later with a pewter mug of ale, which she also set on the table.

"I've been out of the country," Jason said casually. "I haven't been back for a while. I remember you, though, that you worked here in the kitchen."

She eyed him thoughtfully, trying to place him. "Ye look a bit familiar, but I can't honestly say as I recall ye."

He almost wished she did. Perhaps she would also recall the circumstances of the murder.

"There was a night I came in that I recall in particular. Things got pretty exciting—the old duke of Carlyle was murdered."

The cook rolled her eyes, which were round, the skin around them etched with wrinkles. "That were somethin', all right. Poor old fella. What a way to end . . . kilt by his own flesh and blood."

"You saw it, then?"

She shook her head. "I were here in the kitchen when it happened, but it surely sent everyone into a tither."

"They caught him, I remember. Though later I heard rumors that the eldest son didn't really do it. Some say it was the younger."

An odd expression flickered across her face. "I've heard it said, but not in a goodly number of years. There was talk for a while, but eventually it died away. The duke is a powerful man round abouts. Ain't many who'd be daft enough to cross him." Her eyes ran over his face. "Funny, now that I think on it, ye look a bit like him, the old duke's eldest boy, I mean. He were thinner, and I don't remember him bein' so tall. He were paler, softer lookin', not so manlylike, ye know?"

He knew all right; no onc knew better.

She grinned, and he saw that several of her bottom teeth were missing. "Ye ain't related, is ye?"

Jason smiled, though he hoped it looked more sincere than it felt. "I hope not, considering the man was a murderer."

She shrugged. "Like ye said, rumor was he weren't the one what done it. For meself, I wouldn't know. I was down here workin', like I said. Didn't see nothin' till the constable come and dragged the lad away—not that it matters. Boy's dead and gone. Best to let sleeping dogs lay."

Jason said nothing to that, just finished his meal in silence, though his nerves were suddenly taut and he was no longer hungry at all. Perhaps someone here did know something that would help him. Finding out wouldn't be easy, but it stirred a measure of hope. He downed the last morsel, dropped some coins on the table, and stood up from his chair.

"My thanks for the meal, mistress, and the bit of conversation."

"You'll be comin' back, won't ye? To see me gel?"

Jason forced a smile. "Perhaps I will." He was thinking

that he would most certainly return. He would have to be careful, bide his time.

But unless he was swinging from the gibbet, nothing could keep him away.

CHAPTER NINE

∞

*V*elvet stood in front of the cheval glass mirror in her room. Like most of Windmere, the halls abovestairs were barren, the rooms decidedly stark. Even her bedchamber had fallen victim to their lack of funds, her beautiful rosewood armoire replaced by one of simple oak, the exquisite gilt-framed paintings gone from her walls. The peach silk moiré curtains remained, as well as the matching bed hangings and counterpane.

Velvet smiled inwardly, thinking she might wind up wearing the draperies in the fashion of a gown if their finances didn't change soon.

But today was not the time to think of it. Today they were leaving Windmere for the costume ball at Carlyle Hall, the final step in severing her connections with the duke. She thought of him now and an icy shiver ran through her. There was something of menace in Avery Sinclair, something he had kept well hidden until that day in the Queen's Salon. For the hundredth time she silently thanked the highwayman for saving her from a terrible fate in marrying him and wondered where the tall handsome outlaw had gone.

The minute she thought of him, her cheeks heated up. Memories of his hard, burning kisses rose up, visions of his hands on her breasts. Sweet God, she had tried to block them, knelt in the small parish church and silently prayed that the wicked images would go away.

Instead each night she tossed and turned, wishing she could see him again, wishing he wasn't an outlaw, wishing he would ride to her defense as he had swooped down and stolen her that night from the carriage.

Velvet sighed. She had to marry and soon, and it couldn't be to an outlaw, or even a displaced nobleman, if that were indeed what he was. Jason couldn't save her, no matter how attractive he was. She had to find someone else, a wealthy, suitable husband who didn't really need her dowry. Her search would begin at the costume ball.

She would have to be subtle in her efforts, of course. Her main objective was to set the wagging tongues to rest, but with Avery's grudging assistance, she believed the gossip would end. Meanwhile, the Season would begin in earnest very soon. Perhaps there would be a fresh face among the suitors seeking the hand of a wealthy heiress, someone of money and position. If she were lucky, maybe he would spark some feeling in her.

Perhaps one day, those feelings might even turn to love.

Velvet sighed and turned away from the mirror just as her lady's maid, Tabitha Beeson, hurried in carrying her costume for the ball, all that remained to be packed for the journey.

"Just finished, my lady. Lud, 'tis beautiful. You'll be the loveliest gel at the ball."

Velvet hoped so. She had work to do at Carlyle Hall. She smiled to think how disappointed the duke must be that she wasn't the one footing the bill. Pity the poor wretch who would be. Velvet didn't doubt that the duke of Carlyle would be gaining a wife—and soon.

"Thank you, Tabby. Tell Martha she did her usual splendid job." Especially splendid, considering what little she'd had to work with. Which wasn't really surprising. The servants who remained at Windmere had learned to do myriad jobs. Martha sewed splendidly, when she wasn't working as the upstairs chambermaid, and Tabby often helped with the dusting and cleaning. "Tell her the costume is lovely."

She would dress in medieval garb, as the young maid,

Gweneviere, in a plum velvet tunic above an underskirt of amber silk embroidered in gold. A golden girdle had been fashioned for her waist, a small jeweled dagger suspended from it, though the brilliants in the hilt of the ancient family blade were now replaced with paste. The long, pointed sleeves of the gown hung nearly to the floor, and her hair would be loose down her back in the medieval style of an unmarried girl.

A noise in the hall drew her attention from the lovely costume she held in her hands.

"What goes on up there?" Her grandfather's voice rose with impatience. "The carriage awaits us. The footman grows concerned. 'Tis well past the time we should be leaving."

Velvet hurried to the top of the stairs. "We're ready, Grandfather. We won't be another minute more."

True to her word, they were on the road within the quarter hour, barreling along the lane that would carry them to Carlyle Hall. The week before had been bitterly cold, but yesterday a breath of early spring weather had set in. A dome of blue rose above the fields, and a warm sun filtered through the branches of the trees lining the road.

Their late departure had them arriving at the inn midway there well after dark, but their rooms were ready and the fire in the hearth was warm. In the morning they resumed their journey, bowling along the lane at a faster clip than she had expected. Near the Wealdon Forest, they passed a small hamlet constructed mostly of reddish brick, and a skinny gray dog, its ribs protruding, raced along beside the carriage, barking to drive them away.

Carlyle Hall grew nearer, and the closer they got, the more Velvet began to fret. Her mind kept returning to the last time she had traveled this road, the night she had been abducted.

He wouldn't come, would he? Surely he would not dare to accost her again. But she found herself wishing he would, that he would ride out of the woods on his tall black horse, that he would force the carriage to a halt and sweep her up in the saddle in front of him.

By the time they reached the bend in the road where he had appeared before, Velvet was biting her lip, squeezing the fingers she gripped in her lap. A trickle of perspiration slid between her breasts.

Her grandfather eyed her from beneath his bushy white eyebrows, catching the nervous glances she kept tossing out the window. "You look worried, my child. I can see it in your face. You mustn't be afraid, my dear Velvet—this time the bounder will not find us unprepared." He grinned with satisfaction. "We are ready, should he appear. This time the coachy is armed."

"Armed?" Velvet squeaked. "Oh, dear Lord."

"That is correct, my dear. Should the scoundrel accost us again, the man will face the wrong end of a pistol."

Velvet thought of big John Wilton, the coachman seated atop the carriage, and her wish for the highwayman's appearance faded away. *Don't come, Jason, don't come.* Sweet God, she didn't want him killed! She had merely hoped to see him one last time.

She stared at her grandfather, mouthing a silent prayer. She was amazed the aging earl had taken such an action, amazed he remembered the previous trip at all. Then again, that was the way of his illness. One moment he was lucid the next he was not. His memory of the distant past remained crystal clear, but his day-to-day thoughts were as hazy as a London fog.

Riding on the edge of her seat, Velvet fixed her eyes on the trees at the side of the road and tried to control her pounding heart.

In the end, all her worry was for naught. Jason did not appear and the carriage rolled unimpeded toward Carlyle Hall. Apparently, the highwayman had forgotten all about her.

Velvet vowed that once and for all, she would forget about him.

*   *   *

Music filled the magnificent salons and lamp lit corridors of Carlyle Hall. Notes of the harpsichord fluttered delicately across the gilt and mirrored ballroom. Standing in the flickering light of a golden sconce, one of a hundred that lined the majestic ballroom, Avery Sinclair stood for a moment alone, enjoying the brief respite from his guests—and his so-called betrothed.

He caught a glimpse of her small figure dancing, her wavy dark auburn hair gleaming like polished wood in the candlelit ballroom. Avery gritted his teeth until a needle of pain shot into his jaw. The sight of the woman infuriated him. He had been so careful to maintain his image of wealth and power. How had she discovered the truth? Where had she been those days before the wedding when supposedly she had been abducted?

He hadn't the foggiest notion and didn't really care. Wherever she had gone, one thing was certainly clear. She was a conniving little baggage, smarter than he had imagined, and he had underestimated her sorely. He would not do so again.

Avery straightened his black velvet, ermine-trimmed beret, cocking it forward over a thin blond eyebrow, the long wispy feather on top rather dashing, he thought, as he caught his reflection in the mirror. He was dressed as Henry the Eighth, complete with slashed, full-sleeved overjacket, silver brocaded waistcoat, white silk stockings, and silver embroidered codpiece.

He smiled grimly, thinking of the king he portrayed, wishing he could lop off the head of that little bitch Velvet Moran.

He shifted the codpiece to a more comfortable position over his sex. Or perhaps he would do as Henry did—swive the wench a time or two and then behead her.

He mulled over the idea with a surge of satisfaction, his gaze darting toward where she danced the minuet with the aging earl of Whitmore, the earl's randy old eyes fastened wolfishly on her bosom. Good luck and good riddance, he thought, his attention shifting to a far more intriguing target.

A slender blond woman he had seen a few times before, a girl in first blush, attending her first London Season. Her father, Sir Wallace Stanton, was known, on matters of finance, to hold the ear of the king. Over the years, he'd been wildly successful in his business dealings, one of few men known to have actually made money before the South Seas bubble burst. In the decades since, he had turned those profits into a rather large fortune. Stanton had wealth and power, but only one daughter, eighteen-year-old Mary, who would inherit all of his vast holdings.

The aging Sir Wallace had everything most men wanted, but what the old man desired above all else was a title for his little girl. He longed for her to become a member of the nobility, the one thing he had, so far, been unable to give her.

In the past few months, Avery had heard rumblings about her, rumors that the girl and her fortune were for sale. At the time he wasn't interested. He had thought to marry the Haversham heiress. Marriage to a woman not of the peerage was unthinkable, completely out of the question.

Unfortunately, with the loss of his bride and the threat of impending ruin, he was forced to reconsider.

Avery took a delicate pinch of snuff as he studied the young blond girl, then tucked the jeweled silver box back into his waistcoat. He could not say he found her lacking. In her simple milkmaid's costume, she was clear-skinned and comely, in a plain sort of way, not so vibrant as Velvet Moran, but she would also be far more tractable. Last week he had gone to London for a secret meeting with her father. Sir Wallace had nearly overset himself at the notion of his Mary wed to a duke.

A tentative agreement had been reached, including a king-sized dowry and a provision that marriage to Mary would make the duke of Carlyle heir to the vast Stanton fortune.

There was only one catch. Mary Stanton had to agree.

Avery smiled at her across the gleaming marble floor. She was dancing, he noticed, with the earl of Balfour, a handsome wealthy man, it was said, had finally decided to enter the marriage mart. He was in need of an heir, and by the end of the Season, he meant to see the problem resolved.

Avery frowned. He didn't want Balfour anywhere near Mary Stanton. The man had a wicked reputation with the ladies, and though Mary didn't know it, she was already spoken for. Avery would see to it that the earl understood. As soon as he rid himself of his unwanted betrothed, he would turn his considerable charms on Mary Stanton.

Avery smiled. The girl would agree to the marriage—and soon. He would see that she had no choice. He had made a mistake with Velvet Moran. He would not fail with Mary.

He smoothed his false dark-cropped beard and thought of Henry. Once he had money again, his power would grow even stronger. Perhaps, after his position was again secure, he would settle the score with Velvet Moran.

Velvet forced her lips into a smile. She was sick unto death of the earl of Whitmore. He had done nothing all evening but ogle her breasts and leer in the most obnoxious manner. Fortunately, Avery had played his part well for most of the evening, partnering her in the dancing, making it clear that they were still a couple, that nothing was amiss between them. His fawning attentions had saved her from the earl's lecherous advances for a time, but now the duke had strayed.

"You look tired, my dear," the earl said, studying the flush in her cheeks from their latest round of dancing. "Perhaps a moment on the terrace would serve to refresh you."

"No! I-I mean . . . I'm sorry, my lord, but I fear that I cannot." God have mercy! The last thing she wanted was to be left alone with the lustful earl. "I've promised this dance to another. I'm certain my partner will be arriving to claim it at any moment."

She turned to walk away, hoping to escape him, but was halted abruptly by the broad chest blocking her way.

"As you said, my lady," came the rough-smooth voice she remembered so well. "I believe we are partnered for this dance."

Jason! Her heart slammed madly, set up a rapid, oddly cadenced thrumming inside her chest. It couldn't be him. He couldn't possibly be here. He was masked and wigged, yet she had no doubt who it was.

"My lady?" He bowed deeply then tipped his head to the side, motioning toward the dance floor.

It was hard to draw in a breath her mouth felt so dry. "Why, yes, I-I believe this dance is yours . . . my lord." He was dressed in the scarlet tunic and tight white breeches of an officer in the cavalry, his powerful legs encased in high black boots. A silver bagwig covered his wavy dark hair and a black silk loo mask concealed the top half of his face. But even the mask couldn't hide those blazing blue eyes or halt the dizzying effect they had on her.

She accepted the hand he held out to her, his wide palm engulfing her fingers, the warmth and strength reminding her of the imposing force he represented. On legs that trembled beneath her plum velvet tunic, she let him guide her onto the dance floor.

She looked at him, felt the heat of his gaze, and a tiny thrill shot through her. With the force of a blow, she realized how much she had missed him since the day he had left her in the meadow, how often she had thought of him, how worried she had been about his welfare. It was insane, yet her concern for him remained.

It swelled as she watched him perform the movements of the dance, as graceful as any courtier, though he was bigger and taller than most of the other male guests. Velvet nervously glanced past him to the crush of people around them. It was dangerous for him to be there. Whoever he really was, he was surely a villain of some sort. Sweet God, someone he had accosted might recognize him as easily as she had. He might be arrested, perhaps even thrown into jail! Sweet Jesu, even penniless noblemen were not immune to the law.

She tried to focus on the song the musicians were playing, a country dance that seemed to go on and on, but her mind kept shifting to the handsome man across from her. As tall as he was, he moved with the same formidable grace she had noticed in him before, the eyes behind his mask perusing her from head to foot, glittering with heat and some other dark emotion.

She studied him just as boldly, noting the incredible width of his shoulders, his flat belly and narrow hips, the way his breeches outlined his powerful thighs. She saw the way the fabric gloved the considerable bulge of his sex, and her cheeks grew warm. Velvet glanced away, but not before she glimpsed his roguish, arrogant smile.

As soon as the dance was ended, he caught her hand and led her off the dance floor, out toward the terrace above the garden. A hint of spring touched the air and the evening was cool but not cold. Or perhaps it was the heat flowing through her veins that kept her warm.

She let him draw her into the shadows at the end of the terrace, then whirled to face him, finding her voice for the first time since he had appeared.

"For heaven sakes, Jason, have you lost your wits? The duke's home is the last place you should have come!"

He shrugged those powerful shoulders, bunching the muscles beneath his scarlet uniform coat. "I came to see you." He grinned. "I thought perhaps you had missed me."

"Missed you! Why you arrogant, insufferable—" The firm brush of his arm sliding around her waist cut off her words. In the shadows of the terrace, Jason dragged her against him. "What are you—" The sentence was ended by the hot, moist crush of his lips. He kissed her with determined force, molding his mouth to hers, forcing her lips to part before the onslaught of his tongue.

Her stomach fell away and the world began to spin. Her blood pumped faster; her legs went weak. He pulled her tighter into his arms, pressing her the length of his hard-muscled frame, and needles of heat slid through her. Her lips tingled and her skin grew flushed. Pleasure, pure and raw, rolled through her like a wave and her whole body trembled.

"Jason . . ." she whispered, kissing him back, sliding her

arms around his neck. Dear God she was behaving like a fool, yet she could not seem to stop.

Jason deepened the kiss, tasting the inside of her mouth, his tongue sweeping in, his hands roving across her back, circling her waist, then sliding lower to cup her bottom and pull her more firmly against him. His sex was a hard, jutting ridge, warning her to beware, but his kiss was so ravishing, so all consuming, she found herself pressing more solidly against him, cupping his face between her hands and kissing him back as wildly as he was kissing her.

It was Jason who pulled away, his black mask slightly askew, his blue eyes suddenly pinning her with a look of accusation. "You are still betrothed to the duke. I doubt he would appreciate the kiss you have just shared with me."

She dragged in a ragged breath of air, amazed he could suddenly appear so calm. Amazed her own words sounded nearly as cool. "His grace and I have already agreed to part. I wait only a suitable time to satisfy the gossips."

Some of the tension drained from those solidly muscled shoulders. "I hoped you would be smart enough to end it."

She almost laughed. She'd had no choice but to end it. She needed money as badly as the duke did. "Why did you come tonight, Jason?"

He straightened a little, retreating a bit into himself. "To see you, of course." There was more to it than that. She could read it in his eyes. Even his roguish smile did not fool her. "It was worth it, Duchess."

Her cheeks went pink. She shouldn't have kissed him. Worse yet, now that she had, she should regret it. In truth, she did not. "I'll never be a duchess now."

"Do you care?"

She shook her head. "Not in the least. As a matter of fact, I believe I owe you a debt of gratitude. Marriage to the duke would have been hellish. I don't know how I could have missed seeing him for the man he truly is."

The line of his sensuous mouth grew hard. "Avery is a man of many faces. It is not surprising an innocent like you should be taken in."

"You sound as if you know him very well."

"I thought I knew him—I was wrong. It was a costly mistake. One I will not make again."

"I am still betrothed to him. When you came here tonight, how did you know I would not sound the alarm, tell him you were my abductor?"

He smiled that disarming smile of his. It made him look younger, less battle-worn, less weary. The thought occurred that smiling seemed almost new to him, as if it weren't something he did often.

"I didn't know for certain. I believed that by now you knew I had told you the truth about him. I hoped your gratitude would be enough to keep you silent." A dark brow arched up as he studied her. "Or that perhaps you had thought of me on occasion, as I had thought of you."

Her heart twisted, began to beat faster again. She stared into his handsome features and a wave of sadness washed over her. She had thought of him—endlessly—since the moment they had parted. It made not the least bit of difference. She had to marry for money, find a man who could save her family from ruin.

Ironically, she and Avery Sinclair traveled the very same road. In truth, as much as she was loath to admit it, they weren't so very different after all.

"I have to go in," she said, wishing she didn't have to leave. "Will I see you again?"

He shook his head. "I don't think so. 'Twould hardly be the sensible thing to do. I should have left you alone tonight."

She reached up and touched his cheek. "I'm glad that you did not." His eyes seemed to glow with an inner heat. She thought for a moment he would kiss her again, but he did not.

"Good-bye, Duchess." She didn't correct him. The word held a note of endearment and she liked the soft way he looked at her when he said it.

"Good-bye, Jason. Take care of yourself." He turned away from her and she watched him disappear from the terrace into the darkness of the garden, his shadow magnified to gigantic proportions in the flickering torchlight illuminating the gravel paths.

In seconds he was gone and Velvet felt suddenly empty. Moisture burned the backs of her eyes. It was wrong to feel such a powerful attraction for a man she barely knew, yet her chest ached at his leaving and a painful knot of emotion lodged in her throat. All of it was for naught. Even if Jason felt more than simple desire for her, nothing could ever come of it. He wasn't part of her world and she wasn't part of his. Nothing either of them could do could ever change that.

Still, his searing kisses and the memory of his beautiful eyes on her face haunted her until the chill of the crisp night air forced her back inside the house.

Even then she could not forget him.

The costume ball seemed interminable. Velvet smiled and laughed and spoke affectionately of Avery to his guests, all the while feeling weary and out of sorts, and wondering at the real reason Jason had come. As she thought back on it, she believed she had glimpsed his scarlet-clad figure in the hall outside the duke's study. Had he gone inside? Had his motive been robbery, or perhaps something worse? And if it was not, what was he doing in there?

But no answers came. The man called Jason was an enigma, as unfathomable as any wild creature of the forest. She could hire someone, perhaps, to discover who he was, but her funds were dangerously low and it didn't really matter. Jason had no place in her life. He couldn't save her. She had to find a man who could.

Still, it wouldn't happen tonight and as the hour grew late she grew weary.

She searched for her grandfather but found he had already gone up to bed. Tired but still slightly on edge, she wandered the magnificent marble corridors of Carlyle Hall, leaving the guests behind, pausing to view one elegant salon after another, enjoying the beauty of her surroundings.

In the armory, gleaming suits of armor stood at attention, their heavy swords sheathed, their lances anchored by a stiff metal hand. The library was huge, paneled with polished wood and lined with more volumes than she had ever seen in one place before.

An impressive library was a great social distinction. Avery craved social prominence above all else, but she didn't believe he was the one responsible for collecting such wonderful books. She ran a finger along the backs of the leather-bound volumes. Bunyan's *Pilgrim's Progress,* Foxe's *Book of Martyrs,* Baker's *Chronicles.* She found *The Whole Duty of Man, The Seven Champions, The Tale of a Tub,* Turner's *Spectator.* The list was phenomenal. She smiled to think if she had married the duke at least she could have entertained herself in here.

A tall gilt grandfather clock chimed as she wandered back out in the hall. In the distance, harpsichord music still seeped from the ballroom. She turned around in the passage, ready at last to retire to her room, but the house was so vast she couldn't remember exactly which way she had come.

A wrong turn led her into the Long Gallery, a narrow arched passageway with painted ceilings and dozens of gilt-framed portraits on the walls. Four generations of Carlyle dukes and their fathers before them, portraits of wives and children, each of their names proudly engraved on small silver plaques below each painting.

"Beg pardon, my lady." The gray-haired butler stood in the doorway. "I'm sorry to disturb you. I saw you walking this way and thought you might, perhaps, have gotten lost."

She smiled at the concern she read in the old man's thin features, liking him a little more each time she had come to Carlyle Hall. "Thank you, Cummings, I am a bit disoriented. I had no intention of wandering in this direction, but I've been enjoying myself."

He smiled with genuine warmth, turned and pointed to one of the portraits. "That is the second duke, my lady, his grace's grandfather."

"And this imposing man here?" She pointed toward the

stout, silver-haired man in one of the paintings. "That was the present duke's father?" She tried to read the name on the plaque but the light made it hard to see.

"Aye, my lady."

"I wouldn't have guessed. The two look so dissimilar."

The butler moved closer, until both of them stood beside the painting. "The present duke is the old duke's second son. His first wife died in childbirth, and the old duke remarried shortly thereafter. The present duke takes after his mother, Duchess Clarice."

Velvet chewed her bottom lip, her brow arched in thought. "I didn't realize Avery had an older brother."

The old man nodded. "Aye, he did, my lady." He turned to a family portrait that hung off to one side, the canvas not as brightly lit as the others on the wall. "That's him there. The woman sitting next to the duke is his second wife, Clarice. His grace is the blond boy seated on the left below them, his older half brother is the dark-haired boy on the right."

Velvet stepped closer to the portrait, her pulse increasing, her heart beginning to knock against her ribs. The portrait depicted a family of four, the boys just coming into manhood. Each brother's face held a measure of innocence, a look of mischief coupled with the eager curiosity of youth. Avery's blond countenance was unmistakable, the changes in him subtle, his skin still the same pale hue, his build still slender though he had matured.

It was the other youth who had changed, and yet as she lifted a branch of candles from a nearby table and held it beside the portrait, she knew without doubt who it was.

There was no mistaking those piercing blue eyes, that firm square jaw, the strong cheekbones, the curve of those sensuous lips. He looked different today, harder, bigger, stronger. Tougher. A warrior had emerged from the body of a stripling. A man had appeared from what had then been a boy.

Velvet's hand shook as she held the flickering light up next to the painting. "What . . . what was his name?"

"His father named him Jason, my lady, after the first duke of Carlyle."

Velvet's stomach clenched. When she looked back at the butler a sad smile altered his features, making him look years older. "A good boy, he was, young Jason. 'Tweren't true what they said about him. They'll never make me believe it, not till the day I die." Emotion made the old man's voice sound thin and reedy. Something squeezed inside Velvet's chest.

"What happened to him?" she asked, the words just above a whisper.

He simply shook his head. "I'm sorry, my lady. I should not have spoken as I did. 'Twouldn't do for me to gossip. His grace would not approve, and I don't much care to speak of it."

She reached out and gripped his arm, her hold so tight he flinched. "I-I'm sorry." She released her hand and set the branch of candles back down on the table. "I need to know what happened to Jason. I promise what you say will go no further than this, but you must tell me. I beg you, Cummings, please."

He studied her a moment, saw the pallor in her features, heard the quiet desperation in her voice. A resigned breath whispered past his lips.

" 'Twas eight years past, my lady, but I remember it as clear as if it had happened this night. They were arguing, young Jason and his father. The lad had only just turned twenty-one."

"What was the argument about?"

"Lady Brookhurst, I believe."

"Lady Brookhurst?" Velvet repeated with an inward twisting of her stomach. She had met the beautiful countess for the first time tonight. Dressed as Cleopatra in a boldly daring costume of ruby silk and sheer silver tulle, her black hair unpowdered and hanging to her hips, the woman had gained the attention of every man in the ballroom. A woman in her thirties, her skin and figure remained unblemished.

Velvet had been struck by her beauty the moment she had entered the room.

"Aye, my lady, 'twas over the countess, most likely. 'Twas what the servants said. 'Twas known young Jason was involved with the woman and that his father did not approve. At any rate, the boy stormed out of the house and a few minutes later the duke stalked off as well. He followed his son to the inn where the lad and the countess were meeting, and that's where it happened."

Velvet wet her lips. "Where what happened?"

"The argument began again. His grace was shot and killed. They said young Jason did it."

Velvet forced herself to breathe but it wasn't easy. Even in the dimly lit room, she could see the gleam of tears on the old man's hollow cheeks. "It weren't so, my lady. The lad loved his father. He never would have done him any harm."

Velvet's legs shook. They felt ready to buckle beneath her. She clutched the edge of the table to steady herself. "Wh-what happened to Jason?" Half of her didn't want to hear. The other half had to know.

"He was arrested, my lady, tossed into Newgate prison. His brother had followed the duke when he left Carlyle Hall. The younger boy said he tried to stop the shooting. Lady Brookhurst testified against young Jason as well. Only one man stood up for him at the trial—Lord Litchfield. He and the lad had long been friends."

"Litchfield?" Velvet repeated, imagining the marquess's tall dark visage.

"Aye, but it did no good. The lad was sentenced to hang. As God would have it, that never happened. The first night he was there, thieves set upon him. 'Tis a terrible place, Newgate prison, filled with the lowest dregs of the earth. They killed him that night, my lady, murdered the poor boy for a bit of coin and the clothes he was wearin'. Cut him up somethin' awful, they said."

Velvet thought she might be sick. She looked back at the portrait, felt those blazing blue eyes as if he stood in the room. There was no mistaking that face. It was the face of the man who had abducted her, the man who had saved her from marrying the coldhearted duke.

The face of the man who had kissed her tonight on the terrace. A face she couldn't forget.

"Thank you, Cummings." She forced a note of gratitude into her shaky voice. "Now, if you don't mind, perhaps you could guide me back to the staircase so that I may retire to my room."

He nodded gravely. "Of course, my lady." Neither of them spoke as he steered her down the proper passage and she disappeared up the sweeping marble stairs.

Tabby was waiting when she reached her bedchamber. Velvet said little, just let the heavyset woman help her undress, muttered a few words of thanks, then let Tabby guide her up the ladder into the huge four-poster bed.

Once the door was closed, Velvet sank back against the deep feather mattress. Her insides felt leaden, her heart a heavy weight inside her chest.

Not just *Jason,* as she had known him, but Jason Sinclair—the man who should have been the fourth duke of Carlyle. The same man who had come here tonight, the man who had kissed her so fiercely on the terrace.

Not a highwayman but a murderer. Dear sweet God!

Velvet bit down on her lip to stop it from trembling, her thoughts so turbulent it was hard to sort them out. Where had he been hiding all these years? Why had he surfaced now?

One slip, one person recognizing him as the duke's eldest son, and he would be returned to prison. Why was he risking himself? What could be so all-important?

Velvet stared at the amber silk bed hangings above her, at the red silk tassels dangling from the hem, but she couldn't really see them for the face that kept swimming in her vision. Jason Sinclair. The duke of Carlyle.

She remembered his burning kiss, wondered where he was and why he had come this night to Carlyle Hall.

Wondered if he could really be a murderer.

She closed her eyes, but she didn't fall asleep.

CHAPTER TEN

∞

*J*ason climbed the stairs to his bedchamber in the north tower of Castle Running. He was quartered there, away from the main house, where he could come and go as he wished without colliding with a bevy of servants.

Oddly, he felt comfortable here, in the simple, more primitive surroundings in this part of the ancient castle. Heavy Flemish tapestries hung from the thick stone walls, their intricate patterns depicting medieval hunting scenes. A Norman shield hung beside it, a lance, and two crossed swords. The bed was massive, carved of darkened oak with furs tossed upon it and more furs covering the rough oak-planked floors.

A fire crackled in the hearth, placed there by the trusted manservant Lucien had assigned him. He smiled when he saw the beckoning flames, enjoying the heat that pervaded the room, displacing the chill that seemed a constant part of the tower.

He swung his cloak off his shoulders and tossed it onto the wooden bench at the foot of the bed, then turned to discover he was not alone.

Lucien smiled and gracefully rose to his feet. "I suppose I should have stayed at Avery's ghastly affair a bit longer, but once I saw you safely returned from your little sojourn into his study, I took my leave. Dressed as you were, I didn't expect you would encounter any insurmountable problems. Apparently you did not.''

"Only one small problem but that one proved rather more entertaining than bothersome.''

A bold black brow ached up. "Yes . . . I believe I saw the small problem to which you refer dancing with that old lecher, Whitmore, being nearly accosted at the end of a minuet. I hope you extricated the lady before the old fool lost his senses completely.''

Jason smiled. "She *was* rather glad to see me. Now you tell me it was not my winning personality, but Whitmore's leering advances that made her so cager.''

Lucien smiled. "At least he was good for something.'' He moved closer, watched Jason pull a sheaf of folded papers from the pocket of his waistcoat. "From Avery's study?'' he asked.

"Exactly so. As I told you, I knew where the safe was located and how to open it. I wasn't certain what I'd find, but as it turns out, I did rather well.'' Unfolding the papers, he smoothed them out on the heavy oak table. "This document is dated three days after my father's murder. It's a contract between the duke of Carlyle and the countess of Brookhurst. Avery agrees to make her a lump sum payment of two hundred thousand pounds plus a large yearly stipend for life. There's enough money involved to keep the countess in extremely high fashion for the rest of her days.''

"Let me see that.'' Litchfield bent over, carefully examining the document in the flickering candlelight. "Good God, Avery would turn a bilious shade of green if he knew you had gotten your hands on this.''

"By itself, it isn't enough to overturn the guilty verdict, but it's a start, the first solid evidence we've uncovered that shows there might have been some sort of collusion on Avery's part.''

Lucien clamped a hand on his shoulder. "Better than that, this document ties Celia and Avery together. Perhaps its existence will be threat enough to force her to admit her part in the deception and tell the truth of what happened that night.''

Jason shook his head. ''We can't risk it. Celia won't bluff easily. We can't afford for either of them to get suspicious. We mustn't alert them to our movements until we're certain the countess will agree to tell the truth. If she suspects for a moment that I'm still alive, she'll tell Avery. He'll do anything to stop me. My life wouldn't be worth a damnable shilling.''

Lucien frowned. ''We'll have to be careful, but we've known that from the start.'' He smiled slightly. ''As you say, this document in itself isn't enough, but at least we have a beginning. I'm more than pleased about that.''

Jason closed his eyes and tilted his head back against one of the tall oak bedposts. ''It feels good, Lucien, I can tell you. It's the first real hope I've had.''

''This is only the beginning, my friend.''

Jason wished he could be as optimistic. Every day he remained in England the odds of discovery worsened. Sooner or later someone, somewhere would recognize him. The authorities would come after him, haul him off to prison. He would hang for certain—this time there would be no escape. He had to move with the utmost care yet every second that passed decreased his odds of succeeding.

''You've done a good night's work,'' Lucien said, heading for the door. ''Try to get some rest.''

Perhaps he would, Jason thought, moving again to the table, his fingers caressing the valuable documents. He thought of the risk he had taken in going to Carlyle Hall, then smiled to think of his encounter with Lady Velvet. Even if he hadn't found the documents, the risk would have been worth it. He recalled the feel of her in his arms, the lilac fragrance of her hair, and his body quickened with desire. He remembered her soft lips parting under his, her full breasts crushed against his chest, and a dull ache pulsed in his groin.

Perhaps he would sleep, he thought. Or perhaps he would

spend the night in an agony of hunger, reliving the heated moments he had shared with Velvet Moran.

Velvet tossed and turned in the deep feather mattress and didn't fall asleep till just before dawn. When Tabitha finally awoke her, she felt muzzy and out of sorts. A slight headache pounded at her temple.

" 'Is Grace 'as been askin' for ye. 'E wants ye to join 'im and 'is guests."

Velvet nodded. Avery was playing his part to the hilt, thank God. The gossip had dwindled to faint murmurings of consolation for the ordeal she had suffered. Their parting would pass with only the usual amount of speculation as to the cause. Velvet swung her single long braid back over her shoulder and swung her legs to the side of the bed.

"I'll wear the saffron-striped taffeta," she told Tabby, already dreading the day, but even before the sentence had escaped her lips, her thoughts returned to where they had been before. Through the long, sleepless hours of the night, she had thought of only one thing: Jason Sinclair.

Was he truly a murderer? Or was there some mistake that only made him appear the culprit?

Was he guilty? Or was he innocent?

As she completed her toilette, sat on the stool in front of the ornate Sheraton bureau and let Tabby dress her hair, sweeping it up and leaving several fat curls at her shoulder, she tried to convince herself it was possible, that Jason was indeed capable of murder.

Strangely, she didn't really doubt that he was, under the right set of circumstances. It was certain he could be ruthless in accomplishing his ends. He was a hard man, fiercely determined when anyone tried to oppose him.

Jason Sinclair was a dangerous, volatile man. Every sinew in his body spoke of the hardships that had honed him into the driven man he had become. She tried to tell herself he could have callously murdered his father, but nothing inside her agreed. In her mind's eye, she replayed the days they had spent at the small hunting lodge. She had fought him from the first moment of their meeting, yet he had never really hurt her, not even when she had given him cause.

She thought of their encounter in the stable. He had been so gentle with the puppy. And when he had spoken of his father, his words and the look on his face held nothing less than love and respect for the man who had sired him. The butler had said the same thing, that Jason had loved the duke, that he would never have harmed him.

He is innocent, Velvet thought with growing conviction while Tabby closed the fastenings on her wide panniers then helped her into the saffron-striped day dress, growing more and more certain with every breath she took.

A small voice warned that it was wishful thinking, that the man was supposed to have hung, but she could not shake the notion. Jason Sinclair was not a man who could commit such a crime against someone he loved.

Perhaps it was the reason he had finally come out of hiding. Perhaps after all these years, he meant to prove his innocence. She didn't know why he had waited so long, but if he intended to clear his name, he must have found someone to help him, someone he could trust.

Someone like his longtime friend, the marquess of Litchfield.

Her heartbeat quickened, speeding the blood to her throbbing head and making the pounding grow worse. Litchfield had believed in Jason's innocence, had testified in his behalf at the trial. The man who had come to visit him at the hunting lodge was tall and dark. She had glimpsed a portion of his face, and now that she thought about it, she was certain those lean hard features belonged to Lucien Montaine.

Litchfield was a man of substance, a man respected and admired among members of the ton. If the marquess was willing to help him, Velvet was even more convinced that Jason was innocent of the crime.

And Litchfield would know where he was.

"Tabitha! Tabby!" she cried, seeking the woman's return. "I've changed my mind. Come back and help me change." Racing to the ornate armoire, she opened the mir-

rored doors and pulled out a carriage dress of russet silk
faile and a matching silk pelisse.

"Well now," said Tabitha, sauntering back into the room,
"just where are ye headed? I thought ye meant to spend the
morning with the duke."

"I told you I changed my mind. I've an errand to run and
I need something less ornate, more businesslike. Help me
put this on, then get dressed yourself. You can make my
excuses to the duke while I go and summon the carriage."

Tabby knew better than to argue. She helped Velvet dress,
then set off to change into her traveling clothes. In minutes,
they were seated in the Haversham carriage, Tabby across
from Velvet to serve as chaperone. Up on the driver's seat,
John Wilton cracked his whip, and the carriage rolled away,
bowling down the lane to Castle Running, the marquess's
country estate.

She would go to Litchfield, force him to admit he was
helping Jason, and then demand a meeting. For whatever
reasons, however inadvertently, Jason Sinclair had helped
her. Now it was her turn to help him. She would find a way,
she vowed. Litchfield would be the start.

She knew enough about Jason to force his assistance. In
this she was certain to get her way.

Lucien pulled open the doors to the Red Salon, stepped inside, and closed them silently behind him. Seated on a plush
red brocade sofa, Velvet Moran sat waiting, her russet skirts
fanned out around her, her back straight, small shoulders
squared. He couldn't miss the air of determination that surrounded her like strong perfume.

She came to her feet as he walked in, crossed the room
partway to greet him.

"I apologize, my lord, for coming to you without invitation. I have something of importance to discuss with you
and I am afraid it will not wait."

Arching a brow, he took her hand and bowed slightly over
it. "There is no need for apology, my lady. It is always a
pleasure to be visited by a beautiful woman." Her cheeks

bloomed at his words. She thought it was flattery, but he had not lied. There was a lovely, vibrant beauty to Velvet Moran, a robust exuberance that made her golden brown eyes come alive, made her oval face and soft peach lips seem almost irresistible. Even her hair, a rich mahogany hue, crackled with life and fire.

"What I have to say is of an extremely private nature," she said, taking the chair he indicated while he moved toward the sideboard.

"We are private here. You may speak whatever is on your mind." He unstoppered a crystal decanter. "May I offer you a sherry? Or is there something else you might prefer?"

"Sherry is fine, thank you."

He returned, handed her the stemmed crystal glass, and sat down in a chair across from her. "All right, Lady Velvet, what is it you wish to discuss."

Two simple words. "Jason Sinclair."

He nearly choked on his brandy. "Beg pardon, what did you say?"

"I believe you heard me, my lord. I wish to discuss your good friend, Jason Sinclair, the legitimate fourth duke of Carlyle."

He leaned forward, his eyes hooded now but assessing her with a new respect. "My friend was murdered in Newgate prison, Lady Velvet. His passing was extremely painful. The subject is one I seldom discuss."

She was watching him as closely as he was watching her. "But you were his friend?"

"Yes."

"Do you believe he killed his father?"

"What I believe is of rather little consequence, considering—"

"Do you believe he was guilty?"

"No."

She leaned forward, the sherry glass gripped tightly in her hand. "Neither do I, my lord. I believe in his innocence, just as you do."

"That's comforting, my lady, but I don't see what bearing it has—"

"Oh, I think you do. I think that if Jason were alive today, he could still count you among his friends. Is that not so, my lord?"

She was trapping him neatly. He saw it coming, but there was little he could do to stop it. "Yes, it is."

"And we both know that Jason is alive, don't we?"

He thought of continuing the lie, but the look on her face said that she would not believe him. "Why have you come here, Lady Velvet?"

She straightened, her gaze steady on his face. "I want to see him. I believe you can arrange a meeting between us. That is why I am here, my lord."

He mulled that over, noting the determined glint in her eyes that he had seen before. "It would be dangerous . . . for both of you. Why do you wish to see him?"

"If I tell you the reason, you will tell him and then he might not come. Suffice it to say, I wish to meet with him on the morrow. Tell him if he does not appear, I shall be forced to reveal his identity."

He smiled thinly. "I don't believe you would do that, my lady."

A dark reddish brow cocked up. "But you cannot be certain, and you cannot afford to take the risk."

He couldn't help admiring her bravado. Courage and intelligence were intriguing qualities in a woman. No wonder his friend was so taken. "Jason won't like being blackmailed."

"That is my problem. In the meanwhile, perhaps you can suggest a suitable place for the meeting."

He swirled the brandy in the bottom of his snifter, raised the glass and inhaled the rich aroma, but did not take a sip. "There is a lady who lives at the outskirts of the village, a widow of my acquaintance. She is away at present, visiting family in Northumberland." A corner of his mouth tilted up. "It so happens that I have a key to the residence. As we are such good friends, I am certain she will not mind if you use the house for your meeting.''

''Splendid.'' She flashed a smile that was a bit too knowing for a lady of her tender years. ''Be certain to convey my appreciation to your . . . *friend* . . . when she returns.''

He simply smiled. ''Remember that I warned you. Jason will not appreciate your interference in his affairs.''

''And I did not appreciate his interference in mine. As it turned out, I am grateful. Perhaps Jason will be thankful as well.''

He rose from his chair and so did she. He stood a full head taller than she, the top of her head well below his chin, yet there was something about her, a measure of assurance, a strength of will that captured one's notice of her.

''Will two o'clock suit, my lady?''

''Perfectly,'' she said. ''I thank you for your help, my lord.''

His smile was slightly mocking. ''Save your thanks, Lady Velvet, until after you have dealt with my friend.''

She said nothing more, just lifted the russet silk day dress and swept from the room. Lucien watched her go and his smile turned to one of amusement. Jason had met his match in Velvet Moran. Under different circumstances, it would have been entertaining to watch their clash of wills. As it was, Velvet's interference only increased the danger for Jason.

He wondered what his friend would have to say when he learned about tomorrow's meeting.

''God's blood! You are telling me the woman marched into your home, told you she knew I was Jason Sinclair, then demanded a meeting or she would serve me up to the bloody hangman?'' Standing in the small sitting area of his tower bedchamber, Jason fought to control his temper.

Litchfield simply smiled. ''Something like that.''

Jason slammed his hand down on the mantel. ''Well, she can damn well forget it. I'm not about to dance her jig— tell the little vixen she can go straight to hell!'' He paced toward Lucien, stopped and turned, then paced back. "How the bloody deuce did she figure it out?"

"I haven't the vaguest notion."

"She's a smart little wench. I should have known she would be curious. I should have guessed she wouldn't be satisfied just to let the matter end."

"You'll have to meet her," Lucien said. "You can't be certain what she'll do to you if you don't."

"And I can't be certain what I'll do to her if I do."

Litchfield chuckled softly. "She's a handful. Beautiful and full of fire. Makes a man itch to take her in hand."

"Makes a man itch to take her to bed," Jason growled.

"Exactly so," Lucien agreed, and Jason's head snapped up. "Relax, my friend, the girl is all yours. I'm happy with my current mistress and an occasional tumble with the delightful widow Carter when I am in residence here."

Jason turned and stared out the window. "I don't believe she would tell them, but after Celia, I'm not certain of anything where a woman is concerned."

"The meeting might prove interesting. I wonder what she wants."

"God only knows."

"God and you, Jason, at two o'clock on the morrow."

Jason said nothing more, just stared at the green rolling hills between the castle and the village. He was angry—furious—at Velvet's interference. Yet it was hard to deny that deep down inside, part of him was eager for the meeting.

CHAPTER ELEVEN

∞

$\mathcal{D}$ressed in a ruby velvet riding habit cut in the fashionable military style, Velvet prodded the fire she had started in the hearth of the widow's stone house on the outskirts of Hammington Heath. The place was larger than she had expected, slate-roofed and whitewashed, the entire front covered with ivy.

The marquess's key let her into a cobble-floored interior topped by massive oak beams. The drawing room was immaculately clean, the sofa and chairs before the inglenook fireplace were upholstered in a white and rose floral design that gave the home a cheery warmth.

She poked the fire and watched thin tendrils of flame lick the wood. Holding up her hands to absorb the heat, she listened for the sounds of Jason's footfalls, but the creaks and groans of the house were all that surfaced.

It was well past two. Had he called her bluff and decided not to come? Was he that certain she would not give him away?

Velvet sighed into the silence. After yesterday's visit to Castle Running, she had returned to Carlyle Hall to play the part of Avery's dutiful future bride. Today she had made her excuses, then slipped off to the stables and ordered a horse saddled for her ride to the nearby village.

She fidgeted as she walked to the window, tugging at the gold epaulets on the shoulders of the riding habit. Brass buttons formed parallel rows down the front of the ruby velvet in the manner of a uniform jacket, and she thought of Jason at the ball in his scarlet cavalry tunic.

She peered out the mullioned windows to the rolling green fields beyond. God's breath, where was he?

"Looking for me, Duchess?" The deep voice rose from behind her and Velvet nearly jumped out of her skin.

"Sweet Jesu! You scared me half to death! How on earth did you get in?"

He was standing at the end of the mantel, one broad shoulder propped negligently against it, yet she didn't miss the tension thrumming through his tall hard frame.

"Getting in wasn't all that difficult. By now you should know I'm a man of many talents." There was something of menace in his voice, though his tone remained soft and even a bit cajoling.

Then he started across the room in her direction and she caught the flash of fire in his eyes. A muscle bunched in his jaw and the hands at his sides were balled tightly into fists. Sweet Lord, he was angry. Furious in fact. The marquess had warned her, but still she was not prepared.

"I-I know you are upset. I suppose you have a right to be angry, but I had to see you."

"Why?"

"I know who you are."

He moved closer, his jaw set, his eyes piercing. "You threatened me, Velvet. I don't like being threatened."

Her chin went up. "Well, I didn't especially like being abducted, but that didn't stop you from carting me away!"

"I had no choice." He was dressed for riding, in snug buff breeches and a full-sleeved white lawn shirt. His riding coat was tossed over the back of an overstuffed chair.

"So you have acquiesced to my wishes and come here against your will. Did you really believe that I would turn you in?"

His eyes fixed on her face, intense and probing. "I hoped that you would not but I could not be certain. I didn't think

Celia Rollins would stand by and watch me hang, but she
would have done so and gladly.''

Velvet rested a hand on his forearm, felt the muscles beneath his shirt quivering with tension. "Lady Brookhurst
betrayed you, but I would not. I do not believe you killed
your father. I believe you loved him. I want to help you
prove your innocence.''

She stepped away from him, lifted her skirts, and swept
into a deep, graceful curtsy. ''. . . Your grace.''

Jason just stood there. The long muscles in his throat
constricted, but he did not speak. For a silent moment he
held her gaze with his beautiful bright blue eyes. A fine
tremor shook his hand as he reached for her, entwined her
fingers with his own, and urged her to her feet. Then he
swept her into his arms.

"Ah, God, Duchess. No one has called me that in a very
long time.''

Velvet clung to him, sliding her arms around his neck,
feeling his cheek pressed to hers. Tears stung her eyes and
she blinked to keep them from falling. "I want to help you.
That's why I came. I want you to tell me what happened so
I can find some way to help.''

He only shook his head. "I appreciate your concern, but
there is nothing you can do, and involving yourself in my
affairs would only cause you trouble. It could even be dangerous.''

She pulled a bit away, lifted her eyes to his face. "I want
to know about it, Jason. Please, won't you tell me?''

Long moments passed. Each tick of the clock seemed to
echo in the room. With a weary sigh, he turned away, brushing back a lock of his hair as he led her over to the sofa.
He took a seat beside her.

"It's still difficult for me to speak of. I was so naive back
then. I never even suspected.'' He shook his head. "They
planned it from the start, Avery and the countess. They—''

"Avery! Avery is the man who killed your father?''

He nodded. "What did you think?''

"I thought . . . that perhaps he was duped, that there was

a mistake of some sort that convinced him of your guilt.''

''There was no mistake. Celia wanted money. Avery wanted control of the dukedom. They had decided to get rid of both my father and me, perhaps not at the same time, but they were simply waiting, looking for the right moment to put their plan into motion. That night when my father left to follow me to the inn, Avery realized what was happening. He saw a golden opportunity and seized it.'' He laughed bitterly. ''I made it all so easy for them. I fell in love with Celia and I couldn't see the danger. I couldn't think of anything but her.''

Velvet felt a vague stirring she recognized as jealousy. Her chest hurt to think of Jason in love with the beautiful countess. It was ridiculous, but the knifing pain remained.

''I know you were thrown into prison. How did you manage to escape?''

''I didn't.''

''But—''

''The first night I was there, a group of inmates attacked me. They wanted my clothes, my shoes. In Newgate they were worth a small fortune. They beat me nearly senseless, stripped me naked, then left me with only the rags they discarded. One of the men was bigger than the others, tougher. He ended up with most of my things.''

He glanced off for a moment, caught up in his painful recollections. ''Unfortunately, he didn't get to wear them very long. Later that night, the man was attacked and knifed to death, his face badly disfigured during the scuffle. When the guards found him, they assumed the man was me—he was the same size, had the same color hair.'' He shook his head. ''I've often wondered if Avery might have been behind the attack. Lucien was trying to stop the hanging. Avery wanted me dead. He isn't a man to take chances.''

He shrugged those powerful shoulders, the sinews tightening beneath his white lawn shirt. ''I suppose I'll never know.''

Velvet's heart went out to him. ''Oh, Jason.'' She wanted to touch him, to hold him, to banish the haunted look that darkened his handsome face. Instead she waited for him to finish, her chest aching, her throat clogged with tears for the pain he must have suffered.

He stared off toward the window. ''That night, I escaped the hangman, but there were times I wished that I had died instead. In the morning, when they came looking for the prisoner named Hawkins, the man who was killed, I took his place. They transported me to the Colonies. I slaved in the heat and the bugs for four long years before I got away. The only thing that kept me going was the vow I'd made to come back here.''

Velvet didn't realize she was crying till she felt the tears on her cheeks.

Jason leaned toward her. ''It's all right.'' A long dark finger brushed away the wetness. ''What happened is all in the past.'' He tipped her chin with his hand. ''And I told you, there is nothing you can do.''

Velvet looked into those blue, blue eyes. ''You can't be certain of that. I'm staying at Carlyle Hall for one more day. Time enough to have a look around, ask a few questions. I found out about you. Perhaps I'll learn something else that might be of value.''

''And perhaps your questions will stir up Avery's suspicions. If that happens, I'm as good as dead.''

A shiver rippled through her but she forced it away. ''The odds are just as good that you will do something to alert him.''

''I am not fool enough—''

''Point in fact—your appearance at the costume ball. That could have been disastrous. What if someone besides me had recognized you?''

''I was wearing a mask,'' he said stubbornly.

''Yes, you were, little good it would have done if someone had caught you going into Avery's study. And I am not such a fool that I would not take care. You must let me try, Jason. Surely it's apparent the longer you delay in finding proof, the greater the odds of your being discovered.''

The line of his mouth grew grim. "More than apparent, I assure you."

"Let me help you, Jason."

He only shook his head. "No. I don't want you hurt."

"Curse you—I want to help."

"I said no, Velvet, and that is what I mean."

Her chin inched up. "Do you really believe you can stop me?"

Jason's jaw clamped. Anger swept over his features. "You little minx—you are the most willful, stubborn woman I have ever met!"

"I am going to help you, your grace, whether you wish me to or not!"

"Dammit—I should have thrashed you harder!" He reached out and gripped her shoulders, his eyes snapping fire. A long moment passed but neither of them moved. With a groan of defeat, Jason hauled her against him. "But in truth, I would far rather kiss you." He captured her mouth in a ravaging kiss, his lips moving hotly over hers, urging them to part for him.

She should have been angry, should have shoved him away, but she clung to him instead. She relished the heat spearing through her, the feel of his arms around her, the taste of him in her mouth. His tongue tangled with hers, stroking deeply, possessing her as if he owned her. The kiss was hard, rough, hungry. Heat fanned out from the base of her throat, crept over her shoulders, slid into her breasts, making them swell inside her gown.

Jason deepened the kiss, taking her mouth so thoroughly she felt faint. Heat radiated into her stomach, spread out across her skin. His hand moved down to her breast, cupping the fullness, molding it, making the nipple tighten. He worked the brass buttons on her bodice, parted the fabric and slid his hand inside. Warmth invaded her, a melting sensation that wrenched a small mew of pleasure from her lips. His palm abraded her nipple and it tightened even more, forming a painful peak beneath his hand.

Velvet heard him groan.

He was kissing the arch of her throat, pulling the pins from her hair, shoving his fingers into the heavy dark mass that tumbled around her shoulders.

"Jason . . ." she whispered, but his fiery kiss muffled her weak protest and his hands continued their assault. He slid the bodice of the gown off her shoulders, then the strap of her white lawn chemise fell away. The second strap slipped off and he eased down the fabric, baring her to the waist.

"Lovely," he whispered, his hot gaze devouring her naked flesh. When he lowered his head and took a nipple into his mouth, a ripple of heat scorched through her.

"Good sweet God . . ." The words slipped out, but she didn't try to stop him. Instead her body arched upward, pleading for more, trembling when he laved the stiff crest with his tongue. Her fingers dug into his shoulders and hard muscle bunched beneath her hand. She could feel his heart, thundering beneath his flat male nipple, and her touch made the tiny peak grow hard. She trembled and his hand moved lower, shoving up her skirts, working to bunch them around her waist. He swore at her whalebone panniers, smaller for riding but a barrier to his purpose just the same.

His head came up. He dragged in a great breath of air. "We have to stop, Velvet. If we do not, in a few more moments, I won't be able to."

But she didn't want him to stop. She was in love with Jason Sinclair. She had tried to deny it, but the moment she had seen him, the moment he had touched her, she knew it was the truth. He was a criminal on the run, a man accused of murder. Any hour he could be discovered. If he was, his life would be forfeit.

She pulled the thin black ribbon that tied back his glossy dark hair, slid her fingers into the heavy strands, and dragged his mouth down to hers for a kiss. "Make love to me, Jason. Please. I don't want this to end."

Jason groaned. He shook his head even as his hand gently fondled her breast. "I want you, Velvet. I can't remember wanting a woman more, but it isn't . . . we can't . . ."

"Please . . ." she whispered, afraid that if she didn't grasp the moment, seize this last chance to discover true passion, the time would never come again. Jason kissed her, fiercely yet gently. When she opened the buttons on the front of his shirt and slid her hands inside, a shudder rippled through him and she knew that she had won.

With a hand that was suddenly unsteady, he began to unfasten her clothes, releasing the tabs on her skirt and panniers and easing them away, then bending to remove her shoes and stockings. In minutes he had stripped her bare and pulled off his shirt and riding boots. Only his tight brown breeches remained. They covered the thick bulge of his sex, but as he eased her down on the sofa, its hardness pressed into her thigh.

She should have been frightened but she found that she was not. He was a big man and he was powerful, but somehow she knew he would take extra care not to hurt her. His hands caressed her breasts, stroking them, teasing the ends until her body simmered with pleasure. She whimpered when he moved lower, cupping the mound of her sex, his fingers lacing through the curly red-brown hair at the apex of her legs.

The feeling was so new, so intense, she stiffened a little, afraid for a moment. Jason kissed her again, his mouth and tongue gently persuasive, and her fear began to recede. Warmth replaced hesitation, spirals of heat moved over her flesh and coiled low in her belly.

"Jason . . ." She moaned when he parted the slick damp folds at her core and a long dark finger slid inside her.

"God, you feel good." A thorough kiss followed, his tongue thrusting into her mouth with the same sensuous rhythm as his hand. She shifted restlessly, feeling the fire, arching against him. Wanting him, heedless of the consequences.

Suddenly he paused, his gaze moving up to her face. He was breathing hard, his eyes glowing with a hunger he no longer tried to hide. "We have to stop this, Velvet. I won't marry you. Even if I wasn't facing the gallows, I wouldn't wed you. I can't. Stop me now, before it's too late."

Her heart twisted painfully. "Y-you . . . you're married? You already have a wife?"

He shook his head, moving the curtain of dark hair across his shoulders. "No."

He didn't love her. He wouldn't wed her. The thought made her ache inside. Still, she wanted him, wanted desperately to know this one moment of passion. "Then make love to me. It's what we both want."

His features darkened. His jaw clamped. "There are things you don't know, things I can't explain. You'll be sorry, Velvet. You'll regret it. Stop me now while I'm sane enough to listen."

"I want this, Jason."

His eyes bored into her. "You don't know the kind of man I am, the things I've done."

"I don't care!"

He stared down into her face. "I've learned to be greedy, Velvet. I learned years ago to take what I wanted in order to survive." He captured her chin with his hand. "You may regret this but I assure you, sweeting, I won't."

He took her mouth in a savage kiss while his hand cupped her breast, kneading it fiercely, teasing the end. In minutes, she was on fire for him, writhing and moaning as he stroked her damp passage once more.

"You're ready for me, Velvet. Wet and slick. I'll go easy, try not to hurt you. Trust me, love. Let me make it good for you."

She did trust him, she realized. More than any man she had ever known. "Yes . . ." she said softly, gazing into the harsh male beauty of his face. "Yes, please, Jason."

He left her a moment to shed his breeches, then joined her on the sofa, spreading her legs and settling his tall frame between her thighs. He kissed her again, taking her mouth while his fingers worked their magic, then he eased his hardness inside. He didn't stop till he reached the barrier of her innocence.

"I'm a selfish bastard, Velvet," He kissed the side of her neck. " 'Twas a sad day for you when I carried you away."

He plunged deeply and Velvet cried out, but the sound was muffled by his lips.

An instant of pain shot through her, a searing moment that had her clamping her teeth against it. As quickly as it came, it was gone. Jason loomed above her, resting on his elbows, his muscles knotted, holding himself immobile by sheer force of will. "I'm sorry. I tried not to hurt you. Are you all right?"

She swallowed, gave him a tremulous smile. "The pain has fled. I feel only a strange sort of fullness."

His sensuous mouth curved up. "You will feel more, sweeting, that I promise."

And so she did. Slowly he began to move, his hips rising, easing him almost all the way out. Then his buttocks flexed and drove him deeply back in. In and then out. Sinking in until he filled her, then withdrawing until she ached for his return. She could feel every hard inch of him, feel the heavy thrust and drag of his shaft, and tiny vibrations rushed through her. Her body trembled and she arched upward, taking him deeper still. Her hands gripped his sweat-slick shoulders, taut muscle rippled, and the heat in her loins fanned out through her limbs.

Warmth coiled low in her belly. Her body seemed to burn.

In and then out, faster, harder, deeper. Pounding, pounding until the pleasure was unbearable.

"Jason!" She caught her lip between her teeth, her body tightening, shimmering, then shattering into a thousand pieces. Pleasure broke over her, ripples of fire and incredible surges of sweetness. She clung to him, wept his name against his shoulder, held him and let the waves of pleasure wash through her. Jason's body tightened above her. She felt the last of his hard driving thrusts, heard a groan rumble up from his throat.

For long tender moments, he just held her. Velvet clung to him and thought she had never experienced anything so wonderful, never felt so incredibly complete. Whatever happened, whatever life held in store, she would always have this moment, this special gift of passion that couldn't be taken from her.

Then Jason pulled away. "The hour grows late. You had better get dressed." A brusque note rang in his voice she hadn't expected, a remoteness that hadn't been there before. "You've been gone from the house too long already."

Uncertainty fluttered through her. She wanted to reach out and touch him, to take comfort from his solid strength as she had done before. "What we did . . . you did not . . . you did not find it pleasing?"

His eyes swung to hers and he looked at her hard. "Pleasing? Aye, Duchess, pleasing it was, to say the very least. I told you, sweeting, that I would not regret it." He grabbed his breeches and dragged them on, adjusting himself inside them. "I won't apologize for what happened, if that is what you are after. I warned you before we started."

She glanced down, feeling cold now in her nudity, uncomfortable with this harsh side of him, wishing the gentle side would return. "I did not ask for an apology. I am new to this. I was not certain . . . I did not know if I . . ."

He pulled on his shirt, rubbing the scar on the back of his hand as if the skin still burned. "You are quite talented, my lady. The ride was the best I've had in years."

Velvet bit down on her bottom lip, but she couldn't block the soft cry of pain that escaped her throat. She turned away from him, fumbling for her clothes, pulling her chemise on over her head and fighting not to cry. It was a losing battle and tears spilled down her cheeks.

The loving had been so special for her and it had meant nothing at all to him.

She bent forward, her vision blurred, searching for the bodice of her riding gown. Her fingers brushed his as he handed it over.

"Velvet . . . I'm sorry. I didn't mean that."

She looked away from him, forced her arms into the sleeves, and fumbled with the buttons up the front. " 'Twas my idea, your grace. I could have stopped you but I did not. A man cannot think too highly of a woman like that."

She gasped at the fierceness with which he dragged her against him, forced her to meet his piercing gaze. "Do not say that. Do not even think it. This was my fault. I behaved like the animal I have become. I took your innocence. I cared nothing for the price you would pay, only that I hungered to bed you. I tried to warn you. I tried to tell you the kind of man I am, but you would not listen. Now you know."

Stark pain etched his features. Regret shown in the hard set of his jaw. An ache rose in her chest just to look at him. Velvet reached out, rested a trembling hand against his cheek.

"I shall tell you what I know. I know that you are the most passionate and gentle of lovers. I know that you tried to resist far longer than any other man would have, but I would not let you. I wanted you, just as you wanted me. It is you who regrets what has happened, your grace. I promise you, I do not."

He shook his head. "I should have stopped. I should have protected you—"

"I wanted what you gave me. That is all that matters."

He stared at her, searching for the truth, trying to read her face. What he saw must have convinced him, for his eyes closed a moment and when he opened them again, the pain seemed to have faded.

A long sigh slipped from between his lips. "There may be consequences. I should have been more careful but I . . ." He gave her a tentative smile. "I'm afraid, at the time, I wasn't thinking all that clearly."

"I believe I shall take that as a compliment, your grace."

"It was meant as such, my lady."

She smiled softly, feeling suddenly shy. Turning away to finish dressing, she saw that her legs were flecked with virgin's blood. Jason must have realized her dilemma for he left the room and returned a few moments later with a damp cloth and a small linen towel. High color rising in her cheeks, Velvet accepted them. Jason pretended not to notice, turned and walked outside, leaving her alone.

She joined him a few minutes later, dressed once more in her ruby velvet riding habit, her hair smoothed into a bun at the nape of her neck. The stark mode of dress gave her the courage to face him.

"If I should learn anything of value, I shall send word to you through Litchfield."

His eyes went dark, storm clouds on the horizon of a very blue sea. "I told you, Velvet, it's too dangerous. Stay out of Avery's way and whatever you do, don't ask questions."

She smiled sweetly. "Whatever you say, your grace."

"And dammit, don't call me that. Someone might hear you."

"As you wish, Jason. Will you help me up?"

He lifted her easily into the sidesaddle, but his hands lingered a few extra moments at her waist. "Good-bye, Lady Velvet," he said gruffly, his eyes still fixed on her face. "You're a very special woman."

Her throat went tight. "Good-bye, Jason." Already she missed him. Ignoring the ache in her chest and the burning urge to weep, she reined the horse away and did not look back. She had meant what she said—she didn't regret making love to him. It had been the single most astounding moment of her life. She would never regret it. She only regretted that Jason didn't love her. And that it would never happen again.

As soon as she left Carlyle Hall, she was heading for the city. The London Season was underway and she had to find a husband. Jason had made it clear he wasn't interested in marriage, and even if he agreed to return her dowry, she would not wed him if he did not want her.

A fresh lance of pain speared through her. Jason wanted to bed her. He was a virile man who enjoyed the pleasures of a woman's body. He cared little for her beyond that.

It did not mean she didn't intend to help him. Velvet rode back to Carlyle Hall ignoring a thread of loneliness she hadn't expected, and trying to decide the best way to begin.

* * *

Avery stood in the doorway to the morning room, where his last remaining guests had gathered for their breakfast. Pretty little Mary Stanton was among them, seated beside her father, Sir Wallace, at the long, linen draped, silver-laden table.

Avery returned the smile Mary cast in his direction, fighting an unbearable urge to rub his hands together with glee.

In the course of the next thirty days, his problems would be over. He would be married to Mary Stanton, in control of her vast dowry, and heir to her father's fortune. The wheels could be set into motion as soon as his involvement was ended with Velvet Moran.

Avery frowned to see her sitting across from Lady Brookhurst, engaged in what appeared to be a cheerful conversation. Velvet was laughing at something Celia said, her big brown eyes tilted up at the corners with mirth. Avery's frown grew even darker. Celia was hardly a woman of wit, or at least he had certainly never thought so. Most of her humor was ribald and better spoken in bed.

For the past few years, she had denied him even that small pleasure, doling out the lash of her carping tongue without the solace of her body. She constantly badgered him for money, regretted, she said, having ever signed the settlement agreement they had made. Last month, she had somehow discovered the nebulous state of his finances. Only his engagement to Lady Velvet had kept her from baring her vicious fangs at him again.

He watched the two women chatting with a bit too much familiarity and hoped to God the Haversham girl had sense enough to keep her mouth shut about their doomed betrothal. Then he thought of the shrewd way Velvet had manipulated him and relaxed a little. She was a worthy opponent for Celia—and he had far more important matters to attend.

Turning toward the opposite end of the breakfast table Avery started walking toward Mary Stanton.

* * *

Velvet smiled at another of Lady Brookhurst's inane remarks. She had managed to gain a seat across from the countess, but the woman's regard focused mainly on handsome Christian Sutherland, the earl of Balfour. Unfortunately the earl was seated a goodly distance away and Celia soon wearied of trying to capture his attention.

"Faith, but men are a pitiful lot," she said with a sigh. "That one strays from one bed to another with such staggering frequency one would think he must grow dizzy trying to recall his paramours' names."

Velvet glanced down the long stretch of starched white linen, past the gleaming silver centerpiece, to where the blond-haired earl of Balfour chatted with Sir Wallace Stanton. "He is certainly handsome enough."

"La, and a good catch, too. Wealthy in the extreme. At present, he is prowling for a wife, though I doubt he looks forward to being leg shackled."

"If what you say of his constancy is true, he had better choose a woman of great tolerance."

The countess laughed softly. Gowned in bright mauve silk, black Belgian lace flowing from elbow to wrist, she looked elegant and beautiful, cool and unruffled, even though the earl continued to ignore her.

"God's truth, but they all stray sooner or later." Her glance darted to Avery then back to her. "Except for his grace, of course. The duke is obviously smitten. I'm certain he'll be quite the dutiful husband."

The lie came easily. They both recognized it for what it was. Velvet merely smiled. "I'm certain he will, but if he is not, surely once a wife's duty is performed, she should be allowed the same freedom as the man she has married."

Celia's fine black brow arched up. She smiled with obvious approval. "You are far more intelligent than I had guessed, Lady Velvet. Avery is lucky to have found you." But her smug smile said Avery would despise a woman who cuckolded him, no matter how many mistresses he, himself, might have.

Velvet moved the pheasant and eggs around on her plate,

then set her fork down without bringing a bite to her lips. "You knew his brother, I'm told."

The countess eyed her with renewed interest, surprised she had unearthed the long-dead scandal Avery worked so hard to keep buried. She sighed dramatically. "I knew him. We were quite in love, you know. Jason had meant for us to marry."

Velvet nearly dropped the porcelain teacup she had just lifted. "I-I wasn't aware that the two of you were betrothed."

"It was not yet official. I was widowed only just a few months earlier. We meant to wait until after a suitable period of mourning before we announced our plans. That was the reason we were forced to meet in secret."

"I see." Velvet dabbed her napkin against her lips, glad for the moment to compose herself. "Avery rarely speaks of him. I suppose the loss of both his brother and father is just too painful."

"I'm sure it is." She flashed a womanly smile. "But aside from the night of the murder, the memories I hold of Jason are pleasant, indeed." She leaned closer. "He was quite a magnificent lover. Young and virile. Nearly insatiable in bed." She glanced toward Avery. "But I'm certain your future husband —being also a Sinclair—will serve just as well."

Hardly, Velvet thought. Avery's passionless kisses held none of the fire Jason's did. She only wished that Celia Rollins wasn't so obviously aware of it.

"I suppose it was terrible for you, witnessing the murder, I mean, knowing the man you loved would hang and the plans the two of you had made would die along with him."

The countess looked pained. "It was dreadful. Poor Avery was so distraught. Neither of us believed a man like Jason was capable of murder." Another dramatic sigh. "I suppose it was my fault, really. For whatever reason, the duke opposed our marriage. Jason was determined to wed me no matter what his father said. They argued violently. Jason lost his temper, drew his pistol, and shot him. Avery arrived a few moments later, but by then it was too late.''

Velvet's head snapped up. ''I thought Avery said he tried to talk Jason out of it but his brother wouldn't listen. If he didn't get there until the duke was already dead—''

For an instant, the countess looked uneasy then she waved the words away. ''Perhaps he was there before the shooting. I can hardly be expected to recall the exact way it happened after all these years.''

Velvet forced herself to smile and leaned casually back in her chair. She didn't dare press for more, no matter how badly she wanted to. ''Of course you can't. I daresay, I had only heard bits and pieces of gossip. 'Tis a dreadful subject and I was remiss in bringing it up.''

''Yes . . . well, there are certainly more pleasant topics.'' She turned to smile at the handsome earl of Balfour, but he didn't smile back. Another man did, the slender, sandy-haired Viscount Dearing. The countess tossed Balfour a disgruntled glance then began to flirt openly with Dearing.

''As I said,'' the countess remarked to Velvet with a conspiratorial air, ''there are far more pleasant topics. I believe I shall pursue one of them. I'm afraid you will have to excuse me.''

''Of course.'' Velvet watched the countess's graceful departure, accompanied not long after by the slender fair-haired Dearing, who trailed along in her wake. The countess was older than he, but she hadn't lost her allure. She was beautiful, wicked, and incredibly seductive. No wonder Jason had been so in love with her.

The unwelcome thought arose—once he saw her again, perhaps he still would be.

CHAPTER TWELVE

∞

𝒥ason reread the odd little column in the *Morning Chronicle* that hinted at Society gossip, using the first initials of the people it spoke of, telling whatever juicy secrets the writer could unearth. In this case, his grace, the duke of C had been jilted by the fickle Lady V, who could not seem to make up her mind which of her multitude of suitors she wished to wed.

The last line read, "Or perhaps the competition was simply too keen for a mere duke of the realm when matched against the far more romantic figure of the highwayman who carried her away."

Jason crumpled up the paper and tossed it across the bedchamber of Litchfield's town house, where they were now in residence. It slapped against the gold flocked wall then rolled on the thick Turkish carpet. Dammit, he had hoped the gossipmongers would leave her alone. He didn't want her name dragged through the mud and he had believed, as she had, that the amicable parting she had staged with Avery would take the edge off the wagging tongues.

Jason sighed, damning himself and the roll he'd been forced to play in her abduction, cursing himself for giving into his lust and bedding her. Bloody hell, the girl was a virgin! He had never stooped quite so low.

And yet in his heart, it was difficult to regret it. Making love to Velvet had been beyond his wildest imaginings. He couldn't remember when bedding a woman had given him such intense pleasure. The worst part was, he had wanted her again even as she had left him to pull on her clothes.

Even now, the hungry ache remained. And Lucien's suggestion of a visit to one of the private pleasure barges along the Thames somehow didn't excite him. He wanted Velvet Moran in his bed and he could not have her.

Sooner or later he would simply have to accept that.

A knock at the door dragged his attention in that direction. His manservant, a thin man in his fifties named Holcomb, the same man who had served him at Castle Running, stepped in. "A gentleman has arrived, my lord. The marquess requests you join them in his study."

"Thank you, Holcomb." Following the smaller man downstairs, Jason walked past him into Litchfield's book-lined, walnut-paneled study.

Coming around from behind his desk, Lucien looked at him and smiled. "Lord Hawkins, may I present to you Mr. William Barnstable?"

"Good afternoon, milord," said the stout, bull-necked little Bow Street Runner.

"Mr. Barnstable." Jason made a slight nod of his head.

"Lord Hawkins is the man I mentioned. He is equally eager to see the truth of this matter unearthed. With your help, we mean to see our friend Jason Sinclair's name cleared of the blight that has darkened it these past eight years."

Jason lifted the lid off a humidor and offered the little man one of Litchfield's expensive cigars. "How is your investigation coming, Mr. Barnstable? Have you found any information that might be helpful in our endeavor?"

A stubby hand reached in and dragged out a fat black cigar. Instead of lighting it, he stuffed it into the pocket of his sturdy woolen coat. "Eight years has past since the murder. The search has not been easy."

"I'm certain it has not," Jason said.

"We are not questioning the extent of your efforts," Lucien put in. "Though you must know we are eager for re-

sults.'' He had told the Runner that the three men had been
students together at Oxford, that over drinks at Almack's
one night, the two men still living had decided to join forces,
to discover the true villain in the duke of Carlyle's murder
and restore their dead friend's good name. ''Your message
implied that you had unearthed information that might be
of value.''

''That is true, my lord.''

Jason's impatient regard narrowed on the man's pudgy
face. ''What is it, man? What have you found out?''

Lucien flashed him a dark look of warning. *Take it easy,*
it said. *You mustn't appear too eager.*

''Unfortunately, my efforts at the Peregrine's Roost
proved nearly worthless. Most of the servants who were
there that night are gone. The ones who remain recall little
of the actual shooting besides the sound of the gunshot and
the echo of a woman's scream.''

''But you *have* found something,'' Lucien prodded.

''Aye, that I have.'' The little man's smile looked tri-
umphant, like a dog who'd unearthed a juicy bone. ''I believe I've found the man responsible for the murder of your
friend in Newgate prison.''

Jason's muscles went tense. The clock ticked for several
heartbeats. ''Go on.''

''It was a thief by the name of Elias Foote.''

''Is this Foote still alive?'' Lucien asked.

''Aye, that he is . . . or at least he was the last I heard tell.
He's a bad one, I can tell you. A blackleg who spends most
of his time in Southwark or down at the quay. I haven't yet
tried to find him. I thought it best to wait until I had spoken
to you.''

''You did exactly right, Mr. Barnstable,'' Lucien said.
''Lord Hawkins and I will speak to Foote. Just give us a
list of the places he might frequent and we shall do the
rest.''

''In the meantime''—Jason came to his feet—''you just
keep doing as you have been—asking questions and stirring
up answers. Right now that is exactly what we need.''

The stout man took his cue and stood up as well. "I'll send word if I find out anything else." He grinned and patted the cigar that rode in his pocket. "Have a good evenin', milords."

Perhaps he would, Jason thought, relishing the notion that at last he could take some positive action. Except for an occasional foray into the less than fashionable East End where there was no chance he would be recognized, he had been cooped up inside the town house while his friend made the rounds of every fete Avery or Lady Brookhurst might attend.

Jason had yet to venture into Society, though he believed his appearance had changed enough that if he was careful, with a few alterations, he could perhaps move about unnoticed. He wondered what Velvet would think if she saw him, whether she would be glad of his reappearance, or if by now she realized her folly in allowing him the gift of her body.

He hoped to hell he hadn't gotten her with child. He wasn't exactly certain what he would do if he had.

Jason sighed and shoved the unpleasant notion away. Tonight he had something better to do than grow hard with lust for Velvet Moran. Tonight he would begin to search out his first real lead. He wasn't sure where they would find him, only that sooner or later they would. Once they had him, they could discover if indeed Avery had been the man behind the attack Jason long suspected had been meant for him.

He glanced over at Lucien, who studied him from a few feet away. "I take it you are more than eager to go after this villain."

Jason smiled grimly. "More than eager."

A corner of Lucien's mouth curved up. "At least it will take your mind off a certain lady of our mutual acquaintance."

Jason grunted. "I hope so." He hadn't mentioned what had happened between them at the cottage. If he had, his friend would realize that the odds were good the only way he could purge the woman from his thoughts was to bed her until he got his fill. Considering his intentions were entirely dishonorable, odds were even less likely he would be able to do that.

Clasping his hands together behind his back, Avery stood before the window in the drawing room, looking out at the formal gardens off to the rear of the Carlyle town house on Grosvenor Square. Everything was going smoothly. He was free of Velvet Moran, and Mary Stanton was responding to his advances, had already tentatively acquiesced to his subtle overtures of marriage.

More, he admitted sourly, because her father obviously wished it than because she was enthralled with his charm, but it didn't really matter. She would consent to the marriage and they would be wed.

Unfortunately, Mary had made it clear she expected to wait at least a year before the wedding. Avery had smiled and said he understood, all the while calculating how he would force the girl into marriage.

The knock sounded that he had been expecting. He crossed the room and pulled it open, allowing Baccy Willard to step in.

"Well, have you done as I've asked?"

"Aye, yer grace." Baccy had removed his tricorn hat, leaving a wide, flat crease around his black hair.

"All right, then. For the next two weeks, Sir Wallace will be away from the city on business. He has left his daughter in company with her friend, Jennie Barclay. The Barclays and Miss Stanton are scheduled to attend Lord Briarwood's soiree this Thursday next. That should well serve our purpose."

"Aye, yer grace."

"You remember what to do?"

"I'm to see the girl receives word that 'er father 'as fallen ill."

"That is correct. The note is to say that she should tell no one. That she is to seek out the duke of Carlyle, that he will escort her safely to where her father has been taken."

"Aye, I'll take care of it meself."

"Good. And the inn on the road to Windsor—you'll be sure to arrange that as well?"

"Aye, yer grace."

Avery clapped the huge man on the shoulder. "Our troubles are about to end, my friend."

Baccy nodded and turned to leave. Watching the big hulking figure walk away, Avery smiled.

Why should he not? By Friday next, he would be a man of wealth and position again. Pretty little Mary Stanton would be warming his bed. The duke of Carlyle would soon be a happily married man.

Avery waited for the sound of the closing door, but it never came. When he turned, Baccy still stood in the room.

Avery cocked a pale blond eyebrow. "Was there something else?"

"I almost forgot. 'Tis the girl, yer grace . . . Lady Velvet. She was askin' questions at Carlyle Hall about yer brother. I 'eard her talkin' to Cummings. Ye said that I should tell ye if anyone ever asked questions."

"That's right, I did." He smiled. "But in this case, I'm sure Lady Velvet was simply curious about the man who would have been her brother-in-law."

Baccy nodded. "She was real curious, yer grace. I know 'cause after that I followed 'er. I seen 'er talkin' with the upstairs maid, Sylvie Winters. I made Sylvie tell me what they was sayin'. She said Lady Velvet wanted to know about your brother . . . and about what happened the night of the murder."

Avery went still. His heart began thudding uncomfortably in his chest. "I don't like this, Baccy. Why would Velvet Moran be interested in my father's murder?"

"I don't know, yer grace."

"Neither do I but perhaps we ought to find out, eh?" He walked back across the room. "I want you to have one of your men keep an eye on her. If she continues asking questions, I want to know. If anything occurs that seems the least bit out of the ordinary, I want to know that as well."

"Aye, yer grace."

"That's all, Baccy." This time the big man left the room, closing the door behind him and leaving Avery to contemplate this new twist of fate.

Velvet Moran had been a thorn in his side almost since the day he had decided to marry her. Why she was interested in his affairs, he hadn't the foggiest notion, but he wasn't really worried about it. By the end of the week, he would be married to a very wealthy woman. His world would be set right and he would be back in control.

If Velvet turned out to be a problem, he would simply eliminate that problem.

Avery smiled and returned to his peaceful view of the garden.

"You look stunning tonight, Lady Velvet."

"Thank you, my lord." Dressed in an emerald silk gown atop an underskirt of amber trimmed with gold, Velvet smiled up at Christian Sutherland, earl of Balfour, standing beside her at the edge of the dance floor. For the past two weeks, the earl had been paying her court, rather a surprise, considering the gossip about her. And the fact that, in the beginning, he had seemed more interested in Mary Stanton.

"You've been dancing all evening," he said. "Could I get you a glass of punch?" The earl was tall and broad-shouldered with thick, dark golden-blond hair. His skin was swarthy instead of fair, his eyes a keen dark brown, his features not fine but deeply carved. All in all, the effect was virile and very definitely male, the kind of man she might have been attracted to—if it weren't for Jason Sinclair.

Velvet smiled. "I'm not really thirsty. Actually, I should rather have a moment away from the crush, if you don't mind. 'Tis highly unfashionable, I know, but in truth I grow weary of these nightly forays into Society."

His dark eyes lit with amusement. "I believe I've discovered what it is I like about you, my lady."

"And what might that be, my lord?"

"Your honesty. It seems to be a rare commodity among members of the ton."

She arched a dark reddish brow and let him guide her toward the French doors leading out onto the terrace into the cool night air. "A bit cynical, aren't you, my lord?"

"Perhaps, but not without good cause."

Velvet sighed. "Actually, there are times I'm a bit too outspoken. With my grandfather's illness, I've grown used to responsibility. Most men loathe such forthright behavior in a woman. If you do not, then you are a pleasant exception to the rule."

He smiled. "I shall take that as a compliment, my lady." They stopped above the garden, lit by torches above the rows of bright-colored flowers that had just begun to bloom. "All right, Lady Velvet, since we are both plainspoken, I will tell you what I have been thinking."

"My lord?"

"'Tis hardly a secret that I have entered the marriage mart. I am sure you have heard the gossip."

"I loathe gossip. Unfortunately, it is usually difficult not to succumb to the lure of it."

"In my case, the gossip is true. I am searching for a wife, and the fact is, finding one has been devilish hard to do."

"I cannot imagine a man like you having trouble attracting a woman."

"A woman is one thing. A wife is quite another."

She ran her hand along the stone balustrade, feeling the cool rough surface beneath her white-gloved fingers. "For a time, I thought you might be interested in Mary Stanton."

His mouth curved up. "You *are* plainspoken, my lady."

"I warned you, my lord."

The earl sighed. "My family was opposed to the notion of a match between us. They prefer an alliance with a member of the nobility, but in truth I found myself taken with Mary." Something flickered in his eyes, then it was gone. "For whatever reasons, Miss Stanton has made it clear that her interests lie in another direction."

Surely he didn't mean Avery. There was no comparison between the two men.

"Aside from Mary Stanton," he continued, "there is only one other woman who interests me—and that, my lady, is you."

Velvet laughed softly. Thank God she wasn't in love with the rogue. It was hardly flattering to be the man's second choice. "You are telling me, Lord Balfour, that you would prefer to wed Mary Stanton, but that I might possibly do instead?"

He cursed beneath his breath. "Dammit, that is not at all what I meant."

"Then what did you mean, my lord?"

"I meant, Lady Velvet, that I believe you and I would suit. It is purely as simple as that. You were betrothed to the duke of Carlyle, yet I do not for a moment believe it was a love match. I may not be a duke, but I am an earl and a wealthy man. I would like you to consider my offer. If you are interested, we can both put an end to these tedious rounds of parties and get on with our lives."

Velvet said nothing. The earl of Balfour was indeed a plainspoken man. He was handsome and wealthy, he would serve her purpose better than any man she could think of. The earl was the answer to her prayers, and yet it was Jason's image that appeared in her mind.

Jason with his blazing temper and fiery kisses. Jason with his fierce possession and gentle caresses. Jason with the pain in his eyes that never seemed to go away.

She thought of the last time she had seen him, the day that they had made love, and a soft ache rose inside her. Clasping her hands together in an effort to keep them from trembling, Velvet looked up at the earl.

"You have taken me rather by surprise, my lord. I hope you will allow me some time to consider."

"I wouldn't want a lengthy betrothal, Velvet. I need a wife and I want an heir. I find that I'm impatient, now that my mind is made up."

Velvet shivered. Even the duke's businesslike proposal

had not seemed so frankly coldhearted. She turned away from the look in those assessing dark eyes, but he caught her chin and turned her to face him.

"I'll be a good husband, Velvet. You're a beautiful woman and I desire you. Later on, as the years roll past, I'll be discreet in my affairs. I'll never embarrass you as Carlyle surely would have. Think about it, Velvet. I believe we could make a good life together."

Velvet wet her lips. This was exactly what she had wanted and yet . . . "Is . . . is my dowry important to you, my lord?" She wouldn't have asked another man. She would have been afraid to take the risk. Lord Balfour wasn't a man she would dare to deceive.

He looked at her a long assessing moment, then shook his head. "No. I would have wed Mary, a woman not of noble birth. If you were penniless, I would still choose you. I want a wife who suits me and a good mother for my sons. I believe you would serve well as both."

She lowered her lashes, hoping to hide the turmoil swirling inside her. "I suppose that is some sort of compliment and yet I feel oddly disconcerted. Perhaps the truth is harder to swallow than I had believed. Perhaps, like most women, I would rather be wooed with falsehoods than confronted with the plainspoken truth."

Something in those dark eyes softened. "If it makes you feel better, I would not have spoken this way to any other woman. It is only out of respect for you that I did so tonight."

Velvet smiled faintly. "Perhaps you are right, my lord. Perhaps we would suit. I promise I shall give it some thought."

He lifted her hand and pressed his mouth against the back of her wrist. "Thank you, my lady. Now . . . I believe we should go back in before the gossipmongers have another field day at our expense."

"Yes . . . of course . . ." But as she walked inside the house, the knowing glances that swept over them said it was already too late.

CHAPTER THIRTEEN

∞

*J*ason read the small article at the bottom of the *Morning Chronicle* then read it once again. Had the earl of B, it asked, succumbed to the tantalizing allure of the charming Lady V? They had been seen in company on a number of recent occasions. The rakehell earl was looking for a wife and according to the article, the lady in question also seemed eager for the match.

Does a wedding loom on the horizon? Dear reader, we will all simply have to wait and see.

Jason cursed roundly. Damn the little wench. She had only just climbed out of bed with him and already she was dallying with Balfour. The thought infuriated him. He couldn't remember when a woman had made him quite so angry. Then again, Velvet had a way of doing that.

For the balance of the day, she haunted his thoughts and his temper remained at just below simmer. Good Christ, did the lady have ice in her veins? Had she cared nothing at all for him? Or perhaps their one hasty tryst had simply given her a taste for more.

By evening he had worked himself into a slow-burning fury. For weeks he had been lusting after the little wench and yet he had left her alone. She was an innocent, he'd reasoned, he had taken enough from her already. He had tried to protect her from his own base urges when all the while the rakehell earl had been sampling her charms.

Damn her! Damn her to bloody perdition!

Jason began to pace, his fists balled up, when a swift knock sounded and the door creaked open.

"Are you ready?" Dressed all in black as he had been doing on their evening forays, Litchfield stood in the hallway.

"Aye, more than ready. One minute more in this accursed dwelling and I fear I shall explode."

Lucien chuckled softly. "The carriage awaits. We shall find him this night—I am certain of it. The man can't elude us forever."

Jason hoped they would find him tonight. He was itching for a fight and Elias Foote deserved the pounding he would love to mete out.

"Where are we headed?" he asked. They had narrowed the list, but so far had made little progress.

"Bell Yard. An alehouse called Turnbull's, one of Foote's favorites, according to Barnstable."

A section of old Westminster—Thieving Lane, Petty France, The Sanctuaries—the kind of places he hoped he would never see the likes of again. A cold thread of memory snaked through him of places much the same, of crime and poverty, and a past he worked to forget. It had surfaced of late, as they traversed Southwark gutters, scoured Shoreditch, the Spittle, St. Giles in the Fields, Saffron Hill—every rotten slum in the city. Foote was known in those places, they'd confirmed, but they had yet to spot him.

They'd had to be careful, take it slow and easy. If Foote deduced the reason they searched him out, he would run. They couldn't afford for him to escape.

"Perhaps tonight we'll get lucky," Jason said, climbing into the rented hackney that was parked in front of the town house. Dressed in plain brown breeches and a homespun shirt, he carried a battered tricorn though he rarely wore a hat at all. His cloak was of simple brown wool, and yet when they reached the alehouse, they would still look out of place in their seedy surroundings.

Knowing their appearance would cause a stir, they had

let it be known they were searching for Foote in order to hire him. The task they had in mind required a special skill, and they had heard Elias Foote was the man for the job. Jason hoped Foote was arrogant enough to buy it.

It didn't take long to reach the alehouse, a true den of thieves just off a filth-laden alley. A wooden sign swung above the door, creaking in the wind, its red paint chipped and peeling. It was well past midnight, the place crowded with drunken men and bawdy whores.

Jason shoved through the door and tried to ignore the stench of gin-soaked bodies and cheap perfume. It was even harder to shove back the memories that rose as swiftly as the stench.

" 'Ello there, 'andsome." A big-bosomed redhead sidled up to him the moment he stepped inside the room. "Buy a gel a drink, will ye?" She gave him a lusty wink. "I promise ye won't be sorry."

Jason smiled, though it was all he could do not to push the woman away. She reeked of gin and the stale smoke that hovered in patches above the tables and hung in ropy wisps beneath the low beams. Instead he slid an arm around her waist, reached down and fondled her bottom.

"A tankard of ale, sweet lady, and one here for my friend."

The redhead grinned. "Right ye are, ducks. I'll be back afore ye can snap yer fingers." She was gone as quickly as she appeared, leaving Jason to survey the room.

"God's breath, I hate places like this."

Litchfield eyed him darkly. "I daresay I've been to spots I prefer. Though 'tisn't surprising a man like Foote would enjoy a slice of hell like this."

" 'Ere ye are, lads." She set the pewter mugs on the scarred wooden table in front of them. "Drink 'er down, 'andsome. When ye've finished, for a bit o' coin, I'll take ye upstairs for a tumble."

Jason forced another smile. "Much as I'd like to, I'm afraid we're here on business. Perhaps you might be able to help us."

"Business? What kind of business?"

"We're looking for a man named Foote," Lucien said. "We've got a job for him that pays very well. Perhaps you've heard of him."

"Aye, that I have."

Litchfield dropped a coin between the plump mounds rising above the neckline of her blouse. When she giggled and fished it out, Jason caught a glimpse of her red-rouged nipples.

"So it's Foote who brings ye 'ere. Well, Elias has been out of town for a bit. Word is, 'e's due back at the end of the week. 'E'll come here when 'e does—'e lives in a garret upstairs. I can see he gets yer message."

Lucien slid another coin between her breasts. "Tell him we'll be back at midnight on Monday next."

Jason added a coin of his own. "Tell him it will be well worth his while if he meets us."

"I'll tell 'im, ducks. Ye can count on Gracie—I promise ye that."

Jason smiled dryly. "Thank you, Gracie. We'll see you next week."

They left the alehouse, and outside Jason paused to drag in a breath of fresh air. It wasn't much better than the fetid air inside. Still he was glad to be shed of the place, and hopeful that Foote's greed would bring him to their meeting.

"I don't want to dampen your spirits," Lucien said, once they were back in the rented carriage, "but there is a chance, even if we get hold of Foote, what he tells us may not lead to Avery."

Jason's eyes swung to Lucien's face, which moved in and out of shadow as the carriage rolled along in the moonlight. "I know."

But he was no longer thinking of Foote. That problem he would face Monday next. Another, more pressing matter had returned to the forefront of his mind and he meant to do something about it.

Lucien's voice broke the silence in the carriage. "The night is young. We could stop for a nightcap at Madam

Charmaine's. They say she has a new girl who is really quite something.''

"Sorry, Lucien, I'm afraid I'll have to pass." He rapped on the top of the carriage. "Take me to Berkley Square," he called up to the driver, and in the shadows, Lucien quirked a thick black brow.

"Lady Velvet?"

"Aye. The lady and I have some unfinished business.''

Litchfield smiled faintly. "I see."

Jason wondered if he did, wondered how he could when it wasn't all that clear to him. Whatever the case, little more was said and eventually the hack turned onto the square.

"Take me down the alley behind the house," Jason instructed the driver, who let him off near the carriage house at the rear.

"Good luck," Lucien called softly as he walked away, but Jason's thoughts were already focused on the lady he hoped to find upstairs.

Unfortunately, when he checked the carriage house, the Haversham coach was missing. Velvet was probably attending the lavish house party being given by the earl of Whitmore. Everyone who was anyone in the ton was bound to be there. Since her arrival in London, Velvet had made a practice of placing herself in the middle of such affairs.

Jason's mouth twisted into a bitter line. He wouldn't have guessed her to be so taken with Society when she had been at the lodge. Obviously he was mistaken.

Clamping his jaw against the unwelcome thought, he made his way among the shadows, moving quietly through the garden till he reached the rear of the house. Unless she was with Balfour, Velvet would be home sooner or later. Patience wasn't normally one of his virtues, but once in a while, if he had good cause, he could be a surprisingly patient man.

Ignoring the chill in the house, Velvet wearily climbed the stairs. Coal was expensive. They could no longer afford to heat empty rooms, and her grandfather had already retired to his bedchamber.

Pulling her satin-trimmed pelerine from around her shoulders, Velvet pushed open the door to her bedchamber and walked in. A groggy Tabitha hurried in behind her to light the lamps and start the fire, then began to help her undress.

"Did ye have a good time, milady?"

Velvet sighed. "As good as could be expected, considering it was that lecher Whitmore's affair. Lord Balfour's presence helped to fend him off, thank heaven, but I was certainly glad when I could finally make my way home." She'd attended the affair with the earl and countess of Briarwood, friends of Lord Balfour's who, of late, had also become friends of hers.

Tabby hung up her gown and whalebone panniers, then returned to help her put on her night clothes. When Velvet saw the weary circles beneath the stout woman's eyes, she waved her away.

"It's all right, Tabby, I can do the rest myself. Go back to your bed before it gets cold, and try to get some sleep."

"Are ye certain?"

"I'll be fine, Tabby."

"Aye, milady. Thanks be to ye."

Tabby waddled off, closing the door behind her, and Velvet sat down at her bureau to pull the pins from her hair. It tumbled in waves past her waist. She'd just begun to pull the bristle brush through it when a disturbance at the window gave her pause. Turning in that direction, Velvet gasped as the shadow of a man took shape on the balcony, then the doors swung open and a tall broad-shouldered figure stepped into the room.

Jason! Velvet jumped to her feet, her heart slamming hard then setting up a painful thudding. "Jason—what on earth are you doing here?"

In the glow of the lamplight, his features looked harsh, his strong jaw rigid and determined. His mouth twisted into the semblance of a smile. "Why, I came to see you, my lady. Don't tell me you are not glad to see me."

"Of course I am glad. I've been worried sick about you. I was afraid someone would discover who you are."

He started toward her, his impressive height and build nearly overwhelming in the softly feminine room. He was simply dressed, she saw, in course brown breeches and a homespun shirt, his dark hair queued back with a thin black ribbon. He was as plainly garbed as any commoner off the street, yet she had never seen a more handsome man.

When he reached the place in front of her, Velvet stared into his face, taking in his carved male features, her breath wedged somewhere in her throat.

"The hour is late," he said, his eyes roaming over her thin chemise and white silk stockings, all that she yet wore. "You must have enjoyed the evening."

Heat rose into her cheeks at his bold appraisal, a hungry glance that seemed to burn through her scanty attire. Turning away from him, she reached for her quilted silk wrapper and pulled it on, fastened several buttons down the front.

"The evening was not one of my favorites. In truth, I should have preferred to stay home."

A dark brow arched in mocking regard. "Would you?" There was something in his voice, a chord of anger he wasn't quite able to disguise. "Perhaps you would have preferred to be here— if you could have been with Balfour."

"Balfour! You believe I am interested in Balfour?"

"You are telling me you are not!"

"Well, I . . . I, we are acquainted. He has expressed an interest in me and I . . . I have—"

"You have what, my lady? Encouraged his pursuit? Allowed him liberties? Spent time in his bed! Well, you certainly wasted no time." His gaze ran over her once more. "Then again, I discovered what a hot little piece you were when I took you that day at the cottage."

Anger surged with the speed of a bolt of lightning. "How dare you!" Velvet's hand snaked out and cracked across his cheek so loud it echoed against the walls. "Lord Balfour has been a perfect gentleman—which is more than I can say for you!"

Rage darkened his features. Jason loomed above her, his blue eyes glittering, a muscle knotted in his jaw, and for a moment she was afraid. "You are right, Lady Velvet. I am no gentleman. I told you that from the start." His arm went around her waist and he hauled her against him. "I take what I want—and right now I want you!" His mouth crushed down with bruising force.

The kiss was punishing, savage, filled with anger and brutal purpose, yet the fear receded and small fires sparked in its place. Flames licked over her skin and heat scorched through her. She tried to twist free, shoved against his muscled chest, but his unbreakable hold only tightened.

Damn you! She struggled a moment more, but his hard grip never faltered. Beneath her fingers, his heart thundered madly and solid muscle quivered with the fury of his rage. Forcing her lips apart, he thrust his tongue inside, delving deeply, taking what he wanted. Velvet gasped as he gripped the top of her quilted wrapper and ripped it down the front. Her pretty embroidered chemise met that same fate, leaving her in only her dainty pink garters and sheer white silk stockings.

"I want you," he whispered, tearing his lips away, planting hot, damp kisses along the line of her jaw, his mouth moving with purpose down the column of her throat. "God, I can't stop thinking about you."

The admission escaped of its own accord. There was pain in his words and distress in his beautiful eyes. The knowledge ended her struggles. She had hurt him, she suddenly knew, wishing she had told him the truth from the start. He didn't care for her in the way she cared for him, but the pain was there just the same.

"Jason . . ." Sliding her arms around his neck, she gave herself up to his hands and his mouth, letting his closeness fire her passions. She had thought of him, too, and she had missed him. Dear God, how she had missed him.

He kissed her again, gentler now, coaxing instead of demanding. His breath was hot and male. The sweep of his tongue sent tendrils of heat into her stomach.

"I need you . . ." he whispered, filling his hands with her breasts, teasing the peaks until they stiffened, then lowering his head to take one of the tight little crests into his mouth.

Velvet moaned and arched against him, felt his palm cupping her bottom to lift her against his thick arousal. He kneaded her buttocks, slid a finger deeply inside her. Sweet Lord, she was wet and ready, aching for him to take her.

"You want me," he said softly, his voice husky with male satisfaction. "Just as much as I want you."

She didn't deny it, didn't resist when he backed her against the wall and unbuttoned his breeches, cupped his hands beneath her bottom and lifted her up. She moaned as she slid atop his heavy arousal. She was wet but so tight she gasped when he impaled her full length, felt a white-hot jolt of pleasure/pain.

"Easy," he whispered, kissing her deeply, wrapping her legs around his waist then beginning to move inside her. One of his hands laced through her hair. Jason pulled her mouth down to his for a hot, wet kiss, and her tongue slid hotly between his teeth. Tightening her hold around his neck, she let him guide her, lifting her up then plunging her down on his stiff arousal. Each heavy thrust went deeper, pounded harder, demanded more.

Jason! her mind screamed, her nails digging into the muscles across his shoulders, her head thrown back as waves of fire washed over her. He filled her completely, driving hard against her, stroking with fierce determination.

"Jason!" she cried out at the fury and the heat seething through her. Great waves of pleasure tore loose inside, spirals of heat, sparks of fiery sweetness. Her body contracted, tightened around him, and Jason groaned. With a huge force of will, he dragged himself free of her body, and Velvet despaired to realize he had spilled his seed outside her womb. The knowledge left her feeling strangely empty.

The fine tremors of her passion began to fade. Velvet pressed her lips to his shoulder and the sinews there went tense. He let go of her legs and she slid down his tall hard frame till her feet once more touched the floor. Wordlessly, he turned away and began to work the buttons at the front of his breeches. Velvet dragged a white cotton night gown from her top dresser drawer and pulled it on, then turned to face him.

Her breath caught when she saw he stood at the balcony doors. Her heart squeezed. He was leaving. He had taken her in anger, used her like a whore, and one look at his face said that he would not return.

"A pleasure as always, my lady." The line of his jaw appeared carved in stone. "Give my best to Lord Balfour." He started through the doors, but the sound of her voice gave him pause.

"I have to marry Balfour," Velvet said softly. " 'Twill be unfair of me . . . after what has happened this night, but I must do so all the same."

His dark brows drew together. "What do you mean you have to marry him? Are you telling me I have gotten you with child?" He turned away from the doors and long strides carried him closer, the muscles once more rigid across his shoulders. "Or perhaps it is his babe you carry." He paused directly in front of her, his blue eyes dark and stormy.

Velvet did not look away. "I am not with child. I have committed an even graver sin, your grace—I am impoverished. In my world that is a crime of magnificent proportions."

She smiled with bitter despair. "Take a look around, your grace. If the furnishings appear a bit shabby, the walls a trifle bare, that is because they are. Much as I regret to say it. In truth, your brother, Avery, and I were taking the very same journey. I was marrying him because he was wealthy. My father gambled away the Haversham fortune. The only money my grandfather and I have left is what my father set aside for my dowry." When he started to speak, she rushed on, afraid that if she stopped, she might not have the courage to continue.

"Unfortunately, I cannot get hold of the money. Only my husband can do that. The man I marry will receive a small fortune—along with it, I'm afraid, he will also inherit the Haversham debts."

Jason looked stunned. "I can hardly credit what you're saying."

"I assure you, your grace, it is all completely true."

His eyes darted around the room, taking in the barren walls and the sturdy, unpretentious furnishings. "And Balfour is the man you have chosen?"

"I chose Avery. Not a particularly singular choice, as you well know. You saved me from that particular fate, but unfortunately that only means I must find someone else."

Troubled blue eyes ran over her face. "And that man is Balfour."

"Actually, the earl found me. What I told you was true, Jason. He has always played the gentleman. The only man to touch me has been you."

Jason said nothing, but his eyes grew cloudy with pain or perhaps it was simply regret. He looked at her, took in her swollen, passion-bruised lips, the tangled disarray of her hair, and a low groan rumbled from his throat.

He was standing just a few feet away. Two long strides and he caught her against him, buried his face in her hair. "Ah, God, Duchess, I'm sorry. So damned sorry. Good Christ, but you bring out the worst in me."

Velvet clung to him, knowing she shouldn't, that holding him would only make losing him harder, yet craving the strength of his arms.

"I should have told you the truth in the beginning. I suppose I was embarrassed. You had enough problems of your own and mine were hardly your concern."

He drew back to look at her. "It is my concern. I've damaged your reputation. I've taken your innocence. In the marriage mart, those are two of your most valuable commodities. That makes it my concern."

He kissed the top of her head. "If I were any kind of man, I would marry you myself. But odds are, I'll be swinging from a gibbet before this is over. Even if I manage to cheat fate again, there is no guarantee I'll be able to prove my innocence, and even if I do, I won't be staying in England.''

"You're going to leave?" Something painful clenched inside her. He was leaving. Sooner or later, he would be gone from her life for good. "Where . . . where will you go?"

"Back where I came from. The West Indies. That's where I belong, Velvet, not here in England. I'm not civilized enough for that anymore. I just don't fit in."

She thought of the dance they had shared, of how magnificent he had looked at the costume ball. She could have argued that he could fit wherever he wanted, but she didn't. If Jason wished to leave England, she had no right to stop him.

"I can't marry you, Velvet, but I can help you. I have money—quite a goodly sum. I own a plantation on a small island off St. Kitts. I have more than enough to set your debts in order and see that you and your grandfather are comfortable for as long as you need. You won't be forced into marriage. You can wait until you find the right man."

Velvet ignored the dull ache inside her, the pressure building in her chest. She had found the right man. But marriage was not his intention. "In truth, if I had my way, I would not marry at all. I've come to enjoy my independence. Once I marry I shall have to give it up."

"What of children?" Jason asked. "Surely you want a family. All women do."

Velvet shrugged her shoulders. "Actually, I've given the matter little thought. I presumed they would come as a result of the marriage. Other than that, I've not thought overmuch about it." *Until tonight.* Having children with Jason was another matter entirely. She couldn't imagine anything that would give her more pleasure than bearing him a son.

She felt his hand on her cheek. "I'm sorry about tonight, Duchess, but I'm not sorry I've come. Now that I know the truth, everything is going to be all right—I promise you." He brushed her mouth with a feather-soft kiss, their lips clung, and the kiss grew more fierce. "Dammit, I want you again already."

Warmth invaded her cheeks. In truth she wanted him, too.

But Jason turned to leave. "It's getting light outside. I've got to get out of here before someone sees me." A quick glance toward the window, then he looked back at her. "I meant what I said. Everything is going to be all right."

"I don't want your money, Jason. I have money of my own, I simply must marry to get it."

But Jason ignored her. With a last hard kiss, he headed for the door leading out to the balcony. Waving a final good-bye, he swung his long legs over the railing, and began his descent down the trellis he had climbed up. He cursed as a rose thorn cut into his hand, she heard his boots hit the ground, and then he was gone.

Velvet sagged down on the bench in front of her dresser. The clock ticked into the darkness, a hollow, echoey sound, but she did not stir. Since she had met Jason, she had never felt so alone.

Though her body was pleasantly sated, Velvet slept little for the balance of the night. Jason had come to her, made love to her in this very room. Memories of his hard-muscled body surging into hers made her skin grow damp with perspiration. Her nipple tightened to think of Jason's slick tongue brushing over it, to remember the way he had taken the fullness into his mouth. With a trembling hand, she touched herself there, wishing he were still with her.

Instead she lay in bed alone, aching for a man who wanted her but had no interest in marriage, as least not to her.

It was late when she dragged herself from beneath the covers. Crossing to the window, she shoved it open and inhaled a breath of the damp, misty air. Tabby helped her into a simple muslin day dress and she made her way downstairs.

"Good morning, Grandfather."

"That it is, my dear, that it is." Seated at the dining table, his aging countenance broke into a smile. "Slept well, I trust. I didn't hear you come in."

Velvet wasn't surprised. He rarely ever heard her, and even if he had, he likely wouldn't remember. "I slept fine, Grandfather." The lie slipped out without conscious thought. Recalling what had actually occurred made the heat rise into her cheeks. "I hope you haven't been waiting for me. I'm afraid I lazed around a bit this morning."

He nodded, then glanced down at the small white calling card he held in his hand. He pondered it for a moment, then his lined, wrinkled face lit up.

"Blast it, I nearly forgot. You've a visitor coming to call. The marquess of Litchfield, don't ya know. Ought to be here any minute."

"Litchfield!" Her stomach tightened with nerves. Sweet God, had something happened to Jason? "What . . . what does he want?"

"Haven't the foggiest, my dear. Guess you'll find out when he gets here."

Which was, as her grandfather said, not long after. She had only just finished her morning chocolate and biscuits, barely able to get them down for the fear balling tightly in her stomach, when Snead appeared in the dining room doorway.

"You've a guest, milady. Lord Litchfield has come to call. I've shown him into the drawing room."

"Thank you, Snead." Taking a breath for courage, she slid back her chair and came to her feet. *Please don't let it be Jason.*

Her hands were shaking as she walked down the hall and stepped into the drawing room, closing the doors behind her. She felt a hint of relief when the black-haired marquess began walking toward her with a smile.

"Good morning, Lady Velvet."

"Lord Litchfield." They exchanged pleasantries but only for a moment. Then the marquess handed her a wax sealed message, which Velvet immediately broke open. A piece of paper, folded up inside, fluttered neatly to the floor. When she bent to retrieve it, she saw that it was a bank draft for ten thousand pounds.

"Sweet God in heaven." A scan of the paper proved her instincts correct—the money had come from Jason. Velvet's jaw clamped. "Do you know what is in here, my lord?"

"I do, my lady. I hope you realize you may count me among your friends. Your secrets—and Jason's—are completely safe with me."

She believed that was the truth. It didn't lessen the shame she felt that Jason would send her money. She wondered how much Litchfield had been told of their relationship and how much more he had simply guessed.

"You may tell our mutual friend, that however good his intentions, he is gravely in error if he believes I will accept his money." She tore the paper in half, once, twice, three times. Once she got started she couldn't seem to stop until the tiny bits of paper looked more like a handful of confetti than the money she needed so badly. Refolding the message, she dumped the bits of paper back inside, marched over to the marquess and handed him the note.

"You may tell him that he may take his good intentions and shove them up his nose."

A corner of Litchfield's mouth kicked up. "Is there anything else, my lady?"

"You may tell his grace he owes me nothing. What I gave, I gave of my own free will. Money was not then, nor is it now the reason for what happened between us. You may also remind him I have money of my own, that soon it will be used to solve my problems, and I will no longer be in need of his assistance."

Litchfield looked even more amused. "I will tell him, my lady." He started toward the door.

"Oh—and Litchfield."

"Yes, my lady?"

"You may also tell him that I said thank you. I enjoyed our last . . . meeting . . . very much."

The marquess actually grinned. "I will be certain to tell

him, Lady Velvet.'' A word of farewell and the marquess
was gone.

Velvet sank down on the tapestry sofa. The more she
thought about what had just transpired the angrier she got.
How dare he! How dare he try to salve his miserable conscience with an offer of money! She wasn't some doxy! She
wasn't his whore! Just because Jason regretted their passionate lovemaking didn't mean that she did. In fact, she
was superbly grateful she had been given the chance to enjoy such a wondrous experience with a man she cared for
so greatly.

Velvet jumped up off the sofa and started toward the
stairs. She didn't want Jason's money. If he offered it again,
she would tell him to go straight to Hades!

CHAPTER FOURTEEN

∞

$\mathcal{J}$ason paced the floor of his bedchamber at Litchfield's town house. As soon as he heard the door open in the entry and Lucien walk in, he headed into the hallway and down the stairs. Following his friend into the study, he quickly closed the door.

"Well?" he asked, impatient as always.

Litchfield merely smiled. "Hold out your hand."

Jason did as the marquess requested. Grinning, Litchfield turned the once-sealed missive upside down, and tiny scraps of stiff white paper spilled into his palm. Jason knew with an inward grimace exactly what they were.

"You might discern by the size of the pieces," Lucien said, "how pleased the lady was with your offer."

Jason scowled. "What did she say?"

"She said—and I quote—'He may take his good intentions and shove them up his nose.' "

Jason ground his teeth. "And?"

"She also said to thank you. She said she enjoyed your last . . . meeting . . . very much."

"What!"

"That is what she said."

Jason's fist slammed down on the table. "That little vixen. I swear she is unlike any woman I have ever met."

"I certainly cannot disagree. And I am not surprised she

refused your offer of assistance, though from what you have said, she needs that money very badly.''

''There is no doubt of that.''

''Do you still intend to help her?''

''I have to. I owe her that much.''

''What will you do?''

Jason's scowl turned even blacker. He paced back and forth, turned to stare out the window, then began to pace again. Finally he stopped and turned to Lucien. ''I'll do the only thing I can do—what the little hellion has forced me to do. I'll have to marry her.''

Both Litchfield's heavy black brows shot up. ''I thought you said you weren't interested—''

''I'm not. This isn't going to change the way I feel about marriage, but it will solve Velvet's problem.'' He worked a muscle in his jaw. ''And there is something else.''

''Which is?''

''Last night, when I left her house, a man was standing in the shadows. He wasn't there when I went in, which means he must have arrived after Velvet came home.''

''You think he was following her?''

''I don't know. I made sure he didn't see me leave, but he was very definitely watching the house for some reason. My instincts tell me Velvet has been sniffing around, asking questions about Avery. If she has been, she might be in danger.''

''I'll have our man look into it, see what he can find out.''

''Good idea. In the meantime, I'll speak to Velvet.'' An awful thought suddenly struck, twisting hard up inside him. What if she refused his proposal? What if she would rather be married to Balfour? He couldn't really blame her. It certainly made more sense. He didn't intend a marriage in truth, never meant to abide by the vows.

Yet he couldn't shake the queasy feeling that settled in his stomach to think that she might refuse.

Velvet stood for a moment in front of her cheval glass mirror, turning the marquess of Litchfield's white engraved calling card over in her hands. It was the back of the card she read. *Lord Hawkins,* it simply said, the words scrolled in dark blue ink across the stark white surface, the letters etched in a man's bold hand.

Jason had come. Even now he waited in the drawing room downstairs, determined to see her, for what reason she could not imagine.

The card shook in her hands. Jason was here. The thought left her breathless, her skin flushed and warm. He always had that effect on her. Silently she cursed him, then fervently wished she could make him react that same way.

Velvet bent the card in half and then in half again. Damn the man—didn't he realize the danger he put himself in every time he stepped out in public? There was always the chance, however slim, that someone might see him, recall who he was.

She wanted to strangle him. She wanted one of his fiery kisses—both at the very same time. What had he come for? Why had he risked himself again?

Tossing the bent card onto the silver salver it had arrived on, she checked her image in the mirror one last time, smoothed the front of her buttercup yellow silk gown, and pulled open the bedchamber door.

At first she didn't see him, having thought he would be seated in a warm spot in front of the fire. A quick scan of the room and she spotted his tall frame filling a goodly portion of the room at the opposite end. He was standing off to one side, before a row of gilt-framed portraits, pictures of her mother and father, her grandfather and grandmother, and a small porcelain miniature of her as a little girl.

He hadn't heard her entrance, his usual keen awareness apparently eclipsed by his study of the portraits. It was odd the way he looked at them, his features brooding and tense, the muscles taut beneath his dark blue coat. There was something forbidding about him, the darkness she had glimpsed in him before. He appeared every inch the dangerous man he had been the night he had stolen her from the carriage, and insane as it seemed, she was still as wildly attracted to him as she had been that night.

"Jason?"

His dark head snapped up. Burning blue eyes fixed on her face. The darkness left his features, but the tension remained, a different, more palpable sort than she had sensed before.

"Hello, Velvet."

"I-I didn't expect to see you."

A fine dark brow arched up. His mouth looked a little bit grim. "Didn't you? What did you think would occur when you refused my offer of assistance?"

She swallowed. She might be attracted to him, but she wasn't a fool. Jason Sinclair was a hard man, not a man to trifle with. She moistened her lips and hitched up her chin. "I believed you would come to your senses and let the matter rest. I told you I had a means of my own for solving my problems. Once I marry—"

"Did you mean what you said?" he interrupted, surprising her. "You told me you didn't really want a husband. That you valued your independence, that you would keep it if you could."

She meant it. If she couldn't marry for love, she would rather remain alone. Unfortunately, she didn't have that choice. "I meant it."

Unconsciously his broad shoulders squared. "Then I'll marry you."

Velvet's breath hissed out in a rush. "What?"

"I said I'll marry you—at least for a while. Once we are wed, I can see your dowry returned. Your financial problems will be solved, and you'll still have your independence."

Her heart was hammering, fluttering like a bird trapped in her chest. "I'm afraid I don't understand. If I'm your wife, how can I still have my independence? And what do you mean you'll marry me—for a while?"

He simply shook his head. He was dressed quite regally today, in a dark blue tailcoat and tight-fitting breeches. The frothy lace cravat at his throat looked white as snow against his dark skin. The same lace fell from his wrists.

"Once we are married," he explained, "I can help you get control of your dowry. But I can't stay in England. I don't belong here anymore. If I manage to avoid the hangman, I'll be returning to St. Ives, my plantation in the Indies. As soon as I'm gone, you can get an annulment."

Her stomach tightened, astonishment warring with anger. "You expect to marry me, spend time in my bed, then leave me whenever you wish? How convenient, Lord Hawkins. I should imagine there are any number of eligible gentlemen who would be willing to agree to that plan."

"I don't intend to bed you—it shouldn't have happened in the first place. I told you, Velvet, I don't want a wife— and I certainly don't want children—not now, not ever. If you agree, this will simply be a marriage of convenience. You'll have your money and my conscience will be clear for taking your innocence. This is strictly a business proposition."

Velvet's heart twisted. Jason was the third man who had approached her with a marriage proposal that was purely a business arrangement. None of them had loved her. What was it about her that made her so difficult to love?

She swallowed past the lump that rose in her throat. "I appreciate your concern, my lord, but there is no need to trouble yourself. Lord Balfour has also proposed an arrangement that would solve my problem. I have not yet given him an answer, but I intend to very soon."

The color ebbed from Jason's sun bronzed cheeks. A fine tremor shook his big, usually graceful hands. "You are saying you would rather marry Balfour?"

There was something in his eyes, the darkness she had seen before, a shadowy despair that seemed to fill him. It was laced with such regret that she had to glance away. "I did not say that. I merely said—"

"I suppose you are right." He stared at the floor between his feet. "Balfour in surely in love with you. He could give you children, be the husband and father I never could be."

Her heart was breaking, Velvet was sure of it. Dear God

what had happened to him to make him feel this way? "Lord Balfour does not love me. There is every chance he is in love with Mary Stanton."

"Then why does he wish—"

"As you said, it is merely a business arrangement."

The tension in his shoulders seemed to ease. His gaze locked with hers, a blazing blue that would not let her look away. "If that is the case, then you shall marry me. Once I am gone, you'll have time to choose a proper husband, someone who will love and care for you as you deserve."

The ache in her throat went tighter. He didn't love her, but he cared for her in some way. As least more than Avery or Balfour. "I must know, Jason, why it is you feel about marriage as you do?"

His jaw flexed. The darkness inside him swept over him like a wave. He rubbed the scar on the back of his hand as if the skin still burned. "A man like me doesn't marry, Velvet. He doesn't have a wife and children. A man like me wouldn't begin to know how to lead a normal life anymore." He looked at her and the pain in his eyes touched something deep inside her. "I've been gone from England for more than eight years. I've seen things a man should never have to see, done things I'll regret for as long as I live."

And suffered, she thought, looking into his haunted features, as no man should ever have to suffer.

"I could never be a husband to you, Velvet. I could never be a father to your children. This is a civilized country and I'm no longer a civilized man."

"Jason . . ." She reached out to touch him, but he took a step away.

"Give me your answer, Velvet. Will it be Balfour, or will it be me?"

Oh, dear God. Every shred of common sense told her to run as far and as fast from Jason Sinclair as she possibly could. He was certain to hurt her. Already his pain tore into her heart as if it were her own. She loved him. With each passing day, that love would grow stronger. And then he would leave.

Run! her mind said. But her heart whispered the words she finally said to him. "I choose you, Jason. I'll marry you whenever you wish."

The darkness faded as quickly as it had appeared. Uncertainty replaced it. It seemed he was yet unsure of what he was about to do. "Litchfield can obtain a special license. Three days hence, you'll become Lady Hawkins. By the end of the week, you'll be a wealthy woman again."

A wealthy, *married* woman, Velvet thought grimly. In love with a man who didn't love her. Wife to a husband who never intended marriage and meant to abandon her. Wed to a man who would likely hang for murder.

She tried to smile, but inside her chest, her heart hurt just to think of it.

Avery Sinclair leaned against the gold flocked wall of Lord Briarwood's elegant drawing room. A few feet away, his quarry, Mary Stanton, spoke softly to one of her friends, but her eyes were trained on the tall man standing next to the door of the terrace, Christian Sutherland, the handsome earl of Balfour.

Avery's hands unconsciously fisted. Mary had been attracted to Balfour from the start. She had discouraged his suit only to please her father, who had very little use for the man they called the Rakehell Earl. That and the fact Sir Wallace was obsessed with the notion of making his daughter the duchess of Carlyle.

Avery's eyes fixed on Mary, who caught his close regard, flushed and glanced guiltily away from Balfour. Pale except for the rose that now bloomed in her cheeks, she looked exceptionally pretty tonight, gowned in white taffeta trimmed with rosettes of ice blue satin, the dress setting off her pale blue eyes and silver-gold hair. It enhanced her air of innocence, and inside his breeches, Avery began to grow hard.

He shifted a little, easing the pull of fabric, and smiled to think of the evening ahead, of the pleasure he would feel in capturing the prize Balfour had wanted. Pulling his gold watch fob from the pocket of his saffron brocade waistcoat, he checked the time, then smiled as a liveried footman bustled into the room carrying a silver salver. The tall gangly man scanned the crushing throng then headed straight for Mary.

Twenty minutes later she was seated across from him in the sleek black Carlyle carriage, bundled beneath a lap robe, her gentle schoolgirl features marred by worry for her supposedly ailing father. So far his plan had worked perfectly.

The carriage rumbled over the last of the cobbled streets and onto the dusty roadway leading out of the city. Mary's soft, worried voice broke through the clatter of wheels and the jangle of harness.

"I just don't understand it. Even if my father has fallen ill, why would he insist I come to you? It is extremely unlike him to involve outsiders in matters of family. I cannot credit why he would."

"I am hardly an outsider, my dear. It won't be long until I shall be your lawful husband. I am honored that your father already considers me part of the family."

Mary pondered that. "I am certain that must be it, but even so, why was there need for such secrecy? His note was quite cryptic—I was to tell no one but you." She shook her head. "And why would Father wish for us to travel together unchaperoned?" Her eyes suddenly filled with tears. "I am so worried, your grace. Something dreadful must have happened. There is no other explanation for such extraordinary behavior."

Avery reached for her trembling hand and gave it a reassuring squeeze. "You mustn't fret so, my dear, you will overset yourself. In time we'll reach the inn where your father was taken. Soon you will discover the truth of what has occurred and exactly where all of this is leading."

And indeed Mary did.

But not until they had reached their destination, a small thatched roof tavern on a road that led out of town. Not until she had worriedly climbed the stairs to the room where she thought to find her ailing father.

Not until Avery had forced her down on the bed, ripped away her clothing, and pushed himself deep inside her. She had stopped struggling then, had simply lain like a limp, battered doll beneath him, fighting tears of pain and humiliation as he grunted and strained above her.

When at last he was finished, he pulled his flaccid member from between her blood-smeared thighs and announced that they would be married by special license in the morning.

"I am sorry, my dear," he said without a single ounce of sincerity, "but you simply left me no choice." His satisfied smile made her stomach roll with nausea. "I'm afraid I wanted you far too badly to endure a long engagement." It was all she could do to keep from throwing up.

Now, squeezing her tear-filled eyes shut against the sight of him next to the bed, Mary lay rigid while he fastened the buttons at the front of his breeches, strode to the door and pulled it open, then sauntered nonchalantly into the hall.

Listening to his ribald laughter echoing down the stairs to the taproom, Mary knew what her father did not—that the man she would be forced to marry was nothing at all the sort of man her father would have chosen for her husband.

Mary sobbed great wrenching tears into the pillow on the bed, wishing with all her soul she had listened to her heart instead of trying to be a dutiful daughter. She would have chosen a man she loved, a husband who would care for her as deeply as she cared for him. She would have found a man who would make her happy.

Lord Balfour's handsome image came to mind. She had been drawn to the earl from the moment she had met him. He had been kind to her, had responded with tender concern to the gentleness he sensed in her. He seemed to understand the loneliness that dwelled deep inside her, just as she sensed an underlying loneliness in him.

But her father had disapproved.

"The man is a rake," he had said. "The very worst sort of rogue. A man like that will only break your heart, my child. You must trust me to chose which of your suitors will be best.''

And so she had let him. And he had chosen the duke of Carlyle. Mary sobbed even harder into the pillow, trying to ignore the aching bruises that marked her pale skin, the burning pain between her legs.

Her father had chosen Carlyle.

Carlyle, Mary thought, the duke's pale image making the bile rise in her throat.

It was a mistake she would pay for for the rest of her life.

Flat gray clouds darkened the sky overhead. A raven cawed from the branches of the elm tree outside the front door of the small parish church at the edge of the city where Velvet had come to be married. The brief, uninspired ceremony delivered by the short, balding vicar was now at an end. Wind whipped leaves across the porch steps in front of Velvet's silver-shot brocaded skirts as she and Jason descended the stairs leading out of the chapel.

She didn't feel married, she thought. Not in the least. Since he had come for her at the town house, Jason had been polite but distant, his attitude making it clear this would never be a marriage in truth.

She wished her grandfather could have been there, but he had been feeling poorly of late. She had told him about the wedding, of course, explaining she had met Lord Hawkins through the marquess of Litchfield, that they had become close friends, and that Jason had agreed to the marriage simply to help her. Her grandfather had thanked him profusely, and immediately forgotten the reason for Jason's visit.

It didn't really matter. In a way his forgetfulness actually helped their cause. With her grandfather's condition growing worse and no other men in the family, it was obvious to all and sundry that Velvet needed a husband to see to her welfare. Marriage seemed the only plausible solution to a difficult situation.

From beneath her heavy lashes, Velvet looked up at the man she had married, admiring his lean chiseled jaw and solidly etched male features. He was a formidable man, a man who exuded power and presence. Another woman might have been afraid of the danger, the darkness she sensed in him. She was still unsure why she was not.

Walking next to Litchfield, who had acted as a witness, she stepped down from the porch and unconsciously her hold grew tighter on Jason's arm. She discovered she was trembling.

"You're cold," Jason said. Pausing for a moment, he draped her satin-lined cloak around her shoulders. "You'll be warmer inside the carriage."

But in truth she wasn't cold. She was fighting the terrible weight of reality that had set in moments after the wedding. She was wife to Jason Sinclair Hawkins—or so the documents said. A wealthy distant cousin of the Havershams from the Northumberland branch of the family. They had known each other since childhood, an obvious choice for husband, under the circumstances.

Was it legal? For her purpose, she supposed it would do. Once Jason had obtained the dowry from her trust, there was no one to demand its return. Unless he was captured, it was unlikely anyone would question the marriage, and in time, her temporary husband had vowed, the union would be annulled.

The thought brought a tightness to her chest.

Jason helped her mount the iron stairs into the carriage, then he and Litchfield climbed in.

"I suppose congratulations are in order," the marquess said. He had been kind and considerate throughout the morning, a gentle buffer between her uncertainty and Jason's brooding ill temper, which had continued to grow blacker every hour since his arrival.

"Very funny, Lucien," Jason said, his mood still as dreary as the day.

"Thank you, my lord," Velvet said to Litchfield just to spite him.

Jason grunted. "This sham of a marriage is hardly cause for celebration. The sooner it has served its purpose the better for us both—as I am sure my beloved *wife* will agree.''

She smiled just to goad his irritation. ''Oh, I do, my lord. Marriage to a man as ill-humored as you would be a strain on any woman.''

Jason scowled. ''I am sorry if I do not play the role of husband as well as you might wish. Perhaps it is the fact that instead of bedding my beautiful bride this night, instead of burying myself inside her as deeply and as often as I wish, I shall be spending the night alone.''

Velvet's cheeks went hot with embarrassment.

Across from her, Litchfield merely smiled. ''I had a notion that was the reason you are so bitterly out of sorts.''

Jason pinned him with a glare. ''I cannot credit you would be any happier about the situation than I am.''

The marquess chuckled softly. ''I would not be such a fool in the first place. If the lady were mine, her first night of marriage would be spent in my bed.''

A muscle jerked in Jason's cheek, but he said nothing more. Velvet looked away from the men, uncomfortable with the subject, which she knew far more about than she should have on the first day of her marriage. Harness rattled and clanked into the silence inside the carriage, and iron wheels whirred over the dusty lane heading back to the city.

Ignoring the heat still burning in her cheeks, Velvet forced a calm note into her voice. ''You haven't said yet, my lord. Now that we are wed, will you be returning to Castle Running or remaining at Lord Litchfield's town house?''

His eyes took on a mocking glint. ''Why, Duchess, I thought you understood. I'll be moving in with you, of course. I am your cousin, after all, a member of the family. Until we can return together to the country, where else would a loving husband reside except with his new bride?''

''B-but you just said you would be sleeping alone. When we spoke before, you said you did not wish to bed me. You said—''

The mocking twist of his lips slid away and his brooding

scowl returned. "I did not say I did not wish to bed you. It has been all I can do to keep my hands off you since the moment you stepped into the carriage. I said I *would not* bed you, that I did not wish a marriage in truth. The fact that I must stay in the very same house with you is surely God's own curse."

For the first time that day, the dull throb in her chest began to ease. For a moment she said nothing. She had misunderstood. Jason still desired her. *Her*, Velvet Moran. It wasn't simply that he needed a woman in his bed, it was his desire for *her* that had him so out of sorts. Now that he had said so, she realized it had been there in his eyes all along. Beneath his uncertainty of three days past. Beneath the regret and the pain. The knowledge gave rise to hope where there had been none before.

"If you do not wish to stay with me, why are you?"

"Because your snooping has stirred Avery's interest. Someone has been following you, watching the town house whenever you are within."

"There is no way he could have found out. Are you certain?"

"Aye, my lady, that I am. I have learned a great deal in the past eight years, including how to survive. That means knowing when someone is gauging your movements—and finding out the reason why."

"Good sweet God."

"Exactly so.

Litchfied said nothing, but his dark-eyed gaze said that he agreed.

"If you are certain someone is watching, then you most surely cannot stay. The man might tell Avery you are there."

"Jason Hawkins will be there. Jason Sinclair is dead. Avery has no reason to suspect I am alive. He has no reason to believe you are anything more than curious. Unfortunately, even that is too much. My loving brother won't tolerate your interference in any way. Someone has to be there to be certain you are safe."

Velvet didn't argue. If Jason was near, there was hope that she might sway him. She could help him clear his name, and if she could keep him alive, perhaps she could also persuade him not to leave.

CHAPTER FIFTEEN

∞

*L*ucien Montaine slid across the worn leather seat of the rented hackney carriage so that Jason could climb in. A few feet away, a lamp burned beside the door of the Haversham town house in Berkley Square. Lucien could see Velvet standing beside the heavy draperies at the window.

Whipping his cloak out of the way, Jason took a seat on the opposite side of the carriage. "Nasty bit of weather," he said. "Won't be many out in a cold drizzling rain like this."

Lucien's gaze swung back toward the window as the hackney rolled away. "I don't suppose so. Still, I half expected to see your bride accompany you into the carriage."

Jason grunted. "The little hellion actually suggested the idea. She wanted to dress as a lad and wait out in front of the tavern. She could warn us, she said, if any sort of trouble arose, or go for help if it was needed."

He shook his head, his brown hair nearly as dark as Lucien's in the light seeping out of the establishment windows. "Can you believe it?"

Lucien chuckled and leaned back against the squabs. "I believe it. I can only imagine how well that went over with you."

Jason sighed. "The woman is a handful, I can tell you."

"Quite a lovely handful, if I may say so."

"Spare me. If you've an ounce of pity left in your soul,

you won't remind me. I ache for the little wench most of the time as it is.''

Lucien smiled but said nothing more. Circumstances had thrown the pair together. It was up to fate and Velvet Moran whether or not their marriage would endure.

Jason stared out the window. "God's blood, I hope Foote shows. I hope the gold we've offered is enough to entice him.''

"Have no fear. A man like Foote won't be able to resist the lure of a chance for golden guineas.''

Jason said nothing more and the rest of the journey slid past in silence. A heavy mist had begun to fall across the city and even the beggars had bottled themselves up indoors. Once they reached the alehouse in Bell Yard, they paid the hack driver to wait out in front. They then left the carriage, crossed the muddy street, and entered the grimy interior.

The place was as smoky and dim as it had been before, though with fewer patrons crowding between the rough board walls it smelled a bit less earthy.

" 'Ello there, 'andsome.'' Gracie, the big-breasted tavern maid who had been there before, sidled up to Jason and winked. "I wondered if ye'd keep yer word.''

He forced himself to smile. "I said we'd be here at midnight. It's ten minutes till. Is Foote here yet?''

" 'E's 'ere, all right. Waitin' over there in the corner.'' She cocked her head in that direction and Jason followed the movement with his eyes.

Oddly enough, he remembered the big, rough-looking man from prison. He was tall and thick through the shoulders, with a swarthy, porous complexion and pockmarks gouging holes in his face. Eight years ago, Jason had made a point to avoid him. Apparently it was a good thing he had.

"Evenin', mates.'' Foote came to his feet at their approach. "Heard tell you was lookin' for me.''

"That's right,'' Lucien said. They settled themselves on rough plank benches around the table. "You've some information we're interested in buying. You supply it, and we'll make it well worth your while.''

Foote eyed them warily. "I thought you had a job you wanted done."

"The job's already been done," Jason told him. "Eight years ago. What we want to know is who paid you to do it?"

His eyes darted suspiciously from one of them to the other. "I'm afraid you've lost me, mates."

"Newgate," Jason said. "There was a man there, an aristocrat who was accused of murder. His name was Jason Sinclair."

The air hissed out from the space between Foote's front teeth. "Carlyle. 'Tis the bloody young duke you're talkin' about."

"That's the man," Lucien said. "We want to know who paid you to kill him."

The bench scraped as Foote jerked to his feet. Jason's hand clamped on the hulking man's shoulder, shoving him back down in his seat. A pistol pressed into Foote's ribs.

"Easy," Jason warned. "It isn't you we're after. Tell us what we want to know and no harm will come to you."

Every muscle in Foote's body thrummed with tension beneath Jason's hand. For several long seconds, the man said nothing, just stood there gauging the toughness of his opponents. Then he shrugged his beefy shoulders.

"I suppose it doesn't bloody matter. I'm a wanted man already. Another murder more or less won't make a fiddler's damn."

"Who was it?" Jason pressed. "Who paid you to kill Jason Sinclair?"

Foote grunted. "Believe it or not, it was the poor sod's brother. Paid me a bleedin' fortune to see the young duke dead."

"You're speaking of Avery Sinclair," Lucien put in to be sure there was no mistake. "The current duke of Carlyle."

"That's the blighter. A rare bastard, he is. But if you think I'll be tellin' that to a constable, you've got another think comin'. Hangin' from a gibbet weren't part of the

bargain.'' He grinned wickedly. ''Now hand over the coin
and I'll be gone from here.''

''Not quite yet.'' Jason pressed the gun harder into
Foote's ribs while Lucien drew a folded up piece of paper
from the inside pocket of his tailcoat. They had anticipated
Foote's reluctance. The only way he would admit to the
crime was if he could somehow escape the consequences.

''I don't suppose you can read?'' Lucien said.

Foote surprised them with a laugh. ''Believe it or not, I
was a teacher before I took up a life of crime.''

Jason had noticed he spoke passable English. His mark
signed in front of a witness would have been good enough;
this was a bonus they hadn't expected.

''Then you can see this document says nothing more than
what you've already admitted,'' Jason continued, ''that Avery Sinclair paid you to dispose of his brother during the
time his brother was in prison.''

He scanned the ink on the foolscap. ''Aye, that's what it
says.''

Jason nudged him with the gun. ''Sign it and you get the
gold, then you can be on your way. If you're smart, you'll
get out of the country. Refuse and we haul you into the
magistrate's office. Whether you admit to the murder or not,
you're sure to wind up swinging from the three-legged
mare.''

Without waiting for Foote's reply, Jason motioned for
Gracie to come to the table. ''Bring us a quill and some
ink.'' He tossed her a coin and she wiggled away, returning
with the pen and a thick glass bottle. At Jason's insistence,
she remained at the table to witness Foote's bulky form bent
over the paper, his rough hands swirling his signature onto
the page.

Jason allowed it to dry for a moment, then folded it up
and shoved it into his pocket. By itself, the document wasn't
all that much, the word of a murderer, certainly not enough
to acquit him. But combined with the documents he had
found in Avery's safe, it was more than they'd had before.

''I'd suggest, my friend,'' Lucien put in while Jason

handed over a small pouch of coins, "you get as far from London as you can manage."

Foote grumbled something beneath his breath. "Never did much like the bleedin' city."

"You'll like it even less," Jason warned, "if our paths ever cross again. I don't much like paying out gold to a killer."

Foote scowled and clamped his jaw, but he didn't argue. What he saw in the hard lines of Jason's face warned him that he had met a man as worldly-wise and tough as he.

Foote left the room and so did Litchfield and Jason, stepping into their carriage and settling back against the hard leather seat. It wasn't until a voice drifted out of the darkness in a corner of the carriage that they realized they were not alone.

"I am happy to see you and Litchfield are safe, my lord. I had begun to worry that you might have run into trouble."

Jason's head swiveled in Velvet's direction. Fury warred with amazement, making his jaw go tight. "It is you, my lovely little vixen, who has run into trouble this night." He rapped hard on the roof of the carriage. "Driver—take us the bloody hell home!"

Tossing back the hood of her cloak, her head held high, Velvet preceeded Jason into the drawing room, then turned as he slid the heavy doors closed behind him with a thud.

He blew out a frustrated breath. "In God's name, woman, what did you think you were doing? Bell Yard is in the worst part of the city. A woman traveling there alone—I cannot credit you would be insane enough to follow."

" 'Twas not a matter of sanity, my lord. 'Twas simply that this man, Foote, you and Lord Litchfield went after, is obviously a dangerous villain. I thought a person stationed outside the front door to warn you in case of trouble would be the wisest course."

"The wisest course! If one of those degenerates had guessed you were a woman—"

"I hailed a hackney at the corner as soon as you were

gone and instructed him to follow you. I climbed aboard and stayed out of sight. Once I arrived at the alehouse, the driver dismissed your carriage. I simply watched and waited. As it was there was no need of my assistance. Had things turned out differently, you might have been surprised how useful I could be.''

Jason muttered an oath beneath his breath. ''You are insane, Velvet Moran.''

She tossed her damp cloak over a chair. ''Velvet Sinclair . . . Hawkins,'' she corrected softly.

Jason's eyes blazed to life. He gripped the tops of her arms and hauled her so close she could measure the curling length of his thick black lashes. ''I'm a man, Velvet. You are a woman. I am twice as big and more than twice as strong. Believe it or not, I can take care of myself without help from you or anyone else. I have been doing so for the past eight years.'' He shook her. ''Can't you understand— I don't want you hurt!''

Velvet said nothing, just stared into those fierce blue eyes. When he let her go, she surprised him by stepping closer instead of backing away. Sliding her arms around his neck, she raised on her toes and pressed her cheek against his.

''I don't want you hurt, either, Jason. That is the reason I followed you to Bell Yard.''

His powerful muscles went tense. She thought he might push her away. Then he made a sound low in his throat and crushed her against him. ''I don't understand you. You're not like any woman I've ever known.''

Velvet didn't answer, just snuggled closer, pressing herself against his chest, absorbing his solid male strength. His clothes smelled of rain and a faint hint of smoke from the alehouse. She clung to him and felt his heart pulsing against her breast, felt its steady pumping tempo increase, then the thickening ridge of his desire as it hardened to iron and surged against her belly.

Desire slithered through her, warm and enticing. She recognized it now for what it was. She pressed a soft kiss against the side of his neck, tasted a hint of salt and the

warmth of his skin. Her lips moved to the rim of his ear
and a tremor slid through his tall body. She bit down gently
on the lobe then kissed the pulse at the base of his throat.

Jason groaned. His hands moved down her back, settled
around her waist and he drew her even closer. He kissed
her throat, the line of her jaw, then his mouth captured hers
in a searing kiss that scorched the breath from her lungs.

Oh, dear God! She tingled all over. Hot, damp heat slithered through her limbs, pooling in the place between her
legs. Her breasts began to swell, the nipples distending, chaf-
ing against the chemise beneath her gown. She wanted him
to touch her, to soothe the ache he stirred. She wanted him
to make love to her as he had done before.

With trembling fingers she unbuttoned his shirt, slid her
hands across the hard bands of muscle beneath the fabric,
laced her fingers in his curly brown chest hair.

A deep sound rumbled deep in his throat. Big warm hands
slid over her bodice, delved inside the neckline to cup and
mold a breast. He kissed her deeply, his tongue sweeping
in, little swirls of heat tugging low in her stomach. His fingers teased a nipple and her legs went wobbly.

"Jason . . ." she whispered. "Good sweet God . . ."

The hand on her breast grew still. His chest rose and fell
with each of his ragged breaths even as he forced himself
away.

"Hell and damnation!" Gripping her arms, he set her
apart from him, holding her at arm's length as if she posed
some sort of threat. "What the hell do you think you're
doing?"

"I-I was kissing you. You seemed to like it. Surely one
little kiss—"

"One little kiss! In another five minutes, I would have
had you down on the floor. I'd have had your skirts tossed
up and my breeches undone. I'd have buried myself inside
you as deeply and as hard as I could and to hell with the
consequences."

Though a flush swept through her, Velvet's chin went up.
A soft ache throbbed in her woman's place and her breasts

felt tender. " 'Tisn't as though it hasn't happened before. At least now we are married.''

"We aren't married! I told you from the start, this was only a temporary arrangement. I don't want a wife—I'm not cut out to be a husband—not now, not ever.''

Ignoring the heat still thrumming through her, Velvet's gaze came to rest on his face. "I think you would make a fine husband, Jason.''

He only shook his head. "You don't understand.'' He turned away from her, his voice low and gruff. " 'Tis late. Past time you retired upstairs.''

Her heart was beating, thudding with a soft heat that made her ache to touch him. She didn't want to go; she wanted him to kiss her again. One look at those hard, determined features and she knew the wiser course was to leave him be.

"Good night, Jason,'' she said softly.

She got a slight nod and a scowl in return.

He was sleeping in the room next to hers. She didn't hear him enter until several hours later. Once she knew he had arrived, her eyes began to close and she finally fell asleep.

Dressed in a leaf green gown trimmed with yards of white lace, Velvet descended the stairs to the breakfast room. She hadn't expected to hear the sound of her grandfather's gruff laughter or the deep rumble of Jason's own mirth as he joined in. It was a pleasant, happy sound and it drew her toward them like a bird homing back to its nest.

"Good morning, my dear.'' Her grandfather smiled. Both men rose to their feet at her appearance. "Your husband and I were regaling each other with tales of our days at Oxford. Some things never change, don't you know. That school seems to be one of them.'' He chuckled good-naturedly. "My old classmate, Shorty James, was my best friend when I was a student. He was headmaster when Jason attended. They didn't call him Shorty then, as you can imagine. Except behind his back.''

Velvet smiled at Jason and he smiled back. The past was

always easy for her grandfather to recall. It was the present that posed a problem. Apparently Jason had shrewdly discerned the fact and directed the conversation to a subject that put the old man at ease. Velvet's heart filled with gratitude at his compassion.

She watched the pair from beneath her lashes, noticing how comfortable they had already become with each other. If only her marriage were real, if they could truly be the family they appeared. A sweet yearning rose inside her, but Velvet forced it down. She rarely allowed herself to think of Jason as her husband. It would only hurt more when he left.

A light knock sounded. The black-clad butler appeared in the doorway. "Lord Litchfield has made an unexpected arrival. He wishes to see Lord Hawkins. I have shown him into the drawing room."

"Thank you, Snead," Jason said. He turned to Velvet and the aging earl. "If the two of you will excuse me . . ."

"By all means," said her grandfather, but Velvet rose and followed him down the hall.

She caught up with him just before he stepped into the drawing room, stopping him with a hand on his arm. "I'm your wife, Jason—at least until you leave. What Litchfield has to say concerns me, just as it does you."

He started to argue, must have seen some truth in her words, and instead made a slight bow of his head. "As you wish, my lady."

Litchfield stood at the mantel when they walked in, his dark countenance a thundercloud of emotion.

"What is it?" Jason closed the heavy doors, assuring they would be private.

The marquess's steady black gaze swung to Velvet, noting her unexpected presence, but there wasn't the least hesitation. " 'Tis Avery, I'm afraid. Apparently he has married Mary Stanton. The settlement he has gained is rumored to be huge."

"Oh, dear lord, poor Mary," Velvet said.

"Quite so," said Litchfield.

"I had hoped if the gossip of their involvement proved correct," Jason said, "their betrothal would be long enough for her to discover the truth about him."

Litchfield frowned, his bold black brows drawing together. "They say it was a love match. The pair was so taken with each other they eloped while her father was away. I asked our man Barnstable to search out the veracity of the affair and he claims Mary Stanton was forced into the marriage. He says the girl was lured away from the Briarwoods house party on the pretext her father was ailing."

"Sounds like Avery," Jason said darkly. "There's no length he wouldn't go to get the money he needs."

"Sweet God, it must have been terrible for Mary."

Jason's gaze fixed on Velvet. "As much as I pity Mary Stanton, I am equally glad the woman was not you."

Surprise swirled through her. Velvet said nothing, but the protective gleam in Jason's eyes stirred a blossoming sweetness inside her.

Litchfield's face looked grim. "If the man was a fearsome opponent before, with the backing of his powerful new father-in-law and his wealth securely back in place, he is at least twice as dangerous as he was then."

"We'll have to move up our timetable," Jason said.

"You're speaking of Celia," said Lucien.

Jason nodded. "Among other things. At least several dozen invitations have arrived since news of Velvet's marriage leaked out. Half the ton is demanding to meet the lucky man who has married the Haversham heiress. We won't be able to put them off much longer without stirring up more gossip. Avery will be even more curious than the rest. We have to figure a way around the problem and continue to search for evidence against him."

Velvet bit her lip. "You shouldn't have married me. Your life was already at risk. Now the matter has worsened."

Jason shook his head. "It makes no difference. Steps have been taken to release your dowry. As soon as I have it, I shall see it signed into your name. It was a debt I owed you. Soon it will be paid."

Velvet's heart squeezed. A debt he owed. The price of her innocence. She knew that was how he felt, yet it hurt to hear him put it into words.

"In the meantime," he was saying, "I want to speak to Barnstable, see what else he might have unearthed."

Velvet hoped the Bow Street Runner had found something that could help them. Avery Sinclair was a vicious, evil man. Every day Jason stayed in England the chances grew worse that he would be discovered. If he was, he was certain to hang. There had to be a way to prove his innocence. Velvet vowed that she would find it. Once she did he would be safe.

She ignored the jolt of pain that reminded her that once he was, he would also be gone.

Christian Sutherland, earl of Balfour, leaned against the door leading out to the terrace. An hour ago, Velvet Moran, now married to her distant Northumberland cousin, had arrived at the crowded soiree in company with Lucien Montaine along with Lord and Lady Briarwood, who had become her close friends.

Velvet had sent a message to Christian, of course, a letter informing him of her marriage the day after it had occurred. It explained that she had long been enamored of her cousin but hadn't expected that he would make an offer. She asked for his understanding in this, a matter of the heart, and hoped that they might remain good friends.

Christian watched her now, saw her smiling as she paused to speak to the countess of Brookhurst, and found himself wondering at the story that her husband was a bookish, shy sort of man who preferred his scholarly endeavors to the fashionable world of the ton. Not to worry, she had said with what Christian believed was a false amount of gaiety, she and Lord Hawkins were planning a celebration of their marriage in the very near future. Her friends could meet her illusive husband then.

He had offered his congratulations of course, and for the most part, he had meant them. If Velvet was happy, he was

happy for her. In the matter of wives, however, it galled him
mightily that the first two women he had wanted to marry
had flatly turned him down.

It was a thought that drew Christian's gaze to the opposite
end of the crowded salon. Her grace, Mary Sinclair, duchess
of Carlyle, stood like a ghostly waif next to the lean, smiling
figure of her tall blond husband. He was decked out like a
peacock, in a suit of gold and royal blue encrusted with seed
pearls and brilliants. The clothes must have cost him a fortune. It was a statement of his wealth and the power that
his marriage to Mary Stanton had created.

But what of Mary? In truth, Christian had wanted to
marry the girl himself. He was taken with Mary from the
moment he had met her. Seeing her now, looking so pale
and forlorn, stirred a painful throbbing in his chest.

It made him wonder if the gossip he had so far discounted
might, after all, be correct. That instead of a love match,
Mary had been forced into marriage with the duke.

Unconsciously, Christian's hands formed into fists. Mary
Stanton had needed a man she could count on. He had
wanted very much to be that man. Turning away from the
small, fragile picture she made next to Carlyle, Christian
strode out onto the terrace.

The hour was late. Velvet's face felt brittle from the abun-
dance of smiling she had done and accepting the endless
rounds of congratulations. Up until now, she had endured
the evening without complaint, pretending to a gaiety she
did not feel, determined to discover some small shred of
something that might be of value to Jason.

Standing beneath a glittering chandelier at the edge of the
Gold salon, she laughed at a ribald remark her current com-
panion, the beautiful black-haired countess of Brookhurst,
had whispered behind her hand painted fan, an intimation
that the young Baron Densmore was equipped much like a
Scotish bull and with just that much fortitude in bed. The
remark made the heat creep into Velvet's cheeks. She hoped
the countess would not notice.

Celia Rollins had been her quarry from the time of their first meeting at Carlyle Hall. Each time they had spoken, with Velvet's subtle attempts at friendship, Lady Brookhurst's interest had grown.

Velvet laughed at another lusty sally, this one describing Lord Whitmore's male anatomy as compared with that of a shriveled up toad.

"You are delightfully wicked, my lady," Velvet said, wondering if Jason had ever seen this side of the woman. She doubted it. Lady Brookhurst was extremely good at enthralling a man, teasing him to distraction while disguising the true depths of her depravity.

"My dear," she said, "it is past time we ended the formalities between us. From now on you shall call me Celia and I shall call you Velvet."

Velvet forced another of her painful smiles. "I should be delighted . . . Celia."

The countess leaned closer. "I abhor most women, you know. But once in a while, a female comes along who knows what she is about. I sensed that in you, Velvet. You are a woman determined to live as she pleases. I do not know your husband, but whatever manner of man you have married, a woman of your passionate nature will not settle for less than an ardent lover." Her thick black lashes swept down in a way they hadn't before. There was something seductive in the look she cast Velvet that made her suddenly uneasy. " 'Tis another thing we have in common."

Velvet nodded as if she agreed, but for the first time she felt wary. She had done it—formed a tentative friendship with a woman who preferred the company of men. It was odd, but in the past few moments, Velvet could swear that Celia had begun looking at Velvet with the same sultry glances she usually reserved for her unwitting male prey. Surely she was only imagining Celia's softly veiled sensual scrutiny. Surely the whispered stories Velvet had heard about women taking other women as lovers weren't really true. But suddenly she wasn't so sure.

Celia glanced over a creamy white shoulder. "My escort,

the baron, is walking this way. I believe he has plans for me that will require the balance of the evening.'' She flicked the young man a seductive smile, then returned her regard to Velvet.

"You must come to tea,'' the countess said with a seductive lowering of her lashes. ''Perhaps this coming Thursday?'' She smiled. ''I promise I shall have all the juicy gossip on your ex-betrothed's hasty marriage to Mary Stanton. You may count on hearing every sordid detail, right down to the wedding night.''

Velvet's pulse increased. Tea with Celia Rollins. And Avery would be the topic of discussion. It was the chance she had been seeking, the perfect opportunity for her to ask questions, though the notion of an afternoon spent with Lady Brookhurst made her decidedly uneasy.

"I shall be delighted . . . Celia.''

The countess smiled with satisfaction, then her perfect black brow arched up as she spotted the young Scottish bull, Lord Densmore. ''Here he comes now. I daresay, I like the look on his face. I believe his intentions are entirely dishonorable.''

Velvet said nothing as the countess waved and strolled off to meet her lover. A few moments later, Litchfield arrived with Lord Briarwood and his tall, blond wife, Elizabeth, in tow. Balfour had introduced them, so she would have a proper chaperone. Fortunately she and Elizabeth had liked each other at once and even her marriage to Jason had not altered that friendship.

They left the soiree half an hour later, all of them exhausted from the strenuous round of parties they had attended throughout the eve.

All the way home, Velvet thought of her meeting with Celia on Thursday next. She decided telling Jason would not be the wisest course.

CHAPTER SIXTEEN

∞

*M*oonlight filtered through the branches outside the bedchamber window, reflecting off the paving stones and lighting the carriages that returned their occupants to their town houses on Berkeley Square. Jason paced the floor in front of the mullioned panes, stopping to peer into the darkness, but no horse-drawn conveyance rolled up in front of the door.

Velvet had not yet returned from her evening with Litchfield and Lord and Lady Briarwood. It was damned near three in the morning—where the devil was she?

He turned and retraced his steps, listening for sounds in the entry, worried about her, though he knew she was safe with his friend. At least the man who had been watching the house the night he had come to Velvet's room had apparently ended his surveillance—for the present—which put his mind a bit more at rest.

Another twenty minutes passed before he spotted Litchfield's carriage, then he heard Velvet climbing the stairs. Relief trickled through him, followed by an unreasoning anger. Jerking open the door between their two rooms—a door he'd been careful to keep closed until now—he stormed in.

A surprised gasp arose from a candlelit corner. "S-sorry, milord," said Tabby. "I 'eard her ladyship arrive downstairs. I figured she'd be needin' me to help her undress before retirin'."

The stirring of footsteps brought his attention to the door. Velvet stood framed in the opening.

"It's all right, Tabby. My husband can help me undress, since it appears he has been awaiting my return." She tossed him a saucy look tempered with a hint of challenge. He had come into her domain, it said. Now that he had, he could damn well play the role of husband.

Tabby eyed his tall frame from top to bottom, then flashed him a lusty, knowing smile and left the room. If the look on the woman's face was any indication of what she was thinking, the coachman's bachelor days were about to end.

Jason waited till she closed the door. At first he had been worried that she or the coachman might recognize him as the man who had ridden as the outlaw, Jack Kincaid, but the night of his appearance had been cloudy and dark, and it never occurred to them that her ladyship would marry such a man.

Sometimes he wondered at it himself. Velvet was too damned trusting. At the very least she should harbor some hint of suspicion that he might have indeed killed his father. He knew without doubt she believed in his innocence completely. The knowledge did strange things to the area around his heart.

"Was there something you wished to discuss, my lord?" The soft cadence of her voice drew his attention to the woman across the room.

"You bloody well know there is. I want to know what you've been doing that kept you out until three in the morning?"

"Late evenings are the vogue, my lord. Surely you haven't been gone from London so long that you have forgotten."

He tried not to notice the way her lush breasts rose above her sea green gown, the way the cleft formed a dark intriguing shadow, but his body had noticed and the blood began to thicken and pulse through his veins.

"You're supposed to be married. Did no one ask after your husband?"

"Oh, indeed they did, my lord." She sat down on the tapestry stool in front of her dresser and began to pull the pins from her hair. In the light slanting in, it gleamed like burnished copper, and the heat in his blood pooled low in his belly.

"As we agreed," she continued, "I told them you were a bookish sort, far more at home in the country. I told them I had, however, convinced you to host a ball at the end of the month, in celebration of our marriage, and that they could meet you then. That should appease their curiosity for a while."

He watched her face in the mirror, noticed the tiny, heart-shaped patch she had placed beside the corner of her mouth, and knew an irresistible urge to kiss the spot beneath it. Her hands looked small and delicate as they pulled the silver brush through the long curling strands of her glossy dark hair. His fingers itched to touch it, to feel the fine, soft texture against his skin.

He dragged his gaze back to her face, his blood pumping faster, collecting in his groin, making him hard inside his breeches. When he spoke, his voice came out husky.

"Aye, the promise of a ball will soothe them for a while. Perhaps by then I'll have enough evidence to confront Lady Brookhurst. If I do, she'll be forced to admit Avery's guilt—and my innocence."

Velvet pulled her long curling hair forward over one shoulder, then pulled the bristles through it, past the tip of a breast. His gaze fastened there and his mouth went dry. He jerked his gaze away.

"Once my name is cleared," he said thickly, "I'll be able to leave. You can invent some tale of my abandonment and start the annulment proceedings. Lucien can guide you, grease whatever palms he feels is necessary."

Velvet said nothing for the longest time, then she simply rose from her dressing stool, crossed the room, and turned her back, wordlessly asking for his assistance to unfasten the row of tiny buttons.

"I see no reason to hurry," she finally said, waiting patiently for his fingers to do their work. Beneath his hand, he could feel the smoothness of her skin. The faint scent of lilac drifted into his awareness. Inside his breeches he was hard as a stone.

"Perhaps," she said, "I shall grow accustomed to the notion of being married." His head snapped up. The last button popped free and his fingers went still. "Once you have left the country and I am alone, I shall be allowed all manner of freedoms. A married woman who behaves with discretion may do nearly anything she pleases."

Jason clamped his jaw. "Parading around as a husbandless wife wasn't part of the bargain. You agreed to an annulment, Velvet."

"True." She sighed dramatically, turning to face him. Though she held up the bodice of her unfastened gown, her breasts nearly spilled over the top. "But if you truly have no wish to marry someone else, why would it matter? As your wife, I could move freely about without fear of scandal. I could—"

"You could what? Sleep with whomever you wish? Take any number of lovers?"

Velvet shrugged. "I enjoyed our lovemaking, Jason. It taught me that a woman has needs the same as a man. A woman desires to be kissed and caressed—"

"Stop it."

"She needs to feel the pleasure a man can give her. A woman wants to taste—"

"I said stop it, damn you!" He gripped her arms and dragged her against him. "I don't believe this! Are you telling me that after I am gone you intend to take a lover?"

"Of course, what did you think?"

"What did I think!" he nearly shouted. "I thought that you would have our marriage annulled, that you would live with your grandfather until you found a good and proper husband who would treat you with care and respect."

"I have a good husband, Jason. I'm perfectly satisfied with the man I have married. The fact that he doesn't want me—"

"That's not bloody true and you know it. I'm hard as a thundering stone right now! Christ, if I had my way, I'd rip the clothes from your luscious little body. I'd drag you over to that bed, spread your lovely legs, and bury myself inside you. I'd take you hard for the rest of the night and every night until I had my fill. I'd make damned sure I satisfied those needs you were so freely discussing. You wouldn't have to worry about another man in your bed, and if you took a lover, I vow I'd shoot you both!"

For several long moments, she stared at him with astonished, uptilted eyes, her cheeks flushed a pretty shade of pink. If she had thought to shock him, he had neatly turned the tables. He wasn't a proper gentleman anymore and he wanted her to know it. He had done so with a vengeance, or at least he thought so, until she looked him straight in the face.

She wet those soft pink lips. "Kiss me, Jason. I want you to do those things you said."

Jason groaned. God's blood—the woman was killing him! "Can't you understand—I'm doing you a favor. If we make love, you might wind up with a child. I don't know how to be a husband, a father. Once I could have done it. As my father's heir I was expected to do it. But things have changed since then. I'm not the man I was—I never will be again."

She only shook her head. Her next words came out softly. "You just don't see yourself the way I do. You would make a wonderful husband, Jason."

Frustration tore through him. How could he make her see? "If I told you the things I've done, if I had the courage to let you see the man I really am . . . then you would understand."

Small, soft fingers came up to cradle his cheek. "Tell me. Tell me what has happened to you to make you feel this way."

Jason swallowed. Dark images began to appear, screams of agony, sobs of pain, cries for help. He fought against them, tried to block them out. He felt dizzy, sick to his stomach. "I can't." He turned his head away, missing the gentle touch as soon as it was gone. "Don't ask it of me, Velvet. Not now. Not ever."

Velvet looked at him and her eyes grew moist with tears. They were for him, he realized, not for herself, and something tightened inside him. She was standing there holding up her gown, looking at him with a mixture of desire and pity, and it was tearing him in two.

"Make love to me, Jason. Let me help you forget."

Ignoring the pressure in his chest and Velvet's look of compassion, he stepped away, desperate to put some distance between them. "Get dressed," he commanded. "In case it has slipped your mind, you are standing there half-naked. You're behaving like a doxy and it doesn't become you." God's blood, it wasn't the truth, not a shred of it. She was beautiful and desirable and he ached just to hold her. He wanted to make love to her, wanted her in his bed and not just for tonight.

Velvet's bottom lip trembled. Fresh tears welled and a soft sob escaped as she turned and walked away. He told himself to leave her, not to torture himself by listening to the whispery rustle of fabric from behind her dressing screen, not to allow the image of her smooth bare skin to invade the corners of his mind. But his feet remained fixed on the floor, as solidly immobile as if they were nailed to the polished wood.

She finally emerged dressed in a simple white night rail that was every bit as enticing as her disheveled gown. She looked small and fragile, embarrassed and uncertain as he had never seen her. He had done that to her, he knew, with his half truths and his accusations.

He told himself to leave, that it didn't really matter, that it was better if he put an end to the fierce attraction between them. Instead his legs began to move, to stride across the floor in her direction. He knelt beside the canopied bed, reached for her small pale hand, and pressed the back against his lips.

"If we had a marriage in truth," he said, "there is nothing between us you could not say, nothing that would be forbidden. I would cherish your passion, your desire. It is a rare and beautiful quality in a woman, one any wise husband would treasure.''

She turned her head so that she could see him, her dark hair spilling across the pillow. Some of the color returned to her cheeks. "I'm your wife. You are my husband.''

He only shook his head. "I'm not your husband, Velvet, I never will be. Once I was your lover. I was also a fool.''

Turning before she could say something more, something that might convince him to stay, Jason crossed the floor and yanked open the door to his bedchamber. Christ's blood he'd be glad when this whole affair was ended. God knew— if he didn't hang first—he'd be bloody well glad to get home.

Christian Sutherland paused in descending the wide marble stairs. His West End mansion sat across from Hyde Park, his grandfather's lavish gift to the woman he had married. It was Christian's home now, his place of refuge, though at the moment, it sounded as though it were being invaded.

"Please . . . I must see the earl." A small cloaked figure stood just inside the doorway. "I know I haven't an appointment, please, will you tell him I am here.''

"I'm sorry, madam. Lord Balfour is extremely determined when it comes to his privacy. But perhaps if you will give me your name—''

The visitor made a noise of despair that sounded close to a sob. "Say . . . say it is Mary. I believe the earl will come if you tell him Mary is here.''

Christian's heartbeat quickened. He rapidly descended the last of the stairs and stepped into the marble-floored foyer. "It's all right, George. Mary is a friend. She is welcome here. I'll speak to her in the White Drawing Room.''

She stared in his direction, her face well-hidden by the dark recesses of her hood. "Christian," she whispered, hysteria in her voice, "please, you must help me. I'm so frightened. I don't know what to do." It was the first time she had ever used his first name and it told him how near to panic she was.

A knot of worry balled in his stomach. "It's all right, love." Resting a hand at her waist, he guided her into the drawing room. As its name implied, it was done entirely in white and gold, from the lavish ivory silk draperies to the gilt framed pictures lining the walls. "Once you tell me what has overset you so badly I'm certain we'll be able to straighten things out."

He took her mist-dampened cloak and tossed it over a chair, then seated her on a gold fringed sofa.

Mary gripped her hands in her lap. They looked slender and pale, and he noticed that they trembled. "I-I know this is a terrible imposition, but I had to come. I didn't know where else to go, whom I could turn to."

"Where is your father?" he asked gently, knowing they had always been close.

Her blue eyes clouded with tears. They were lackluster as he had never seen them, the life in them completely gone. "My father is dead."

Christian's jaw went tense. "I'm sorry, Mary." He squeezed her hand. "Sit here a moment, love. I'll be right back." Moving to the sideboard, he poured her a small glass of sherry, then returned to the sofa. "Drink this." Kneeling, he pressed the stemmed crystal into her trembling hand. "Just a sip or two will make you feel better." When she accepted the glass, he sat down on the sofa beside her.

The glass shook in her slender fingers. She took a sip and set it on the table. "I miss him," Mary said brokenly. "Already I miss him so much."

"Mary, I'm so sorry. How did it happen?"

"There was an accident . . . the carriage veered off the road and went into a pond. My father drowned." Tear-filled eyes lifted to his face. "*He* did it. I know he did. Somehow Avery killed my father."

Stunned silence enveloped him. An icy shiver ran down his spine. "Mary, surely you are mistaken. The news of your father's death has come as a terrible shock. It is understandable that you are upset. Surely the duke would not—''

Her fingers bit into his arm. ''You don't know him as I do. You don't know how ruthless, how cruel he can be. I think my father had begun to see. I think he had started to worry he had made a mistake in choosing Avery.''

Christian's head came up, the words gripping him even more fiercely than her unexpected accusations. ''Your father was the one? You did not wish to marry the duke?''

Pain washed over her features. Her eyes slid closed and a flood of tears washed down her cheeks. ''I wanted to please him. He was an old man and I wanted to make him happy.'' She leaned toward Christian, her anguished gaze fixed on his face. ''I would have married you, my lord. I was in love with you.''

Christian's chest went tight. ''Mary . . .'' He took her gently in his arms, whispered soft words of comfort, and let her weep against his shoulder. He held her and his heart squeezed with pain. For Mary. And for himself.

''The night of the Briarwoods' party,'' she started raggedly, ''he tricked me into leaving. He took me to an inn. I thought my father was there, but it wasn't the truth.'' A heart wrenching sob slipped out. ''Avery tore off my clothes. He did things . . . terrible things. Dear God, it was so awful, so horribly vile.'' She shook her head and a fresh cascade of wetness rolled down her cheeks. ''I always imagined that it would be beautiful.''

Anger knifed through him, and a fierce jolt of regret. It would have been, Christian thought bitterly, if he had been the man making love to gentle Mary.

She drew away from him then, pulled back to look him in the face. ''I can't stay there a moment more, my lord. I can't face him, knowing what he's done.''

''You can't be certain the duke is responsible, Mary.''

''I know it—in here.'' She rested a hand over her heart. ''He wanted my father's money. As my husband, with my father gone and his fortune left to me, Avery controls every schilling. Can't you see? It was Avery. Somehow he found a way to get what he has wanted all along.''

Christian wasn't sure he believed the duke would go so far as to kill the old man, but it didn't really matter. The duke of Carlyle had already done more than enough to earn the earl of Balfour's loathing.

"He beat me," she whispered, and his whole body went rigid. "He was careful to be sure the marks did not show. I try not to anger him. I try, but I cannot seem to please him." She looked up at him with teary pale blue eyes. "Please, my lord, will you help me? I have nowhere else to go."

Christian worked to stay calm. He wanted to kill Avery Sinclair with his two bare hands. "Mary . . . love, of course, I will help." His mind worked frantically, sorting through the possibilities. "But even if you weren't married, you couldn't stay here. I'm a bachelor. The gossip would soon leak out that there is a woman staying in my house."

"Wh-what am I going to do?"

What indeed? He needed the help of someone he could trust. Someone who would understand. "There is a woman who may be able to help us. I believe the lady may have discovered the truth of Avery's cruelty. Perhaps that is the reason she ended their betrothal."

"You are speaking of Velvet Moran."

"She is Lady Hawkins now, but yes that is the woman I speak of. Do you know her?"

"We have met on several occasions. She was always kind to me."

Christian urged Mary to her feet. Picking up her cloak, he enveloped her in its deep, disguising folds. "Avery won't like being thwarted. As soon as he discovers you have left him, he'll be looking for you. With the money he now has at his disposal, he can hire an army if that is his wish."

"I left him a note. I told him I was too grief-stricken to stay in London. I told him I was returning to my father's house in the country, that I would await him there. The funeral is set for the end of the week."

"Avery will make a point of being there. If you go, he will know that you suspect him. He will see it in your eyes. There is no telling what he might do."

"I know. That is the reason I came here."

Christian nodded. "We've some time yet. You'll have to stay out of sight until we can figure out what to do."

Mary rested a slight, shaking hand on his arm. "Thank you, my lord."

A tender smile rose to his lips. "I liked it better when you called me Christian."

Mary's cheeks grew flushed, soft spots of color in a face that was otherwise pale. She gave him a tremulous smile, the first he had seen. "I shall be forever in your debt . . . Christian."

He ran a finger along her jaw, admiring the fine delicate bones. "I shall remember you said so, Mary." He made no further comment, just guided her toward the door and ordered the butler to have his carriage brought round. All the while his mind was turning, wondering how he could possibly right the awful wrongs the duke had done to his Mary.

In a modest India calico house dress, Velvet sat in the drawing room across from a pale-faced Mary Sinclair. The notion struck her that by an odd twist of fate, Mary was her sister-in-law, though of course she did not know it. Christian Sutherland stood at her side, protective in his stance as she had never seen him.

The earl had come to her less than an hour ago. He had asked if they could be private, uncertain how he should proceed in front of her new husband. But Jason wasn't at home.

Velvet had ushered Balfour into the drawing room, along with the small cloaked figure he had helped down from his carriage. Halfway through the incredible discussion that painted Avery Sinclair even more a villain than she had believed, Jason had returned from his meeting with Litchfield and the Runner, Mr. Barnstable.

At Jason's appearance, Lord Balfour had stiffened protectively over Mary, but Velvet had assured them her husband would be most sympathetic to their cause—and that they could totally trust him.

She wasn't afraid either of them would guess whom Jason was. He had told her that he had met Christian Sutherland only once in passing more than ten years ago, and he had never met Mary Stanton. Mary glanced across at Jason, who listened to the tale of her forced marriage, his jaw clamped hard, a muscle bunched in his cheek.

If the situation hadn't been so awful for poor dear Mary, Velvet might have smiled at his bookish disguise—tiny wire-rimmed spectacles perched on his straight, well-formed nose, his dark hair hidden by a plain gray bagwig that made him look years older than he was. He was dressed more like a tutor than the wealthy Northumberland noble he was supposed to be, in a plain brown velvet coat, white jabot, and beige breeches, his muscled calves encased in white clocked stockings.

''There is more to the story than I have told you,'' Mary suddenly said, and Velvet's gaze swung sharply in the slender blond woman's direction. ''Lord Balfour does not wish me to say this, since as yet I have no proof, but if you are willing to help me, you should know the extent of what you risk.''

''Go on,'' Jason prodded. ''Whatever you say will go no farther than this room.''

Balfour seemed to relax, but Mary looked even more tense. ''I told you my father is dead. I did not say that I believe my husband was somehow responsible for the deed.''

Jason's face turned grim and Velvet's stomach knotted. Mary went on to explain about the inheritance Avery would control and that she thought her father had begun to grow suspicious of Avery's ill treatment of her.

''I never told my father the truth about him. I didn't want him to blame himself and I knew that he would.'' She began to cry softly, and Balfour rested a comforting hand on her shoulder. ''I should have gone to him, told him the truth about Avery. My father would have found a way to protect me. He would have used his influence to ruin the duke, if that was what it took. Instead, now he is dead.''

Balfour handed her a handkerchief, then turned the full measure of his regard on Jason and Velvet. ''My mother and brother are in residence at my country estate in Kent. Mary can't stay here in the city. I am at a loss as to what I should do.''

''Windmere,'' Velvet said with a glint of determination. ''It shan't be luxurious, certainly nothing of what she is used to as the wife of a duke.'' Balfour's shoulders went stiff, as if the words were a painful reminder that Mary did not belong to him.

''Velvet is right,'' Jason put in. ''Windmere will serve well enough. There are only a handful of servants in residence, but that should work in your favor.''

''And those who are there are extremely discrete,'' Velvet added. If Balfour thought it odd that the wealthy Haversham heiress lived a frugal existence in what was thought to be a lavish country estate, he did not say so.

''Mary will be safe at Windmere,'' Velvet finished. '' 'Tis a place the duke will never think to look.''

Balfour came to his feet and so did Mary. ''Then Windmere it shall be. You will never know how much your help has meant to Mary and to me. If there is ever a favor you need, anything at all that I can do, do not hesitate to ask.''

Jason nodded. ''The time may well come, and not in the far distant future. If it does, it is good to know Velvet and I may count you among our friends.''

The time may well come. Balfour did not ask what the cryptic words meant, just nodded and shook Jason's hand, then bundled Mary up inside her cloak. ''If you'll send word ahead, I'll see Mary arrives there safely.'' He glanced down at the top of her head, invisible beneath her hood. ''It's been a difficult time for her. Perhaps I shall stay until she is settled in, if that is all right with you.''

''Of course,'' Jason said. They watched the two of them leave, and the moment they were gone, Velvet went into Jason's arms. He did not turn her away.

"He has killed someone else," she said, her cheek pressed against his solid chest.

"We do not know that for certain."

"You know it—I can see it in your face. And again there is no way to prove it."

A muscle tightened in his jaw. "Sooner or later, his greed will make him careless. When it does, we'll be ready."

Velvet pressed closer. She could feel Jason's heart beating heavily beneath her hand. Her own heart was pulsing in a sharp uneasy rhythm.

And suddenly she was afraid.

CHAPTER SEVENTEEN

∞

*T*hursday arrived, but instead of having tea with Celia Rollins, Velvet sat next to Jason in Litchfield's borrowed black carriage, jostling along the muddy road on the way to the Peregrine's Roost.

She'd had to beg Jason to let her come with him.

"I won't be a burden," she'd argued. "I can help you. If I dress as a chambermaid, I can move freely among the servants. They love to gossip. I can get them to tell me things you couldn't begin to ferret out."

He scowled. "You don't look the least bit like a servant. There isn't a one of them you'd be able to fool."

Her chin went up. She flashed him a saucy bright smile, clamped her hands on her hips, and tossed her head. "I'd 'ave to differ wi' ye, gov. I'd 'ave to say I could do a right foine job o' makin' 'em believe me, if I were a mind to."

Jason's jaw dropped. "How in God's name did you learn to talk like that?"

Velvet grinned. "Have you ever listened to Tabby? John Wilton isn't much better. With as few servants as we had left at Windmere, we all grew fairly close."

Jason shook his head. "I don't like it, Velvet."

"You don't have to like it. You can pretend you don't know me. I'll arrive on horseback, say I'm headed for a job at Castle Running—or better yet, Carlyle Hall. That will give me an opening to talk about the duke. I'll say my cousin works there, that she got me the job. The rest I'll play by ear.''

''I don't know . . .'' Jason rubbed the late afternoon shadow of beard that darkened his jaw. ''Avery's even more dangerous than we believed. If he somehow got wind that you were sniffing around again, if he started putting things together—''

''That isn't going to happen. The man isn't omnipotent. There is no way he could know we were there.''

Jason said nothing for several long moments. ''I still don't like it.''

Velvet grinned. ''But you'll do it—right, gov?''

A hint of amusement then a frustrated sigh whispered out. ''I have to find out if anyone at the inn actually saw the murder. As a servant, you might have a chance at the truth. Besides, I'll be there to make sure you don't get into trouble.'' He pinned her with a glare. ''Isn't that right, my love?''

Velvet's lashes swept down. ''Of course, my lord.''

She wasn't about to argue. She wanted Jason there, wanted to be with him as much as she possibly could. She was determined she could make him care for her enough to stay in England—or if he left, to take her with him. Being married to her, she had decided, was in his best interests as well as her own.

And so they'd set out the following day, Jason driving Litchfield's stylish one-horse phaeton, a bony gray saddle horse tied on behind for Velvet's hopefully inconspicuous arrival at the inn. Jason would be playing the part he had played before, Jason Hawkins, a member of the landed gentry just passing through.

Less than a mile from the Peregrine's Roost, he pulled the conveyance off the road and helped Velvet down, then settled her astride the old gray horse, pulling her simple woolen skirt down to cover her legs as best he could, then scowling at the portion of trim, stockinged ankle still exposed.

''I'll follow at a distance,'' he said, his face still dark, "make sure you get there safely. An hour later, I'll join you."

"All right." She was dressed in a brown woolen skirt and an unbleached muslin blouse, a mobcap hiding most of her dark auburn hair.

Jason caught the horse's rein as she started to ride away. "Dammit, I don't like involving you in this. Are you sure you want to go through with it?"

Velvet flashed him a jaunty smile. "Whot ye think, gov? I can 'ardly wait to get there."

Jason flinched. "Steer clear of the taproom. The men in there might find a woman traveling alone a bit too much temptation."

"Right ye are, gov."

Reluctantly, he grinned. "As charming as you look in that getup, I'm afraid I'd turn out to be one of them."

Twin spots of color rose into Velvet's cheeks. Then her warm smile slowly faded. "Good luck, Jason." She blew him a soft pretend kiss, and reined the bony old horse away.

Jason watched her ride off with a mixture of unease and admiration. She had more brass than any two men he knew. She was loyal and she was fiercely determined. If he was the man he had been eight years ago, he would be proud to claim her as his wife. Then again, if he was that naive young man, he would have married Celia Rollins. He wouldn't have been smart enough to recognize the qualities he admired in Velvet. He would have been too busy listening to his little head instead of thinking with his big one.

Cursing himself, Jason rolled along behind Velvet in the phaeton, then waited in a leafy copse of trees for the hour to pass so he could follow her into the inn.

When he finally arrived, he spotted her old gray nag in the stable. Tossing the stable lad a coin to see to his own horse and rig, he made his way across the courtyard to the entrance of the inn. Ivy covered the thick stone walls and hung down over the low wooden door. He ducked his head and stepped into the flagstone entry.

At first he didn't see her, not until he walked past the

door to the kitchen. Spotting her small form hidden behind
a cloud of steam erupting from the stove, he was amazed to
see her working. Apparently she had traded a night of lodg-
ing for a day of labor.

It shouldn't have surprised him but it did.

Jason felt the pull of a smile. At least he knew where she
was and what she was doing. Hopefully it would keep her
out of trouble.

He made his way to the taproom, a low-ceilinged room
crisscrossed with heavy wooden beams. Though the place
was old and a bit age-worn, the flagstone floors were neatly
swept, the walls newly whitewashed since his last visit. He
remembered the proprietor had always done his best to keep
the place clean. Apparently, he still did.

Settling himself at an empty wooden table in the corner
where he could watch the comings and goings in the room,
he leaned back and called for the serving maid, then ordered
a tankard of ale. The balance of the day and most of the
evening, he spent either at his table or milling about the inn.
He spoke to the barkeep and the serving wench in the taproom, spoke to several of the inn's longtime patrons, but
decided to take it easy, to wait a while, let Velvet have a
go at the servants before he pressed too hard.

Leaning back against the wall behind his roughhewn table, he pulled the gold watch fob from his pocket, flipped
open the lid, and checked the time. Fifteen minutes before
eleven. Time for his rendezvous with Velvet in the stable.

Having learned that the stable lad had already gone to
bed in a nook above the carriage house, assuring they would
be alone, Jason left the inn by a small door at the rear of
the taproom and crossed to the barn. Only a sliver of moon
lit the night, and odd-shaped passing clouds occasionally
obscured even those few puny rays of brightness.

Moving through the shadows, his long strides lengthened.
He was eager to find out what Velvet might have learned.
He wanted to be sure she was all right, and that she had a
decent place to sleep. If nothing had been discovered, to-

morrow he would try again, press until he had the answers to his questions.

Pausing inside the door, he could just make out the faint glow of a lantern, the candle behind the thick glass burning so low there was barely the hint of a flame. Then he caught a glimpse of Velvet's mop-capped head. Even in the dimly lit stall where she waited, he could see damp strands of her long dark hair, loose and glinting red at her temples, see her cheeks flushed pink with exertion.

"Jason," she called into the darkness. "I'm over here in the corner." He could see that she was. He could see as well that her blouse was moist with the heat of the kitchen and clinging seductively to her bosom. Without the panniers she usually wore beneath her skirts, her hips were rounded, womanly, incredibly alluring.

He approached her in the stall where she stood in front of a worn leather saddle, but paused a few feet away, not trusting himself to get closer. "Did you have any luck?"

She dabbed at the perspiration on her forehead with the back of a hand. "Not as much as I had hoped. At least not yet."

He wasn't surprised, yet disappointment coursed through him. "We knew it wouldn't be easy. We'll try again tomorrow." His eyes ran over her clinging, rumpled clothes. Hard work agreed with her. He wouldn't have believed it. In truth she looked as pretty in her simple working garments as if she were gowned in silk.

"What I meant to say," she amended, "was I didn't find out as much as I wanted, but someone here knows something, Jason. Someone at the inn saw something that night— I'm certain of it. There is no doubt in any of the servants' minds that the old duke's murderer was not his eldest son."

Jason's heart began pumping. He fought down a surge of excitement. "Do you think you can find out who it is?"

"I'll find out, sooner or later. I told the cook I had several more days before my new job started and she said she could use the extra help. In a few more days—"

Jason frowned. "In a few more days, you'll be back in

London. I can't stay past tomorrow without arousing suspicion and I'm not about to leave you here alone."

The line of Velvet's jaw went firm. "Don't be ridiculous. This is the chance we've been waiting for. I'm not about to leave until we find the person who can help you clear your name."

"I said, you're leaving with me."

Her small hands clamped on her hips. "I'm staying till I find out which of these people saw your father murdered."

"You're leaving."

"I'm staying."

His jaw flexed. The woman was a menace. She was also the most appealing little baggage he had ever seen. "If you were really my wife, I would beat you."

She cocked a brow, a slow grin forming. "I don't think so."

A corner of his mouth tugged up. "Oh, you don't? If I remember correctly, you made that mistaken presumption before."

She flushed prettily but remained where she stood, not one bit daunted by his words. Then the teasing note in his voice slid away. "You don't know me, Velvet. If you did, you wouldn't be so sure."

She stared at him for long silent moments, her eyes running over his face. "You're wrong, Jason. You're the one who doesn't know who you are. I know that you're a good and noble man. You're a man of principle. You're gentle and decent—"

"That is what you think, Velvet? That I am a man of principles? That I am gentle and decent?"

"Yes."

Velvet watched him move closer, his eyes fierce now, burning with a hungry light that darkened them almost to pitch. "If that is what you believe, perhaps it is time you found out exactly how wrong you are. Let me tell you what it is at this moment that I am thinking."

She moistened her lips, nervous now as he loomed above her, yet somehow strangely intrigued.

"I am thinking that you have never looked more enticing to me than you do at this very instant. I am thinking I should like to pull the cap from your hair and drag my fingers through it. I would kiss you, roughly, ravish that sweet mouth and plunder those ripe, seductive lips." His jaw tightened. Desire blazed in his eyes like a flame burning out of control. "Then I would take you—right here in the stable. I would bend you over that saddle, lift your skirts and plunge myself inside you. That is what I am thinking. That is exactly what I would like to do. Is that the gentle man you imagined? Surely even you are not too blind to see there isn't an ounce of gentleness left in me."

The pounding of Velvet's heart made it difficult for her to speak. The heat pumping through her made the inside of her mouth feel hot and dry. "We could do it that way . . . make love as the horses do?"

"Sweet God, aren't you listening! You're a lady, forgodsakes. Surely you don't want me to take you right here!"

"You have done it that way before, have you not?"

"Of course, but—"

"No one is here. If I were your lover instead of your wife, would you make love to me here in that way?"

Glittering blue eyes bored into her. "Aye. I would take you now . . . here . . . take you as I have wanted to every day since the first moment I saw you."

Velvet reached for his hands, slid his wide palms over her breasts. Her nipples went hard at his touch and she heard him groan. "From the start, you have been more than clear in the fact that I am not your wife. Once I was your lover. Please, Jason . . . I want to be your lover again."

He shook his head, but he didn't move his hands, his fingers curling instead around her, testing the firmness, the fullness.

"I'm only a man," he said roughly, his gaze intense. "God knows I have tried to be a better one, but it appears once more I have failed."

His arm slid around her. Jason hauled her against him, his mouth coming down hard, slanting over hers. A hand swept the cap from her head and he dragged his fingers through her hair, scattering what few pins remained, setting it free to tumble around her shoulders. Heat raced through her. The smell of man, horses, damp straw, and leather all combined to swamp her senses.

She clung to him and kissed him back, accepting the sweep of his tongue, the flood of warmth it stirred, the feel of his rock-hard torso crushed against her breasts. His hold on her shifted. He jerked the tie on the simple blouse she wore and dragged the material down to bare her breasts, then lifted one into his hand. He pebbled the end with his fingers, bent his head and sucked the nipple into his mouth, gently biting the crest.

Velvet swayed against him, arching her back, her nails digging into the thick bands of muscle across his shoulders. Good sweet God! Her breast swelled into his mouth; her nipples ached and distended. Her head fell back and he kissed the pulse at the base of her throat, trailed kisses across her bare shoulders.

"God, I want you." Then he was turning her around, hauling up her simple brown skirt, jerking up her thin lawn chemise, leaving her legs and hips bare. She felt the smoothness of the saddle pressing into her stomach as he bent her over the seat. Her knees brushed the low rack it sat on. She heard the buttons on his breeches popping open one by one, then he was freeing himself, his hardened arousal pressing with resolve against her hips.

"Spread your legs for me, Velvet."

She did as he told her, trembling with excitement, with heat and unbearable need. She whimpered at the hot flood of sensation when his fingers found the entrance to her core and he began to softly stroke her.

"You're so wet." His hands smoothed over skin, softly caressing. "So tight and hot." He sank a finger deep inside, probing carefully, preparing her for him. Another finger sank in, stroking even more deeply between the plump, slick folds.

"Jason . . ." Her stomach contracted, the muscles tightening as a shattering climax tore through her. Pleasure rolled over her, whispered through her limbs, and she worried her legs might give way beneath her. For a moment she forgot where she was, knew only that sweet fire coursed through her in thick, mind-numbing waves. Then a stiff, pulsing heaviness slid deep inside and the waves of sweet sensation began to build again.

"Jason . . . ?"

"Hang on, love." Surging into her fully, his groin came hard against her bottom, his heavy shaft filling her, sliding out and then filling her yet again. Scorching heat broke over her, gooseflesh crested on her skin. His palms cupped her breasts, his fingers plucking the sensitive ends, then he settled his big hands at her waist and began to ride in earnest.

Dear sweet God! His deep, plunging rhythm had her hips arching upward, pulling him farther inside. Velvet's eyes slid closed as wave after wave of pleasure swept through her. Sweet, sterling moments passed. Velvet moaned, her body constricting around him. Jason groaned and his muscles went rigid as he reached his own release.

At the last possible instant, he withdrew, spilling his precious seed onto the straw-covered floor beneath them. Breathing hard, he held her against him, his body still flush against hers.

His lips brushed the nape of her neck, the rim of an ear. One big hand smoothed over her hair. Then he was turning her into his arms, cradling her gently against his chest. They stood like that for long, silent minutes.

Idly, his hand cupped a breast. There was no tension there now, only a tender caress. "We have to go in, love."

Velvet snuggled closer. "That was incredible, Jason. I can hardly believe the things you make me feel. If I cannot have you for a husband, I am more than happy to settle for this."

She felt his muscles tighten and wished she had kept the thought to herself. He drew away from her, pulled her blouse up over her breasts, then began to refasten the buttons at the front of his breeches.

"That was a selfish thing to do," he grumbled, "yet I cannot regret it."

"I do not regret it. In truth, I already await the moment that it will happen again."

He whirled on her, his expression dark once more. "No, dammit! If we keep this up, sooner or later there is bound to be a babe. What the devil would you do if I got you with child?"

Velvet blinked at the unexpected sting of moisture in her eyes. "I would love it, Jason. I would love to have your babe." Her hand trembled where she pressed it against his chest. "I could love you, Jason . . . if you would let me."

His face went paper white. Jason gripped her shoulders. "Don't you understand—I don't want you to love me. I don't want you to have my child. What I feel for you is lust—nothing more. You're a beautiful, desirable woman and I want you. That is all there is between us. That is all there ever will be!"

Pain jolted through her. She knew he felt that way and yet it hurt, dear God it hurt so badly. He turned and stalked away from her, pausing a moment at the door. He didn't turn around. "Where are you sleeping?"

She swallowed past the ache that had risen in her throat. "I . . . have a room in the attic upstairs."

"Will you be all right there?"

"The place is clean and neat. I'll be fine."

He still did not turn. "Is there a lock on the door?"

"Yes."

"Use it." And then he was gone.

Jason watched from the shadows beside the barn until Velvet appeared through the stable door then disappeared inside the back door of the inn. He returned to the taproom, his chest feeling leaden. Dammit, what was there about the girl that he couldn't seem to resist her? Christ's blood, she was young and naive. Why did he continue to take advantage?

But even as he said the words, his mind said Velvet was a woman not a girl. She was strong and determined and she knew exactly what she wanted. Still, he did not want to hurt her.

He settled himself heavily at a table to the right of the hearth. A group of soldiers, infantrymen from the fourth regiment just back from India, had arrived earlier in the evening, hard-drinking men, half of them drunk as lords by now, the other half well on their way to joining them.

Four of them were joking with the tavern maid, one of them a thick-chested sergeant with stripes on the sleeves of his red and white uniform. He reached over and pinched the skinny girl's bottom. She jumped, spilling a tankard of ale, then turned to slap his hand.

"Mind your manners, sergeant."

I'll pay ye," he whispered, the words more a loud hissing slur. "Give me a tumble and I'll pay ye, lassie . . . more'n ye make here in a week. 'Tis months since me and the boys here been with a woman."

Jason shifted uneasily, thinking of Velvet, not liking the direction of the men's conversation. There weren't that many women in the tavern and several of the soldiers had remarked on the "ripe little dark-haired beauty" they had spied in the kitchen when they came in.

The girl eyed the silver in the palm of the big sergeant's hand. She glanced over her shoulder at the barkeep, then nodded. "Aye, I'll meet you. I'm through here in an hour. I'll meet you out in the stable. No one ever goes out there this time o' night."

A guilty flush warmed the back of Jason's neck. Christ, he wasn't much better than the sergeant, taking an innocent young girl like Velvet out in the stable, treating her like the doxy he had once called her. God's breath, they had made love three times and never shared a proper bed. Worse than that, each time he had left her, he was already hard and wishing he could take her again. Good Christ, what was there about her?

At the table beside him, the sergeant grumbled something to the effect that an hour of waiting for a wench was too damned long, and the girl sauntered off to fetch another round of drinks. Jason ordered one as well, a mug of rum he finished far too quickly, then a second mug that finally had the desired effect and began to make him groggy.

He must have nodded off, for when he awakened a few minutes later, the sergeant was gone and two of the soldiers were haggling over a bet. One said the sergeant would slake his lust long before the hour was up, while the other man's coin said the girl would refuse him, no matter how much money he offered.

A third man said it wouldn't matter. The girl would wind up beneath him, whether she wanted it that way or not.

"Damn shame, you ask me," the lanky corporal said. "The sergeant's a rough one, when it comes to the women. Pretty little thing like that oughtn't to be treated that way."

Jason's heart slammed hard against his ribs. Whatever effect the rum might have had was gone in a instant. He jerked to his feet so fast he knocked over his chair, and then he was running, his booted feet pounding toward the servants' stairs at the back of the taproom.

Velvet awakened slowly, her eyes trying to adjust to the darkness of her small attic room. A noise had aroused her, the sound of metal grating, or perhaps it was the lifting of the latch on her door. She knew that couldn't be. She had locked the door soundly. It must have been another door down the hall.

Rolling onto her back, she worked to get comfortable on the narrow, corn husk mattress when an odd prickling rose at the nape of her neck. Someone was in the room with her—she was sure of it. Someone was watching. Cold fear snaked down her spine, making her hands feel clammy. She bolted upright in her tiny single bed, her mouth opened wide on a scream.

A meaty hand clamped over her lips, stifling the sound, nearly gagging her. A heavy male body, ripe with the smell of sweat and rum, forced her back down on the bed.

"Hello, lass." He twisted a lock of her hair around his callused thumb, and fear made her shiver. "Ain't you a pretty little thing. You and me gonna get real well acquainted.''

His breeches were already partly unbuttoned, she saw. A thick roll around his waist hung over the band at the top. The fear increased, making her nauseous. He was twice her size. Even if she could pry away the hand and manage to cry out, the walls were thick and there was no one up there to hear her.

She started thrashing beneath him. God, he was so heavy! His foul breath filled her nostrils and tears began to burn behind her eyes. He let go of her long enough to grab the front of her night rail and Velvet jerked away, desperate to free herself. A scream erupted, but his hard slap muffled the sound. A second slap split her lip and made her ears ring. His long blunt fingers ripped her nightgown down the front, then he cruelly twisted one of her breasts.

''Ye better learn to please me, lass. Ye'll learn quick enough, Sergeant Dillon don't take no sass from a woman.''

She wet her lips, tasted the coppery flavor of her own blood, then steeled herself for another violent effort. She bucked and kicked, but couldn't dislodge him. Her scream died beneath his thick, punishing lips. The bile rose in her throat and she thought she might be sick.

Grabbing a fistful of his hair, she bit down hard on the tongue he forced into her mouth, and he jerked backward, swearing violently, his fist lashing out, slamming against her jaw and knocking her nearly unconscious back down on the bed.

''Ye bloody little vixen. Ye'll pay for that, ye will.''

''You're the one who is going to pay,'' said a soft, deadly voice from the doorway. ''I'm going to kill you, Sergeant. I'm going to do it with these two hands.''

Velvet whimpered. The room spun crazily, yet there was no mistaking the tall forbidding figure standing in the shadows across the room. Jason had come. She blinked to clear the tears from her vision. Thank God, Jason had come.

The sergeant straightened away from her, his eyes now trained on his new quarry, and Velvet held her torn and bloody nightgown together over her aching breasts.

"The girl is mine, bucko. If I have to take ye down before I can have her, so it shall be."

"Stand away from her," Jason warned with deadly calm. For the first time, Velvet's eyes came to rest on his face. She almost cried out at the cold-blooded menace she saw there, his eyes so piercing they looked black, his mouth no more than a hard, grim line. Every muscle in his powerful body quivered with fury. His hands were so tightly balled his knuckles looked as though they would pop through his skin.

She wiped at the blood oozing from the corner of her mouth, but she didn't notice the pain. Instead she stared at the deadly combatants, then caught the glint of steel as the sergeant reached toward his boot and withdrew a thin silver blade.

"Jason! Look out!"

He jerked back just in time, the blade missing him only by inches. A corner of his mouth curved up in a predatory smile that gleamed with brutal purpose. Velvet wet her lips, her whole body shaking. She had never seen him like this, never could have imagined the ruthless determination that twisted his handsome features into a cold mask of rage.

Jason circled, but in the small room, there wasn't much room to maneuver. The big sergeant grinned with malice.

"She's a ripe one, ain't she? Ye can bet I'll take 'er hard."

Jason's pupils shrank to pin dots. His jaw flexed, but the soldier's words did not hamper his steely control. If anything it seemed to settle even more deeply.

"I'm going to kill you," he repeated. "I'm going to carve you up with your own knife, and I'm going to relish every drop of blood I spill from your worthless carcass."

Velvet made a keening sound in her throat. She didn't know this man. She was nearly as fearful of him as she had been of the sergeant. She backed herself into a corner just as the barrel-chested soldier lowered his head and charged into Jason like a bull.

Velvet bit hard on her lip to stifle the scream that lodged in her throat. The side of her face ached, her head pounded, and her jaw throbbed, yet she felt none of those things. She was too caught up in the horror of watching two fierce male opponents determined to take each other's life.

The men crashed over a rickety table near the corner. Jason captured the sergeant's knife hand and twisted the viscous blade away, but the moment the soldier's hands were free, he wrapped them around Jason's neck and began to squeeze.

"Jason!" Fear nearly blinded her. Watching his face turn a vivid shade of red, she began to search desperately for some sort of weapon.

Then his fist lashed out, pounding into the sergeant's face, bloodying his nose and smashing his lip. Jason rolled free and the two men staggered to their feet. The sergeant landed a heavy blow to Jason's ribs but he merely grunted. His fist lashed out, taking the sergeant square on the chin and knocking him over backward. Jason grabbed him by the lapels of his scarlet coat, dragged him to his feet, and began to smash one fierce blow after another into the sergeant's bloody face.

Grunts of pain erupted from between the man's bleeding lips. Blood spurted from his nose. Frantic to save himself, he clawed the floor above his head until his fingers closed around the handle of the knife. He swung it down fiercely, but Jason caught his wrist and wrenched it away as if it were no more than a simple distraction.

Smiling coldly, he gripped the handle and pressed the blade against the sergeant's fleshy neck. "I'm going to slit your throat. I'm going to let you bleed to death like a butchered pig."

"Jason!" Velvet screamed. Bolting forward, she gripped the hand that held the knife gouging into the sergeant's flesh. "Forgodsakes, don't kill him!"

He didn't seem to hear her. The thin edge of steel bit cleanly into the soldier's mottled skin, leaving a fine trail of blood in its wake.

"Have pity, man—she's only a serving wench!"

Jason's eyes blazed. "The woman is my wife." The blade cut deeper; blood began to flow.

"Jason!" Velvet started crying. She could barely see for the tears flooding her eyes, just a hazy blur of his tall, powerful figure that appeared to be edged with crimson. "Please . . . I'm begging you . . . please don't kill him."

His hand shook, but the pressure remained. The knife blade wavered but did not move.

"Jason . . ." she whispered, still gripping his arm. "Please . . ."

His breath hissed out. His dark head dropped forward against his chest. He tossed the knife against the wall with a steely clatter, grabbed the sergeant's jacket, jerked him up and hit him so hard his head bounced loudly on the floor.

"H-he's unconscious," Velvet whispered between her dry lips, staring with horror at the blood-covered figure on the floor.

Jason staggered to his feet. "He'll stay that way for a while." He weaved unsteadily toward her, his lip bloody, his coat torn. Unconsciously, she flinched when he reached out to touch her, and his eyes shot up to her face. They were clouded with concern, she saw, dark with worry and fear for her.

Staring into her stricken features, the look slowly faded, changing into something she could not read. The muscles in his face went taut. He seemed to collect himself, withdraw somewhere inside. "Are you all right?"

She wasn't all right. Every part of her ached and throbbed. She was shivering with shock and fear and she wanted to cry more than she wanted to draw the next breath of air.

"I-I don't want to stay here. I-I can't. Please . . . I want to go with you."

He surprised her with a shake of his dark head. "You can't mean that. Not after what has happened." His eyes remained dark, forbidding, the bleak eyes of a stranger. "Not after what you've seen."

She didn't understand, couldn't seem to make her foggy mind function. "What I've seen?"

"I would have killed him, Velvet. God, I would have slit the bastard's throat. If it hadn't been for you I would have done it."

"Yes."

"Now do you understand?" He glanced away from her, no longer able to meet her eyes. Stark pain outlined each of his features. "Now do you see the kind of man I am?"

Oh, dear God. Her legs were trembling so badly she feared they might collapse, yet she forced herself to move. Stepping over the sergeant's unconscious body, she walked unsteadily toward him, feeling the same thrumming ache for Jason that pounded through her bruised and battered body.

She stopped in front of him, waited until his eyes came to rest on her face. "Yes . . . I saw what you did. I understand you cared enough for me to risk your life defending me. I saw that you are even braver than I had imagined."

He gripped her shoulders. "I would have killed him!"

"Yes. Or you would have died fighting to protect me, if the sergeant had had his way."

His eyes bored into hers. "I don't understand you. How can you still believe in me? Surely now you have doubts . . . surely you must wonder—"

"Did you kill your father?"

He only shook his head. "No."

"This man beat me. He would have raped me. You were angry, blinded by fury at what he had done. You were trying to protect me!" Still clutching her torn and bloody nightgown, she closed the distance between them. "Take me out of here, Jason. Please. Take me out of here now. I know with you I will be safe."

Jason stared hard. For a moment, he didn't move. Then a low sound came from his throat and he reached out to touch her, enfold her in his arms. He buried his face in her hair. For seconds, he just held her, then he lifted her against his chest, kicked open the door, and stepped out into the hallway.

"We'll be safe in my room." His boots echoed down the stairs. "We'll get your things in the morning."

Velvet didn't argue. Shock had claimed the last of her reserves and she had started to shake all over. When they reached his room, he drew back the covers on the bed and rested her carefully in the middle. He lit a candle on the bedside table, then went over and locked the door. Pulling a pistol from his satchel, he checked the load and set it on the table next to the candle.

Seating himself carefully on the edge of the bed, he reached toward her. His hand shook as he gently lifted her chin, turning it into the light so that he could survey the bruises. He blanched when he realized the extent of the sergeant's cruelty.

The muscles in his throat constricted. He couldn't seem to speak. "God, I'm sorry. So damned sorry."

"It doesn't matter," Velvet said softly. "You came for me. That is what is important." But she was still shivering and she was still frightened inside.

He gently parted the front of her nightgown, saw the bruises beginning to darken around her breasts. "Christ, he really hurt you." His eyes slid closed. "God damn the bastard to hell." His gaze was piercing. "I never should have brought you here. It's my fault this happened."

Velvet gripped his hand, felt the tension thrumming through it. "Do you think everything that happens is your fault? Just because you are a duke does not make you responsible for every bad thing that occurs."

But the look on his face said he believed that it did.

"Even your father wasn't perfect. If he had controlled his temper, if he hadn't followed you to the inn, he might not have been killed—or do you believe that is your fault, as well?"

His head dropped forward. A weight seemed to settle on his shoulders. "I don't know what to believe anymore."

Velvet blinked back tears. She rested a hand on his cheek, felt the hard line of his jaw beneath her fingers. "I am still shaking. Please, Jason . . . I am so very tired but I know I shan't be able to sleep. Will you hold me?''

She thought he would argue, that he would refuse. Instead, he turned away, bent down and began to pull off his boots. His shirt and breeches followed. With his broad chest bare, wearing only a pair of tight-fitting cotton drawers, he climbed into bed beside her. Velvet snuggled into his arms, rested her head against his thick-muscled shoulder.

''Thank you,'' she whispered. In minutes she was asleep. As she had said, she knew she would be safe. And that Jason would not close his eyes before the sun rose the following morning.

CHAPTER EIGHTEEN

∞

Velvet awoke to the sound of Jason moving about the room. She cracked open an eye and discovered he was packing. Her small satchel, apparently retrieved from upstairs, sat on the seat of the ladder-backed chair beside the bed.

She levered herself upright, wincing at the pain shooting through her. Her breasts ached, her head pounded, and her lip was puffy and scabbed.

"Jason, what are you doing?"

His head came up. He looked at her over his shoulder. "Taking you home."

"What of the sergeant?" she asked, ignoring this last. "Is he . . . ?"

"The soldiers have all gone. At least we don't have them to deal with." He stuffed a full-sleeved linen shirt into his satchel as she swung her legs stiffly to the side of the slatted wooden bed.

"We don't have to leave just yet. I'm sure Mrs. Mc-Curdy—that's the name of the cook—will understand my being late to work, once she learns what happened."

His eyes widened with incredulity. "Are you mad?" He started toward her. "You look like hell and there is little doubt you feel the same way. You can't possibly go down there and work. I shouldn't have let you come in the first place. Now I'm taking you home before something else bad happens."

He had a point; she couldn't deny it. Working was the last thing she felt like doing today, but this was the chance they had come for and she wasn't about to quit until she had the answers they sought.

"Just give me a couple of hours. As battered as I look, the servants are bound to be sympathetic. Maybe they'll confide in me, tell me what we need to know."

"No. Absolutely not." He went back to his packing, tossed in his stockings then the pair of bloodstained breeches he had worn the night before. "We're leaving and that's the end of it."

Velvet slid to her feet, wincing at the jolt of pain that shot through her body. Luckily he was looking the other way. "We have to see this through, Jason. We have to take this final opportunity. The soldiers are gone. Please . . . let me have one more chance to see if I can find out the truth."

The leather strap on his satchel whirred through the buckle as Jason tightened it down. His eyes came up to her face. "I've already hurt you enough."

"I told you before, what happened wasn't your fault. Now I'm asking you . . . please . . . for just this one small favor. Give me three more hours. Three hours, Jason, then we can leave."

He stomped around the room, his expression dark and stormy. Then he gripped the satchel and tossed it onto the bed. "That isn't fair and you know it."

"Let me help you, Jason."

He moved toward her, stopping so close they almost touched. He clamped his hands on his hips and stared down at her. "Three hours, Velvet. Then I'm dragging you out of here. There'll be no excuses. If you won't leave, I'll toss you over my shoulder and cart you off like a sack of potatoes." He bent down nose to nose with her. "Do I make myself clear?"

Velvet smiled. "Very clear, my lord." Turning away from him, she dressed quickly, donning her servant's clothes, ignoring the aches and pains that came with every movement.

"I'll meet you at the copse of trees just beyond the inn.

If you aren't there in exactly three hours, I'm coming back to get you.''

"I'll be there," Velvet called out, making her way down the stairs. As soon as she was out of his sight, she gave in to the groan of pain she had held back until then. Sweet Lord, she hurt all over.

Mrs. McCurdy was busy washing a heavy iron skillet when Velvet walked into the kitchen.

"Good heavens, luv, ye look even worse than I thought."

"You heard—I-I mean, ye 'eard what 'appened last night?" Velvet asked, sliding into her thick Cockney accent.

Mrs. McCurdy nodded. "We all heard about it. Some of them soldiers was talking about the fella what come to help ye, but nobody seemed to know who he was." Her eyes suddenly twinkled. "Of course some of us got our notions."

The heavyset woman made a clucking sound and waddled toward Velvet like a mother hen appraising an injured chick. "They said they had to carry that big beefy sergeant out of here on a stretcher." She surveyed the dark purple bruises on Velvet's jaw and frowned. "Too bad the bloody sod was still breathin'."

Velvet didn't add that if Jason had had his way, he wouldn't have been.

"What can I do to 'elp ye?" Velvet asked, and Mrs. McCurdy's frown deepened.

"Ye don't plan on workin'?"

"I need the blunt, Mrs. McCurdy."

The stout woman sighed. "Me Betsy's just back from the village. She can wash the pots and pans. Ye can sit right here and I'll bring ye some tea towels to mend."

It wasn't much of a task. Velvet was grateful for the older woman's charity. They talked for a while, until Betsy arrived, a lovely red-haired girl about Velvet's same age with a bright, winning smile. They got on well and like her mother, Betsy was more than sympathetic, as were the other servants, most of whom eventually wandered in. By the end of the second hour, Velvet had eased the conversation in the direction she wanted.

"The man who helped me . . ." she casually mentioned, "he said he was here some years back . . . the night the old duke was murdered. He said he didn't much approve of the inn's clientele."

Mrs. McCurdy crowed. "I knew it were him—that handsome young squire what came in yesterday. He come once before to see me Betsy."

Velvet frowned. Jason hadn't mentioned Mrs. McCurdy's pretty red-haired daughter. "He was very gallant," she said, though the words came out a bit more grudgingly than they might have. "He risked himself to save me." The conversation moved forward, inch by inch, Velvet directing them little by little to the night of the old duke's murder.

"I think someone here saw what happened that night," she confided in low tones. "I think someone knows the young duke was innocent."

Betsy glanced both ways as if to be sure no one could hear, then leaned down close to her ear. "I saw it," she said. "I was only ten years old, but I saw this man climb the back stairs holdin' a pistol. I saw him point it through the window and fire." Thinking of it, Betsy shivered. "I was only a little girl but I won't never forget."

Velvet stood immobile. Inside her chest, her heart was hammering, pounding nearly through her chest. "Did you see who it was?"

Betsy blinked and glanced around. "It was *him*, the slimy toad. His grace, the duke of Carlyle. Only then he weren't no duke."

Velvet's knees nearly buckled beneath her. She dragged in a long slow breath of air, her heart thumping madly. She had done it—she had found a witness! She turned at the crack of a deep male voice booming through the open kitchen door.

"You're late," Jason thundered, his expression tight and drawn.

Velvet crossed to the place where he stood with his long legs angrily splayed and smiled into his scowling face. "I'm sorry. The hours slipped past more quickly than I imagined, but I think you'll agree that the time was well spent." She was smiling so brightly he said nothing more and didn't resist when she reached for his hand and led him into the kitchen.

"Lord Hawkins . . . there is someone I would like you to meet." She frowned, fighting a sudden, unwelcome surge of jealousy. "That is if the two of you haven't met already."

They had done it. They had actually succeeded in finding a person who had witnessed the murder. Though the girl had only been a child at the time, it was one more precious card in the deck Jason was stacking against his brother.

As he guided the phaeton along the lane returning them to London, he glanced down at the small figure sleeping against his shoulder. With tender care, he pulled the lap robe up to her chin and carefully tucked it around her to ward off the chill. In the watery gray sun seeping in between the clouds, he could see the dark purple bruises on her face, and anger rose inside him.

He knew only too well how she must be hurting. He blamed himself for it, yet if she hadn't come with him, Betsy McCurdy would never have been discovered. She would never have agreed to testify against his brother.

As it was, against her mother's wishes, with Velvet's gentle persuasion and Lord Hawkins's guarantee of safety, the girl had finally agreed.

"I have to, Mum," she'd said to her mother, sniffing to hold back tears. "I wish I had told someone then. For years I've felt so guilty. Lord Hawkins wants to clear the young duke's name and I mean to help him. I've a chance to tell the truth and this time I'm going to take it."

Perhaps she would only have to tell her story to the magistrates. Jason hoped so. But it eased his mind to know he could count on Betsy McCurdy, and he believed he could.

Velvet made a sound in her sleep and snuggled closer. Jason gently lifted a windblown strand of her burnished hair and tucked it behind an ear. She was small, not much bigger than a child, but she was so much woman. Even now, her face battered and bruised, her lip cut and swollen, he wanted her with a desperation close to obsession.

He had tried to stay away from her, to protect her from the lust he always felt when she was near, but so far it had been a losing battle. And she certainly didn't make things any easier.

Kiss me, Jason. I want you to do those things you said. Inwardly he groaned. God's breath, the woman set his blood on fire. She was a tempting little baggage with a passion to match his own. True, she was headstrong and a goodly bit of trouble.

But she was also brave and intelligent, as loyal a friend as he had ever known. A friend who had suffered gravely because of him. What was he to do with her now?

Jason admitted he wasn't really sure. By the time they returned to London, the papers would be ready for the release of Velvet's dowry. She would have the money she needed, and he had enough evidence to confront Celia Rollins.

He should move out of her town house, get away from her before he gave in to his lust again. But staying with Velvet had proved the perfect cover. A shy, bookish husband from Northumberland, a distant cousin that the ton was curious about but little more. Through Velvet and Lucien, he could follow Avery's movements. And living in her town house, he could keep an eye on her, as he had intended from the start. He didn't want to see her hurt again.

He would stay, Jason decided, his body already clenching to think of the nights he would have to spend in the room next to hers. It wouldn't be for long, he told himself. In a few more weeks, his goal would be attained—or he would be hanging from a tree on Tyburn Hill. Either way, his time with Velvet would soon be at an end.

Jason found himself oddly depressed by the notion.

Candlelight flickered on the lavender watered silk walls of the countess's bedchamber. The massive white and gilt canopied bed, draped in the same lavender silk, had been turned back in anticipation of his arrival.

Avery almost smiled. The woman was ridiculously transparent. Celia knew he had money again—vast sums at his disposal—and she wanted to win back his favor.

"It's been far too long . . . your grace." The low seductive voice came from the doorway of her luxurious marble dressing room at the opposite end of her bedchamber. "Avery, my darling, I've missed you."

She was wearing a sheer purple nightgown, a shade darker than the lavender silk walls. It set off the whiteness of her skin, the blackness of her hair, her ripe, succulent figure, and Avery began to grow hard.

Though he schooled his lust not to show, inwardly he admired her efforts and how skillfully she used them to gain the desired effect. But two could play games of seduction. He was tired of his insipid, unresponsive little wife. He was glad she had crept back out to her country house—his house now, he corrected. And Celia had always been a marvel in bed.

He arched a pale brow in her direction. "What's the matter, my dear? Densmore already flagging in his traces? Pity . . . I imagined the old boy would last a bit longer than he did." He pulled off his plum velvet tailcoat and tossed it over a nearby chair. "Then again, your voracious appetites have been known to emasculate the hardiest of men."

Her ruby lips drew together in a soft seductive pout. "You wound me, your grace." She floated toward him, a vision in her sheer, flowing gown, her bosom nearly spilling from the bodice. The sight of those ripe, creamy breasts made his shaft begin to throb.

"And even were it true," she continued, "I do not remember it ever being so with you."

Avery laughed lightly. "Such flattery, my dear. The likes of it should not go unrewarded." He moved toward her, meeting her at the foot of the bed, drawing her into his arms. He didn't bother to kiss her, just cupped each of her heavy breasts and began to upbraid the nipples. Celia gasped as he harshly tweaked the ends.

Her breathing quickened. She had always enjoyed rough play. Celia smiled as she helped him remove his silver brocade waistcoat. He tossed it away, then bent and kissed the smooth white skin at the base of her throat. The hands he placed on her shoulders urged her down on her knees and Celia instantly complied. She freed him, then smiled with satisfaction at the stiffness of his arousal.

"How shall I please you, your grace?" Her smile was lurid, full of promise. Her slender hand stroked up and down his sex. "I believe I know just the way."

Avery groaned as she took him into her mouth, her soft lips closing around him. Pleasure coursed through him at the feel of her tongue skimming over his rigid flesh. She wanted money. She would do whatever it took to ensure she got it. Still, she meant to end their love play in the simplest, most expedient manner.

He didn't intend to make it so easy.

Grabbing a handful of her hair, he pulled her away from his arousal, then began to remove the balance of his clothes. "We've all night, my dear. There is really no hurry—is there?"

A momentary pique flared in those lovely green eyes, then it was gone. He wondered which of her lovers she intended to meet after she had finished with him.

"No hurry at all . . . your grace."

A flicker of irritation trickled through him. There was something in the way she said his title, a slightly sarcastic edge. It had always secretly annoyed him. Tonight the bitch would pay.

"Get on the bed," he commanded and Celia instantly obeyed. Her mood was changing, her eyes beginning to gleam. She had sensed his anger and she knew what it meant. He would take her roughly, perhaps even cruelly. Her reluctance had turned to anticipation.

"Turn over onto your stomach," he told her, climbing up on the bed beside her. Rolling up a pillow, he stuffed it beneath her hips with a cool, malicious smile. He would take her Greek style. Celia never much favored that.

Satisfaction at the thought made his shaft rise up even more. Celia was conniving to get her hands on more of his money. All she would get was a good hard swiving, some aches and some bruises.

He imagined it would be the last time she welcomed him into her bed.

Silver clanked. A footman busied himself removing the breakfast dishes from the linen draped table in front of them. A teacup rattled noisily in its saucer as it was carted away. Outside the mullioned window a storm had begun to brew, thick clouds settling in, a heavy mist distorting the view of red peonies blooming out in the garden.

"Friday is Sir Wallace's funeral," Velvet said to Jason, who sat at the head of the long polished table. Her grandfather had eaten earlier and retired to the study to read, one of his favorite pastimes. "Do you think Mary will go?"

Jason glanced up from the *Morning Chronicle* he had been reading. "I hope not. Balfour will be hard-pressed to protect her if Avery demands she return with him to the city."

"Poor Mary."

"Aye, that she is, married to the likes of my murderous brother. Perhaps she has found a champion in Balfour. For Mary's sake I hope so."

"What will they do?"

" 'Tis hard to guess. If she is serious about ending her marriage, she can try to obtain some sort of dissolution. Unfortunately if, by some miracle, she should succeed, she would be a ruined woman. It seems unlikely that Balfour would offer marriage. If he did, Society would shun him as well. At any rate, with the power Avery commands as duke, odds are, such an action would never be granted."

"You are saying there is no hope for them?"

His sensuous mouth curved up. "If I am successful in my endeavors, there is every hope for them. However inadvertently, their destiny is now tied to mine. If Avery is proved guilty of my father's murder, he'll lose everything—perhaps even his life. Under those circumstances, if she isn't left a widow, an annulment would undoubtedly be granted."

And if you fail? Velvet did not have to ask the question.

"If I fail," he said as if she had actually spoken, "most

likely I'll be dead. Mary would have to flee the country in order to escape him.''

Velvet said nothing to that. Her chest felt tight to think of Jason dead. It suddenly hurt to breathe. "When will you speak to the countess?"

"I'm not certain. I have to be absolutely sure I can force her to tell the truth. If instead she should go to Avery, tell him I'm still alive, he'll do everything in his power to see I don't stay that way long."

Velvet made no comment, but her stomach felt leaden. Jason couldn't go to Celia until he was certain how she would respond. But Velvet could. Only that morning, she had sent a note to the countess asking if they might not reschedule their tea. A note had arrived in return, inviting her to come that very afternoon.

The bruises she still carried from her unfortunate encounter at the inn were nearly faded. She could disguise the faint yellow tint that remained with a bit of rice powder, as she had been doing, and be on her way.

At three o'clock, she would join the countess at her Hanover town house. Velvet would use the time to try and decipher the way the wind was blowing between Avery and the countess. With the duke's recent marriage and the death of his wealthy father-in-law, the subject would be an easy one to broach.

"Perhaps I could speak to her," Velvet said just to test the waters. "We've formed a tentative friendship. Perhaps I could discover—"

"No," he snapped. "I don't want you anywhere near that woman. 'Tis certain she feels not the slightest qualm about murder. God only knows what else she might be capable of doing."

An uneasy shiver ran through her. The woman was dangerous, of that there was no doubt.

"Stay away from her," Jason repeated. "When the time is right, I'll take care of Celia myself."

Velvet toyed with the napkin folded across her lap. Jason and Celia. He had loved her once. "Perhaps you look forward to the meeting. Perhaps you still find her attractive.''

His head whipped in her direction. The newspaper rattled
in his hands. ''I despise the woman. Beauty means little
when it is mired so deeply in evil. When I think of Celia
Rollins, I feel an overwhelming urge to wrap my hands
around her lovely white neck.''

Jason went back to reading his paper, his eyes mostly
hidden beneath the clear glass lenses he wore perched on
his fine straight nose. Noticing the brooding scowl that still
darkened his features, she shoved back her chair, rounded
the table, and walked up behind him. When she slid her
arms around his neck, bent and pressed a soft kiss on his
cheek, his startled blue gaze swung up to her face.

''Do not worry, my lord. One way or another, we will
find a way to convince her. Soon, the whole of England will
know you are innocent of any wrongdoing.''

He gently unwound himself from her hold, his grip implacable, though he did not hurt her. ''Hardly that, Velvet.
I am guilty of more misdeeds than I wish to recall. My
father's murder, however, is not among them.''

He picked up the paper and rose to his feet. ''Now, if
you will excuse me, I am off to see Litchfield. I won't be
home until late. Don't bother to wait supper. I'll get something to eat while I'm out.''

Velvet watched his tall retreating figure striding across
the room and out the door. He'd been polite but distant ever
since their return from the inn. She missed the hours they
had spent together, the comfort and warmth of sleeping beside him as she had that night at the inn.

Velvet sighed into the quiet of the empty room, lonely in
a way she had never been. Jason was determined to avoid
her, but today it was just as well. She had a date with Celia
Rollins. Perhaps she could learn something that would be
of help.

CHAPTER NINETEEN

∞

$\mathcal{J}$ ason climbed the iron steps into the carriage Litchfield had provided for his use while he was in the city, settled himself in the seat, and leaned back against the tufted leather squabs.

His meeting with Lucien had come to an end. They had gone over the evidence they had collected, but the word of a woman who had been a frightened child of ten, the written statement of a killer, and a financial agreement between Lady Brookhurst and his brother was hardly enough evidence to convict the reigning duke of Carlyle of his own father's murder.

Jason steepled his fingers, brooding over the problem, knowing what he had to do. Barnstable had uncovered nothing new. What they needed was a credible, reliable witness

What they needed was Celia Rollins—damn her black-hearted soul—to tell the bloody truth!

It was risky—damned risky—he knew, to approach her. But Celia was the key and time was running thin. There really was no other choice. Litchfield's place wasn't far from her town house near Hanover Square so he ordered the driver to head in that direction. Already tension rippled through him. What he planned was dangerous in the extreme, but in order to clear his name, he would have to take the chance. Somehow he would have to convince her he had enough evidence to convict her and Avery of the murder.

The coach rolled along toward its destination. Oblivious to the inkseller hawking his wares beneath a plane tree in the middle of the block and the beggar who was singing at the corner, Jason watched without seeing the city creep past. It wasn't until they reached St. George Street that he realized he had almost arrived at his destination. Speaking through the small opening beneath the driver's seat, he ordered the coachman to turn down the alley at the rear of the house, then signaled a halt in front of the stable.

"Wait for me here," he told the driver. "If someone comes, go round the block and I'll meet you on the street at the north entrance to the alley."

He would approach the house through the servant's entrance. If the coachy thought it odd, he didn't care. He wasn't about to give the woman notice he was coming. His resurrection from the grave would arrive with the same amount of warning he'd had of her treachery and betrayal.

Moving silently, making his way toward the back of the town house, he skirted the garden and headed for the small door at the rear of the house. Seeing no one, he pulled it open and silently stepped inside, then paused to listen for the sound of footfalls coming in his direction.

No noises. No servants roamed about. Jason remembered it was Celia's custom to dispense with unnecessary help when she anticipated some sort of intimate liaison. He wondered whom she awaited and hoped Celia's paramour wasn't already upstairs.

Voices traveled along the corridor leading down to the kitchen below, but the stairs leading upward were deserted. Making his way stealthily along the passage to her second story suite of rooms, he paused outside to listen, then quietly walked in.

He remembered her extravagant tastes, but not the clutter. Silver candelabra crowded cut crystal dishes. Dozens of ornate snuff boxes covered the entire top of an ivory inlaid table. There were gilt clocks, chiming clocks, featherwork friezes, cut paperwork, small Japanned vases—to say nothing of the larger pieces like the ornate clavichord she had shoved against the wall.

Apparently the lady's penchant for expensive baubles had grown in proportion to her sexual appetites, which over the last eight years were rumored to have risen to legendary extremes.

Quietly crossing the room, his footsteps silenced by the thick Oriental carpet, he made his way toward the bedchamber. He stopped at the door but hearing no voices or movement, pulled it open and walked in.

A soft gasp alerted him of a female presence and he turned toward the sound. Celia sat at a rosewood dressing table beside the door to her sienna marble dressing room, an extravagance she'd had built at great expense to her late lamented husband, the doddering earl of Brookhurst.

Her eyes took in his plain but well-tailored clothing then began a keen appraisal of his form. She hadn't yet realized who he was.

"What are you doing in here? Who gave you permission to enter my room?" She was gowned more simply than he might have expected, in a mint green taffeta day dress, something she might wear to a ladies' tea. But her straight black hair fell loose around her shoulders and her bosom nearly spilled from the top of the gown. He wondered again whom she was expecting.

He smiled grimly. "Hello, Celia."

Her eyes swung to his, clashed and held. She rose from her dressing stool as he walked closer, her hand sliding to the base of her long slender throat. "Jason! My God—is it really you?"

He wasn't wearing his glasses. No bagwig hid his hair. He knew she would know him. He wanted her to know who he was. He drew himself up to his full height, taller and nearly three stone heavier than he had been eight years ago. Intimidation was his game and he had learned to play it well.

His eyes remained locked with hers, icy cold and dark with determination. "It's been a long time, Countess."

"Dear God—it is you!"

The smile twisted, became almost brutal. "I'm afraid so, my love."

She cringed away from him, terror now in the eyes that clung to his. She whirled and tried to bolt past, but he caught her arm, halting her flight before it ever got started. With a firm grip on her shoulders, he forced her against the wall.

"Leaving so soon, my love? How disappointing. And here I thought you'd be overcome with joy to discover I'm still breathing."

Her gaze darted furtively toward the door. Celia moistened her full ruby lips, preparing for a scream.

"Don't even think about it. I doubt there is anyone around to hear you and even if there were, I doubt they would give the sound much credence, considering the sort of behavior that goes on in here on a fairly regular basis."

She tossed her head in a way he remembered, her fear receding since thus far he had not hurt her. "How would you know? You abandoned me, left me to whatever ruthless measures fate had in store. What right have you to condemn me?"

"*I* abandoned *you?*"

"That is correct. Obviously you escaped from prison without the slightest concern for what was happening to me. You left me to face the judges, to deal with Avery and the scandal the two of you created. You cared nothing at all for me while I was devastated with grief at the thought that you were dead."

Anger pumped through him, so fierce it made him dizzy. "You testified against me at the trial, remember? You verified Avery's story of the murder—or has that minor detail slipped your mind?"

She looked up at him through long black lashes, her red lips pouty and imploring. "I was confused. Everything happened so quickly. By the time I had sorted things out, they told me you were dead."

His hands bit into her shoulders. He wanted to shake her till her teeth rattled inside her empty head. "I am not a boy anymore, Celia. You can't make me believe your lies by batting your beautiful eyes or tempting me with the ripeness of your bosom. You and Avery planned my father's murder for months before it happened. I've come to insure the two of you pay for what you've done, and I have the evidence I need to do it.''

Shock and panic filled her deep green eyes. "What . . . what are you talking about? There is no proof. Your father's been dead eight years. What proof could you possibly have?"

"There was a witness, Celia. And the man Avery paid to kill me in prison has also come forward." His mouth twisted maliciously. "And of course there is the document Avery signed the day after the murder—blood money he agreed to pay to you for the rest of your miserable life."

"It isn't true, Jason!" She threw herself against him and began to bitterly weep. "I loved you. I've always loved you." Desperate green eyes pleaded through lashes spiked with tears. "I love you still."

Jason stared down from his considerable height above her. "Do you, Celia?"

"Yes—oh, Jason, yes! Truly, I do. You must believe me. I knew nothing of what your brother was planning. The night of the murder, I was frightened, terrified he would kill me, too. He said he would if I told anyone the truth. After the trial, I thought you were dead. The money was his insurance that I would keep my silence."

Jason worked a muscle in his jaw. How could the woman invent such outrageous tales when both of them knew exactly what had happened? Watching her now, he clamped down on an urge to strike her. He had never hit a woman before, but he itched to leave the imprint of his hand across her perfect cheek.

"So you were frightened," he taunted, "too terrified of my brother to tell the truth."

"Yes."

He ran a knuckle along her jaw. "But you'll tell the truth now, won't you, Celia? Because you know that if you don't, you will hang right alongside of Avery."

She swayed toward him, slid her arms around his neck and pressed her heavy breasts into his chest. Her nipples were rigid, he saw with a feeling of disgust. She was aroused by his anger. She wanted this tougher, stronger, unyielding version of himself that she had never seen. And she wanted the control over him that she had had before.

"Avery is an animal. I loathe the very sight of him." Her hand slid down to the front of his breeches. "It's you I love, Jason." She cupped his sex and began to stroke him, but his fingers caught her wrist and he pulled her hand away.

"Those days are past, Celia. At present, all I want from you is the truth. I intend to set up a meeting with the judges at Old Bailey. I'll send word of the date and time, then come for you myself. I'll expect you to tell them it was Avery who killed my father. You'll do that—won't you, Celia?"

When she hesitated, he squeezed hard on her wrist.

"I'll tell them."

"If you try to leave London, the judges will take that as a presumption of your guilt along with Avery's. If you try to warn my brother in any way, I'll see you pay equally for the crime he committed."

He gripped her arms, dragged her up on her toes, and shook her—hard. "Do you have the least doubt I mean what I say?"

Celia looked into eyes as icy as death itself, and a shiver of fear snaked through her. "No."

"Then I shall count on your unparalleled sense of self-preservation, Lady Brookhurst, to ensure you abide by your word." He started toward the door, then stopped and turned. "One more thing."

She wet her lips, which looked stiff and pale around the edges. "Yes, Jason?"

"Should you, for any reason, decide to cast your lot once more with Avery, it will not be a naive young duke you'll be facing but a man who will track you to the ends of the earth just to squeeze the life from your lovely, traitorous body." Turning, he stalked out of the room.

At the alley, he paused. His carriage was gone. He walked

to the corner, spotted the conveyance, and climbed in. At last, the tide was turning in his favor. With Celia to testify in his behalf, proving his innocence would be assured. His lands would be restored, his good name returned.

For the first time since he had returned to England, the tension drained away and relief trickled through him.

Then the carriage rounded the corner, rolling past the front of the town house. He spotted the Haversham crest on the door of Velvet's smart black coach, and tension knotted in his stomach once more.

Velvet had never been to Lady Brookhurst's town house. From the outside, the narrow structure in Hanover varied little from the others packed shoulder to shoulder along the tree-lined street. The inside of the house was another matter entirely.

The residence had been done in an elaborate French motif, the extravagant gilt and silk-upholstered furnishings interspersed with Oriental pieces that looked slightly out of skew in their surroundings. The resulting mix might have been bearable had there not been so much of it. As it was, except for a small open area in the middle of the drawing room, scant inches stood between the hodgepodge of expensive objects.

The butler quirked a busy gray eyebrow in Velvet's direction. "Her ladyship awaits you upstairs, Lady Hawkins. She wishes you to join her for tea in her private drawing room." He turned and started walking, expecting her to follow, his pointed nose stuck high in the air.

As she trailed him up the corridor, she noticed there appeared to be an odd lack of servants, just the butler and a serving maid moving through the empty halls downstairs.

The unease she'd felt when she had earlier left the house returned as she approached the door to the countess's private suite. When the butler opened the door to the drawing room, eyeing her with an air of disapproval, it settled like a cold stone in her stomach. It churned there, mixing with anticipation. Perhaps today she would uncover some scrap of information that would prove helpful to Jason.

Velvet sat down on an ivory brocaded sofa and surveyed the drawing room, as overdone and gaudy as the rooms downstairs. She fidgeted, trying to get comfortable in her stiff panniers, fiddled with her apricot embroidered silk gown, and wondered why the countess kept her waiting.

The door leading into Celia's bedchamber was firmly closed yet Velvet started at the sound that came from within. Furniture moving, the muted sound of voices. A scraping noise and something heavy hitting the floor. Dear heavens, what was going on in there?

On tiptoe, she crossed the carpet, straining to make out the dull mix of sounds coming from behind the thick wooden door. Moving closer, she pressed her ear against it, but the noises had abated.

Velvet chewed her lip, curiosity warring with concern. Perhaps the countess had fallen. Perhaps she had been injured. Perhaps she needed help. Steeling herself to the anger she might well face on the opposite side of the door, Velvet turned the silver knob and eased it open, then leaned forward and peered inside.

"Good sweet God!" The breath wedged in her chest at the sight of Celia Rollins sprawled across her huge canopied bed, her skin as pale as the sheets, her head bent back at an oddly canted angle. Velvet rushed toward her—just in time to see a man's tall figure moving out through the French doors onto the balcony. As large as he was, he traveled swiftly, climbing over the rail and making his way down the trellis. She raced to the window only to find he had disappeared behind the tall box hedges in the maize at the front of the garden.

Velvet gripped the bedpost, her breath coming fast now, harsh and erratic. She could see the countess wasn't breathing, that there wasn't the least rise and fall of her chest. A survey of her face, a glance at the deep green eyes staring in lifeless horror, the strangely bent angle of her head, and Velvet realized Celia's neck had been broken.

Great dark bruises were already forming, indentations of the deadly work done by a man's powerful hands.

Her hold on the bedpost grew tighter, her whole body shaking. Dear God—the countess had been murdered. And Velvet had seen the man who had done it. Who was he? Why had he killed her? Sweet Lord, what should she do?

Looking away from Celia's limp, twisted figure, she fought to gather her wits, to make herself think. Images of Jason rose in her mind, a tall man, dark-haired and incredibly strong. *I despise the woman,* he had said, had even mentioned a desire to get his hands around her *lovely white neck.*

Velvet shivered. The killer was as big as Jason, perhaps even larger, and his hair was dark, mayhap even black.

It couldn't have been Jason. Surely not. Jason would never have killed her. But the trembling worsened and her head felt so light she thought she might faint.

A noise at the door kept her standing. She turned in that direction and saw Jason's tall frame outlined in the opening. He stood rigid, unmoving, his blue eyes wide in an expression that mirrored disbelief. His face was as pale as her own.

"My God!" He strode into the room, not stopping till he reached the foot of the bed. "For the love of Christ, what has happened?" He stared a moment more at the limp and lifeless figure, then his gaze swung in Velvet's direction. He noticed the pallor of her cheeks, saw her sway unsteadily toward him, and caught her as her legs went limp beneath her.

If she swooned it was only for an instant. "I-I'm all right. I didn't mean to do that. I can stand on my own."

He just kept walking. "I'm taking you out of here. You can tell me what happened to Celia, then we'll figure out what we're going to do."

They didn't leave by the front stairs as she had expected. Instead Jason carried her down the servants' stairs at the rear. His carriage was waiting in the alley behind the stables. He loaded her aboard, then ordered the driver round front, stopping only long enough to send Velvet's coach back to the Haversham town house.

"How . . . how did you know where I was?" Velvet peered up at him from the seat beside him, but Jason didn't answer. He was staring out the window, his jaw set, lines of distress making him frown.

"Jason?"

He turned at the sound of his name, seemed to gather his concentration. "I'm sorry. You asked how I knew you were there." He scowled down the length of his nose. "I came here to see Celia. I hoped to convince her to tell the truth. I saw your carriage as I was leaving. I figured I had better go back and see what mischief you were up to."

His features looked strained, the skin taut across his cheeks. Turbulent blue eyes fixed on her face. "What happened, Velvet? What were you doing in there?"

Velvet leaned back against the seat of the carriage, which rattled along the crowded streets, the noise of the wheels absorbed by the rattle of carts and wagons, the thud of footman's boots carrying wealthy patrons in sedan chairs.

"Lady Brookhurst invited me to tea," Velvet said. "She promised to give me all the latest gossip on Avery's marriage. She thought that would interest me, since we were once betrothed."

A muscle jumped in his cheek. "Go on."

"When I got there, the butler said the countess wished me to join her for tea in her suite. I thought that rather odd, but since I was there for a purpose, it didn't really matter."

"So it was you she was waiting for. I thought she was planning a lover's tryst."

Velvet's cheeks grew warm with embarrassment. "I was wondering . . . it sounds rather silly, but is it possible . . . could Celia possibly have had those sorts of designs on me?"

Jason's hand slammed down on the windowsill. "God's blood, Velvet—I told you to stay away from her! The woman was completely depraved! The thought of you exposed to a creature like that makes my skin crawl. I can't imagine what the devil I ever saw in her. I can't believe I was ever fool enough to fall prey to a woman like that."

"She was very beautiful, Jason," Velvet said softly, unable to suppress an image of Celia's broken figure sprawled atop the bed.

He sighed heavily, raked back a lock of his thick dark hair. "Tell me the rest," he said.

Velvet took a steadying breath, neatly folded her hands in front of her. "I waited in her private drawing room, but Celia never appeared. Then I heard noises coming from her bedchamber. I opened the door and found her, lying on her bed, just as you saw her. That's when I saw the man—"

His head whipped around. "You saw him! You saw the man who killed her?"

"I got a glimpse of him, yes."

"And I suppose he also saw you."

Misery washed over her in long thick waves. She had been trying not to think of that. "Yes."

"I told you to stay away from her, dammit! I was afraid something would happen. Bloody hell, Velvet—don't you ever do a single thing I say?"

She straightened on the carriage seat, drew herself up. "Not when I have a chance to do something that might help you. I had to go, Jason, can't you see? I—" *Love you,* almost spilled out, but she clamped down on the words. "I wanted to help you. If Celia hadn't been killed, I might have discovered something useful."

Jason held her gaze for several long moments, then turned to stare back out the window, resting his head against the back of the seat. "It was Avery, wasn't it."

"No."

His gaze swung in her direction, darker now, intense. "If it wasn't my brother, then who? What did he look like?"

"In truth, he looked a great deal like you."

"Me! You think I am the one who killed her? Celia was the only hope I had of clearing my name. Why the devil—"

"I said he looked a lot like you. I didn't say it *was* you. His height and build were the same. He might have been bigger, thicker through the torso. His hair was as dark or darker than yours. I never saw his face.''

The muscles tightened beneath his dark brown coat. ''But you aren't sure, are you? You think I might have been the one who killed her.''

''You said you were there.''

''I decided it was time to face her. Time was running out. I hoped I could pressure her into telling the magistrates the truth.''

''And?''

''Celia agreed . . . not that it matters now.''

Velvet reached for his hand, felt the tension, the bitter frustration running through him. The muscles across his cheekbones stretched his dark skin taut. Thin lines etched his forehead.

''I know you didn't do it. If I'd had the least suspicion, it would have been allayed the moment I saw your face. There was no doubt you were as surprised to see her dead as I was. And even if that had not happened, I do not believe you are capable of murdering a defenseless woman.''

Something flashed in the depths of his eyes, the darkness that was constantly with him, a glimpse of something grim and forbidding she had seen in him before.

''You might be surprised, Velvet, what a man will do, under the right set of circumstances.'' He shook his head, moving a tendril of his hair, and some of the darkness faded. ''But, no, I didn't kill her. Avery might have arranged it. Perhaps he has learned I am alive and meant to ensure her silence, or perhaps he was simply tired of paying her off.''

''Or perhaps there is no connection at all. Perhaps she had other enemies that we know nothing about.''

Jason stared out the window. ''My instincts say no, that Avery is the man behind this. At any rate, the woman is dead and with her any chance I had of clearing my name.'' His shoulders seemed weighed down. His eyes had turned a dull bluish gray, bleak and defeated. ''To make matters worse, the killer has seen you. He knows that you can testify against him. There is every likelihood he will now come after you.''

Unconsciously, Velvet's fingers gripped his arm. "I'm frightened, Jason—for both of us. What are we going to do?''

"I won't let him hurt you. I promise you that. I'll hire men to guard the town house. I'll see that someone is with you whenever you go out.''

Velvet didn't argue. She hardly wished to end as Celia had done. "What about the murder? The butler must have found Lady Brookhurst by now—or if he hasn't he very soon will. He knows I was there. I shall have to report the murder, and it would probably be best done sooner than later.''

"Aye. You've no choice in the matter. As soon as we get back home, we'll send a messenger to the constable's office. We'll tell him you were frightened when you discovered Celia's body, that you rushed back to the town house, then sent word of the crime as quickly as you could.''

"Surely he'll want to speak to my husband. What should I do?''

"Tell him I'm gone. You can say I had business in Northumberland, that I won't be back for several more days. That should put him off for a while. If the man in charge of the case had no connection to my father's murder eight years ago, he won't know who I am and I'll be able to speak to him if that is what he wants. Otherwise, we'll cross the bridge when we come to it.''

Velvet still clutched his arm, his biceps so large both hands wouldn't wrap around it. He could have killed Celia, broken her neck as easily as snapping a twig. Yet she knew he was innocent, just as she had known he was not guilty of killing his father. Perhaps she was biased. She loved him, after all, more each passing day. But she believed in Jason Sinclair as she had from the start. His pain was her pain and seeing him now, she knew he was suffering.

"We'll find a way," she whispered softly. "I know we will. You can't give up, Jason, I won't let you.''

Penetrating blue eyes swung to her face. There was tenderness there and a world of regret. "I'm a lucky man, Velvet, to have been your husband even for a very short time." His hand brushed her cheek, lingered there a moment. Their arrival at her town house ended what else he might have said.

The tenderness fled his eyes as the carriage rolled to a halt and despair settled in once more. He had lost hope now and she couldn't let that happen. He didn't deserve to be punished for a crime he didn't commit. She wanted to help him, yet every moment he remained in England he was in danger.

A sharp pain throbbed under Velvet's breastbone. She loved him. She wanted him to stay with her, but in the end, unless he was dead, he was certain to leave. His mind was made up and she knew now how implacable he could be.

The pain dug deeper, twisted inside her. He would die or he would leave. Either way she was going to lose him.

Descending the iron steps of the carriage, she took the arm he offered and let him guide her toward the door of the house, but the ache remained, rose as a bitter lump in her throat.

Dear God, she was going to miss him.

CHAPTER TWENTY

∽

Sitting behind the desk in the study of his town house, Avery looked up from the papers he had been reading and motioned for Baccy Willard to come in. The big burly man approached with his battered tricorn firmly gripped in his big knobby hands.

"Well, man, is it done?"

Baccy swallowed, his Adam's apple stretching up and down. "I done it. I kilt her . . . just like you told me." He stared at a place on the wall above Avery's head. "You never said she was so pretty."

"Pretty?" Avery rudely grunted. "Pretty as one of those damnable India cobras. Good riddance to bad rubbish, I say." He shoved back his chair and stood up. "No one saw you? You got in and out without a problem?"

"I watched 'er for more'n three days. Today she let the servants go home early. It were a good time to see it done."

"Good thinking, Baccy."

He shuffled uneasily, shifting from one foot to the other.

"What's the matter?" Avery fiddled with the papers stacked on his desk, impatient now that he knew the task was completed.

"There were a woman. She come into the room just as I was leavin'."

"Did she see you?" Avery leaned over the desk.

"She seen me. Not me face, but she seen enough."

"God's teeth! We'll have to find out who it was, get rid of her before she has time to cause trouble."

"I know who it was."

"You do?"

He nodded his shaggy black head. "It were the girl what you was supposed to marry."

"Velvet? You aren't talking about Velvet Moran?"

"That were her."

"Good God, what would Velvet be doing with a woman like Celia?" Leaning even farther over the desk, sunlight glinted through the window onto his powdered blond hair. "You're certain it was she? You couldn't have been mistaken?"

"It were her."

Avery realized he was sweating. He didn't like the feel of it trickling down his sides beneath his linen shirt. "You've got to silence her, Baccy. Your life could be in danger." As well as his own. Velvet had been nosing about before, digging for information about his father's murder. If she had formed a friendship with Celia, there could only be one reason.

"Kill her," he commanded. "Get rid of her before she makes trouble."

Baccy shuffled his big feet. "I don't like killin' women. Specially pretty ones."

"Listen to me, you big oaf! You get rid of that girl before she opens her mouth and you are carted off to Tyburn Hill!"

Baccy looked sullen, his black brows pulling down until they met in the middle of his forehead.

"Go on," Avery urged. "Get it done and the sooner the better."

Baccy scowled then slowly nodded, his features dark with brooding resignation. Hanging was his secret fear. He would do what Avery said. Moving quickly for a man of his size, he lumbered to the door, then closed it carefully behind him. Avery stared at the place he had been, but his unease didn't lift as it usually did. What was Velvet after? Why was she seeking information about an eight-year-old murder?

If Baccy killed her, he would never find out.

Then again, once she was dead, it wouldn't really matter. Avery smiled with satisfaction and sank back down in his chair.

Picking up the final sheaf of papers needing the duke of Carlyle's signature, he dipped the quill into the ink bottle and scrolled his name across the bottom. Ink splashed carelessly on the pristine pages, but he didn't care. His carriage was waiting out in front, his trunks already packed and loaded. He was leaving London as soon as he was finished with this last bit of business, departing for his most recently acquired estate in East Sussex, the former home of Sir Wallace Stanton.

He had a funeral to attend.

Avery flashed a second satisfied smile, at his marriage to Mary Stanton and the death of her father, the most profitable endeavor he had undertaken in years.

Christian Sutherland stood at the bottom of the staircase leading up from the entry at Windmere. A drizzle had begun to fall outside the windows, the air chill and oppressive, the sky thick with dark spiraling clouds.

He glanced up at the sound of Mary's footfalls, slight, soft, padding steps approaching with a hint of trepidation.

"Mary . . ." His breath caught as it had begun to of late whenever she appeared, a slender, golden wraith, a childlike figure of loveliness he found more alluring than the most sought after courtesan.

His attraction to her had strengthened in the days since their arrival at the Haversham country home, hours spent in the gardens, or sharing a simple meal together before the hearth. He had found her sweetly honest and unfailingly sincere. Her shyness was endearing, and she was generous to a fault. More than that, she seemed to fit him, her softness in contrast to his strength, her gentle demeanor a buffer to his bold determination.

"I'm ready, Christian."

He took her hand, helped her descend the last of the stairs.

"Are you certain, Mary? Is there nothing I can say to dissuade you?"

"He was my father, Christian. I loved him. I must say my final farewells. I couldn't live with myself if I didn't."

Anger filtered through him, fury at Avery Sinclair. "If the duke is there, if he orders your return with him to London, there is no way I'll be able to protect you."

Her small frame trembled. Christian could feel the fear spinning through her. "I must go," she whispered. "Please don't be angry."

He was far beyond angry. He was livid with rage and frustration. Mary Stanton should have been his, not Carlyle's. She would have been treated with care and respect. Instead God only knew what suffering she might endure at the hands of the duke.

"If it hadn't been for you . . ." Her voice rose just above a whisper. ". . . If it weren't for these days we have shared—the courage you have lent me—I do not know what I might have done. But you are wise and you are strong, and some of that strength and wisdom now resides in me."

Her pale eyes grew luminous with tears. They shimmered on a fringe of golden lashes then spilled onto her cheeks. "I shall never forget you, Christian. Through all of the years of my life I will remember these special days that I have shared with you."

Something sharp knifed through him. "Mary . . ." He took her into his arms and sheltered her there, his chest aching with bitter regret and no small amount of fear for her. "My love, I am begging you. Please . . . say you will stay here where you are safe. In time, we will find a solution, some way out of this muddle Carlyle's treachery has immersed us all in. There is always a means if one is—"

"Do you love me, Christian?"

He cupped her face between his hands. "I care for you, Mary. You know how deeply I care."

He felt the faintest shake of her head. "It doesn't really matter. I am a ruined woman, no longer pure, not the sort of female a man like you would marry."

Christian gripped her arms. "That is not true. There is nothing Carlyle could do to make you anything less than you are—sweet and kind and innocent. Do not talk that way again."

Mary looked at him, sadness brimming in her eyes. "You are the strongest, bravest man I have ever known and I love you with all my heart. If you loved me in that same way, there is nothing I would not do so that we might be together."

"Mary, please. I am not a man who loves easily. My feelings for you are deep and irrevocable, but love? I do not know, and I will not lie to keep you."

Her throat constricted. More tears slid down her cheeks. "That is why I love you, Christian. And why I always will."

A knot formed in his chest. "Don't go, Mary, please."

"I must, my lord. Please don't make this harder than it is already."

He dragged in a harsh breath of air. If he loved her, perhaps she would stay, try to find a way for them to be together.

If he loved her.

But did he? He had never loved a woman. He wasn't sure he knew how. Perhaps he should have lied. Christian tossed the notion away. Whatever happened, it wouldn't be fair to Mary.

Setting his jaw against the pressure building inside him, he directed her into the carriage, settled her in the seat then sat down across from her, stretching his long legs out for the journey to her East Sussex home.

He wanted her there before the duke's arrival, wanted it to appear that she had been in residence all along. Christian would accompany her for most of the way, then send her on alone.

The thought made the tightness in his chest expand until his ribs seemed to press into his lungs. Somehow he would help her, he vowed. Somehow he would find a way.

* * *

It was dark outside, only a sliver of moon lit the empty London streets outside the Haversham town house. An occasional carriage, returning its occupants home, and the lonely hooting of the owl who had built its nest in the stable were the sounds that filled the chill night air.

It's over. After all these years, it has finally come to an end. He was weary, so unbelievably tired. Defeat hung like a shroud around his shoulders. In the silence of his bedchamber, Jason felt the walls of failure closing in, an implacable, invisible prison.

Only a single candle flickered in the room, the flame burning low, guttering in the pool of wax that had been building as the hours crept past. Sitting in a chair in the corner, his long legs sprawled in front of him, his hair unbound and hanging around his shoulders, he lifted the brandy decanter to his lips, taking a long pull of the soothing liquid straight from the bottle.

Tonight he needed the solace, needed to drive the demons of hatred away.

Not since the beginning, eight years ago, had they stalked him as they did this eve. Back then, when he had been thrown into prison, when he had been forced to endure the suffering, the pain and humiliation, he had done so for a single burning purpose—to see his brother pay.

Vows of vengeance had seen him through the torturous weeks aboard the inmate-crowded brig, days he was so seasick he slept in his own vomit, too weak to lift his head from the hammock he slept in, forced to drag in fetid air from the seven-inch space between him and the next odorous male body.

Hatred of his brother had given him the strength to survive blistering days in the fierce Georgia sun with little to eat and barely enough water to keep him alive, long days of backbreaking labor, fighting the bugs, the sweat, and the death that lurked in the malignant swamplands.

When he thought he couldn't go on, when he thought he would rather be dead than face another sunrise, thoughts of Avery living in Carlyle Hall, dining on pheasant and champagne while he ate weevily rice and watery soup made for fifty men from a single ox bone kept him going. Thoughts of Avery squandering the Carlyle fortune, of him destroying their father's good name, of him sleeping with the woman Jason had once believed he loved.

Determination was his ally, a need for revenge so strong just thinking about it could make him sick to his stomach.

Always he had believed he would win. Always. Tonight, in the shadows of his quiet room, he sat in the darkness facing the terrible certainty that Avery was going to be the victor. There wasn't enough proof to clear him. With Celia gone, he would have to leave England without the justice, the vengeance he so desperately wanted. If he didn't, sooner or later he would hang.

Then Avery would have won even that final, empty victory.

Jason took a long, steady pull on the bottle, scoffing at himself in the process. Who was he kidding? His brother had won years ago with his cruel betrayal. He had lost a part of himself during those terrible years in Georgia, in the days after his escape into the vicious swamplands, moving just ahead of the baying hounds. Days he was more animal than man.

Survival was all he lived for then, a will so strong it overrode all he ever was, any traces of decency still left inside him. It was during those final bleak days that he gave up any chance for the kind of life he'd led before, to be the man he was before.

Jason flicked a glance at the door, his thoughts turning to the woman in the room next to his, the petite dark-haired beauty, Velvet Moran. Velvet Sinclair, he corrected. His wife—for all intents and purposes save one. A true and bona fide, God-sanctioned marriage.

That he could not have—had sworn with an oath of blood he would never allow himself to have.

He took a drink of his brandy. Once he had wanted such a union, dreamed of children and home and sharing his life with a woman who belonged to him, as his father and mother had done. Those dreams died on the blood-soaked deck of a captured British barkentine, destroyed forever by a conscienceless act of violence and death that placed him among the vilest men who walked the earth.

Even as the thought occurred, images appeared, the echo of a cannon blast, the smell of gunpowder hanging in the air, the shrieks of the women dragged out onto the burning deck.

Jason shook his head, fighting the memories, the terrible images, his fingers tightening around the neck of the brandy decanter, the cut glass edges beginning to saw into his flesh.

With a force of will, he shoved the gruesome thoughts away, set the bottle on the floor, stood up, and began to peel off his clothes. Shedding his wrinkled tailcoat, then his waistcoat, he shrugged out of his white lawn shirt. He still wasn't drunk enough to sleep, but perhaps he would be able to rest a little. Even an hour would help. Whichever path his fate now took, he needed his wits about him if he intended to survive the days ahead.

Weariness and the brandy made his movements sluggish and awkward. He cursed when he brushed the edge of the table, tipping it sideways, and an untouched brandy snifter, placed there for his use, went crashing to the floor.

He cursed his bad luck, which seemed to mirror the events of the day, and barely had the will to bend down and pick up the pieces.

Velvet heard the splintering of glass in the room next to hers. Jason was still awake. But she had suspected as much. He was mired in depression at Celia's murder, certain his last hope for proving his innocence had died along with her.

Velvet had tried to cheer him at supper, had described in detail her meeting with the constable and relayed the news that the man seemed satisfied with her tale of the murder. The killer was a footpad, the constable was certain, intent on stealing the countess's jewels. They were safe for the moment, she had told Jason, but he had only nodded, excused himself, and retired upstairs to his room.

A few minutes later, a servant was summoned and a bottle of brandy sent up to his bedchamber. There had been no word from him since.

Listening now, the sound of Jason's movements carried through the wall between their rooms. Knowing she shouldn't, her heart throbbing softly in warning, Velvet swung her legs to the side of the bed, drew on her quilted wrapper, and walked to the door leading into his bedchamber. It wasn't locked. With Celia's murder so near at hand, Jason was worried about her safety. He wanted to be able to get in quickly if trouble arose.

Quietly lifting the latch, she opened the door and stepped in.

Long dark shadows filled the chamber, and the dim, yellow flicker of a candle burned low. Jason knelt beside a small piecrust table, facing away from her as he worked to pick up the broken shards of a brandy snifter, his sun-darkened torso burnished in the faint light of the candle. He was naked to the waist, she saw, wearing only his breeches and boots.

He straightened from his task at the sound of her approach and started to turn, but not before she saw the crisscross of jagged white scars that formed a vicious patchwork across his back.

A gasp escaped before she could stop it. Jason swore an oath, set the bits of broken glass down on the table, and started in her direction. "What do you want, Velvet. Did you ever think of knocking?"

Her bottom lip trembled. She felt sick to her stomach. "Y-your back. Dear God, Jason—what in heaven's name has happened to you? What have they done?"

He stiffened, stopped a few feet away and came no closer. His face looked hard, his features closed up and remote. "I was flogged. It happens to criminals, Velvet. I am not a particularly humble man. Taking orders was difficult for me, a man raised as heir to a duke. It took a while for them to break me, longer than most."

Her eyes filled with tears. How could she not have noticed? How could she not have guessed? Then again, they had only made love a few times and she had been too caught up in the things he was doing. Or perhaps he had simply been careful that she did not see.

Velvet closed the door with a soft thud behind her and made her way toward him across the room. Inside her chest, her heart thumped painfully, hurting for him, each breath tight with knots of pity.

"Turn around," she whispered and saw him bristle even more.

"It isn't pretty, Velvet. I hoped you would never have to see."

"Please, Jason." Her throat felt so thick, the ache there so harsh she could barely speak. "I want to see how badly they have hurt you."

His muscles quivered, strained with the tension that poured through his powerful body. She thought he might refuse, then slowly he moved, his shoulders straight as he turned so the candle shown on the deep grooves and ridges. They were lighter than his darkly tanned flesh, a maze of thin lines that crossed the heavy muscles, some deeper than others where the lash had cut more than once. Broad valleys of flesh had been ripped out in places then partially grown back only to be torn out again.

Her breath constricted, seared down her throat. Oh, dear God, the pain he had suffered. Tears stung her eyes, spilled in scalding droplets down her cheeks. She couldn't begin to imagine the torture, the relentless agony he must have endured. Her hand trembled as she lifted it toward his scarred and battered flesh. She rested it gently atop one of the grooves, bent and pressed her mouth against the taut brown skin.

She heard his hissed intake of breath, felt the muscles tighten. Twice more her mouth brushed his flesh as if she might take away the pain, banish the horrible anguish he had suffered.

He turned then, his eyes penetrating, dark with terrible memories, with anger that now seemed directed at her.

"I'm a criminal, Velvet. I tried to explain that, tried to make you see. I didn't kill my father, but I've committed other crimes, dozens of them, worse crimes even than murder."

"No . . ." It was a barely whispered word. Velvet shook her head. "It wasn't the same. You were innocent. You were fighting to save yourself. You didn't deserve what they did."

He gripped her shoulders, his fingers biting in, tight and unrelenting. "Why can't you see? Why is it so hard for you to understand?" He looked down at his scared left hand, made a fist that showed the back and held it close to the candle flame. "I got this while I was in Georgia. I stole money, Velvet—from a small parish church. I assaulted the vicar to get it, an old man who happened to get in my way. I was trying to escape the rice plantation that was my prison. I needed money to do it—I didn't care where I got it. When they caught me, they heated up a long length of iron and they branded me."

Velvet stood frozen. A scalding fire seemed to be building in her stomach. Dear sweet God!

He rubbed the melted web of skin on the back of his hand. "I was bigger by then and stronger than two smaller men. I was worth more alive, as convict labor, than I was dead— or they simply would have hanged me."

Her heart seemed to crumble. Pity for him choked her, nearly made her gag.

"When I finally escaped three years later, I held my hand over the flame of a candle to burn away the big *T* the men had put there. A big ugly *T*, Velvet. Everyone in Georgia knew the letter stood for Thief."

A sob escaped. "I can't bear it. I simply cannot." Velvet took the final step between them, slid her arms around his neck, and pressed her cheek against his shoulder, trying to absorb some of his pain.

Bitter sobs shook her. She felt his hand, tentative at first, then stroking gently down her back. "It's all right, Duchess. Those days are past. The scars don't hurt anymore."

Velvet only cried harder. Sweet God, how had he been able to bear it? How had he survived?

"It's all right," he whispered. "Please don't cry. I'm not worth your tears, Velvet. A man like me isn't worth it."

He had said something like that before. She pulled back to look at him, saw through a film of tears. "These aren't the only scars you carry, are they, Jason? The ones locked up inside, those are far worse. Tell me what you've done that is so terrible it has nearly destroyed you. Whatever it was, you had reason for it. You were fighting for your life, fighting to right the wrong that had been done to you. Tell me, Jason, let me share your awful burden and in time the pain will fade."

He only shook his head. Already the darkness had begun to appear in his eyes, to sweep across his features. "Don't ask that of me, Velvet. If you care for me at all, you won't ask me about it again." The turbulence in his expression betrayed an agony that ran soul deep. It was etched so sharply Velvet's heart twisted painfully inside her.

She wanted to hold him, comfort him. She wanted to take away the hurting, erase the terrible memories. "It's all right, Jason. You don't have to tell me anything you don't want to." She reached up to touch him, brushed an errant lock of his wavy dark hair back from his cheek.

Turning away, she began to unbutton her wrapper. It took longer than it should have with her fingers trembling so badly. Jason said nothing as she eased it off her shoulders and let it fall, nothing as she crossed to his big four-poster bed and drew back the covers.

He stood unmoving in the shadows, but she felt his eyes on her, a searing, glittering blue, dark with heat and his turbulent emotions. Ignoring the pulse beating hard inside her chest, the warmth beginning to run through her veins, she clasped the hem of her night rail and dragged it off over her head.

His gaze, a deep blazing blue, watched her toss it away and climb up in his big four-poster bed.

"Please . . ." Her fingers worked the single plait of her

hair, unbraiding it then loosening the strands. She spread it around her shoulders. "I need you, Jason, just as I know you need me. Make love to me this night. Help us both to forget, if only for a while."

Long moments passed. Jason said nothing. His heart was beating, slamming like a hammer in his chest. He stood rigid, almost afraid to move, staring at the girl who was no longer a girl because of him, at the woman he had married who wasn't really his wife.

He closed his eyes against the tempting sight she made lying there in his big bed, her luscious body naked atop the milk white sheets. Thick dark red hair framed her finely etched features and full pouty lips. Pale ripe breasts thrust upward, crested by soft pink nipples. In the light of the candle, a forbidden triangle of silky auburn hair nestled between her legs, challenging him to caress it.

"Come to bed, Jason." Golden brown eyes begged him not to refuse her again.

Already hard, his body throbbed with heat. Blood rushed to the stiff ridge of flesh pressing uncomfortably against the front of his tight-fitting breeches. He had tried to block his desire for her every day since they had left the inn. There were times he had actually succeeded. This night was not among them.

She ran a small hand in invitation over the vacant place beside her. "Neither of us can be sure what the future will bring. I need you to hold me, touch me, make me feel safe. Will you do that for me, Jason?"

His breathing quickened, came in shorter, faster cadence. His hunger grew with every heartbeat, fired by the glow of her skin, the uptilt of her breasts. He watched, her nipples hardened into tight little peaks against the chill that invaded the room, or perhaps it was the knowledge that he wanted her so badly.

His arousal strengthened, ached with every breath. He wanted to pull that tight little bud between his teeth, to suckle and tease until she writhed and begged him to take her. He wanted to rape that sweet mouth, to invade it with

his tongue. He wanted to spread those shapely legs, to fill
her with his hardness, to thrust into her until the lust he
constantly fought was finally sated.

"Jason . . . ?"

Christ's blood, he was only a man. And he needed her so
damned badly. With shaking hands, he reached toward the
buttons at the front of his breeches, popped the first one
loose and then the next, sat down and tugged off his boots.

Perhaps he would pay for his lust. Odds were he was
destined to burn in hell—what difference would one more
sin make in a life that was shadowed by more than he could
count?

He whispered her name as he sat down naked on the bed
beside her. "God, Duchess, I want you so damned much."

A soft smile touched her lips. Her eyes moved from his
face, spanned the width of his shoulders, moved across his
hair-roughened chest. Her hand skimmed over the flat slab
of muscle across his stomach, paused as her gaze traveled
down to the jutting ridge of his sex.

"You are so beautiful. So strong, Jason, so incredibly
male. Even the scars you carry cannot dim your beauty."

He found himself smiling at her sincerity. "I am supposed
to say something like that."

She looked up at him from beneath those thick black
lashes. "Do you think I am beautiful?"

"I think you are incredible." He kissed her then, taking
her mouth gently at first, though what he wanted was to
conquer, to claim, to possess the very essence of her. He
wanted to fuse his body with hers, to make her so much a
part of him that she would never forget him.

She kissed him back far less gently, demanding he show
her his strength, or perhaps merely sensing his need as she
so often seemed able to do. He groaned at the feel of her
small tongue sliding into his mouth, and his control slipped
badly.

His hands roamed over her body, felt the smoothness of
her skin, the sweet hills and valleys that marked her a
woman. He kissed his way down to her breasts, took one

into his mouth, tasted and caressed until she writhed beneath him. His hand found her softness. She was wet and hot. He stroked her deeply, felt her body beginning to tremble, felt her small hands gripping his shoulders.

"Jason," she whispered as he rose above her, parted her legs with his knee. "I need . . . I need . . ."

"It's all right, love, I've got what you need." He entered her in a single stroke, filling her completely, locking them both together. Their mating was swift and fierce, driven by long-denied passion, or perhaps desperation. Afterward they lay entwined.

He took her again just moments later, more slowly this time, almost gently, savoring the closeness, knowing it was wrong and yet the pleasure was so fierce, the joy so overwhelming he did not care.

He slept after that, the deepest, most trouble-free sleep he could remember. Tomorrow he would face the problems that remained, the worries about Velvet's safety and his own, make whatever painful decisions he must make.

Tonight there was only this one small woman and the kind of peace he hadn't known in years. The last thing he remembered was the pleasure he felt at having her curled in his arms.

CHAPTER
TWENTY-ONE

∞

It wasn't yet sunrise, but stark lines of gray crept over the horizon. Velvet had slept for a while, her body sated from their powerful lovemaking, but her mind could not rest.

Thoughts of Jason haunted her, images of the scars she had seen on his back, visions of the torture he must have endured. Sadness filled her, a bruising ache for Jason that throbbed deep down inside and would not end.

Until last night, she hadn't known how desperately she had come to love him. As the Haversham heiress, she had never really expected to fall in love. She believed she would know only the sort of feelings that came with an arranged marriage, had hoped at best to find a kind, indulgent husband with whom she could live a peaceful life.

She hadn't known these burning emotions existed, this yearning, wrenching, all-consuming attachment for another human being. She would love this man forever. She knew it as surely as she knew he would leave her—or that he would be killed.

She thought of the lovemaking they had shared. He had taken her fiercely, then with such exquisite care tears had surfaced in her eyes. Yet each time they reached their peak, Jason had withdrawn, pulled away from her to spill his seed outside her body.

He didn't want a child he would have to abandon. The

message could not have been clearer. It left a hollow emptiness inside.

He cared for her, but not enough to stay. He would leave, even if his innocence was somehow proven, his title and estates restored to his name. And he would not take her with him.

A bitter lump rose in her throat, but Velvet forced it down. What they shared could not last. Sooner or later she would lose him. It hurt to think of it—dear God, it hurt so much. She wished she could bury the love she felt for him, but she could not.

Instead she wanted desperately to help him.

As the sun began to lighten the gray horizon, Velvet vowed as she had before, that she would find a way.

Lucien Montaine tossed the *Morning Chronicle* onto the seat of the carriage. News of Celia's murder rose in big bold letters across the page. Lucien had known about it, of course. It was the talk of the ton, relayed with the speed of a Southwark fire. He had received a message from Jason as well, its tone dispirited, as his own spirits were at the news.

That, however, was yesterday. Today he had sent word to the Haversham town house requesting an audience with Lord and Lady Hawkins. Defeat was not his nature.

And he had come up with a plan.

"All right, Lucien, let's hear it." Closing the door to the drawing room, Jason eyed him through the clear glass spectacles he was now wearing. "Your step is far too jaunty. What are you up to, my friend?" He looked weary. Shadows shone like bruises below his deep blue eyes, but Velvet looked hopeful.

"Yes, my lord, please, if there is something you have learned, some news that might be useful—"

"I'm afraid I know nothing new. I truly wish I did. What I've come to propose is daring, and there is no small amount of danger, but at this point—"

Jason leaned forward, caught his shoulder. "If you've a

plan that might clear my name, the danger is of little consequence."

"I thought that would be your position."

"What is it, my lord?" Velvet asked. "What can we possibly do?"

Lucien eyed his companions, took a deep breath and dove in. "The way I see it, we've gathered some very good evidence against your brother, but unfortunately not enough to convict him. Celia's testimony could have done it, but she is dead. That leaves only one person."

Jason pulled the spectacles from his nose. "Avery? You think we can force my brother to tell the truth?"

"That isn't exactly what I had in mind. More likely we might be able to trick him into admitting the murder. If a magistrate happened to be present at the time, combined with the evidence we have already, it would surely be enough."

The haunted look faded from Jason's features. Even in his somber clothes and wearing the gray bagwig, he looked younger. Then he grinned. "You're a genius, Lucien."

"Yes, but we knew that all along."

Jason laughed. It was a rich, husky sound Lucien hadn't heard in far too long.

"How do we do it? When and where?"

"Easy, my impatient friend. It's going to take some planning and some time. We'll have to move carefully, make certain we think through every possible detail. A single wrong move and your life could be forfeit."

Velvet went pale.

Jason merely nodded. "We'll start today," he said, "hammer out a plan then try to find the faults in it. As you said, we don't want to move until we're certain the plan will work. On the other hand, the ton is breathing down Velvet's neck to meet her mysterious new husband. She's been holding them off by telling him I'm busy with business and traveling often out of town. But if we don't act soon, they'll be arriving in droves at the door just to get a look at me."

Lucien chuckled. "Then perhaps they shall . . . or at least

we will make them believe that they are about to."

"I'm sorry, my lord, I'm afraid I don't understand." Unconsciously, Velvet's hand came to rest on Jason's arm. Lucien noticed his friend did not pull away. "We can't possibly let all those people see him. Even dressed as he is and looking somewhat different than he used to, someone is sure to recognize him, recall who he is."

Lucien merely smiled. "You promised them a ball to introduce your shy, retiring new husband. We can't do that—but we can send the invitations." He cocked his head. "Let me see . . . the date will be set for . . . shall we say three weeks hence? That should hold them at bay for long enough to carry out our plans."

Velvet smiled brightly. "You really are a genius, Lucien." She looked radiant today, womanly in a way he hadn't seen her. He knew that look, the softly feminine countenance of a woman well-loved.

Jason had broken his promise not to take her. If he had, it wasn't something his friend had done lightly. That he desired her was obvious in every look he cast her way, but Lucien was sure there was more. Jason cared for Velvet. Lucien wondered just how strong his friend's feelings were.

And how badly Velvet would be hurt if Jason left England without her, as he was determined to do.

The fire popped and sizzled. An ember pinged against the hot metal grate. Outside the window, night had set in with an icy chill. Resting her embroidery on her lap, Velvet fidgeted in front of the fire in the drawing room. The weather was damp and a stiff wind whipped the branches of the trees, but inside the house wasn't cold anymore, not since Jason's arrival.

There was coal enough to keep the fires burning. The candles that now lit the room were fine beeswax tapers instead of the tallow she had been using these last desperate years.

She wasn't destitute anymore. Jason had returned her dowry, but even then he had not let her spend the money.

He had provided well in the time he had been there, playing the part of husband, at least in that respect.

In other ways, he was still the same remote, stubbornly determined man he had been before. He hadn't slept with her again. Last night she had been waiting upstairs when he finished his late-night meeting with Litchfield, hours spent working out more of the details of their plan.

Wearing a diaphanous pink silk gown that had been part of the trousseau meant for her marriage to Avery, she'd stood silently in the doorway, praying he would accept her blatant invitation.

Jason hadn't approached her, had merely stood in the middle of his bedchamber and simply shook his head.

"I am trying my damnedest, Velvet. If we keep making love, sooner or later there is going to be a babe. Sooner or later—" He paused midsentence, his eyes suddenly hard, piercing her with accusation. "Or perhaps that is exactly your intention. You think that if you are with child, then I will not leave. If that is your game, Duchess, you are sorely mistaken. A child would hasten my departure not deter it. I want nothing to do with a babe—mine or anyone else's. I made that clear from the start."

Her heart beat painfully. Most men wanted a child of their loins, a son to carry on his father's name. Why was it that Jason did not? Was it part of the dark secret he harbored? Velvet was sure that it was.

" 'Twas not my intention to trap you, my lord. If your care of me is not enough to keep you here, then I would rather that you leave."

Jason said nothing.

" 'Twas simply that I desired you." At least it was partly the truth. "You have taught me to enjoy the pleasure a man can give a woman. The last time we made love, you seemed to enjoy it as well. I thought perhaps . . ."

"You thought perhaps what, Duchess? That I would like to bed you again?" He crossed the room toward her, moving with his usual animal grace, stopping so close she could see the heavy pulse beating against the long muscles running down the side of his neck.

His eyes raked her, hunger evident in the dark glittering blue. "You are no fool, Velvet. You know how much I want you, that when I see you dressed as you are 'tis all I can do to keep from tearing off your flimsy garments and taking you right here." His hand came up to her cheek but he didn't touch her. Instead he let the hand fall away. "There is nothing I would rather do than bed you. I am asking you—as the friend you have become—to abide by the agreement we made."

A soft knot of despair rose up. He didn't love her but he had accepted her as his friend. And he trusted her, she knew. For a man like Jason, friendship and trust did not come easy, yet somehow she had earned both those things. The knowledge gave her an odd sort of comfort even as it forced an end to the desperate game she had been playing, the dangerous game of the heart that she had been hoping to win.

She cupped his cheek, felt the late-night bristles of beard along his jaw. "I will not trouble you again, my lord." She smiled sadly. "Sleep well, Jason." Then she turned and walked away.

Now as she sat alone by the fire, she couldn't help remembering, wondering at his secrets, wishing he trusted her enough to tell her what they were. Her grandfather's shuffling footfalls drew her attention to the door.

"I say, my dear, where is that handsome rogue you have married?" He walked into the drawing room, a leather-bound book in his thin, veined hand. "Thought I might entice him into a game of chess."

"He had a meeting with Litchfield," Velvet reminded him, though he had asked that same question less than an hour ago. "He won't be returning for some time yet."

"Yes, yes, that's right, Litchfield. Sorry, I seemed to have forgot."

She smiled at him with tenderness. "That's all right, Grandfather."

He scratched the thinning white hair on his head. "Seems

there was something else . . . something I was supposed to tell you.''

Unease trickled through her. ''What was it, Grandfather?'' Odds are he wouldn't recall. She hoped it was nothing important.

He snapped his fingers. ''A message! By jove, that's it! Remember now. Put it on the desk in the study. I'll just go and fetch it. Won't be a moment. Back in a trice.''

Velvet waited impatiently, toying with the embroidery in her lap but unable to concentrate on the delicate work required to fill in the complicated pattern.

The aging earl stuck his head through the door. ''Damned if I haven't forgot what I went after.''

''A message, Grandfather. You said you left it in the study. Why don't you wait here and—''

''Right! The message that came for your husband. Won't be a moment.'' He left mumbling under his breath. This time he returned with the note he had apparently received sometime that morning, a wax sealed message addressed to Lord Hawkins.

Velvet studied it only a moment, then tore it open with suddenly nervous hands. This wasn't the time to stand on formality. The message might be urgent.

Which was exactly the way it appeared.

Scanning the neatly folded paper, Velvet read the note then read it again. The words on the page were scrolled with great care, as if the writer had ordered them penned, not written them himself. The sender wanted a meeting, the message said. He had heard of his lordship's search for information regarding the murder of the duke of Carlyle eight years past. For a price, the information could be his.

Come to the alley beside the Swan and Crown. You will find it in the Strand, a block off Bury Lane. Ten o'clock— no later. Come alone.

Velvet bit her lip and her eyes strayed toward the tall polished ormalu clock that had barely escaped being sold with the rest of her family's possessions. Sweet Jesu! Already it was a quarter past nine and Jason might not return home for hours. He was meeting with Litchfield but she wasn't sure where. He was tired of being cooped up indoors and had mentioned that they might go out for a late-night supper.

"What is it, my dear?" Her grandfather's voice interrupted her thoughts. "You're looking a little bit piqued."

Velvet eyed the note in her hand. How had the sender discovered Lord Hawkins's interest? How had he known where to send the note? Perhaps Mr. Barnstable's investigation had alerted him. Or perhaps he was acquainted with someone at the Peregrine's Roost.

Whatever the case, it was obvious the man knew something. It could be information that was vitally important. If Jason didn't arrive to collect it, the man might disappear and they would never find him again.

"There is someone I must see, Grandfather. If Jason should come home before my return, give him the message. The note will tell him where I have gone." She pressed the paper into his frail, wrinkled hands. "Can you remember that, Grandfather?"

"Course I can."

But odds were he would forget. Perspiration dampened her temple. She thought about summoning the butler, but the fewer people who knew of this the safer for Jason. Besides, she would take along the man Barnstable had hired to watch the house and would probably be back long before Jason's return.

She glanced at the clock, heard the seconds ticking like a countdown to a deadly race. Whirling toward the door, she called for a footman to summon her carriage, then grabbed her hooded cloak and went to find the Runner standing guard outside the house.

Ten minutes later they were careening along the crowded streets, passing beneath the big painted signs suspended above them, making their way toward their destination. The Swan and Crown wasn't in the best part of town—far from it, but the man in the battered hat seated across from her was above average in height, sturdily built, and appeared as though he could defend them if trouble arose.

He stirred on the black leather seat. "I don't mean to speak out of turn, milady, but it's a bit late for a woman to be travelin' about, especially in this part o' town. I don't think your husband would approve."

Now there was an understatement if ever there was one. "I'm afraid I have no choice, Mr. Ludington." She smiled at him sweetly. "Besides, I am sure I am perfectly safe as long as I am with you."

Even in the dim light of the carriage she could see his chest puff out. "Aye, well, right ye are, I suppose, now that ye put it that way."

"And I shall only be a moment. As soon as I have concluded my business with the man I have come to meet then we can be on our way."

He didn't argue, just grunted and settled his thick body more solidly against the seat. Outside the carriage, a heavy mist had begun to drift over the muddy streets, but it was the odor that Velvet noticed, a sour, dead-fish smell rising up from the docks. The buildings along the dirt lane they traveled were soot-blackened, the windows often boarded up, and rubbish rose in piles against the crumbling brick walls.

Velvet shivered at the damp air seeping through her cloak, making her skin feel sticky and cold. She wasn't afraid, not exactly. But she was decidedly uneasy.

The sign for the Swan and Crown rose out of the mist ahead. "There it is!" Velvet rapped on the roof of the carriage then instructed the driver to pull over in front of the building on the left.

"I don't like this, milady. Your husband will be having me head if something should happen to ye."

"Nothing is going to happen, Mr. Ludington, not with you standing right here beside the carriage. I will simply shout for help if I find myself in need of assistance." She had told him nothing of the rendezvous, only that she had a bit of business in a rather disreputable part of town and needed him to accompany her.

"I'm not staying here," he said, hefting himself up off the seat. "I'll be comin' right along with ye. I wouldn't be doin' me duty, if I didn't."

Hiding a look of frustration, she accepted the man's rough hand and let him help her down from the carriage. "I understand you are trying to protect me, Mr. Ludington, but unfortunately, this is something I must do alone."

He stubbornly shook his head. "Your husband hired me to protect ye."

"That is correct, Mr. Ludington. My husband is paying your wages. If you wish to keep earning them, I suggest you follow his wife's wishes." That convoluted logic was undoubtedly the opposite of reality. Jason would be furious to discover she had gone—even with Ludington to accompany her. But what else could she do?

She pulled the hood of her cloak up over her head and picked up the small brass lantern she'd had the foresight to bring along. "I won't be long, sir. And you will be able to see the light from here."

He shifted uneasily, his eyes darting toward two drunken seamen staggering into the tavern. Velvet gave him a confident smile and no more time to argue, just turned and briskly made her way toward the alley beside the alehouse. Raucous singing, the music of a bawdy sea shanty, drifted out from inside the building, but the alley looked deserted. Except for a blind man, a beggar who sat in the shadows, a moth-eaten blanket pulled closely around him, she saw no sign of the man that she was supposed to meet.

Her unease built, stretched her nerves. She whirled at a noise in the darkness, saw the furry bodies of two big gray rats scurrying behind some empty boxes, and fought down a shiver of fear.

The crunch of gravel beneath a man's heavy boots sent a second shiver through her. She glanced toward the carriage, saw the vague outline of the Runner, but the fog was closing in and he seemed a long ways away.

"I-is anyone here?" she called out, heart thumping now, her fear growing with each rapid pulse. "I've come in the stead of Lord Hawkins. Please . . . if anyone is here . . .'' A shadow loomed above her, tall and heavy across the shoulders, dark and sinister in the swirling white mist.

Velvet cried out as a thick arm snaked around her shoulders and he dragged her hard against him. His hand came up, callused and blunt-fingered. She caught the glitter of a blade, felt the man's muscles tighten, screamed and tried to twist free, but his grip was a solid band of iron clamped around her.

She tried to scream, but his muscled forearm choked off the sound. With a flash of clarity, she realized the man who held her was the man who had killed Celia Rollins and that she was about to die.

''Sorry, miss,'' he mumbled with genuine regret, then the blade swept down, down in an arc toward her throat. Velvet closed her eyes against the moment of anticipated pain, but it never occurred. Instead, the arm was wrenched upward, away from her neck, as dear Mr. Ludington stepped into the fray.

With a grateful cry, Velvet twisted free of her huge attacker and slammed back against the wall, her feet going out from under her, tumbling her into the dirt of the alley. She scrambled to right herself, her heart pounding with fear for the stocky Bow Street Runner who was fighting so valiantly to save her.

''Run, milady! Save yourself while ye can!''

She wanted to, but she could not leave him to die. Instead she frantically searched the alley for a weapon, finally found a rusty curved length of iron that had once been part of a wheel and whirled it toward the huge man gripping poor Mr. Ludington by the neck.

The Runner was unconscious, she saw, already dead or very near to dying from lack of air. Saying a prayer for the strength she needed, she swung the heavy iron with all her might, catching their assailant hard across the ribs, and heard the satisfying crack of bone. A vicious curse erupted. Ludington's unconscious body slumped to the ground and Velvet nearly fainted as the huge man whirled and started toward her.

Hefting the heavy piece of iron, her hands trembling so badly she wasn't sure she could hold on, she faced him, certain she and the Runner were both going to die in this filthy, rat-infested alley. Instead the big man took two lumbering steps and froze. Staring over her head, he clenched his fists, swore something foul, turned and raced off down the alley the opposite way.

For several long seconds, Velvet just stood there clutching the rusty length of iron, shaking with fear and the first sweet stirrings of hope. It took a moment for her to recognize the echo of long, pounding strides slamming against the ground behind her, approaching at nearly a flat-out run. An instant later she recognized whose they were and spun with overwhelming relief toward the sound.

"Jason!" The coachman ran along beside him, carrying one of the carriage lanterns into the gloom of the alley, lighting the harsh set of Lord Hawkins's face. Jason raced past in pursuit of her attacker, halting some distance away, his dark gaze searching the thick, swirling mist that had swallowed the man as if he had never been there. Turning, he retraced his steps, stopping in front of her, his tall hard body just inches away.

In the glow of the lantern, the coachman knelt beside the Runner still sprawled on the ground, and Velvet heard Ludington groan.

"Is he all right?" Jason called out to the driver, never taking his eyes off Velvet's face.

"He'll be fine, your lordship. Just some nasty bumps and bruises. I'll help him back to her ladyship's carriage."

Jason merely nodded. In silence, he reached for the heavy piece of iron still clutched in Velvet's hand, pried it loose from her stiff, aching fingers. His eyes roamed her face, worry gouging lines across his forehead. "Are you all right?"

She nodded, her throat too tight to speak.

"What in the name of God did you think you were do-ing?"

Velvet didn't answer, couldn't force the words past her lips.

"You could have been killed, dammit! How could you do such a crazy thing?"

Tears collected. She still didn't speak.

"God, Duchess . . ." Jason's hand came up to her cheek. She noticed that it trembled "What am I going to do with you?"

Hold me, she wanted to say. *Please, Jason, I'm so frightened. Won't you please just hold me?*

But she didn't say the words. She didn't have to. With a low groan, Jason hauled her into his arms, cradling her tightly against him. "How could you be so reckless? How could you risk yourself that way?"

She sniffed to hold back her tears and sucked in a shaky breath. "There wasn't time to wait for you. I hoped the man would know something that could help you. I had to take the chance."

"You little fool," he said, but there was no harshness in the words and mixed with them was a thread of fear and something else she could not name. He held her a few minutes more, his heart beating nearly as hard as her own, then he eased her away and together they walked back toward his carriage.

She paused outside the door. "I guess Grandfather remembered to give you the message."

His hands came up to her shoulders, gripped them so hard she winced. "What if he hadn't, Velvet? Or if I had arrived a few minutes later? Do you realize you would probably be dead?" A sliver of moon slid out from behind a cloud. In the watery light Jason's face looked drawn and pale.

His words brought the ugly scene rushing back in and Velvet started trembling, her muscles turning rubbery and weak. Limp from the remnants of exhaustion and fear, she reached out to him, caught his arm to keep from falling, and heard his softly muttered curse.

Hard arms went around her, swept her deeper into the folds of her cloak and high against his chest. "God's blood, Duchess." Carrying her into the safety of his carriage, he settled her on his lap and held her protectively against him all the way home.

Velvet could feel the tension still running through him, the remnants of anger and fear he fought to control.

"I suppose it was a trap," she finally said, breaking into the silence.

His hold tightened nearly imperceptibly. "I suppose it was. I'm still not certain if it was meant for you or for me."

Velvet shifted, turned to look into his face. "It was the man who killed Celia so he must have been after me."

Jason shook his head. "The note was sent to me. If your grandfather had remembered to give it to me, I would have gone to the Swan and Crown instead of you. My brother must have sent the message. He probably discovered I'm still alive and set a trap for me."

"But it was the man who killed Lady Brookhurst—I'm sure of it."

"That's right. Undoubtedly my brother's henchman. It would appear he intends to see both of us dead."

Velvet said nothing, but an icy shiver ran through her. Turning her face into Jason's heavily muscled shoulder, she snuggled deeper into his arms, but this time even Lord Hawkins's powerful presence could not make her feel safe.

CHAPTER TWENTY-TWO

The day of Sir Wallace's funeral dawned windy and cold, flat gray clouds hanging over the small family plot on the hill above Stanton Manor.

The service itself was brief, a short memorial in the nearby parish church, not the flowery elaborate pageant in a London cathedral her father would have wanted. But Mary thought that in this Sir Wallace would forgive her. She wasn't up to facing the hundreds of members of the ton who would have been obliged to attend, now that his daughter was married to a duke.

Standing beside the grave, waiting for her father's ornate silver casket to be lowered into the earth, she thought of Avery with his carefully contrived, sympathetic expression, and his black satin armband, and the image brought a bitter taste to her mouth.

The duke of Carlyle felt no sympathy. And he certainly felt no remorse. Avery had done this—she knew it in the depths of her soul. The duke of Carlyle had murdered her father. He had no scruples, not a single ounce of compassion when it came to getting what he wanted.

Standing rigidly beside him, Mary fervently wished that she were her father's son instead of the weak, spineless woman she felt like in that moment. She wished she had the courage to plunge a knife into Avery's ruthless black heart.

The service came to an end and he reached over and pat-

ted her arm. "Come, my dear." His long, sad-faced countenance only heightened her loathing. " 'Tis time we left all
this sorrow behind and returned to the city."

Her stomach clenched, then rolled over. "I-I had thought
to stay here, your grace, at least for a little while longer."

Avery shook his silver-wigged head, moving the fat rolled
curls beside his ears. "Nonsense, my dear. 'Tis time you
returned. You've responsibilities, now that you are a duchess. Giving me an heir is one of them. It is well past the
time I planted my seed and got you heavy with child."

Mary nearly swooned. Avery's hold around her tightened
and the moment passed. "I am sorry, my lord. 'Tis merely
that I grieve so for my father. Can you not see your way to
leaving me here until the feelings pass?"

His mouth pursed with disapproval. "You'll go home
with your husband. That is the last I wish to hear on the
subject." Avery turned away from her, walked over to one
of Sir Wallace's closest friends, and began a discussion of
the profitable investments the man had helped her father
make over the years.

Mary watched them for a time, reading the distaste for
the duke her father's friend was obviously feeling. At last
she turned away and on legs that felt wooden, made her way
back to the house. Avery would be leaving that very afternoon. Now she would have to go with him. Christian had
warned her, but she wouldn't listen. Now she was paying
the price.

She wondered where the earl was and what he was doing,
wondered if he worried at least a little about her. His tall,
golden image appeared in her mind as plainly as if he stood
there, and tears burned behind her eyes. She knew it was
more than grief for her father that caused them to wash
down her cheeks.

Jason leaned over the sketch Lucien had made of a warehouse building the marquess owned on the London docks.
They had chosen the place as the meeting point for their
rendezvous with Avery.

"There is a small room here at the rear." Litchfield pointed toward the back of the building. "Avery won't be able to see it. We will position the magistrate inside the room. He can see through a small unobtrusive window and listen to what is being said without anyone knowing he is there."

"Have you spoken to him yet?" Jason asked. "He may not be all that eager to help." They were working in the study of the Haversham town house. Since the attack on Velvet outside the Swan and Crown, Jason had been loath to leave her.

"No, but he'll do it. He is somewhat in my debt for a favorable investment I suggested to him several years back. Thomas is a member of a card club I belong to. I plan to speak to him before the meeting tomorrow night."

"Are you certain we can trust him?"

"I believe him to be an honest man. I don't think we can trust him to know the truth of your identity, at least not until after Avery's confession. He would be duty bound to turn you in."

What if my brother doesn't confess? Jason was thinking. What if he doesn't admit to a bloody thing? But he didn't say the words out loud. Both of them knew the answer to that.

"If what happened last night is any indication," Jason continued, "we can be fairly sure my brother knows I'm still alive. He won't be particularly surprised to receive a message suggesting we meet."

"True. Unfortunately. Since it eliminates the element of surprise. It would have been better if he hadn't found out until we were ready. 'Tis certain the man would have been badly unnerved to see you in the flesh after all these years."

Jason mouth curved bitterly. "I'm sure it would."

"In any case, we shall have to rub on. We need the bastard's confession, and one way or another, we're going to get it."

Jason stroked the side of his jaw, feeling the slight rasp

of beard though he had shaved just that morning. "I wonder how he found out I was here."

A noise sounded a few feet away. "I'm still not certain he has." Velvet stood just inside the study door. Jason had been so lost in thought he hadn't heard her arrival.

"I'm afraid I don't follow," he said, his eyes running over her, an unexpected jolt of pleasure assaulting him at the sight of her.

" 'Tis simply that the more I think about what happened, the less I'm convinced your brother knows anything about you."

Jason scoffed. "He knew enough to damn near get you killed."

She walked farther into the room, her dark auburn hair pulled back in a simple knot at the nape of her neck, her apricot taffeta gown brushing gently against her ankles. He watched her and his body tightened with longing. He forced the unwanted response away.

"There is another possibility, you know," she said.

"Which is?" Lucien shifted his position beside the mantel.

"Which is that the note we received was real. There really is a man who saw something the night of the murder. He didn't reveal himself to me because he wanted to speak to Jason."

Jason frowned darkly. "And the presence of Celia's assassin—that was merely a coincidence, I presume."

"You know it was not. He was watching the town house, just as you expected him to do. When he saw me leave, he simply followed, hoping for a chance to do me in."

"Which he very nearly succeeded in doing," Jason reminded her with a scowl.

Lucien pushed away from the mantel, his long-limbed frame moving with elegant grace across the carpet. "You know, old friend, she may very well be correct. There is no reason for Avery to suspect your return from the dead. The countess might have told him before she died if Avery had been the one to kill her, but he sent his henchman instead.

I doubt if Celia would have said anything to him.''

Jason pondered that. He looked at Velvet and a hint of respect curved his lips. ''You never fail to amaze me, Duchess.'' To Lucien he said, ''I think in this the lady is correct. I shouldn't have jumped to conclusions. Unless my brother stumbled across the information by accident, he has no reason to suspect I'm still alive.''

Lucien's mouth curved up. ''Which puts the element of surprise back into our plan.''

''It also means there may be someone else out there who can help us,'' Velvet added. ''Someone who knows the truth. Perhaps he'll try to contact us again.''

''Perhaps,'' Lucien agreed. ''In the meantime, I'll finalize the details of our meeting and speak to Thomas Randall about it.''

''What will you say?'' Velvet asked.

''That I suspect the duke of Carlyle may be involved in a smuggling operation, that he may be using my empty warehouse for nefarious gain. I'll tell the magistrate I've arranged a meeting that could establish the duke's guilt and ask Randall to stand as a witness.''

Velvet smiled. ''Except that the crime Avery will be admitting to won't be smuggling, it will be murder.''

''If all goes well,'' Jason reminded them, his hands unconsciously balling into fists.

Velvet lightly touched his forearm. ''It will, Jason—it has to. You're innocent. It's beyond time people knew the truth.''

But Jason wasn't so sure. So much could happen. So much could still go wrong. Part of him wanted to forget the vengeance he had been seeking for so long, to return instead to his West Indies plantation and continue the simple life he had been living these past few years. But there was Velvet to consider. Until he found a way to stop Avery, her life would be in danger.

An image flashed of the night before, of Velvet in the darkened alley, of her terrified face, of deadly glittering steel. He closed his eyes against a vision of her lying in a spreading pool of blood, dead in the rat-infested alley.

His stomach tightened and the bile rose into his throat. In an instant the awful vision shifted and began to change. The pool of blood ran toward him, across the canted deck of a tall-masted ship. He could hear the women screaming, begging them to stop, begging someone to help them.

Jason braced his hand against the table to steady himself, to push the vision away, but the crimson pool kept spreading, forming a bloody pool at his feet. "No . . ." he whispered, but the screaming only grew louder. He tried to block the sounds, but the blood kept creeping toward him. He wanted to run, but he couldn't move. He had to escape. He had to—

"Jason? Jason, are you all right?"

Her soft voice filtered in, sweetly soothing. The crimson pool began to fade and the screams slowly retreated, withdrawing themselves into the back of his mind.

"Jason?" Her hand encircled his arm and he realized he was trembling. "Dearest, are you all right?"

The gentle endearment slid over him like a balm. He shook his head to clear it, found himself still standing in the study. The heat of embarrassment felt warm at the back of his neck. "Sorry. I was just . . . I didn't mean for that to happen."

"It's all right." She didn't press him to explain as he thought she would, just rose and placed a soft kiss on his cheek. "I'm sure you've just grown weary. You've accomplished what you meant to, and the marquess was just leaving."

He felt his friend's solid grip on his shoulder. "Get some rest. I'll take care of everything. As soon as the pieces are in place, we'll be ready to send word to your brother."

Jason just nodded. His thoughts were still in turmoil, the images of blood and death remained, making his worry for Velvet even stronger.

God's breath, if anything happened to her, the fault would be his, another sin added to a long, weighty list.

It was a thought too awful to even consider.

*   *   *

Christian Sutherland, sixth earl of Balfour, felt like a complete and utter fool. He was standing in the garden of the duke of Carlyle's town house, waiting in the shadows like a lovesick pup for a glimpse of Mary Sinclair.

It was the second night he had been there, lurking among the potted plants, hiding behind the geraniums, hoping to catch her attention and garner a moment alone. He knew she had returned to the city. She was in deep mourning for her father so she hadn't gone out, but the duke had made no secret that he had brought her home.

"The chit knows better than to gainsay me," he had said. "She does as I tell her, and a damned good thing. The girl has no love for the marriage bed, more's the pity, but I'll see she does her duty, and she had better not complain. A man needs a son, by God. A few days more to mourn her old man, then she'll spread her legs and be glad of it—until I'm sure she carries my seed."

Carlyle had made the remarks across a green baize table in the gaming parlor at Brook's.

It had taken Christian's full control not to hit him.

Instead he had wound up here, waiting like a fool in the garden, hoping no one would discover his presence, except, of course, for Mary.

Movement in a room upstairs. It was far too early for the duke to be home. Christian watched the flicker of a candle as it floated out of a bedchamber and down the stairs. The light disappeared for a moment, then reappeared in the library. Flattening himself against the wall outside the window, he peered into the interior and smiled with relief to see Mary.

Christian rapped lightly on the tall mullioned window and the candle lifted in that direction. Another soft tap. He stood away from the bushes, allowing her to see him. Recognition dawned. Mary's hand flew to the base of her throat then she hurried toward the window and threw it open.

"Christian? Whatever are you doing here? You must leave immediately, before someone sees you."

Instead he took her hand, urging her over the sill and out into the garden. "I-I'm not properly dressed. My hair is unbound. I-I must look a frightful mess."

Christian smiled. With her silver blond hair and pale blue eyes, she looked like a delicate angel. "You look beautiful."

Her hand relaxed in his and she let him lead her into the darkness and up the stairs of the gazebo at the far end of the garden. "What's wrong, Christian? Why have you come?"

"I had to see you, Mary. I had to be sure you were all right."

Mary glanced away. "I'm fine. The duke insisted I come back with him, just as you warned me. I should have listened to you, Christian."

"It isn't too late. We can go away just as I said. We can leave England, Mary. Start over somewhere else."

She looked at him with pale, sorrowful eyes. "You would give up all that you have? Your home? Your businesses? Your family? Why, Christian? Why would you do such a thing?"

His hand came up to her cheek. It was as soft as the down of a dove. "I've thought of nothing but you since the moment I left you. I love you, Mary. I was a fool not to see it. I love you and I want us to be together—no matter what it costs."

Her gentle blue eyes filled with tears. "I love you, Christian. More than my own life. And that is the reason I cannot go with you. Since I left Windmere, I've had time to think things over. Whatever Avery has done, I don't believe my life is in danger. I've no choice but to stay, to make the best of the life God has seen fit to give me."

Christian shook his head. "Mary . . ."

"Please, Christian. I am a married woman. There is nothing else I can do. In time, I shall learn to tolerate Avery and eventually there will be children. I can find solace in that."

"Your children would also be mine, if you would come with me."

She simply shook her head. "It is too late for us, Christian. I won't let you suffer for what the duke's greed and my father's mistaken intentions have done. I know what I must do."

A sharp pain rose in Christian's chest. He found it difficult to breathe. "Are you certain, Mary?"

She nodded. "It is better this way. At any rate, I would have made you a very poor wife. Avery has destroyed whatever passion I ever thought to feel for a man. I loathe the act of loving and always will. You deserve a better sort of woman than that."

His hand shook as he cupped her cheek. "That is what you think? That you have no passion?"

She tried to glance away, but Christian would not let her. Instead he turned her face to his and gently settled his mouth over hers.

It was a soft kiss, unbearably gentle, but Mary felt it like a warm, teasing wind through her body. His tongue slid along her lips, coaxing them apart, then slipping inside. He tasted her, urged her to taste him, and knowing she shouldn't, knowing it was the wickedest thing she had ever done, tentatively she did so. Christian eased her closer, tighter in his embrace, his hard body pressing the length of hers. He deepened the kiss, and she found herself clinging to his shoulders, swaying even closer against him.

His hand found her breast, but instead of a brutal squeeze, his fingers lightly brushed the side. He cupped the fullness and a soft sweet warmth unfurled in her stomach, began to seep through her limbs. It was incredible, so wonderful she found herself pressing more fully against the bands of muscle across his chest. It was Christian who pulled away.

"There is nothing wrong with you, Mary. Nothing gentleness and patience could not cure."

Her breath came in short, breathy little gasps. "I shouldn't have let you . . . I know it was wrong, but once you touched me, I didn't want you to stop."

Christian ran a hand through her hair. "I'll teach you

passion, Mary. Come away with me. Make a life with me somewhere else.''

She wanted to. Dear Lord, she had never wanted anything so badly. But Christian would be ruined. They both would be. They would have to give up their homes, the land of their birth, their families.

"I cannot, Christian." She pulled away from him and turned away, started down the stairs of the gazebo, stopped and looked back at him over her shoulder. Tears sparkled on her lashes. "Go on with your life, my love. Find a way to be happy."

Christian said nothing, just stood there in the darkness, his chest aching, his throat closed up. He would go on. He was that kind of man. Perhaps he would even find happiness of a sort.

But he would never love again, never risk the sort of pain he felt in losing his Mary. Christian knew that as certainly as he knew he would draw in the next breath of air.

CHAPTER TWENTY-THREE

∞

*V*elvet closed the door to her grandfather's bedchamber and started down the stairs. On the landing, she passed the thin graying butler coming up.

"Good morning, Snead, I'm looking for the earl. Have you perhaps chanced to see him?"

"Good morning, my lady. As a matter of fact I haven't seen him since he broke his fast."

"He isn't in his bedchamber, and I didn't see him in the study. I thought perhaps he might have gone out."

"I don't believe so, my lady. The carriage has not been summoned and both footmen are still here. He must be in the garden."

Velvet nodded. Her grandfather rarely went out and never without a footman to accompany him. His memory was far from reliable and he usually preferred reading or chess to spending time out of doors. She checked the garden, but he wasn't there. She checked the carriage house. Jason's borrowed coach was gone, but the Haversham carriage remained. She spoke to the groom and the coachy, but neither of them had seen the earl.

Beginning to worry, Velvet returned to the house and went downstairs to the kitchen. She spoke to the cook and several of the serving maids, but again found no trace of the earl.

"You still haven't found him, my lady?" Now even Snead looked worried.

"No, I—"

Just then the chambermaid called down from the upstairs rail. " 'E was with yer 'usband, milady. I seen 'em talkin' together this mornin'."

Velvet smiled, felt unweighted with relief. "Thank you, Velma." She turned to Snead. "I'm sure that's where he is. He has undoubtedly gone off with Lord Hawkins. Jason said he had some errands to run. I imagine he took the earl with him and simply forgot to mention it before he left."

The butler smiled. "I'm sure that is it. Shall I order you some breakfast, my lady?"

She sighed. "I suppose I might as well. Unless Grandfather tires, Jason won't be back until late afternoon." It was the first time he had left her since the attack, and at that he hadn't been happy about it.

"I've hired two extra men to watch the house," he'd said. "I'll leave Ludington inside and the others on guard front and rear."

"I'm sure I'll be fine."

He frowned. "Celia wasn't fine. Perhaps I should take you with me, keep an eye on you myself."

Velvet set a hand on her hip. "I should like nothing more than your company, my lord, but I refuse to let your brother frighten me in my own home."

Jason sighed with resignation. "Perhaps you're right. Besides, you are probably safer here. On top of which, I've a great deal to do and I'll be finished a lot faster if I'm not distracted." He gave her a wicked smile. "And you, my dear Duchess, can be very distracting."

She hadn't seen him again before he left, but as the afternoon wore on and she completed her long list of household duties, she almost wished she had gone with him.

At four o'clock, Jason came home, striding into the study with his usual purposeful strides, drawing her appreciative gaze to his tall, masculine figure.

"I see you survived without me," he said, but relief lightened the blue of his eyes.

"As did you, my lord. I presume my grandfather is also none the worse for wear."

"Your grandfather? How would I know how your grandfather has fared?"

The blood drained from her face. "I thought he was with you."

"Well, he isn't. I wouldn't have taken him along without telling you. Are you saying the earl is not here?"

Velvet moved unsteadily toward him. "H-he's been gone since this morning. Oh, Jason, where on earth could he be?"

"It'll be getting dark very soon. We had better get busy and find him. We'll start with the men on guard outside. Hopefully one of them saw him leave."

Velvet chewed her lip. "I should have thought of that."

"You would have if you hadn't believed he was with me."

Probably true. At any rate, the important thing was to find out where her grandfather had gone and bring him back where he belonged.

Jason took her hand. "Come on, love. We'll find him. I promise."

Velvet shoved down her worry and let him lead her toward the front door of the town house. As he predicted, one of the guards out in front had seen the old man leave.

"He came out right after you left, milord. Set off toward the square, he did. He were whistlin'. Looked like he knew where he was goin'."

Velvet gripped Jason's arm. "Even if he did know, he should have been home by now. Oh, Jason, we've got to find him!"

"We will, love. I've already summoned the carriage."

Thank God. With Jason in charge, some of her terror receded. At least it did until she remembered the man who had followed her to the tavern the last time she had left the house. *Oh, dear heavens, Grandfather!*

"You don't . . . you don't think anyone would hurt him?"

They were riding along in the carriage, searching the most likely paths he would have taken.

"You mean like one of my brother's henchmen? No. I don't see any reason to think he might be in that sort of danger."

Velvet chewed her lip. "Perhaps your brother doesn't need a reason. Or perhaps he has had Grandfather abducted in order to get to me."

"Or to me. We still don't know for sure he hasn't discovered I'm alive. I'd say it's possible my brother is involved, but until we exhaust all the other possibilities, I don't think we should become obsessed by the notion. The earl may have simply wandered away."

"He wouldn't do that. He never goes off by himself."

Jason gently squeezed her hand. "Memory loss like the earl's is common among people his age. I'm afraid it will continue to worsen. We can't know for certain what the earl might do."

But Velvet wasn't consoled. For the next four hours, they searched without stopping, throughout Mayfair into Piccadily, and on to St. James's, asking if anyone had seen him, searching for any sort of clue.

A man in Pall Mall thought he had seen the aging earl early that morning, and another man thought he had seen someone who fit the earl's description late in the afternoon. The search continued until both of them were exhausted and Velvet overwrought with worry and fear. At eleven o'clock, against her wishes, Jason ordered their return to the town house.

By midnight, Velvet was nearly inconsolable.

"Dear God, where could he be?" She paced the floor of the drawing room, her eyes fixed on the darkness outside the window.

"Unfortunately, he could be anywhere. He probably had money. Perhaps when it got dark, he had sense enough to let some sort of room."

"And what if he has been injured? What if even now he is lying in some gutter, beaten and hurting, wondering why

no one has come for him? Or worse than that, what if he
has been abducted? What if the man who attacked me—''

"Stop it!" Jason gripped her arms and brought her up
short. "Stop it right now. We don't know if anything re-
motely like that has occurred. Until we know exactly what
has happened, I'm not going to let you stand here and torture
yourself.''

Velvet's eyes filled with tears. "I'm so frightened. I have
to find him, Jason—I have to. My family is dead. My
mother and father are gone.'' She started crying and he
eased her into his arms. "He's all I have, Jason. He's all I
have.''

"We'll find him, Duchess. Please don't cry. I promised
you, remember? As soon as it's light, we'll start looking for
him again. Lucien will come, and I'll hire men to help us.''

Tears soaked his white lawn shirt but Velvet couldn't stop
crying. Her fingers curled into the lapels on his coat. "He's
always been so good to me. The earl is the only real family
I've ever had. Mama died when I was young. My father was
always gone. If it hadn't been for the earl, I don't know
what I would have done.''

He tilted her chin up, brushed a finger along her jaw.
"You would have endured. You would have been strong,
just as you've always been.''

Velvet shook her head. "I don't think so. The earl taught
me that. He gave me the courage to face the world head-
on. When my father died and we discovered he had lost all
of our money, Grandfather was the one who convinced me
I could save us.'' She looked up at him and tears rolled
down her cheeks. "You'll be gone, Jason. If the earl is gone,
too, I'll have no one. I'm not nearly as strong as you think.''

He pressed a soft kiss on her forehead. "You'll have me,
Velvet. Even if I'm not here, you can always count on me
to help you. If you ever need anything, all you'll have to
do is ask.''

Velvet stared up at him. "I need someone to love me,
Jason. Will you be able to give me that?''

Something flashed in his eyes, something painful and elu-

sive. Jason made no reply, only stood there and watched
her, a dozen unreadable emotions reflected in his face.

As the silence stretched between them, Velvet eased herself away. "Tomorrow will be a very long day," she said
on a shaky breath. "I suppose we should try—"

He stood up before she could finish. "Yes . . . I suppose
we should." Sliding an arm possessively around her waist,
he urged her out of the drawing room and up the stairs.
When they reached her bedchamber door, instead of leaving,
he followed her in. Wordlessly, he turned her around and
began to unfasten her gown.

"What . . . are you doing?"

He finished the last of the buttons and started on the laces
of her corset. "I'm taking you to bed. I'm your husband, at
least for the present. I can love you for as long as I'm here.
I'll try to be careful. If there are consequences we'll deal
with them later."

Heat washed through her. Her nipples puckered and tightened. "Do you want this, too?"

His eyes came to rest on her mouth. "I'm a man, Velvet.
I've wanted this from the moment I met you."

But she thought that if she hadn't lost her composure,
hadn't seemed so utterly lost, he wouldn't be here with her
now. "What about Grandfather?"

The line of his mouth seemed to soften. "The man you've
described wouldn't want you to worry. If you're in bed with
me, you'll be too busy to think about it." Giving her no
time to argue, he pulled the tabs on her panniers and tugged
the stiff whalebone cages down over her hips. He drew off
her chemise, set her on the bed and took off her shoes and
stockings. Pulling the pins from her hair, he spread the
heavy curls around her shoulders.

"Your turn. I think it's time you learned how to undress
a man."

The thought was delicious, but the chance to escape her
worries, to enjoy the pleasure he promised, warred with her
conscience. Grandfather might be in danger. Still, there was

nothing they could do until the morrow and she needed the solace Jason's lean hard body could provide.

Velvet smiled. "I've always enjoyed the challenge of learning something new." Moving closer, she eased his tail-coat off his thick-muscled shoulders, then began to work the buttons on his silver brocade waistcoat. It wasn't that easy. Not when his hands were skimming over her breasts, when his palms were squeezing her bottom, when his mouth was kissing the line of her jaw.

"I can't . . . I can't do this unless you stand still," she said breathlessly, her hands trembling with the hot sensations coursing through her.

Hungry blues eyes bored into her. "All right, Duchess, as you wish." Standing with his legs slightly braced apart, he let her remove his waistcoat and cravat, pull the studs out of his shirt, and strip the fabric off his shoulders. Brawny muscle gleamed in the candlelight, darkened by a thatch of curly brown chest hair. She ran her hands over his small flat nipples and watched as they firmed into buds. Everywhere she touched, hard muscle bunched and tightened.

"I'm glad you're enjoying yourself," he said, a gruff note tingeing his voice. "But I believe it is time you removed my boots."

She glanced up at him, saw the amusement—and the hunger—in the taut lines of his face. He sat down on the foot-stool, stretching his long legs out in front of him, and Velvet removed his tall black Hessians, then drew his stockings down over his muscled calves, enjoying the long lean sinews that connected ankle to knee.

Jason stood up when she had finished. "The breeches, Duchess. I believe those are next."

Velvet wet her lips. Her hands shook as she began to work the buttons at the front of his pants, his heavy arousal straining toward her touch. At his quick intake of breath, it occurred to her the power she held, and a wicked smile rose to her lips. Cupping the thick bulge of his sex, she gently squeezed and began to stroke him, felt the stiffness increase beneath her hand.

Jason's sensuous mouth curved faintly. "So you like being in charge, do you? I never doubted that you would." Jason caught her wrist. "But I think your eagerness might better be put to use somewhere else."

Velvet stood by as he stripped off the balance of his clothes then naked, carried her over to the bed. Several deep, feverish kisses followed, his tongue plunging in, his hands caressing her breasts, making her nipples tighten.

"Aye, Duchess," he teased between small soft kisses. "I thought you would enjoy being in command."

"No, I—"

But her words fell away as his big hands encircled her waist and he lifted her astride him. His fingers found her softness. He stroked her there, and heat rolled through her. She was wet and hot, aching for him when he lifted her again, bringing her down in one smooth motion, impaling her on his shaft.

"Aye,'tis well past the time you took charge. Tonight you will ride me for a change."

Spots of color rose in her cheeks. Velvet moistened her lips, slightly swollen from his kisses. Her body felt full and overly warm. Tentatively she moved, and the heat where they joined spiraled upward. She raised herself, then took him full length again, felt the heat pulsing, raised herself, felt the heat, and began a feverish rhythm.

"Sweet Jesu . . ." Jason groaned as she plunged herself down on him again and again, rocking sensuously, riding him in earnest now, enjoying the heat and the blossoming pleasure.

Enjoying the power she held.

Her dark auburn hair formed a curtain around them, blocking all save the glow of the candle. A harsh sound came from Jason's throat and she realized with satisfaction he was fighting for control.

"Good Christ," he muttered, reaching for her, gripping her bottom and driving himself upward to meet each of her impaling movements. A hot, pervading sweetness began to build. Velvet's head fell back, her hair teasing his groin, and release shattered through her. Beneath her, Jason stiffed, reaching his own release. He dragged her off him at the last possible moment, easing her down at his side, stroking a shaky hand through her hair.

They slept for a while, awakened and made love again, gently this time, making the most of their passion.

Though worry for her grandfather still hovered in the back of her mind, Velvet fell into a deep, drugging sleep. It was the rest he had promised to give her, the sleep she so desperately needed. Jason had kept his word.

Though Velvet lay quietly sleeping, Jason could not. He was worried about the earl. For whatever reason his brother might concoct, the old man might well be in danger. As soon as it was light, he would gather his forces and set out to find him. He prayed the old man wasn't another victim of his brother's greedy bloodlust.

Jason shifted beneath the sheet, then eased Velvet once more against his side. Her flame-dark hair spilled over his shoulder and several silky tendrils wrapped around his hand. He watched the rise and fall of her breathing and thought that he had never derived this kind of pleasure from a woman.

Perhaps he shouldn't have broken his pledge not to take her. But he would never forget the tears in her eyes when she had spoken of the earl. *He's all I have, Jason.* He had always thought of Velvet as unbreakable. As strong and resilient as a sapling in the wind. Now he realized no matter how strong she was, she was still a woman. Subject to a woman's fears, a woman's wants and needs.

What she needed was a man, someone to look after her. As long as he was her husband, he would have to be that man.

The decision was made. Their parting would be harder for it, but they would each survive, and in time they would forget each other.

And she would be better off without him.

That thought disturbed him in a way it hadn't before. He thought of Velvet's stubborness, her headstrong nature, her penchant for getting into trouble. The wrong man would want to break her. Might even abuse her. Avery would have. A weak man wouldn't understand her, wouldn't realize that for all her strength there were times she couldn't cope, times she needed the help and guidance of a husband she could love and respect.

It occurred to him that he was the sort of man who could handle her. She was strong, but so was he. Against all reason, she believed in him and that translated into respect. And he was beginning to understand her needs, just as she seemed to understand his. For a fleeting instant, the thought crossed his mind that he might take her with him when he returned to his plantation.

The notion was so sweet, so full of yearning a painful ache rose inside him.

Jason pushed the notion away. Even in the darkness, he could see the folly of his thinking. She respected him now because she didn't know the truth. Once she did, whatever she felt for him would disintegrate like ashes in the wind. Only bitter distaste would remain.

And sooner or later, there would be children. After what he had done, he could scarcely look upon a child without being riddled with guilt. How could he possibly have one of his own?

The fact was he had no choice but to leave her. No matter what he wanted, no matter what she believed she wanted, it would never work out between them.

Even if he was stupid enough to fall in love.

Velvet made a soft sound in her sleep, snuggled closer against him, and he brushed her lips with a tender kiss. Emotion and longing rose in his chest, and Jason felt the sharp sting of despair as he realized with sudden, absolute clarity, that falling in love with her was exactly what he had done.

CHAPTER
TWENTY-FOUR

∞

The sun shone well above the horizon when Velvet awakened the following morning. And she was in bed alone.

Worry for her grandfather rushed in. Scrambling out from beneath the satin counterpane, she grabbed her blue silk wrapper, yanked open the door, and raced out into the hallway, unmindful of her wild, unkempt hair, rosy cheeks, and overall recently bedded appearance.

Her terrible hours of worry turned to naught. For when she reached the top of the stairs, the aging earl of Haversham stood in the entry, dressed in yesterday's unkempt, wrinkled clothes.

"Grandfather!" Velvet raced headlong down the stairs, hurling herself into the old man's frail arms. "Dear God, where on earth have you been? What happened to you, Grandfather? We were worried sick."

Jason stepped in before the old man could answer. "The earl's had a long night, Velvet," he said gently. "I imagine he would like to bathe and change."

He looked weary and bedraggled. Pity formed a thick knot in her throat. "Yes," she said, forcing a note of brightness into her voice. "That is a capital idea."

The old man merely nodded, his shoulders sagging as she had rarely seen them. Snead appeared as if by magic to lead the aging earl away. It was all she could do not to follow them.

Instead she turned to Jason. "What happened? Where has he been?"

"At the bootmaker's shop in St. James's. With a man by the name of Elias Stone. Apparently Stone was working late when your grandfather arrived, unable to remember where he lived."

Velvet's heart constricted. Dear Lord, she had always dreaded this day.

"They gave him a place to sleep, searched out his residence this morning, and were good enough to see him safely returned." Jason's mouth curved up. "Since Mr. Stone refused compensation for his assistance, I have ordered six new pairs of boots for myself and a dozen pairs commissioned for you, my lady."

Velvet grinned at Jason and he smiled back. Then she released a sigh of relief. "Thank God your brother was not involved."

Jason's smile slid away. "No, not in this. We have finally discovered something of which the bastard is not guilty."

For that Velvet felt untold relief. By afternoon the household had settled back to normal and by nightfall, the earl's good humor was restored. By bedtime he had already forgotten his misadventure and the servants put on guard so another such happenstance was unlikely to occur.

But trouble had arisen from a totally different direction and Velvet was once more brooding and out of sorts. As soon as supper was ended, Jason approached where she sat in the drawing room.

He lifted her chin with his finger. "You should be dancing on the table instead of moping around, you know. Your grandfather came through unscathed, and my murderous brother's plans for our demise so far have been thwarted."

She gave him a smile that quickly slipped away. "Mary Sinclair has returned to the city. Apparently she has reconciled with the duke."

Jason frowned and leaned back against the sofa. "No one reconciles with my brother. He has commanded her presence and she has obeyed. Apparently Balfour was not prepared to throw caution to the wind and spirit her away.''

"Or Mary wouldn't go with him.''

Jason grunted. ''Then the lady is a fool.''

''Do you think that she is in danger?''

''Possibly. Probably not. My brother isn't crazy. He knows what he wants and he is simply ruthless enough to use any means at his disposal to get it. At present he wants an heir. He has a wife, so in his mind there is no problem to overcome.''

Velvet said nothing for the longest time. ''Mary is in love with Balfour.''

Jason's eyes swung to hers. ''Then perhaps that is the reason she remained with my brother. She is married to a duke. The scandal of her leaving would ruin Balfour. He would lose everything he has worked for. Perhaps she loves him enough that for his sake she is willing to give him up.''

There was something in his eyes. Something she hadn't seen there before. In some dark way it had something to do with her.

''I want to see her,'' Velvet said, ''discover if she is all right.''

''You know you can't do that. Your life would be in danger.''

''Surely the man wouldn't murder me in his own home.''

''Avery is unpredictable. God only knows what he might do.''

''But we aren't even sure he is the man behind Celia's death. Surely if Mr. Ludington accompanies me—''

Jason reached out and grabbed her arm. ''I said no. It's too dangerous for you to go there. I forbid you to go and for once in your damnable life you are going to obey me!''

Velvet swallowed hard. He had never spoken to her in quite that tone of voice. Perhaps in this he did know what was best.

She lowered her gaze. ''As you wish, my lord.''

A sleek dark brow arched up. Jason read her acquiescence, apparently believed she was telling the truth, and his hold on her gentled. ''Thank you.''

Surprise at his words, then a tentative smile touched her lips. "Will you stay with me tonight?"

Jason didn't hesitate. "Yes."

"For me or for you?"

"Because it's what both of us want. Now that I've accepted my failings, I've decided to stop trying to behave like a saint." He cocked his head toward the doorway. "I believe I know a remedy for brooding, my lady. 'Tis a slightly different version of the cure for worrying. Shall I show it to you?"

Velvet wet her lips, anticipation making her suddenly warm. "I believe I should like that."

Jason's vivid blue gaze ran over her, hot now and utterly disturbing. His eyes came to rest on the twin mounds rising above her bodice.

"Come," he said softly. "It is past the time for us to be abed." Resting a proprietary hand at her waist, he urged her forward and Velvet went with him, out the door and up the stairs.

"The plan is set then?" Jason paced toward Litchfield, who stood beside the mantel in the study.

"Yes. The magistrate has agreed. It is simply a matter of luring your brother into the trap."

"How have you planned to do that?" Velvet asked. She was seated on a comfortable leather divan sipping a cup of tea, but Jason could tell she was nervous.

"We shall send him a message," Litchfield told her. "We shall tell him we have uncovered information that will prove he is the man who killed the duke of Carlyle. We will offer to keep the information secret for the sum of ten thousand pounds."

"And you think he will believe that?"

"He'll believe it. Blackmail is the sort of thing Avery might attempt himself, under a similar set of circumstances. He'll believe there is someone willing to keep silent for a price. How he'll react to the threat we've posed is the unknown factor in the equation."

Velvet's teacup rattled. "I presume you expect him to arrive at the warehouse alone."

"I doubt he'll come by himself," Lucien countered. "For all his machinations, Avery is a coward. He'll probably bring one of his henchmen to protect him, but odds are he won't bring anyone else. He won't want to risk discovery, should the proof being offered be real."

Velvet set her nearly untouched cup of tea down on the table. "What if my theory is incorrect? What if he knows that Jason is still alive? What if he guesses that his brother is involved in this?"

Jason sighed. "Unfortunately, that is the rub. If he has somehow discovered my involvement, there is no telling what he might do."

Velvet rose and walked toward him, slid her arms around his waist and simply held him. "I'm frightened, Jason."

He kissed the top of her head. "It's all right to be afraid. The trick is not to let your fear deter you from your purpose."

"There is no doubt the plan is fraught with danger," Lucien agreed. "But if it works, Jason will be free."

Her tall dark husband touched a big hand to her cheek. "I have to take the risk, Velvet. For my father. For me. Time is running out."

"We'll take Barnstable and Ludington with us," Lucien added, "post them outside as guards. If they sense any sort of threat, anything at all, the men will signal and we will simply scuttle the plan and withdraw."

"I don't like it, Jason. Nothing is ever that simple."

Lucien walked toward them, his elegant strides carrying him gracefully in her direction. "Chin up, my lady. The plan is a good one. With Avery's overblown ego convincing him he is untouchable, we have every reason to believe our scheme will work. All we need is one slip, one indication that he is less than pure in regard to the murder. If we can keep him talking, he might very well incriminate himself. Combined with the evidence we have, it would be more than enough to clear Jason's name."

"That's right." Jason ran a finger along her jaw. "We have to push him, Velvet, goad him into telling at least a portion of the truth." He turned to his friend. "The meeting is set for tomorrow night?"

"The note is being delivered even as we speak. Tomorrow night at the docks, we shall discover if our plan will work."

Avery read the missive his footman had just delivered then read the note again. His fist slammed down on the top of the table. For all his careful planning, for all the time he had spent making certain he was safe, someone knew something about his father's murder. Damn and blast! He didn't need trouble like this.

Half an hour later he was ensconced in his study, seated behind his desk, Baccy Willard standing on the opposite side, his thick legs slightly splayed, knobby hands clasped in front of him.

Avery waved the message like a flag of infamy. "Eight years and I'm still not free of it. Whoever he is, the bastard has the gall to demand a meeting. Can you believe it? He says I'm to bring the money to an abandoned warehouse down on the docks. He says that I am to come alone."

"Ye oughtn't to go by yerself."

"I know that. Do you think I'm a fool?"

Baccy just stood there.

"I want to know who this man is. I want to know what he has discovered." He fanned the note, his mind spinning, pondering events that had occurred over the last few weeks. "That damned girl is involved in this—I can feel it. I don't believe for a second it is merely coincidence that just a few weeks before this note arrived, Velvet Moran was prowling about, trying to dig up information. Her friendship with Celia was too convenient, too timely. She was looking for something—but what? Why would she want to know about an eight-year-old murder? What would she possibly have to gain?"

"Maybe someone else wants to know."

Avery glanced up. Sometimes Baccy was a lot smarter than he looked. "Like who for instance?"

He shrugged his beefy shoulders. "I dunno. Maybe 'er new husband. Maybe he's the one who wants the money."

Avery shook his head. "The man is married to the Haversham heiress. He has no need of money." Suddenly he frowned, his mind whirling, picking up pieces, trying to fit them together. "What other reason would a person have, Baccy?"

The big man shrugged "I dunno."

"Revenge, that's what. Perhaps the man she married was a friend of my father's. Or perhaps a friend of my brother's. Or perhaps he's related, maybe even some by-blow of my father's I never knew about."

Baccy said nothing, but Avery came to his feet. "You've seen him. What does he look like?"

"Who?"

"Velvet's new husband. Who the devil have we just been talking about?"

"Oh." He shuffled one big foot. "Tall, I guess. Almost big as me. Brown hair." He glanced up. "He wears spectacles. But I seen his eyes that night in the alley. Blue eyes. The bluest eyes I ever seen."

The last words hit him like a blow to the stomach. "Blue eyes? The man she married has blue eyes?"

"Brighter than the sky. Like sapphires, they was. The bluest blue I ever seen."

Avery sank down in his chair. "No." He shook his head. "It isn't possible. There is no way it could possibly be him." Springing to his feet, he rounded the desk, stalked past Baccy and headed for the door. "Come with me."

Down one hallway after another, Baccy loping along in his wake. Avery led him into the Long Gallery past a row of family portraits to a painting that sat slightly off to one side. "Take a look at that, Baccy. Is that him?"

"Who?"

"Velvet's husband, you ninny. You said you saw him. Is that the man you saw?"

"That's you in the picture."

Avery ground his teeth, desperate to hold on to his temper. "Yes, that is me on the left. Take a look at the dark-haired boy. He'd be older now. A full-grown man nearing thirty. Imagine him taller, bigger. Is that him, Baccy. Is that the man you saw?"

Baccy took several steps closer to the portrait. Then he turned and grinned. "That's 'im, the man in the alley. It were foggy, but I seen him before at the house, and that night I seen him real good."

The big hulking bruiser could be wrong, of course, but something told Avery he wasn't. Turning, he stared once more at the painting, and suddenly he knew without the slightest doubt that the man he would confront in the warehouse was his supposedly long-dead brother.

Seconds passed. Baccy didn't move and Avery just stared at the portrait.

Then he smiled. "It's got to be him. It all fits together. The abduction, Velvet's hasty marriage—my brother always did have a way with the women." His lips curved. "The bastard's come back from the dead but he won't stay alive much longer."

"Who?" Baccy asked.

"My brother, you dunce!"

"Oh."

"He thinks he's got me, but the truth is I've got him. I was always smarter than he was." He chuckled without mirth. "I guess some things never change."

It was a quiet night on the quay. The sound of water-soaked planks slapped by a brackish sea cut through the moonless evening. The smell of dead fish and mildew rose into Jason's nostrils as he rode in the carriage with Ludington and Barnstable, making his way toward Lucien's abandoned warehouse.

Litchfield would be arriving with the magistrate, Thomas Randall. The marquess planned to take him directly to the empty office at the rear of the building without ever seeing the others. Lucien wasn't taking any chances Randall might recognize the man who was once the young duke of Carlyle, even though he had carried the title for only a few brief days before his supposed murder in Newgate prison.

Jason moved across the room and lit a half-burned white candle that sat atop a crate. He pulled his watch fob from his pocket and checked the time. Lucien was due to arrive in twenty minutes. Everything was set. Success or failure loomed just around the corner.

Now all they had to do was wait.

Velvet glanced up at the ornate grandfather clock in the drawing room. Only five minutes had passed since the last time she had looked. This was turning into the longest night of her life.

"I should have gone," she muttered, setting her embroidery aside with a sigh, then picking it back up and stabbing the needle determinedly through the fabric. "I should have made them take me with them."

"What's that, my dear? Did you say something?" The earl looked up from the book he was reading.

"No, Grandfather. I'm just . . . I'm just a bit out of sorts tonight."

He marked his place in the book he was reading. "Why don't you have Cook fix you a nice warm glass of milk then go on up to bed? That's what I like to do." He stood up from his chair and set the heavy leather volume on the pie-crust table. "As a matter of fact, I think I'll do just that— go on up to bed."

Velvet stood up, too. "I don't think my stomach is up to much of anything, but I'll fix a glass for you. I'll bring it up when it's ready." She crossed to where he stood, went up on her toes and kissed his frail cheek. "Sleep well, Grandfather."

He mumbled a sleepy good night, yawned, and left the drawing room, leaving Velvet alone with her turbulent thoughts. Good as her word, she started belowstairs to heat the milk, but Snead appeared as he so often did, and the task was accomplished for her.

At the butler's insistence, she drank a glass herself, but the usually soothing balm did nothing to calm her nerves. Instead they mounted with every heartbeat. When an insistent knock rapped at the door, Velvet nearly jumped out of her skin.

Snead appeared in the entry at the same time Velvet arrived. With a hand creeping up to her throat, where a rapid pulse pounded, she watched as he checked the peephole then drew back the bolt and pulled open the door.

Cloaked from head to foot, Mary Sinclair, reigning duchess of Carlyle, stood in the opening. "I-I'm sorry to bother you at such a late hour, but I . . . May I come in?"

With Jason gone to meet Avery, Velvet's worry soared to gigantic proportions. "Of course, your grace." She forced herself to stay calm. Snead removed the lady's hooded cloak, and in the light from the branch of candles on the marble-topped table, Mary's pale face and trembling lips did nothing to allay Velvet's fears.

"Lady Hawkins, may we be private? The matter I wish to speak of is urgent."

Oh, dear Lord. "Follow me. We can speak in the drawing room." Velvet turned to her as soon as the door was closed. "Tell me what has happened."

Mary wet her lips, which were tinged with blue and drawn thin with worry. "Your husband is in danger. I-I overheard them speaking in the Long Gallery yesterday afternoon—Avery and one of the men who works for him. At the time, I didn't understand enough to sort the matter out, not until I saw the two of them tonight, preparing to leave for some sort of meeting."

The fear in Velvet's stomach expanded into her chest. "Tell me what you know."

Mary clenched her hands. "Not enough, I'm afraid. Apparently the duke has discovered some sort of secret about your husband. I believe Avery is going to confront him and that Lord Hawkins is in danger."

The fear tightened now, clenched into an icy knot. Avery knew Jason was alive. God only knew what he planned. "I have to warn them." She glanced at the ornate clock. "Oh, dear Lord, there isn't enough time!"

"Perhaps there will be, if I go with you. My carriage is just outside."

Velvet paused only a moment. If Mary was discovered helping Jason, God only knew what price the duke might extract. But time was running out. Readying her carriage would take precious moments Velvet did not have.

"All right. Let's go. And pray we get there before it's too late."

The single white candle flickered on the empty crate. Jason flipped open the lid to his heavy gold pocket watch and tried to read the dial in the wavering yellow light. "He's late."

"Patience, my impatient friend," Lucien said from the shadows beside him. "Avery is playing cat and mouse. He intends to be the cat in this game and not the other way around. He is making certain the meeting place is safe."

Jason thought of Ludington and Barnstable, posted in the darkness across the street. If Avery spotted them, he wouldn't come inside and the game would be over before it got started. "Randall?"

"He's in position. And as ready as everyone else."

But the minutes ticked past and still the duke of Carlyle did not arrive.

Where the devil is he? Jason felt like pacing, but forced himself to stand still. Had his brother discovered the trap? Had he simply declined to come in the belief that the evidence implied in the note was false?

A shuffling sound drew his attention. Litchfield stepped farther back into the shadows as the sagging warehouse door swung open and Avery Sinclair walked into the eerie circle of light thrown by the candle.

For a moment he just stood there, an elegant slender figure cloaked in black, his pale face crowned by his queued-back golden hair. "All right, you bloody scum. I'm here, just as you asked. Now it's your turn. You'll have to show yourself, if you expect me to give you the money."

Jason stepped out of the shadows. The fear and shock he had hoped to witness on his brother's face never appeared, only a smug, satisfied smile.

"Ah, so it is you, dear brother. I thought so, but of course I couldn't be sure."

Jason tensed. Damnation. Avery had known all along. "You don't seem the least bit surprised. Considering the lengths you went to to be certain I was dead, I find that rather amazing. Then again, most of your brutal tactics have amazed me."

"Brutal tactics? What brutal tactics? As I recall, you are the murderer in this family. You are the one who was sentenced to hang."

"But you are the one who is guilty of the murder. Both of us know that. And now I have the evidence to prove it."

"Do you?" Avery's laugh rang with menace in the empty room. "I don't think you have the least chance of proving me guilty of a crime you committed."

Jason's muscles tightened even more. The surprise they had hoped for had failed them. Avery had guessed his brother was the man behind the note. Jason had known it could happen. They were praying it would not.

Lucien stepped out of the shadows, continuing to press for some misspoken word that might salvage the situation. "There was a witness, Carlyle. You may have known Jason was alive, but I'm sure you weren't counting on that."

Unease shifted across his features then it was gone. "If there is a witness, it is someone you have bribed to lie in my brother's defense." He smiled with malice. "If you had any real evidence you wouldn't have set up this meeting. You would have gone straight to the authorities."

Jason said nothing. His brother was right. Except in financial matters, no one had ever accused Avery of being stupid.

"Now that I think on it," Carlyle continued, "your witness magically appears—and my witness has conveniently been murdered.'' A noise sounded outside, a rumble of voices that began to build.

Jason glanced at Lucien. There had been no signal from Ludington or Barnstable to alert them. Avery must have discovered their presence and somehow silenced the pair.

''Let's go,'' Lucien commanded.

Jason nodded even as he started for the low door hidden in the shadows, the escape route they had provided.

''Leaving, gentlemen?'' Avery's voice cut across the room, reaching them just as Jason ducked his head and started through the opening. Avery laughed. ''I don't think so.''

''Jason!'' At the side of the building, Velvet stood in the dark beside Mary Sinclair. Both women were held captive by a pair of stout man's arms. ''It's a trap! Run, Jason! Run!''

But even her tear-filled warning could not save him from the small army of men that surrounded the building, constables and watchmen, men in Carlyle's pay.

''Stay right where you are!'' a voice of authority shouted from behind them.

Lucien shoved one of the men aside and Jason bolted in that direction, only to encounter half a dozen more a few feet ahead of him. He swung a solid blow to one man's jaw, kicked out at another, punched a man in the stomach and whirled to run. Three men blocked his path. Someone brought a thick oak club crashing down against the side of his head. Still he fought on. He battled a watchman, took on two more of his brother's henchmen, went down in a tangle of arms and legs, grunts and groans, and a shower of blows than battered him until he could no longer stand.

The last thing he remembered was the toe of a big black boot landing full force in his stomach, the painful cracking of his ribs, and Velvet's tearful sobbing.

''Jason!'' With a great burst of effort, she tore free of the man who held her and raced to the man on the ground. He was covered with blood, and lying in the dirt unconscious.

Heedless of the mud soaking into her skirts, she knelt beside him and carefully smoothed back his hair.

"He is innocent," she whispered, looking up at the constable and the magistrate who now joined them, tears running freely down her cheeks. "The duke is the man who is guilty of murder."

Thomas Randall looked hard at Lucien. "What is the meaning of this, Litchfield? I came here under the impression I was to stand witness to the unveiling of a crime. Instead I find you are in league with a man who was sentenced to hang for murder. Do you realize you are aiding and abetting a criminal? That in itself is a serious crime."

"I realize that, my lord." The marquess straightened to his rather imposing height. "Unfortunately, it was a chance I had to take. You see, Lord Randall, Lady Velvet and I have evidence that will prove without a doubt Jason Sinclair is innocent of the murder of his father."

A grumble of disbelief ran through the men.

"Then you should have come to my office with the information. You may do so at ten o'clock in the morning, at which time you may address your claim to the Crown court justices. In the meantime, the prisoner will remain in custody in Newgate prison."

A whimpering sound escaped Velvet's throat. Lord Randall turned a hard look on Jason, who had finally begun to stir.

"Take him away, men," he ordered, and Velvet was forced to stand by while they hauled Jason to his feet and dragged him away.

Lucien's hand came to rest on her shoulder. " 'Tisn't over yet," he said softly. "We shall hire the best barrister in London. Perhaps what we have will be enough."

Velvet shook her head. "You know it won't be. Not against a duke. And now you are also in danger." Velvet looked up at him. "Dear God, Lucien, they could throw you into prison along with Jason."

His hand squeezed gently. "Rest easy, love. I brought Thomas Randall into this, one of the most respected magistrates in the city. That in itself will show my sincerity. I don't think I am in danger. It is Jason we must watch out for.''

A thought occurred and Velvet's head snapped up. ''And Mary,'' she whispered, turning just in time to see the duke leading his errant wife back toward the ducal carriage. ''Sweet God, what will he do to her?''

Lucien frowned. ''I wish I knew. We can only pray that she is able to convince him she was worried for his safety as well as that of Lord Hawkins.''

Velvet looked over at Jason, whose arms were now tied behind his back. His face was bleeding and he winced with every step they forced him to make. With a harsh jab in the ribs and last rough shove, one of the men thrust him inside a waiting carriage. The door slammed closed and the vehicle lurched away. Velvet blinked back tears.

''Jason is telling the truth,'' she said, ''but no one will believe him.'' Her gaze swung to the ornate Carlyle carriage, just beginning to roll off down the street. ''And even to save herself, Mary Sinclair will not be able to lie.''

CHAPTER
TWENTY-FIVE

∞

It was a bluff, pure and simple. Velvet knew it and so did Litchfield. The evidence they had was questionable at best: the word of a serving maid who was only a child at the time, a murderer's sworn statement, a financial agreement tying the duke of Carlyle to the countess of Brookhurst, the sort of document that might mean any number of things, even the price of an expensive mistress.

It wasn't enough and both of them knew it. Still, along with the barrister they had hired, the Honorable Winston Parmenter, they made their way into a private chamber where they would face the six magistrates who sat as Crown court judges in cases involving a sentence of death. It was a large oak-paneled room, well lit by tall mullioned windows. The judges, fully robed and wearing long white periwigs, sat at a narrow wooden table while Jason sat alone at a table across from them, his face battered and bruised, one eye swollen nearly shut.

He didn't turn to face her when she walked in, just kept his vision trained straight ahead, looking neither right nor left. Velvet bit hard on her lip to keep the tears in her throat locked up inside, to keep from crying his name. She knew how much he needed her, though from his carefully controlled facade, no one else would know. Perhaps he didn't even know himself.

Dressed in an austere gray silk gown trimmed with black,

she tore her gaze away from his battered face and took a seat at a table next to Litchfield and the barrister. Parmenter, a tall, imposing man in his late thirties with brown hair graying at the temples and a brow that seemed furrowed a good deal of the time, took a moment to review his notes, then glanced up at her and gave her a confident smile.

The usual formalities were observed, then Thomas Randall, acting as chief magistrate, came straight to the point. "Let me start by reminding you all this is simply a hearing, a presentation of heretofore unknown evidence in a crime that was tried eight years ago. The charges in this matter are grave ones. Accusations made against a man as prominent as the duke of Carlyle are serious indeed. Coming from anyone other than a member of the nobility, a man whose reputation is as sterling as that of the marquess of Litchfield, they would not be given the slightest amount of credence."

He shuffled the sheaf of papers sitting on the heavy oak desk in front of him. "On the opposite end of the spectrum, the duke of Carlyle has accused his brother not only of the murder of his father, for which the prisoner has already been found guilty, but also the murder of the countess of Brookhurst."

Velvet gasped. Jason made a guttural sound in his throat. Beside her Litchfield tensed.

Good sweet God. Anger mixed with the fear coursing through her, making her almost dizzy. She didn't dare look at Jason, but turned instead to the marquess, who reached over and squeezed her hand.

The barrister came to his feet. "Charging my client with the murder of Lady Brookhurst is ridiculous, my lord. There are absolutely no grounds to believe the man who killed Celia Rollins was Jason Sinclair."

"According to the duke, there is. It seems there was a witness who saw the murderer leaving the countess's residence. He has asked that the lady be sworn in, that she give us a description of the man she saw leaving the scene of the murder."

Oh, dear God, they were speaking of her! Velvet thought she might actually faint.

"Surely you aren't referring to my client's wife," said the barrister, aware that Velvet's presence that day at the countess's mansion was a matter of record.

Avery spoke up from the corner, where he and the barrister who represented him had quietly taken a seat. "I am indeed referring to my brother's wife—if a wife is in truth what she is."

The implication was clear. Litchfield slammed his hand down on the table. Murmurs arose in the chamber, and the magistrate rapped his gavel.

"Here, here!"

"Your lordship, there is no reason to malign the lady's integrity," the barrister said calmly, which was apparently the reason for hiring such a man. "The marriage is a matter of record. We would certainly be willing to provide the necessary documentation, should the magistrates require it. However I do not see how my client's marriage is relevant one way or another at this time."

"Your point is well taken," said Thomas Randall. "The lady's testimony is all we seek."

Velvet shook her head. "No," she whispered. "I won't do it. They'll twist my words. They'll make it sound as though it was Jason I saw. I-I can't—"

"My lords—" Litchfield came to his feet. "The lady is obviously too distraught to give testimony. I remind you, as Mr. Parmenter has said, the man you accuse is her husband. Aside from that, she has already been questioned by the authorities. At the time the crime was committed, she described the man she saw to the constable who handled the case. Surely that is enough to satisfy the court."

Randall motioned toward one of the clerks. "Perhaps it is. I believe you have the notes Constable Wills was good enough to provide. Read the lady's description for us, if you please."

"Aye, your lordship." The stocky little clerk cleared his throat then began to read from the notes of Velvet's interview with the constable after the murder. " 'He was a tall man, powerfully built. He had long dark hair, unpowdered and tied back with a ribbon. I didn't see his face.' "

"No!" Velvet stood up from her chair. "It wasn't Jason! I would have known him! I would have recognized him!"

A gavel rapped for order. Another magistrate broke in. "You said yourself, my lady, that you did not see his face. Either you did, or you did not? Which is it?"

Velvet's heart nearly pounded through her chest. Lying would only make things worse. "I-I did not."

"Thank you. Please sit down."

She did as he commanded, her mouth gone dry, the rapping of the gavel still ringing in her ears.

"I remind you all," Thomas Randall said, "these proceedings are informal. The prisoner has already been sentenced. We are only here to deliberate what new evidence may have been gathered and decide if it is enough to alter the circumstances of the court's decision. Mr. Parmenter, you may proceed with your presentation."

Perched on the edge of her chair, her whole body trembling, Velvet watched in terrified silence as the scant bit of evidence they had gathered was presented to the six Crown court judges.

"If it please the court," Parmenter said, "the witness, Betsy McCurdy, will be arriving from the country with all haste. Her testimony will verify the claims being made and resolve any doubts the magistrates might have as to the villain in this case."

He went on with confidence and skill to present the balance of the evidence, but Velvet feared, as she knew Jason did, that it wouldn't be enough.

"I should like to ask a question of Lord Litchfield." One of the magistrates peered at him over the top of a gold-rimmed quizzing glass. "I should like to know why you did not come directly to Lord Randall with this information? What did you and the prisoner intend to accomplish by Lord Randall's presence at an empty warehouse?"

"We had hoped to gain the duke's confession, my lord.

It would have made your task all the simpler.''

Velvet glanced at Lucien. If uncertainty was what he was feeling, not a trace of it showed in the depths of his silvery eyes.

''Yes, it would have,'' said Randall. ''A confession coming from the prisoner would also simplify our task. Unfortunately, neither party seems willing to grant us that favor. Since that is the case, we must make our decision based on the evidence at hand.'' He looked down at his notes, then at Jason. ''Until such time as we have finished our deliberations, the prisoner will remain in custody at Newgate prison.'' He rapped the gavel.

Velvet's throat went tight. Newgate. Hell itself was reputed to be only the least bit worse. And he had already suffered so much.

The barrister rose to his feet. ''Please, your lordship. We should like to request special custody until the matter is resolved. The last time my client was thrown into jail, someone tried to kill him.''

Randall sighed. ''I am sorry, but the prisoner has already escaped his sentence once before. Since that is the case, the ruling of this court must stand. As soon as we have reached a decision, word will be sent to you.'' Another rap of the gavel and the men rose to their feet.

For the first time, Jason looked in Velvet's direction. The bitter resignation carved in his face made a tight knot squeeze in her chest. She started toward him, but the barrister blocked her way.

''I'm sorry, my lady. You cannot speak to him here, but you will be able to visit him as soon as he is settled.'' In prison, he meant. Dear Lord, she felt like she was living in a nightmare. ''You will want to pay the garnish, of course, and money enough to make certain he is comfortable.''

''Yes . . .'' Velvet said just above a whisper.

''I'll see to it, Velvet,'' Lucien said gently, taking her arm and beginning to guide her away. ''We'll do everything we can to see him properly settled.''

But it wouldn't be enough. Not unless they found a way

to save him. At the moment, only God seemed able to do that.

The gray stone wall pressed into his back. The dampness in the cell seeped through his white lawn shirt, clinging like a layer of film against his skin. A watery ray of sunlight trick-led into the cell next to his, but only the faintest trace reached his dirty straw pallet on the cold stone floor.

A rat skittered across the cell, making a scratchy, tapping noise with its tiny clawed feet. Fetid air wrapped around him, a mixture of sweaty, unwashed bodies and filthy, rot-ting clothes, the ripe smell of urine and feces, the rancid smell of sickness. He'd been led into the bowels of the prison, though Lucien had paid the garnish and demanded he be housed in the master's side instead of the common side of the prison.

But in Newgate, money only bent the rules as far as it pleased the guards. For the coin they'd been provided, they would move him, they said, in a few more hours, a larger, cleaner cell would be ready, and they would take him there. Of course hours might mean days, days might turn into weeks. In the meantime . . .

In the meantime, he would sit here in the darkness, in-haling the foul gutter smells, trying to ignore the dampness, the layers of slime on the stones beneath his feet.

Trying not to remember another time in this same fetid prison, a time that had nearly destroyed him.

And there were other memories he tried to avoid, at least in the beginning. Thoughts of Velvet, the woman who had invaded his life with such passion, invaded his bed, and finally his heart. Thoughts of her smile, her laughter, her courage in the face of danger. Her loyalty and trust. He tried not to think of the way it had felt to kiss her, to caress her beautiful breasts, the pleasure of being inside her. The way her small woman's body wrapped so tightly around him.

He didn't want to remember her, to make each minute, each second even more painful, now that he was alone.

But the darkness had come, pushing into his mind, suck-

ing him back into the agonizing past, back to the first time
he had been there. Back to the terrible years that followed.
The awful day in May when he had ceased to be a man and
become something far less human.

To keep the memories at bay, he gave in to his need for
Velvet and allowed his mind to concentrate on the days he
had spent with her, the laughter they had shared, the hours
of passion, the priceless gifts she had given him: her innocence, her friendship, her unfailing loyalty and support.

For a while, he was able to keep the darkness away, keep
from remembering the blood and the death and the agonized
screams. In the end, the fetid odors, the filth and the blackness in the cell began to steal his will and thoughts of Velvet
slipped away.

The long tunnel of darkness dragged him in, burying him
in the past, leaving him alone with his demons. Ugliness
and despair sucked him down, wrapping him in tentacles of
misery, and this time they would not go away.

She had to see him. Not in the morning, when Lucien
planned to take her. Not tomorrow. Not the day after that.
She needed to see him tonight. Now. No matter what anyone
said.

Velvet dressed hurriedly, wearing the plain brown woolen
skirt and simple cotton blouse she had worn at the Peregrine's Roost, sturdy shoes, and a serviceable hooded cloak.
The Haversham carriage was ready and waiting out in front.
Ignoring Snead's worried expression, Velvet went out the
door, down the front porch stairs, and settled herself in the
shadowy interior. Mr. Ludington sat in the darkness across
from her. He and Mr. Barnstable both sported lumps and
bruises from their encounter with Avery's men.

Surprisingly, even fully aware for the first time of Jason's
true circumstances, both had remained steadfast in their support, certain the man who fought so valiantly to prove his
innocence—and to protect the people in his care—couldn't
be guilty of murder.

The big Runner shifted against the seat, uncomfortable in

the lavish, red velvet interior of the carriage. "Are ye sure ye want to do this, milady? 'Twould be safer for ye to wait for his lordship to come for ye in the morning."

"My husband needs me. Something is wrong. I can feel it. I can't wait until morning."

Ludington made no reply. Something was wrong—there was no doubt of that. The lady's husband was about to be hanged. He wished there was something he could do to change things. Since his efforts so far had done not an ounce of good, seeing the lady safe to Newgate was surely not too much to ask.

The carriage rolled through the darkened streets, the clatter of the city growing louder as they neared the prison. Ragmen and coal sellers, chimney sweeps and beggars crowded the lanes and alleys along the way. Gutter smells drifted through the windows of the carriage, the sound of street criers hawking their wares. They passed beneath the big swinging signs of gin shops and alehouses and finally reached the prison.

Ludington helped Velvet down from the carriage, surprised when she caught his arm, rested her hand near his elbow. He must have felt it trembling and realized she needed his support for he straightened, drawing himself up, then walked her protectively to the deputy warden's office.

Money changed hands, a goodly sum, even more than she had expected. It didn't matter. She'd been prepared to pay whatever amount it required to accomplish the purpose she had come for. She left with the warden's promise—ensured by the lure of even more golden guineas—that a new cell would be readied and Jason moved by morning. Then she and Mr. Ludington were shown through a heavy wooden door that led into the bowels of the prison.

A fat, bearded jailer carrying a smoky lantern led the way. Even from a distance, she could smell his ripe, unwashed odor, the sweat and the filth on his clothes. It mingled with the rancid stench around her, making her stomach roll. As they descended the dark stone passageway, the walls slick with mold, and damp against her cloak, she found she could no longer separate the smells.

The vilest dregs of humanity crouched in the cells they passed along the way. The bile rose in Velvet's throat at the bawdy remarks her appearance garnered, the clawlike fingers reaching out to her through the bars, the moans of the sick and dying. Her hand grew tighter on Ludington's arm, but she kept on walking, forcing herself to look straight ahead, not to think about the pitiful wretches living in a place far worse than any St. Giles gutter.

She was shaking by the time she reached the door to Jason's cell, and not from the icy chill that swept down the passage.

" 'Ere ye are, miss." The fat man stuck a long iron skeleton key into the heavy lock and the metal made a tortured grating sound. He reached for a small white tallow candle that sat beside the door, lit it, and passed it over to her. "Ye've an hour with the prisoner, no more."

Velvet nodded, accepting the candle with unsteady hands. "Thank you."

Ludington stepped up beside her. "I'll be right here, milady. Right outside the door. Ye just call out if ye need me."

She forced a smile. "I'll be fine." But she wasn't fine. She was sick with despair at the thought of Jason being held in a place like this. And that it had happened before. For the first time, she understood the roots of the pain that ate at his tortured soul.

Oh, beloved, if only I could have saved you from this, she thought, wishing there was something she could do to free him, vowing as she had a dozen times that she would find a way.

Steeling herself, taking a breath of the fetid air in an effort to bolster her courage, Velvet stepped into the darkened cell. The key grated as the guard locked her in.

"Jason?" Wondering why he hadn't come forward, she lifted the candle to search the room. "Jason, it's Velvet, where are you?"

Still no answer. A scuffling noise, then tiny clawed feet

skittered across the slick stone floor. Velvet bit hard on her lip to stifle a scream. Only a rat. The least of her worries down here. She pointed the light toward a distant corner. Where was he? Had the guard mistaken the cell?

Then she saw him, sitting on the floor, a heavy iron manacle chaining his ankle to the wall. His eyes were open, but he didn't see her, just stared straight ahead into the shadowy darkness.

"Oh, dear God." A sob rose into her throat, along with a thick knot of tears. Velvet set the candle down on the floor with trembling hands and slowly approached him. Kneeling at his side, she slid her arms around his neck and pressed her cheek against his.

"Jason, my love. It's Velvet. Everything is going to be all right."

Jason said nothing, just stared sightlessly ahead.

"Jason, please . . . it's Velvet."

He stirred then, a whisper of movement. She felt him inhale a deep breath, then another, forcing more and more air into his lungs. He blinked several times, then shook his head as if pulling himself from a dream. She eased away and looked into his face, saw the small black pupils of his eyes slowing beginning to focus.

"Velvet?"

"Yes, my love. I'm right here." She brushed away the tears that had started to slide down her cheeks, leaned forward and pressed a soft kiss on his lips. "Are you all right?"

A deep sigh of despair followed by the clank of his chains. "You shouldn't have come here, Velvet."

"Where were you, Jason, when I first arrived? What were you seeing?"

His gaze swung to hers in the light of the candle, intense blue eyes, stark in a face etched with deep lines of pain. "The past," he said simply. "The reason you shouldn't have come."

"I had to come. I had to see you. I had to be sure you were all right. You're my husband, Jason." Her gaze locked with his and refused to leave. "And I love you. I was afraid to tell you before, but now . . . now I want you to know. I love you, Jason. I have for a very long time."

The muscles in his throat moved up and down, but he didn't speak. His head dropped forward, and in the glow of the candle, she saw his strong jaw was darkened with bruises, his lips cut and swollen.

Slowly he lifted his head. Big dark hands reached out and framed her face. "I never wanted you to love me. I tried to tell you, tried to protect you. I'm sorry for the pain I've caused you, the terrible trouble I've brought."

"I'm not sorry. I love you. I treasure every moment we have shared. I pray for the hour you are free so that we can be together again."

He only shook his head. "That isn't going to happen, Velvet. Even if some miracle occurred and I got out of this place alive, it's over between us. Whatever we shared is past."

"No! Don't say that. I—"

"You don't love me. You only think you do. The man you love doesn't exist. Not anymore. He hasn't for a very long time."

"That isn't true. You're exactly the man I believe you are and more."

He ignored her words, his finger running over her bottom lip, the touch as light as a feather. "I've been selfish, Duchess. I should never have touched you, never should have married you. I should have left you alone. If I had, you wouldn't have gotten hurt." Jason glanced around the dingy, rat infested cell, saw Velvet kneeling beside him on the filthy straw pallet, and his heart twisted painfully inside him. She didn't belong in a place like this, should never have known such a place existed.

He was the reason she was there. It was his fault—again.

He ran a finger along her jaw, wishing he didn't have to hurt her yet again, wishing he could spare her the truth. But it was far too late for that.

"You want to know what I was seeing while I sat here in the darkness? You want to know the truth? Well, I'm going to tell you, Velvet. Then I want you to leave this godforsaken place and never come back again."

CHAPTER
TWENTY-SIX

∞

$\mathcal{E}$ight long years had passed. Yet for him it seemed only yesterday. It had happened late in May. He'd been in Georgia for three torturous years, days of heat, and bugs, and backbreaking labor. He was full of hate back then, blinded with it. He wanted his freedom and he would do anything to get it.

He'd tried to escape, of course, but the dogs never failed to find him. They had flogged him, beat him nearly to death, but even that could not stop him. Jason was determined to get away.

The fourth time he tried, odds were they would kill him, but his luck had finally changed. In the dense pine forest not far from the camp, he crossed the path of an ancient black man, also on the run. Samuel needed a man with a strong enough back to pole his flat-bottomed boat through the Georgia swamplands. If there was one thing he had it was strength.

"I had the power and he knew the swamp," Jason told Velvet. "Samuel headed north once it was safe. I went south to the Carolinas, a place I had heard of called Charles Town. There were ships there, I'd heard, sailing for ports around the world. England was out of the question, of course, but there had to be somewhere I could go, someplace I would be safe."

He rested his head against the cold gray stone, staring up

into the darkness, letting the memories rush in. "As it turned out, legitimate ships were on the lookout for escaped convict labor. If I'd tried to leave aboard any boat in the harbor, the captain would have turned me in."

Velvet's hand found his in the darkness, warm and gentle and comforting. He wondered which exact moment she would pull the hand away.

It took the full force of his will to continue, to tell her of the ship he'd finally found anchored just outside the harbor, a ship of privateers, the captain, Miles Drury, told him. Desperate men, Jason saw, men willing to ignore the limits of their conscience.

The *Valiant* was a British barkentine. It wasn't until later he discovered it was stolen.

And the men weren't privateers. They were nothing but black-hearted thieves. Jason remembered them well, misfits and drunkards, cutthroats and pirates, the lot of them. Any other time, he wouldn't have set foot aboard a ship crewed by such men, but at the time he didn't care. He'd spent three long years with riffraff just like them and he had survived. He would survive again.

Six days out of port, the pirating began, a brigantine headed for Bermuda. It was the first of half a dozen such ships, the crew growing fat off the stolen bounty, Jason ignoring his conscience. He deserved a share, he told himself, for the grave injustice he had suffered. He could use the money to return to England, to prove his innocence and Avery's guilt. To set things right for his father.

And so far, except for men injured fighting to protect their goods, no one had been needlessly killed.

His riches grew and an odd sort of friendship developed between him and Captain Drury, a Welshman who had come to the Colonies as an indentured servant.

"You're a gentleman," the stout, gray-haired Drury proclaimed one night after supper as he stood at the wheel smoking his long-stemmed clay pipe. "And educated in England. Hard commodities to find, my friend, for a man in my business."

And so they sailed on, until that ill-fated morning in May, that warm, breezy unsuspecting day when the passenger ship, *Starfish*, bound for Barbados, sailed over the blue horizon.

"She's a choice one, eh, mate?" Black Dawson, the beefy first mate, strode up to where he stood at the taffrail.

"Aye, that she is," Jason replied uneasily. "But perhaps our time would be better spent looking for a ship laden with goods instead of one that's simply carrying people." Merchant ships were one thing. Passenger ships another. He didn't like the notion of Drury's bloodthirsty crew descending on a boatload of innocent travelers.

Black Dawson grunted. "They'll be money and goods aboard 'er. A handsome bit more than ye think."

The rest of the crew felt the same. Jason grew more nervous as the *Valiant* closed on the big full-rigged ship in the distance, then a little after noon, they sailed into position.

"Fire the forward cannon across her bow," the captain commanded. "We'll see if the blighter hoves to."

Jason tensed at the roar and splash that barely missed the front of the ship, but the *Starfish* didn't slow, just continued to lumber forward in its dogged attempt to escape, her captain making a courageous but futile effort to avoid the rapidly gaining barkentine.

It took several more carefully placed rounds of cannon shot before the *Starfish* finally ran up the white flag of surrender and the *Valiant* lowered its topgallant sail and began to hove alongside her.

"Have your passengers come up on deck," Drury commanded the captain of the *Starfish*. "Tell them to line up along the starboard rail."

Black Dawson watched eagerly from beside where Jason stood. "Take a look at that, mate." A thick elbow jabbed him in the ribs. "Ye see them skirts? I been three months wi'out a taste of wagtail. Looks like me dry spell is ended."

Jason felt suddenly sick. Even from a distance, he could see half a dozen pale-faced women standing near the starboard rail. Wordlessly, he left the bulky first mate and made his way toward the stern of the ship in search of Captain Drury.

"Your men mean to rape the women. You have to do something to stop them."

The captain peered at him from over the top of his pipe. "You aren't cut out for this, Hawkins. You never were. I shouldn't have taken you on." He turned to assess the crew, who were set to board the *Starfish* the moment the grappling hooks were in place and the two ships brought together.

Captain Drury pulled the pipe stem from between his teeth. "I'm sorry, lad. I may be the captain, but I can't stop them from taking what they've earned. Besides, most of those women are married. A little bedsport won't hurt them. They've had a man between their legs long before this."

"It was far more than bedsport," he told Velvet, the pain of that day washing over him in thick, aching waves. "They dragged the women down on the deck and tore off their clothes. The men who fought to defend them were sliced open with cutlass and saber, ripped from bowel to sternum then tossed overboard to feed the fish."

Velvet made a sound in her throat. The hand that held his began to tremble. Still, he forced himself to continue, to describe the scene on the deck, a scene out of Dante's Inferno, a scene he had begged the captain to stop, then unsuccessfully tried to stop himself. For his trouble, he wound up unconscious, lying in a pool of his own blood atop the shifting holystoned deck.

Several hours later, he awakened to the sound of bawdy laughter and raucous singing, the men drunk on the kegs of rum they had found in the hold of the *Starfish.*

His head throbbed, his vision blurred, but he dragged himself upright and stared out over the rail. The *Starfish* bobbed like a ghost ship in the rising sea, her deck completely deserted. Every man aboard had been tossed overboard, every woman used by the crew until she lay bleeding, then tossed into the water to join the men.

Standing next to the captain, a gash on his head and one along his jaw, Jason stared at the bloody deck of the *Star-*

fish, his foggy mind unable to believe what had occurred. That was when he saw her. A young girl no more than eleven or twelve, a slender, wraithlike creature with huge, frightened green eyes and long chestnut hair. Black Dawson had found her below, hiding somewhere in the belly of the *Starfish,* which he had just finished setting ablaze.

Now he dragged the girl triumphantly toward his ship-mates, brandishing her slender form like a succulent prize, one he intended to ravage himself before passing on to the crew.

Jason started forward, fury nearly blinding him, a rage so great he could barely control it. Drury's hand clamped like a vice on his arm.

"There's nothing you can do."

Jason swung on the man he had once considered a friend. "You have to stop them. She's only a child."

The captain shook his head. "It's too late for that. If it's any consolation, you were right. We shouldn't have stopped the ship. I regret it, but what's done is done."

"But the girl—"

"They'll take her, every man jack of them. Then they'll get rid of her, just like they did the others. They're running on bloodlust now. If you try to stop them, they'll kill you, and the girl will still wind up dead."

"No! You can't just let them kill her!" Jason shook his head in utter disbelief. "She's a child, forgodsakes. A child!" Whirling away, he started across the deck, but hard arms clamped around him from behind.

"Ya ain't goin', mate. The cap'n wants ya to stay alive and so ya shall." Serge Baptiste was a mountain of a man, a big Portuguese sailor the crew called the Baptist. As big as Jason was, the Baptist was bigger. Coupled with the strength of Patsy Cullins, another stout member of the crew, they jerked his arms up behind him and forced him down to his knees on the deck.

"Her clothes were ripped off," Jason continued in a voice that was flat and toneless. "Four of the crew held her down and Black Dawson knelt between her legs."

Sick at the sight, he had tried to look away, off toward the building sea, but the thin blade of a shark's fin cutting through the surface of the water did nothing to give him ease. A shrill, terrified scream brought his eyes swinging back to the girl.

He would regret the next few moments every second of his life for as long as he lived, and yet he would do it again. With a bellow of outrage, Jason wrenched an arm free of his captor's hold, grabbed the pistol the huge sailor carried stuffed into his belt, raised the gun, and aimed it at the girl.

One shot was all he had. It wouldn't help her to kill Black Dawson, though he itched to lay the crosshairs over the man's thick skull—a dozen more waited to take his place. Jason aimed and fired the pistol, the sound reverberating across the deck of the ship.

"The ball hit squarely," he said, his voice little more than a whisper. "I remember the way her eyes slid slowly closed. She'd been so frightened. Now her pretty face looked almost peaceful." His voice cracked on this last. "Whatever they did to her now, at least her suffering was ended."

"Jason . . ." Velvet whispered his name, but he didn't hear her. He was remembering the way he had dropped the gun and looked away, remembering the slickness of tears sliding down his cheeks.

He didn't care who saw them. He didn't care if they killed him. He wished he were dead. Wished he were the one lying in the spreading pool of blood instead of the pretty little girl.

But Black Dawson only laughed, a sharp bark of mirth that went on and on and finally had the whole drunken crew falling to the deck in gales of uproarious laughter.

Miles Drury's hand came to rest on his shoulder, but Jason jerked away.

"I'll have you put ashore the first chance we get," Drury said. "Your share will ensure some sort of future. Until then keep your mouth shut and stay below as much as you can. Maybe I can keep you alive until we get there."

Jason didn't answer. He didn't want the captain's blood

money. He didn't care if he lived or died. He didn't care about anything but turning back the clock to the day he boarded the cursed ship, and God knew he could never do that.

Instead he was as cursed as the ship was, as doomed as the men aboard her. He would never forget what happened that awful day, never forgive himself for what he had done.

And he knew then as surely as he knew now, no one else who knew the terrible truth would be able to forgive him either.

Soft sobs drew his attention from the darkness of the past, a warm touch lingered against his skin, her small hand still tightly clutching his. A gentle voice whispered his name, and the sound was thick with tears, heavy with undisguised anguish. Slender arms slid around his neck, a cheek wet with tears pressed against his own, and their salty tears mingled.

"Jason . . ."

"Forgive me," he whispered, knowing she never could, knowing only God could do that and he hadn't had the courage to ask. Hadn't felt he deserved forgiveness, even if God were good enough to grant it.

Against him, Velvet's body shook with grief, her chest moving in and out, the muscles in her throat constricting.

But no words whispered past her lips. There was only the soft sound of her weeping. He shouldn't have asked her, shouldn't have pressed her for something she could not possibly give him. It only made his pain all the greater.

Something warm touched his cheek. A trembling hand tenderly cupped his face, a gentle touch, a soft caress he never thought to feel again.

"Beloved Jason. You don't need my forgiveness. You never did. That day on the ship, you did what you thought was best. You risked your life to help her."

"I killed her. I murdered her."

"You saved her. You saved her the only way you knew how, and wherever she is, she knows that. I would have welcomed your bullet and so did she."

Jason shook his head. "She was only a child. *A child.* She never had a chance to live."

She pulled back to look at him, her cheeks shiny with wetness in the faint light of the candle. "What about you, Jason? You haven't really lived a single day since that girl died."

He didn't answer. His throat hurt too much to speak.

"You're only a man, Jason. Only a man. Sometimes you make mistakes, just like any other man. Sometimes you have to make choices. You made a choice that day, a terrible choice between two unthinkable, inhuman courses of action. You knew they would probably kill you, yet you chose to help that innocent young girl, to ease her suffering the only way you knew how."

He dragged in a shaky breath of air. God, he hated for her to see him cry.

"You're only human," Velvet said. "God knows that. Make your peace with God, Jason. As for me, I love you even more than I did before. And I was right. You're everything I believed you were and more."

A painful ache rose in his chest. He turned her into his arms and crushed her against him. "Ah, God, Duchess." His hands slid into her hair, destroying her careful coiffure, tearing the pins loose, allowing the heavy curls to tumble down her back. "I love you, Duchess. I love you so damned much."

She was crying again. He could feel her small body shaking, but when she looked up at him, in the faint light of the candle, he could see her smile.

She pulled a handkerchief from the pocket of her skirt and dabbed at her eyes. "You love me. You mean it wasn't just lust."

"I kept hoping it was."

The smile returned, brighter this time. She started to say something more, but the guard rapped hard on the door.

"Time to go, miss." The key grated and the door swung wide.

Velvet's eyes clung to his face. "The darkness can't hurt

you now, Jason. It can't hurt you ever again. You've come out of the dark into the light, and the past is no more than a memory.'' Her hand cupped his cheek. "Promise me you will remember. When the darkness threatens, think about the light, Jason. The light is love. Will you remember?''

He swallowed past the tightness in his throat. "I'll remember,'' he said softly.

She kissed him then, a kiss of love and tenderness, a kiss of promise and determination. Jason kissed her back with all the love, gratitude, and hope he felt in his heart. He thought that he had never known a woman like her. And that if he lived, he would never let her go.

CHAPTER TWENTY-SEVEN

∞

Christian Sutherland couldn't sleep. Not even at two in the morning. Not since he had heard about Lord Hawkins, who wasn't Lord Hawkins at all, but the duke of Carlyle's older brother, the man who should have been duke, a man sentenced to hang for his father's murder.

Christian didn't believe it. Not since he had come to know Jason Sinclair. Not after the too-convenient deaths of Celia Brookhurst and Sir Wallace Stanton. Not after what Mary had said.

Too many coincidences, too much good fortune for the duke, a man Christian now realized was nothing but an unprincipled, utterly ruthless fraud.

But what to do about it? How could he help Sinclair? And what should he do about Mary?

Standing at the window of his bedchamber overlooking a corner of Hyde Park, Christian thought of the woman he loved and knew the choice she had made in staying with Carlyle was a drastically wrong one. Considering the things the duke had done, she owed him nothing and neither did he. And he feared that Mary was in danger.

Christian had heard the story of the meeting Litchfield had arranged with the magistrate at the docks, as had everyone else in the ton. He had also heard of Mary's untimely arrival with Velvet Sinclair and her efforts to help Velvet's husband. Mary had gone against Carlyle. Avery must have been furious. God only knew what he might have done.

The thought of Mary suffering at the hands of the ruthless duke made Christian sick to his stomach.

Unconsciously, he braced his hands on the windowsill, his fingers curling into the wood. He would send her a note, he thought, demand that she meet him as soon as she could leave without causing undo notice. But what if Avery intercepted the message? God's blood, anything might occur. It was simply too dangerous for Mary.

Clenching his jaw in frustration, Christian began to pace in front of the window. He had to see her. He would carry her away by force if that was what it took to get her out of there. She loved him and he loved her. In time he could make her see reason.

He strode up and down, his hands balled, his jaw tight with anger and worry. He might have worn a path in the carpet if the butler hadn't knocked just then at his bedchamber door.

"Excuse me, milord." George Marlin, the Sutherland family butler for more than twenty years, blinked heavy-lidded, sleep-filled eyes, his stocking cap bobbing atop his head.

"Yes, George, what is it?"

"I'm sorry to disturb you at this time of night, milord, but the lady who came here before . . . I believe her name is Mary?"

Christian went tense. "Yes, yes. What about her?"

"She is arrived downstairs."

Christian's eyes slid closed on a momentary pang of relief. "Thank God." It lasted only an instant, turning rapidly to worry. Had something happened to Mary? Was she injured or in some sort of trouble? Christian strode toward the door, the little man racing along behind him.

"I know 'tis highly irregular, your lordship. Under normal circumstances, I wouldn't have admitted her at such an hour, of course, but after the last time—"

"You did exactly correct, George."

"I've shown her into the White Drawing Room, sir."

Christian nodded his approval. Descending the stairs two at a time, he slammed into the drawing room, nearly colliding headlong with Mary. Pale blue eyes, wide and uncertain, flew up to his face.

"Christian . . ."

"Mary, thank God you have come." She didn't fight him when he gathered her into his arms. "Are you all right? He hasn't hurt you? He hasn't . . . ?"

Mary glanced away. "He was so angry. He said I had betrayed him by trying to help Lady Hawkins. I have never seen him so enraged."

"Tell me he did not hurt you. I will kill him if he has harmed a single hair on your head."

"He meant to punish me. I think he would have forced himself on me, but his man, Willard, arrived and apparently he had more important matters to attend to than dealing with an errant wife. He's been busy since then, but I knew that as soon as he was finished with whatever he has been doing . . ."

Christian held her away from him. "You're not leaving," he said in a voice steel-edged with determination. "If I have to tie you up and carry you away in order to keep you with me then that is what I will do."

Mary gave him the gentlest of smiles. Tears collected in her lovely blue eyes, and a single drop slid down her cheek. "I'm not leaving. Not without you. Not if you want me to stay."

Christian's gaze was fierce. "I want you, Mary. I've wanted you from the first moment I saw you. I should never have let you go back to Carlyle."

A shudder slid through her small frame. "He's a murderer, Christian. He killed my father, and now I am convinced he killed his own father as well."

"I think you're right, Mary. I should have listened to you in the first place." Christian held her tightly again.

"We have to help Jason and Velvet. What can we do?"

"I don't know. The judges haven't yet made their decision. There is always the chance he will be acquitted."

"There isn't the slightest chance of that happening and you know it."

Christian sighed. Mary was right. The judges would never acquit, not against a duke, not without more evidence. "Whatever happens, first we must make certain that you are safe. I shall send you to my family in Kent. Once they understand the circumstances of what has occurred and that we are committed to being together, they'll do everything in their power to help us."

"I can't leave yet. Not until Avery is made to pay for the crimes he has committed."

Christian started to argue, but the look in Mary's eyes warned him not to.

"I've an idea, Christian. I think I might be able to be of some help."

"Go on," he said.

"The authorities seem to have abandoned their efforts to find the man who murdered Lady Brookhurst. Apparently, they have little to go on. But if Avery is behind the deed, as I suspect he is, then it must have been done by one of his men. The gossipmongers are saying Jason is the man who did it, that even Velvet's description of the murderer fits her husband."

"Ah . . . yes, I see where you are leading. Whoever committed the murder must be similar in appearance, or at least a man of Jason's approximate height and build."

"And with his same dark hair." Mary tightened her hold on his arm. "There is just such a man in Avery's employ. He rarely comes to the house and almost always uses the outside entrance to Avery's study when he does, but upon occasion I have seen him. His name is Willard, the man I mentioned before."

Christian mulled that over. It was possible. Then again, it might be merely coincidence. "It's a long shot, but I suppose it's better than doing nothing. And if we can find the man who killed Celia, odds are he'll lead us straight to Avery."

"My thoughts exactly. Surely it is worth a try."

Christian gently kissed her. "Anything is worth a try, my
love." Unfortunately that didn't include calling the murderous bastard out, Christian thought with a hot surge of malice. The notion of a duel held a strong appeal. Stronger by
the moment. Christian was a crack shot and Avery's death
would save everyone a whole lot of trouble.

But the fact was, with the duke out of the way, there
would be even less evidence to help clear his brother.

Jason Sinclair would almost certainly hang.

As promised, Litchfield arrived promptly at ten o'clock the
next morning to accompany Velvet to the prison. She was
dressed and ready, and waiting anxiously for his arrival. She
wanted to see Jason, make certain that he was all right.

At the sound of the marquess's heavy footfalls in the entry, Velvet hurried to greet him. His haggard, tightly drawn
expression sent her heart slamming up against her breastbone.

"Lucien—dear God, what has happened?" Wordlessly,
he took her arm, guiding her into the drawing room and
firmly closing the door. "Please, my lord, you must tell me
what has occurred."

"Perhaps you should sit down, my lady."

"Lucien, please, you are scaring me."

He took a weary breath, the muscles tense along his jaw.
"I'm sorry, Velvet. An hour ago, the magistrates sent word
of their decision. Their deliberations took even less time
than expected." His face looked even grimmer, and Velvet
sank down on the sofa.

"Dear Lord, they still believe he is guilty." Tears stung
the backs of her eyes. She blinked to hold them steady, but
they started to slide down her cheeks.

The marquess sat down beside her, gently captured her
hand. "You mustn't give up, Velvet. Avery is guilty. Somewhere there is evidence to prove it. There is still time for
us to find it."

The words passed through her mind as if they had not
been spoken, muffled by the ringing that had risen in her

ears. "The original sentence . . . it is to stand?"

"Yes."

"When?" It came out as the merest whisper.

Lucien gave a soft sigh of regret. "Monday."

Monday. Of course. Execution Day. Four more days and Jason would be hanged.

"The evidence we presented was simply not enough to sway them against a duke of the realm," the marquess continued. "And there was the matter of Celia's murder to contend with. It was simply more expedient to lay the blame for that at Jason's feet as well."

Velvet bit her lip, barely able to make sense of Lucien's words. Jason would hang. In only four more days.

"We'll continue our search for more information," he was saying. "Barnstable and Ludington are working round the clock. They're bound to turn up something."

Velvet tried to smile, to agree with him, make both of them feel better. But the corners of her mouth began to wobble. She turned away and began to cry instead.

Comforting arms surrounded her, held her close against a solid chest. She sobbed like a child against his shoulder.

"Easy, love," he whispered. "You mustn't give up yet. It isn't fair to Jason."

Her throat ached. Her chest felt so tight every breath sent a fearful jolt of pain into her lungs. Still, she forced a measure of steel into her spine and sat up straighter on the sofa.

"You're right, of course. We must be strong for Jason." He handed her his handkerchief and she dabbed it against her eyes. "Does he . . . has anyone told him the judges decision?"

"There was no point in waiting. Parmenter went to see him. He knows by now."

Her chin went up. "Then we must go to him with all haste. He mustn't give up. We must not let him."

Lucien didn't argue, though in truth he believed his friend would prefer to be alone. There were things a man needed time to adjust to, and coming to grips with his own mortality was certainly one of them. Facing the hangman for a crime he didn't commit was a task he couldn't imagine.

Still, Lucien knew better than to argue. Velvet would go to the man she loved and nothing he could say would stop her. It was the kind of love he had never really believed in. In a way, he envied his friend.

"I must caution you, my lady. By now Jason should have been moved from the common side to the master's side of the prison, but the place is still unbearable. The experience won't be a pleasant one."

"I'm well aware the vision of hell Newgate is, my lord. Mr. Ludington accompanied me there last eve."

"What!"

"Jason needed me. I had to go."

"But they had yet to move him. Surely you didn't go down into—"

"I had to see him. I went where he had been taken."

The marquess grunted some unintelligible response, then shook his head. "Jason said you were a handful. I am only just beginning to see what he means. Remind me to choose a pleasantly docile wife when the time comes for marriage."

Velvet forced a smile, little more than a weary curling of the lips. "A docile wife would bore you in a thrice, my lord, but I suppose we shall have to wait and see."

She hadn't slept at all these past few nights and her body ached with worry and fatigue. But the marquess already felt responsible for her. He was worried enough without adding to his burden.

Litchfield made another unpleasant sound. Accepting her cloak from the butler in the entry, he draped it around her shoulders, offered her his arm, and they set off for the prison.

Jason stared through the bars of his cell. The stone-walled room was spacious and swept amazingly clean; he remembered from before how much better life was on the master's side of the prison.

Money was the key, as it seemed to be in most things.

Yet no matter how much a person had, it couldn't seem to change what fate had in store for him. Perhaps it was true that money was the root of all evil.

Or was it merely the lengths to which some people would go in order to get it?

Like his brother, Avery, driven to the murder of his own father. Like arranging Celia's death, and that of Sir Wallace Stanton.

Jason looked out through the bars on the window of his cell, letting the sunlight lessen the chill that no amount of heat could completely dispel. From where he stood, he could look down at the prisoners prowling the courtyard, see them crabbing about in their dismal rags, dirty specters trading for scraps of food or tobacco, or another tattered bit of clothing. Jason preferred to look upward, toward the patch of blue he could see above the gray stone walls, to the turrets and windows, domes and spires of London.

Such a vibrant, sprawling city. Until his return, he hadn't realized how much he'd missed England. The lush, rolling green fields, the moors and forests, the cooling mists that hung over the verdant landscape. Even the fog that crept with such stealth through the crowded streets of the city.

England was lost to him now, like the dream of revenge he had come home to attain. In only four days, he would hang. Only four more days.

There was a time he wouldn't have cared, a time he longed for death, would have accepted its arrival as a friend. The years had changed that.

And the days he had shared with Velvet.

Jason thought of her now, thought of how much he had come to love her, and regretted as he had a dozen times, the pain he had caused her. He had never meant to hurt her, yet from the beginning that was exactly what he had done. He recalled her visit the night before, the secrets he'd laid bare before her, and his chest painfully tightened. She had driven his demons away, brought him into the healing light, if only for these last few precious days.

It was the most cherished gift she had ever given him.

An image of her face rose up as if she were there, the soft pink lips and tilted golden brown eyes, the fringe of thick dark lashes, her fiery auburn hair. If he closed his eyes, he could remember the exact feel of her skin, the full, perfect curve of her breast. She had tempted him from the moment he lifted her up on his horse. Thoughts of her tempted him still. Yet he should have left her alone.

Jason set his jaw, his mind firming with solid determination. She would listen to him in this, he vowed. He would give something back to her for all that she had given to him. In this, his final request, she would do as he commanded. He would have it no other way.

Velvet walked the dank, thick-walled passageways in silence, grateful for Lucien's solid support. She had come to treasure the marquess's friendship, would need it, she knew, to make it through the days ahead.

In the meantime, there was Jason to consider. Velvet did not intend to let her despair show through to the man she loved. She would do anything to prevent that. Pausing for a moment outside the cell, she felt Lucien's silvery eyes on her, the light in them dark with regret and concern.

"Are you sure you are ready for this?"

She lifted her chin and forced herself to smile. "Of course I am ready."

Lucien nodded to the guard, who unlocked the door, and she and the marquess walked in. Jason was waiting, a smile on his face she hadn't expected. Wordlessly, she went into his arms, felt them tighten almost painfully around her. He held her for long, heartrending moments, then eased himself away.

"Before either of you gets too morbid," he said, "I'm fine, now that I'm on this side of the prison where at least I am able to see. Parmenter has been here. He has relayed the bitter news, so you are spared that painful duty. I am happy to say, the man remains optimistic, just as I do, that something will turn up before the sentence is carried out on Monday."

"Barnstable and Ludington are working full-time," Lucien said. "They've half a dozen extra men at their disposal, more if they need them. I've told them not to leave a single stone unturned."

Velvet moved closer against him. "We'll find something, Jason. And even as we speak, Lucien is attempting to set up a meeting with the king and his ministers. There is every chance that his majesty may step in on your behalf."

But Lucien had warned her against hoping too strongly for such a move. The king had far less power these days, acting only on recommendations from his ministers. The ministers needed support from parliament. Odds were slim they would risk parliamentary disfavor by going against six powerful judges of the Inns at Court.

Jason smiled again, looking almost cheerful. Too cheerful, Velvet suddenly realized, and her heart lurched painfully up under her ribs. He fully believed he was going to die this Monday next, but he was determined to protect her from the truth for as long as he could.

Velvet simply could not bear it. For a moment she feared she might burst into tears, but Jason's presence so close at hand gave her the strength to stay calm.

Instead she glanced up and merely returned his smile, allowing him to play the game, hoping it would somehow help to ease him.

They talked for a while, speaking of their strategy, things Lucien and his men were looking into that might turn up the evidence they needed to free him. Things none of them believed would really work.

Then Lucien left them alone. "I've business to attend," he said. "I'll return in a couple of hours to see Velvet returned safely home." He cocked a brow at Jason. "Do you think it's safe to leave her, or is there a chance your wife will attempt a jail break while I'm gone?"

Jason smiled. "If she tries it, I hope she succeeds."

Even Velvet smiled. "If there was the slightest chance for success, you may be certain I would try it. However, from the number of guards posted outside Jason's door, I doubt there is much hope of his escape.''

Lucien clamped Jason on the shoulder. "Hold good thoughts, my friend.'' With that he quit the cell.

Velvet surveyed the barren interior, noting the low rope bed in one corner with its narrow corn husk mattress, the single wooden chair and scarred wooden table.

"I can't believe you are actually here,'' she said into the silence. "It's as though I am in some sort of trance. Any moment I expect to awaken.''

"Perhaps you shall,'' he said softly. "Lucien has always been a miracle worker.''

Velvet shook her head, trying to clear away the numbness she'd been fighting since the night of Jason's arrest. "It isn't fair. You don't belong here, Jason. You didn't eight years ago, and you don't now.'' She glanced up at him. "Mr. Barnstable is working to find new evidence. The moment he does, we shall take it to the judges. The court will put an end to this nonsense once and for all, and then you can come home.''

She reached toward him, smoothed back a lock of his dark hair, felt the strands curling softly beneath her fingers. "We'll be a family, Jason. A real family, just as I once dreamed.''

He smiled at her sadly. "Was that your dream, Velvet? That we would be a family?''

She looked into his dear, handsome face. "I used to think how it might be, if only you would stay. I want to have your children, Jason. I want to wake up beside you and know that you belong there, that you will not leave.''

"I love you, Duchess. I don't think I could have left you even if I had tried.'' He kissed her then, a tender kiss full of love and sadness, heavy with regret and promises they knew he could not keep. Jason deepened the kiss, claiming her mouth as he might have claimed her body, imprinting a memory of himself upon her for all time.

"Make love to me, Jason,'' she whispered, clinging to his shoulders. "Here. Now. Give me your baby.''

In the past, he would have drawn away, wouldn't have wanted the closeness. Now she saw that he was tempted. Hunger and need glittered in the fierce blue of his eyes. Love for her he made no effort to hide.

Slowly he pulled away. "I want to, Velvet, but I can't. Not here. Not in this foul place. I want your memories of me to be sweet ones, filled with the passion and love we shared." He eased her farther away, holding her at arm's length so that he could look into her face.

"I want you to promise me something. It is the last favor of you that I will ever ask."

Her heart squeezed. Her eyes burned. He was saying what she did not want to hear—that he would not be returning home. Velvet shook her head.

"You can ask it of me once you are out of here. Tomorrow I'll come back and—"

"No." His grip grew tight on her shoulders. "The favor I want is for you to stay home. I don't want you to come here again."

"No! You can't ask that of me. I love you. I want to be with you. I—"

"I don't want you to see me locked up in this place and I don't want you to watch me hang. I want your word, Velvet. I want your promise that you will do this for me, grant me this one last request."

Her throat closed up, ached until she couldn't speak. Tears filled her eyes and a flood of moisture slid down her cheeks. "I can't. I have to see you. I have to be with you."

"Please, Velvet. Do it for my sake. Do it because you love me."

The ache in her throat spread into her chest. Oh, God, she ached all over. "Jason . . ."

"I love you, Duchess. If things were different, if I was able to come back home, I'd be the husband of your dreams. I'd do everything in my power to make you happy. I'd never leave you, Velvet. Never." He pressed his mouth over hers, softly stilling the tremor in her lips. "But that isn't going to happen. And because it is not, I want your word, your solemn promise that you will never come here again.''

She clung to him, unable to keep from crying, holding him while her body shook with tears. ''I love you,'' she whispered.

''Then do this last thing I ask. Do it for me, Duchess. Do it for me.''

She didn't want to say yes. She wanted to be with him every hour, every minute that they had left. But it wasn't what he wanted, and so at last she agreed. ''I'll do as you wish.''

''And you won't come to Tyburn. I couldn't bear to think of you there.''

''No, I won't come to Tyburn.''

''Do you promise?''

''Yes.''

Powerful arms crushed her against him. He held her while she cried, neither of them speaking, neither pulling away. Finally he released his hold, his eyes touching hers one last time, then going over her head to the window in the door to the cell. Lucien had returned. It was time for her to leave.

Lifting her chin with his hands, he gently wiped the tears from her cheeks. ''You've always been strong, Velvet. Stronger than any woman I've ever know. Be strong for me now.''

Velvet blinked to clear her vision. She could hardly bear to look at him, to gaze into those blue, blue eyes she might never see again. Raising on tiptoe, she kissed his mouth, her lips trembling, the kiss a sweet farewell filled with yearning and all the love she felt for him. It was all she had left to give him, all he would allow her to give.

Jason returned the kiss with a slow, aching tenderness that burned a hole straight into her heart.

''I won't let you die,'' she whispered. ''I won't let them take you from me.''

Jason pressed a kiss against her forehead. ''God go with you, my love.''

Turning away, moving like a sleepwalker toward the open door, Velvet left the cell.

She didn't look back. She did not dare.

Instead she let Lucien guide her down the passageway, the heavy stone walls blurred by a thick veil of tears.

"He asked me not to return," she whispered. "He made me promise."

Lucien sighed. "I thought he might do that."

"We have to save him. We have to find a way."

But Lucien did not answer. There was nothing left to say.

"At last! After all the misery my beloved brother has caused me, the time for his comeuppance is finally at hand." Avery smiled as he tossed the *Morning Chronicle* onto his desk and stared up at Baccy Willard, who stood on the opposite side. It was all he could do to keep from gleefully grinning. "The bloody bastard hangs on the morrow."

Baccy made no reply. He hated hangings, felt sorry for any poor sod who wound up on the three-legged mare. It bothered him that his master always seemed to enjoy other people's misfortunes. Even the death of his own brother.

"What about the girl?" Baccy asked, unable to keep the dread from showing in his face. "You still want me to kill 'er?"

Avery had already pondered the question. "For the present, leave her be. With my brother gone, there's no more reason for her to stir up trouble, and even if she does, no one will believe her. The magistrates will hardly be willing to admit they hanged an innocent man."

"What about yer wife?"

Avery stiffened. The subject was a sore one. The mousy little bitch had the unmitigated gall to run away. "We know where she has gone. And everyone else believes I have simply sent the frail little creature back to the country. Since time is not a factor, I shall deal with Balfour at my leisure and once I have done so, take my errant wife in hand and see that she is brought home." And beat her silly once he got her there. The woman would learn the hard way the consequences of trying to best him. She would not try it again.

"In the meantime," he added with malicious satisfaction, "we shall simply sit back and enjoy the hanging."

Baccy frowned, but Avery could hardly wait.

CHAPTER
TWENTY-EIGHT

∞

*I*t wasn't possible that the four days, each one a seeming eternity, could now all be passed. Only these final hours remained, hours of sorrow too deep for tears, a day of broken dreams and shattered pledges.

Velvet couldn't remember when she had last broken her word. Perhaps a promise she had made as a little girl, some mischief she was forsworn against, or perhaps it was the time she had vowed never to play in the brook without Grandfather's permission but kept her fingers crossed because she knew she would.

To break a solemn pledge, given to Jason in love and respect for his wishes, wasn't something Velvet did lightly, yet allowing her husband to face the gallows without her was simply not something she could do.

And so she steeled herself against her conscience, and prepared herself for the ordeal ahead. She wasn't going to cry. Not today. She had cried endless tears through the long, bitter hours of the night, cried until she was empty, hollow inside, as parched of emotion as a dried-out husk of corn.

And so she readied herself to face this day, dressing in the simple gray silk gown trimmed with black that she had worn to court.

The plain black carriage Jason had borrowed from Litchfield waited out in front. Velvet made her way outside the town house, climbed in, and pulled the curtains, sealing herself inside, sealing her emotions in as well. For the next few hours, she would simply exist, survive simply for Jason, a vessel of strength for the man she loved. She wouldn't let him see her, wouldn't let him know she was there or watch him die at the end. She would keep her word as much as she could.

But she had to be there, believed he would be able to feel her presence even if he could not see her, to draw strength and courage from it.

And Litchfield would be there as well, seeing to Jason's comfort in any way he could, bringing his body back home once Jason's life was ended, as good and loyal a friend as any two people could have.

Velvet leaned back against the carriage seat, trying not to think, trying to harden herself for what was to come. But she had never been to a hanging, wasn't prepared for the fairlike atmosphere, the gaiety of the throng gathered atop Tyburn Hill.

She wasn't prepared for the line of expensive carriages filled with the social elite, all there to enjoy a day of amusement.

Staring out the window, she wasn't ready for the long string of carts carrying prisoners to their deaths, each man riding atop his own coffin.

"Jason . . . oh, dear God."

Even from a distance, she could see him, taller than the rest, his shoulders broader, thicker, and purposely squared. There wasn't an ounce of weakness in the set of his spine, the resolute lift of his head, as she had known there wouldn't be.

As the cart he was in rolled along, the crowd surged around him, a motley throng of the morbid from the lowliest pickpocket to the highest-ranking members of the ton. High-born ladies peered through opera glasses, their powdered hair piled high above their painted faces. Coxcombs in silver buckled shoes and tight satin breeches dismounted from sedan chairs. Ladies in Mantua silk, men in Manchester velvet stood mere paces away from shuffling rag merchants, brushed shoulders with chimney sweeps, followed after milkmaids, and rode next to whores.

Tyburn Hill at Marble Arch. Velvet knew of it, everyone in London did, but her wildest nightmares couldn't have imagined the reality. She couldn't have envisioned people dancing and cheering as the hangman slid the rope around the victim's hooded head. Couldn't imagine them singing bawdy tunes or mildly watching a peepshow while a few feet away, men where dying.

She couldn't possibly have conjured the smell of burned apples as a woman moved through the crowd, her tin pan filled with coals, roasting the fruit she carried for sale in a basket atop her head.

The aroma wafted toward her and Velvet's stomach rolled with nausea. For a moment she thought she might be sick. Then the moment passed and she leaned forward once more, steadying herself on the windowsill.

A vicar passed along the line of carts, mumbling prayers for those who wished them. Jason patiently waited his turn, looking neither right nor left, heedless of the jeering mob around him, as if for him they didn't exist. It was all she could do not to go to him, to touch him one last time. He wouldn't want that, she knew, and she would respect his last wishes.

Instead, she searched the crowd for Lucien, certain he was there, but she couldn't see him. Perhaps it was better, since he would hardly approve if he knew she had come.

And so her gaze returned to her tall, handsome husband, willing him her strength, wishing that she had been able to save him. A movement caught her eye in the row of carriages parked farther along the road leading up the hill. Velvet spotted the Carlyle crest, big gold letters emblazoned on the duke's carriage door. Even from a distance she could hear the sound of Avery's laughter and that of the overblown doxies who had accompanied him to the hanging.

Rage swept over her, so strong she could taste it in her mouth. It surged through her blood, blotting the aching numbness, making her body come alive for the first time in days. Avery was here. He had come to see his brother hang. Fury overwhelmed her, made her blind to everything but the sight of the ruthless, fraudulent duke, the man who was killing her husband.

Velvet reached for the small silver door handle, turned it and slammed the door open, then descended the narrow iron stairs.

The cart had halted its long winding journey up the hill. Jason barely heard the rattle of his heavy iron chains, or the guard unlocking the long length of metal that fastened his leg to the aging wood. His ankles were still shackled, his wrists manacled as well. The skin was chaffed raw beneath them, oozing bright spots of blood.

Jason ignored the pain. He had steeled himself for this occasion and he was ready to see it done. He wished he weren't so filled with regret, that his ending could be more peaceful, but it was hard to find peace when his father remained unavenged, when his brother continued to elude the hangman and enjoy the fruits of his murderous treachery.

And there was Velvet, always Velvet. She needed him, just as he'd needed her. She was strong, yes. But she was innocent and vulnerable as well. She needed a man, a husband, and he was exactly the right man for her.

He knew that now with absolute clarity. Unfortunately, the knowledge came too late.

" 'Urry it up, man. Ye be next, don't ya know. Next in line for the gallows."

But hurrying wasn't so easy with the weight of the chains, even if he had felt the need to rush. Instead his pace remained unhastened, his steps as dignified as he could make them, considering the heavy iron weights. Still he reached the platform all too soon. Jason paused at the bottom, took a deep breath for courage, and started the long climb up the stairs.

Velvet's heart thundered. The anger felt good pumping through her veins, as if she were finally alive, a living, breathing person for the first time in days. She started forward, wishing she had a weapon to use against Avery, rage driving her, an urge she relished as the moment of her husband's death drew near.

The rage protected her, gave her strength. The courage to be strong for Jason.

She had almost reached the four high-stepping grays standing in their traces at the front of the carriage, the animals snorting their displeasure at the noisy, raucous crowd, when a clawlike hand wrapped around her wrist. The pressure of bony fingers bit through her haze of anger, bringing her to a reluctant halt a few feet from the carriage. In her blinding rage, it took a moment for her mind to decipher what was happening.

"Penny for a blind man," the beggar asked, squatting on his haunches, holding a tin cup out in front of him. He was dressed in rags, a cloudy eye sightlessly staring up at her, the other covered by a long dirty hank of graying hair. "Spare a coin for a man in need."

She started to turn away. Jason would die any moment, Avery was just ahead, and rage still boiled through her.

"Help an old man, lady," the beggar intoned. "A coin or two for a bite to eat."

The rage began to fade. She wanted to call it back but her eyes swung to Jason and her throat clogged with tears. She had thought she would never cry again. Brushing at the wetness on her cheeks, she reached into the pocket of her skirt, pulled out a small pouch of coins, and tossed one into the old man's cup. It rattled then fell silent.

"Thanks be to ye, milady." He straightened, taller than he appeared, his flesh so spare bones protruded their sharp edges through the fabric of his shirt. He tossed back the dirty lock of hair. "Ye've a good heart, milady, just like ye husband. Always gave me a coin whenever he come to the inn. Not like his brother. Never was like that. I'm the one what seen 'em, milady, the one what sent ye the message. It was the younger one what done it, the younger one what kilt the old duke that night at the inn."

For a moment, Velvet couldn't move. Then she swayed and feared that she would surely swoon. Her knees started shaking and her mouth felt dry. "You saw him? How could you? You're blind."

"Blind in one eye, me love, not both."

"Oh, dear God." Reaching out, she captured the old man's wrist and bolted forward, half expecting him to balk and jerk away. Instead he followed along in her wake while she raced toward the stairs, battling her way through the crowd toward the platform at the top of the hill. Pickpockets and cutthroats, thieves and prostitutes parted before her driving force, clearing a path ahead.

"Make way!" she shouted. "I have to get through!" The urgency of her voice seemed to reach them and the path opened wider. Hurrying, stumbling, pressing on up the hill, Velvet dragged the old man forward, praying they would make it, that his words would garner some sort of reprieve.

Time. Even that small concession was more than she dared to hope for.

The word of a beggar against that of a duke.

It was insanity of the wildest sort, and yet she pressed onward. Hope rose in her heart. She tried to press it down, but it wouldn't go away, though she knew with awful certainty that hope would surely die along with Jason.

On the platform in the distance, she looked up to see the noose being settled around his neck. He wore no hood, but faced the crowd with all the quiet dignity of a true duke of Carlyle.

"Stop!" Velvet shouted. "You must stop at once!" But she was still too far away, the crowd too noisy for the hangman to hear her. Perhaps he wouldn't stop if he did.

Velvet's lips began to move in silent prayer. With each step she took, she prayed for God's intervention. *He is innocent. He's a good man. Please, won't you help him?* She was almost there, almost at the top of the hill. The crowd had begun to still, mumbling now, enthralled by the act of death they were there to witness. The hangman was checking the rope around Jason's neck.

Velvet opened her mouth to scream, but a buxom, aproned woman stepped into her path, colliding with surprising force, sending both of them flying. Velvet went down in a tangle of flesh, rough cutting pebbles, and dust. Ignoring the woman's curses and the pain stabbing into her leg, she was back on her feet and running, the beggar's thin arm gripped tightly once more.

But oh, dear God, she was going to be too late!

A dark blur of movement whipped past the corner of her eye. A man was running flat-out toward the platform. Lucien, she saw, taking the stairs two at a time, reaching the top just as the hangman knocked the block out from under Jason's feet.

"Nooo!" she screamed, a wave of agony breaking over her, a soul-deep anguish that made her stomach roll with nausea. But Lucien didn't slow, flying instead across the platform, hurling himself across the wooden floor and catching Jason before he came to the end of his deadly descent.

"Oh, dear God." Tears spilled onto her cheeks, a great cascading flood of them.

Other men were running through the crowd. The earl of Balfour led two of the magistrates through the masses, which had fallen to silence at the scene they had witnessed on the stage.

"Cut that man down!" one of the magistrates commanded. She saw it was Thomas Randall, the man who had come with Lucien to the warehouse. "Cut him down, I say. Do it and be bloody quick about it!"

Velvet thought her legs might give way beneath her. Her body was shaking, but her hold on the not-so-blind beggar never faltered.

"Your lordship!" Velvet raced the last few feet to the front of the platform, gasping madly for air, dragging it into her lungs. "This man was a witness to the duke of Carlyle's murder. "Please—I know his word holds little stock against that of a duke, but combined with the other evidence that we have collected—"

"Quite so, my lady. Thanks to your sister-in-law, Mary

Sinclair, the earl of Balfour was able to track down a man
named Bacilius Willard. At Lord Balfour's . . . ah, persuasion . . . the man has been guided away from the path of sin.
He has been shown the light of truth and justice and con-
fessed to the murder of the countess of Brookhurst. He
named his employer, the duke of Carlyle, the man who ordered it done. Combined with the evidence already presented—''

A gunshot sounded just then. A puff of white smoke rose
out of the crowd and several women screamed. Standing
next to Lucien, Jason ducked away from the lead ball whiz-
zing past his ear so close he could feel its trailing wind.

''It's Avery!'' Lucien pointed toward the man who
pushed and shoved, forcing his way back through the crowd.
''We've got to stop him!''

Jason swore an oath as the last iron shackle fell onto the
wooden planks at his feet. He paused only an instant before
jumping off the stage and landing neatly next to Velvet. He
kissed her full on the mouth then started running. Fighting
his way through the crowd, which was enlivened again by
this latest round of events, he pushed and shouldered his
way toward Avery. Flanked by Lucien and a small army of
watchmen, jostling and weaving his way in and out, he raced
toward the man who had fired the gun.

Avery headed straight for his carriage, fool enough to
believe he hadn't been spotted. Or that if he had, he could
buy his way out of trouble as he had done before.

He never reached his destination. Jason tackled him before he could reach the door, dragging him into the dirt,
rolling over and over, winding up on top of him. He landed
a harsh blow to his brother's jaw, and Avery grunted in pain,
his head slamming hard against the ground. Jason grabbed
the front of his white frilled shirt, dragged him up, and hit
him again, splitting his lip and splattering blood all over his
gold satin tailcoat.

''I'll kill you,'' Avery threatened, wrapping his hands
around Jason's throat and beginning to squeeze. Jason
knocked his hands away and simply hit him again. A crowd

had gathered around them, cheering the two men on, though Avery was no match for Jason's superior strength. Coming to his feet, Jason dragged his brother upward, determined to control the fury surging through him, the need for revenge sweeping hotly through his veins. He wanted Avery alive. He wanted his brother brought to justice, to see him pay for the things he had done.

Someone jeered, the crowd surged forward, and Avery twisted away. Reaching into his coat, he pulled something from the inside pocket, and a pistol appeared in his hand.

"I've always said, if you want something done, you have to do it yourself." He cocked the hammer.

Jason knew he stood too close for Avery to miss. Good Christ, he couldn't let the bastard win again. Diving to the side, his body tensed against the impact of the ball, Jason hit the dirt and rolled. A thunderous shot resounded, then another. It took several seconds to realize the first shot had come from behind him, taking Avery square in the chest. The second was the sound of his brother's weapon, discharging harmlessly into the air.

Silas Ludington casually stuffed his spent pistol into his breeches. "Good riddance," he said without the least amount of pity.

Jason's gaze swung back to the man in the dirt just a few feet away. A last breath whispered past his brother's thin lips. Avery's sightless eyes stared upward, as if they followed the wasted arc of his spent lead ball.

"Is he dead?" Lucien asked when he reached them.

"Yes."

Litchfield gripped his shoulder. "Then it's over."

Jason nodded, feeling as if a weight had been lifted from his chest. As Lucien said, at last it was over.

Justice had finally been served. The waters muddied by Avery's greed at last ran clear.

He started back up the hill and on the opposite side of the crowd, Balfour saluted. His own ends had been served this day along with those of Mary Stanton. No two people deserved it more.

At the bottom of the platform, Velvet waited beside Thomas Randall. Her eyes were wet with tears, but there was so much love and hope shining through something warm unfurled inside him.

"Your husband is a very lucky man," the magistrate said. "Twice this day, he has eluded the jaws of the grim reaper. "I am pleased to see that justice has been so well served." He turned his attention to Jason. "I believe, your grace, it is time you took your lovely wife home."

Velvet bit her lip. For the first time she looked uncertain. "Are we for home, your grace?"

Jason reached for her, drew her against him. "Aye, Duchess. Home to Carlyle Hall." His hand came up to her cheek. "I meant what I told you. I love you and I'm not leaving. You're stuck with me, Duchess, for as long as I live."

His mouth curved into the tenderest smile. "Thanks to you and some very good friends, that looks to be quite a long time."

The crowd on Tyburn Hill was cheering again. For the man on the hill, the rightful duke of Carlyle, who had stared death in the face and lived to tell the story, and for his beautiful, fiery-haired duchess, who was kissing him so fiercely.

Even the mob on Tyburn Hill turned buffle-headed for a happy ending.

*E*PILOGUE

∞

ENGLAND, 1765

*T*he last late-afternoon rays washed the horizon in faint shades of gold. Autumn was setting in, the first leaves falling, the evenings turning chill.

Preparing to bathe and change before their guests—Lord and Lady Balfour and their two small children, Michael and Sarah—arrived for a week's end visit, Velvet watched her husband through the bedchamber window.

On the grassy knoll below the terrace, he was leading a dapple gray pony ridden by his four-year-old son, Alexander Jason III. Alex's sister, two-year-old Mary toddled along at her father's feet, occasionally throwing her arms around his legs, hanging on for dear life and refusing to let go. The third time it happened, Jason laughed good-naturedly, bent and lifted her up on his shoulders, and Mary squealed with delight. Across the yard, the earl of Haversham, a contented great-grandfather now, watched with unabashed pleasure.

Velvet smiled softly, feeling a tug at her heart. Jason was a wonderful father, better than she could have imagined. He had finally overcome the dark secrets of his past, and as the rightful duke of Carlyle, become the man he was destined to be. The years he had suffered gave him a strength of character, an insight into people few men ever had. He was kind and caring, capable and fair. Having survived such a

desperate existence, he understood his peoples' problems as
few aristocrats ever could.

A knock sounded. Velvet turned away from the window
and started for the door, but Tabby reached it first.

"Well, lads, 'tis high time ye got 'ere." The heavyset
woman pointed toward the copper bathing tub in the corner
and the boys marched dutifully in that direction. "Hurry,
now and don't be spillin' as ye go."

Velvet stood by while the bathing tub was filled. The two
boys left to return downstairs, and Tabby helped her off with
her pink silk wrapper. Naked, she slid into the tub.

"Will ye be needin' me 'elp?"

"No, Tabby, I'm fine."

"Enjoy yer bath, yer grace." The heavyset woman quietly left the room, closing the door behind her.

Velvet sighed and leaned back against the rim of the bathing tub. The water felt warm and soothing, easing away the
problems of a busy day, a day filled with children's laughter
and a husband's loving warmth.

Soon they'd be returning to London. Jason was a member
of the House of Lords and he viewed that duty with deadly
earnest. His main interest was the judicial system. He knew
its failings and he never ceased to speak for the plight of
the common man.

After Avery's death, he had even helped Baccy Willard.
When the man would have hanged, Jason petitioned the
court for leniency, asking instead that Willard be sentenced
to prison. Avery was the real criminal, he believed, poor
ignorant Baccy simply a pawn in his brother's deadly
games.

Velvet sank deeper into the tub, letting the water slosh
over her breasts, thinking how happy she was.

"Daydreaming, my love?"

She felt his hands, big yet gentle on her shoulders. She
hadn't heard him come in, but then he had always moved
with pantherlike stealth.

She turned to look at him, saw the way his gaze traveled
over her bare shoulders, the tops of her breasts just above

the water. "I was dreaming of you," she said, smiling into his handsome face, warmed by the heat in his gaze he made no effort to hide.

"I'm glad to hear it. That makes what I have in mind much simpler to accomplish."

She cocked a brow. "Oh? And exactly what is that?"

"Seduction, my love. It wasn't my intention when I arrived, but since you are already dressed for the occasion . . ."

Velvet shrieked as he bent and scooped her out of the tub, water sloshing over his tall black boots. "Jason Sinclair, have you lost your wits?"

He grinned, his eyes bright blue with mischief. "I don't believe so. There is nothing crazy about a man making love to his adorable wife." There was a hunger in his gaze as well. She knew what it was for she felt that same stirring, a fierce ache for Jason low in her belly that never quite seemed to go away.

Ignoring the water dripping from her naked body, he carried her over to the bed and came down on top of her, his tall hard body nestled snugly between her legs.

"You should have at least let me dry off."

He gave her a soft kiss on the lips. "I'll dry you off." Lowering his dark head, he licked droplets of water from a nipple then sucked a breast into his mouth.

Velvet moaned at the sweetly hot sensation, her body arching upward, wanting even more.

Instead he shook his head. "I'm not through drying you yet."

Oh dear Lord. His mouth trailed over her breasts, sucking the water from each one, then he kissed his way down to her navel. He drank deeply there, his tongue dipping in, swirling and laving, then moving lower, parting the soft auburn curls between her legs. His mouth settled over the tiny sensitive bud, sucking and stroking, determinedly probing until he had her writhing beneath him.

In minutes she had reached a powerful climax, her hands fisting in his thick dark hair, her body arching up off the bed. Her body still tingling all over, she lay there for several long moments, weak and sated, listening to his chuckle of male satisfaction, watching him strip off his clothes.

He came down on top of her, his hard-muscled frame pressing her into the mattress. "I love you, Duchess." He kissed the side of her neck. "Have I told you that lately?"

Velvet smiled. "Once you told me that saying you loved me was the hardest thing you ever did." She pushed back a lock of his thick chestnut hair. "But it isn't really that hard, is it?"

He grinned wickedly and pressed her hand against his heavy iron-hard arousal. "As a matter of fact, Duchess, it is."

Velvet laughed, and he dragged her beneath him, covering her mouth with a kiss, beginning to make love to her again. There was a time he believed he didn't want a wife, didn't want a family. Now if luck held, that family was about to grow larger again.

Velvet knew without doubt her husband would be pleased.

Award-winning, bestselling author Kat Martin currently resides in Missoula, Montana and Bakersfield, California. She's a graduate of the University of California, loves history, travel and snow skiing. Over three million of her books are in print and she is published in a dozen foreign countries. You can visit Kat at her website:

HTTP://www.Katbooks.com